Beyond the Doors

By J.K Scot

Disclaimer.

This book isn't a memoir.
It doesn't reflect the author's present recollections of past associates, nor should anyone assume that anything within this book is a personal experience or other than the product of the writer's imagination.

The novel's story and characters are fictitious.
Certain long-standing institutions, agencies, and public offices are mentioned but the persons and the activities described are wholly & completely imaginary.

All characters, organisations, events, and criminal enterprises, which might resemble any entities or real people, living or dead, in actual locations, past or present, are coincidental and absolutely fictional.

No paratroopers were harmed in the writing of this book.

Acknowledgements.

Gratitude: To all who hacked their way through my grammar & spelling to give encouraging feedback. Particular thanks to; CM of France, Ann, Alexandra, Marta, Horse-Lady, Tina, Lindsey, Jamie, Patsy B, Valik, Mishka, Mr. Fudge, Mr. Lubyanka, Bailey, Albo, Nick the Greek, 3rd Bn. Shane, PJ the Para, Ms. Robertson of Dunoon Grammar School, Stuart Evans & RS Security. Also, Kyokushin Champ Chris, Liz Ratcliffe, Chris Thrall & Stephanie Hale for the detailed, professional notes.

Research: I'm grateful to both Mr Haisman & Mr Kelly for all of the hospitality, anecdotes, advice and introductions as well as their profound psychological insights into the mores of gangland.

Content: This story contains graphic scenes of gratuitous sex, violence, substance abuse, kink, foul language, suicidal thoughts, mental health issues, illegal activity, racial slurs, toxic masculinity and gender bias. The imperfect persons portrayed in this book are theoretically trained professionals, so please do not try any of this at home without first consulting a qualified medical practitioner, a legal representative & at least one responsible parent.

Table of Contents

Chapter 01 -Initiating a Project.

Jamie trudged with other passengers up the gangplank to grunt, 'Good morning,' at a ticket collector before dumping himself onto an uncomfortable bench beside a porthole. Taking a last look across the sea loch to his village, he sighed.

It was dawn o'clock in the morning, and at his mother's insistence, he and his rucksack were on their way to a city as far away from his home as he could go without needing a passport. He resented the trip, and if he'd known any of the dangers that fate had planned for him, he'd never have gotten on the boat.

He'd only switched off for a minute when a former teacher plopped next to him to ask in the happy-chatty tone of a morning person, 'Hi? Where are you off to?'

'University,' he replied curtly, then added a more friendly, 'England.'

'Oh, that's great. Where, what are you studying?'

Jamie forced a half-hearted smile but groaned inside, mumbling, 'Engineering.'

He didn't want to appear rude but usually felt more comfortable observing people than talking to them. The following conversation was a struggle as he'd hardly spoken to anyone in the previous six months, apart from the winch operator he'd been working with in the woods. Going from a limited vocabulary yelled into his walkie-talkie of "Haul-in, Haul-back and Stop," to using whole sentences early in the morning was hard, and it took a while for his brain to warm up.

She asked, 'What made you choose that? Is it something you've always wanted to do?'

'Naw, no really,' he shrugged, grinned, then misquoted something she'd said to him in class, 'I'm a blank sheet of paper writing my own adventure.'

For the propriety of politeness, the pair maintained banal conversation for the half hour it took to cross the Clyde by ferry, and as they parted ways at the train station, she told him, 'Well, nice to see you again. I hope you realise all of your ambitions.'

Those words rattled around in his mind as he continued southwards to England. He had no ambitions. At best, he was disinterested in seeing the world on the other side of the loch, and he was only becoming a student in response to his mother's relentless pressure to leave what she called,

'A dead-end job in a place where people went to die of boredom.'

Twelve hours later, at the final train station of his journey he was stiff, red-eyed, and groggy from sleeping curled up on a seat. He called home to say he had arrived safely then took a disorientating cab journey through a warren of identical houses to an address in a long street of red brick. Sadness overwhelmed him when he realised that he'd swapped life in a place of deer on the hills where no one locked their doors, for a grubby red-light district where the only feral wildlife were muggers and pimps. He turned the key in his new home, but instead of the rich smell of freshly baked bread he was used to, the stink of garbage assaulted his nose. He hated it already. When a mouse scuttled past him in the hallway, he'd seen enough of the place.

In the hundred square feet of dilapidation that was his bedroom, he dumped his bag on the floor and lay down with his head on an uncomfortable pillow.

There, staring at a damp, stained ceiling he sulked himself to sleep. It felt like he'd closed his eyes for only a second when his quiet was shattered by someone ringing a cowbell while repeatedly bellowing, 'Beer! Beer! Beer!'

It became apparent that he had flatmates. Bursting into his room, they made introductions and became insistent in their eagerness for Jamie to come out drinking with them. They didn't take, 'Erm...Ahm no sure,' for an answer and he was soon carried on a wave of enthusiasm to a tiny bar opposite the local fire station.

Inside, the students were pressed together so tightly that he couldn't move without stepping on someone, so he hung back from his new acquaintances and stood in an alcove by the entrance where at least there was a cool draught. From there, wherever he looked, it was packed with colourful people. All fluttering past and chattering away with what he interpreted as cosmopolitan cool. At home in Argyll, he might only see half a dozen different people per week, but now everything was overpowering; too strange, too noisy and too hot. He was considering leaving to return to his bedsit when one of his housemates thrust a pint of lager into his hand with the words, 'It's alright, isn't it?' and dragged him into the swirling mass and towards the beer garden.

Five lagers later, the students Jamie had arrived with had drifted away. He was now alone, people-watching and slumped against a wall with two full pints in his hands. He felt fuzzy headed as he pressed one cold glass against his skin. It sent a refreshing and tingly spasm of ice down his spine, and he tried to stand straight. Instead, he managed only a slight stumble that cracked the back of his head on some masonry. A female voice purred, 'You okay?'

Looking around, Jamie saw a tanned girl with one of the pub's spot lamps illuminating her head like a halo. She was beautiful, stylish, dripping in gold jewellery and fashionably dressed in a black designer blazer. She seemed serene, out of place in a sweaty student pub. She took a step closer and opened her mouth to say something but was interrupted by a grumpy sound from behind barking an order, 'Mate, go over there!'

The words came from a doorman, a forbidding-looking man who repeated the command and startled Jamie with a sudden hand gesture. That made the drunken student back away, bump into the girl, and spill his lager on her. He began spluttering apologies while looking at his feet, feeling mortified.

The girl chuckled and said, 'Es la fiesta, no to worry cutie!'

She punctuated the statement with a pirouette and clapped her hands above her head like a flamenco dancer, 'I am Maria. What is your name?'

Inebriated, surprised she was talking to him, it took him a long time to mumble, 'Hi,' but anything else he might've wanted to say was interrupted by the doorman snapping, 'Go!'

Jamie was a happy compliant drunk that stumbled again, slapped a wall for support and staggered a few paces away. From this new position, he tried to look for the girl who'd just spoken to him, but all he could see was a group of menacing-looking workmen arguing with the doorman.

Their shifts in body language were mesmerising for Jamie and he became absorbed in watching as the words changed to insults. When they were told to leave, an intimidating man at the back of the group yelled, 'Make us!'

Another made the point-blank threat of, 'Do one, or you'll get a kicking!' while encouraging his associates to move forward with little waves of his hand.

'Not so big on your own, are you?' said a fat pimple in dirty jeans and grubby t-shirt. The men were getting braver, daring the doorman to react in one direction so that they could surround him from another.

They only hesitated to rush him because they could see what Jamie couldn't.

The doorman was gripping something under the hem of his jacket. It was the handle of a Kukri blade. Another thing he was unaware of was that these workmen had a lucrative criminal side-line in local pubs. Their usual method was to take over an area's supply chain of drugs by arriving en masse and causing enough trouble to intimidate individual pub landlords into turning a blind eye to their trade.

'You know I could just shoot you?' growled the ringleader seated at a table.

The man looked confident with his friends flanking him and didn't bother to get up.

The doorman didn't seem concerned and casually answered in a mocking tone,

'Yer whatever Fatty, I've had more rounds come at me than you've had fry-ups!'

That was when Jamie spotted the weapon and woke up to what was happening.

He muttered, 'Uch jeez, not now,' and scanned around for a safe avenue of retreat.

Then the girl Maria caught his attention. She was surprisingly tranquil and outstretched her hand, beckoning him with one finger; cooing, 'Sweetie, come to me.'

His legs found the impulse to wobble forward to where she stood behind the man at the table, but as he squeezed past, the ringleader gave him a sneering glance.

It was the look a bully might reserve for the harmless but it distracted Jamie enough that he missed his footing and dropped one of his pints.

What happened next began like a set of dominos falling as his arms and legs floundered in a slow drunken sequence. It ended with one of his hands smashing a glass off the table and his other grabbing the man's shoulder for balance. At that moment, he was neither worried nor particularly aware of what was happening because as he looked up, his eyes met those of Maria. Her strangely peaceful smile captured him. It didn't matter that she was also shaking her head at him.

The look of mirth on her face made him feel warm and snuggly drunk. He grinned back at her without realising that to everyone else in the pub, it was the crazy-eyed grin of a boy holding the edge of a broken glass to a terrified man's neck.

Jamie locked into her gaze. He was only mildly aware that he was still draped over someone and had spilt his lager. Then his befuddled mind caught up with some of what had happened, which prompted Jamie's conditioned response of apologies,

'Oh, very sorry. Sorry. Sorry.'

One of the workmen yelled, 'Don't move, John, DON'T MOVE!' and Jamie saw the blood and realised he'd nicked the man's chin. He wasn't concerned for the man, having already marked him down as a bad person, but it wasn't in him to be impolite about it either so said, 'He was...'

To clarify his meaning, he nodded towards the seated man with a clumsy gesture and accidentally head-butted him. Then he yawned and blinked before announcing to Maria, 'I am so tired and yir lovely by the way. Oh, and my name's Jamie.'

Just then, a seven-foot-eight giant in a red tie and blazer arrived from inside the pub and scattered everyone like skittles. Jamie watched, too slow of thinking to be afraid as the hulk growled, 'Whatcha looking at,' and gawped as the monster rushed at him with a massive arm outstretched. It was as if with each step, the earth shook.

The ringleader wasn't sneering anymore. Jamie was brushed aside as the Giant gripped the seated man around his jaw and lifted him above his head. Holding him aloft, he told the crowd, 'I haven't started work yet, but once I clock on, I've a generous helping of pain for anyone what don't look studenty.'

Unwilling to confront the doorman the workmen screamed, 'Let him go!' but backed off. The Giant roared, 'Orders are to clean this pub of dealers. Nothing personal dickheads! Now fuck off.'

Taking a deep breath and still holding the man in one paw, he sunk his other into his victim's ribs with a sickening crack. The ringleader dangled like a toy doll, and with only a slight flex in his legs, the giant lobbed the man to splatter at the feet of his mates and tell them, 'Don't come back, or I'll be round to wake you up one morning with a hammer.'

As the men left, Jamie sat down on the vacated table. Everything was a bit wobbly, and he briefly rested his head on the beer-stained table to stop the world from spinning.

An adrenalin dump took over. The last thing he remembered being told was, 'You can stay.'

He dozed off and dreamt of a girl talking to him in a sweet purring voice while his head rested on her arm as a pillow. When he finally woke up, he was lying on a pool table upstairs surrounded by doormen in uniforms with a rolled-up dog blanket under his head. Spread around him in the bar was a blur of inquisitive faces and the shaven skulls. Their shifts had finished in other pubs around the city, and with their red ties removed and clipped to their blazer pockets, they'd congregated for after-hours drinks in the now-closed pub.

One of them mimicked in a threatening tone that changed to laughter,

'Did you touch one of my students?'

And with a grin, he asked Jamie, 'Pint? I'll get it.'

'Could ah huv a black coffee, please,' he told the man while stretching.

One of the men threw his wallet onto the pool table and told him,

'There you go, had to check who you were. Don't worry, it's all there.'

Jamie sighed and decided to be relaxed about having his pockets rifled.

He didn't bother checking it, as he had no idea how much he'd spent that night.

One by one, the identically dressed men introduced themselves,

'I'm fifty,' said a grim looking thug. The man beside him pointed at his badge number and declared, 'Thirty-two.' Then the group of uniformed lads called out their numbers in turn as if it was a hilarious joke.

A scarred face told him, 'I've known Nine since school. I still dunno his real name.'

'I dunno it and I'm his nephew,' said another who choked laughing.

Jamie stared around the faces, and they explained why they used numbers,

'Don't want names shouted across a pub. That's a step closer to getting known or nicked.'

The Giant told him, 'I'm Ginger. It be hard to be anonymous when you are British prisons powerlifting champ. Non-drugs free obviously.'

It was as if he wanted a reaction to the words' Prisons' and 'Drugs,' but Jamie's face stayed blank. As they chatted, it felt like he was an honoured supper guest surrounded by cannibals who all knew some secret he didn't.

He was their after-hours entertainment, but it all seemed okay.

One asked, 'So how come you stuck a glass in matey's neck?'

Still tired, he slipped into his semi-intelligible Scottish dialect to say,

'Uch, him, Ah don't 'hink he wiz awe that nice. Ma name's Jamie. I'm a student at the university,' then he yawned to punctuate his reply.

The doormen then all spoke at once in a barrage of questions with garbled Hampshire accents, and one asked,

'Can you say eleven? Go on, say eleven. No, no say purple burglar alarm for us.'

He knew what they were talking about but feigned ignorance about the comedy show they were referring to and switched in his mind to pronounce every syllable slowly in clear English. Another of the doorman asked, 'Can you say film, no. Say poem?'

The first doorman he'd seen that night, badge number 22, placed a pint of lager in front of him and said, 'Thanks, but you shouldn't have got involved.'

'Any coffee?' Slurred Jamie as he tried to process what they were saying.

Another interrupted, 'Well mate, I started working on nightclub doors at fourteen, but I don't think I have ever seen anyone fall asleep halfway through a glassing before.'

The Giant grabbed Jamie by the collar and pulled him closer to declare,

'Fair play. You did good! Ya helped us. Don't worry about the Muppet you glassed.'

'Yer but you were a bit too psycho, a bit too soon,' suggested Twenty-two holding an imaginary sugar cube in front of his eyes and grunting, 'A little.'

Jamie forced himself to speak without his dialect and jokingly replied in an impersonation of an English one, *'Air well it t'was all terribly, terribly upsetting don't you know.'*

One doorman called out to a large shaven-headed Buddha sprawled on the next sofa, 'What about him for that student thing?'

The man didn't look over but nodded his agreement with, 'Why not.'

The Giant explained, 'We need someone who speaks student. Next Tuesday morning for a couple of hours work. Few quid for someone using their social skills, won't be any trouble?'

Jamie replied with another yawn, 'I don't have any social skills.'

The Giant beamed, 'Yer mate, good one. So go to your campus Tuesday, meet us at the reception at eleven in the morning, white shirt with a collar.'

'Okay. I kin dae that,' he said, without really thinking about what he'd agreed to.

All he was clear about was that he'd no real lectures in the first week.

'Good lad, now repeat the order in fucking English. So, I knows ya understand.'

'College reception, Tuesday at eleven am, white collar shirt, I understand,' he said quietly and slowly without his accent, perhaps a little uncomfortable to be the centre of attention.

From behind the bar, he heard, 'Jamie, where are these kettles? Please to help?'

The lads around chuckled, 'Go on through Matey. She's been waiting all night for you.'

He walked over and pushed open the lower door that led him into the kitchen, and as soon as he saw her, he froze like a rabbit in a set of headlights. The woman reached forward, gently held his ears and kissed him on both cheeks while saying, 'Hola. Niño Bueno.'

He had no clue what to say in reply. It was a new feeling for him, a weird nervousness that made his stomach tense and his neck retract into his shoulders. Mostly he was startled by the surprise familiarity rather than any sudden shyness, and for a moment he could only manage to stare into her eyes, mesmerised in silence. Then, when she spoke, he didn't understand a word. All he heard was a rapid undulating melody of seductive Spanish and totally forgot about wanting a drink.

A doormen yelled out, 'Oi, are you two fucking in there!'

Jamie turned, his face flashed red with his nostrils flaring. The magic spell was broken but Maria touched his arm and whispered,

'Do not to mind them, they only is jealous-o. I did not want to stay but I cannot leave you. I don't think all boys are so nice here,' and with a soft grip on his wrist, she asked,

'Was that okay if I said I am with you?'

There was nothing in him trying to be cool. Truth blurted out, 'God yes!'

A man called out something about him and Maria but it was like the buzzing of a mosquito on the other side of a window to Jamie. For an hour, they chatted on a sofa in a quiet corner of the pub. No one disturbed them except for the Giant, who brought them a lager and a glass of house red.

Suddenly Jamie asked, 'You want to go?' which was his merely brain catching up with what Maria had mentioned earlier rather than a confident attempt to go somewhere with her. She chuckled, 'Do I bore you?'

Enunciating every word clearly, he replied, 'I...No...I didn't mean that. It is very late,' and he became slightly flustered while searching for something better or nicer to say.

'It is morning,' said Ginger clapping him on the back with a thump.

Jamie looked at his watch, 'Oh, we have to go.'

'I'll take you. Don't want ya getting mugged,' said Twenty-two, 'To show I'm nice.'

'Yes, we go now. I am a little tired,' Maria said tugging his sleeve.

Twenty-Two drained his pint, jingled his keys and asked, 'Tell me where?'

In the car, Jamie sat in the back seat. Her thigh touched his, and for some reason, he moved his hand to touch her leg. She responded by wrapping her little finger around his. That was when the most surprising thing of his eventful evening happened and Maria murmured in his ear,

'I like you, Jamie, you not pretend to be someone. I want to see you again. Okay?'

He nodded, and after that, neither of them spoke until they arrived at her house where she told the doorman, 'Thank you for taking us home.'

'My pleasure Doll-face,' he replied with a sleazy grin, 'Anytime.'

Maria ignored his awkward flirtation and softly pecked Jamie on his cheek, 'Soon Cariño,' then turning around she joked, 'You Meester twenty-two, I need to watch.'

As her shadow disappeared into her flat, the doorman asked,

'How did you pull a bird like that?' but Jamie didn't respond the rest of the journey except to mumble directions with feigned tiredness. He didn't want to explain that for him, Maria wasn't a bird, she was intrigue at first sight. Once at his house, he tumbled into bed, falling asleep and happy to be in the grubby little city and wrapped up in a blanket of contentment about the woman he'd just met. What he didn't know was that the man he had nearly glassed was someone who thought of himself as a big-shot hoodlum. He was a thug who was already plotting revenge against the slender student.

'Open up Mush!' bellowed a Hampshire accent banging on his door.

'I'm coming,' replied Jamie as he stumbled half-awake towards the noise. Barefoot and dressed only in his black pyjama bottoms, he opened the door to find Ginger the Giant blocking out the sun. Startled, he asked, *'I thought I was meeting you on Tuesday?'*

'No mate. We're off to Don's! Hurry up!' he replied herding him back towards his room. His first weekend was supposed to be a time of exploring the city and making schedules, but instead, he was rushed to get dressed. In jeans and an 'Alba gu bràth,' t-shirt he climbed into the Giant's car only to discover that the driver's seat had been removed to make room for Ginger's enormous size. Even with him driving from the rear there was still not enough space and Jamie soon found he was to be pressed against his window every time the Giant changed gear.

They sped along a route of grey concrete and tarmac, descending in levels of housing prices while Ginger talked about stalking deer, bulldozers, nightclub fights and fishing for carp. He wasn't sure if it was the same story, as he got confused by all the times the huge man repeated the same sentences. It sounded like he forgot most of what he'd said within a second of saying it.

They ended up in the kind of suburb where curtains always twitched behind draughty windows, but nobody called the police about the sins they saw.

'We're here!' he grinned beeping his horn, 'Right Mush, here's me keys. Keep an eye on me. If I give you the nod, run to the car and drive away.'

Jamie asked, 'That don't sound good. How come?'

Ginger began a grunting effort to struggle out of his car and explained,

'Don invites everybody, not just employees. We got girlfriends, ex-wives, and assorted hoods that have been stabbing each other for years, and then there are his other cousins. Half the thieving gypsies in Hampshire will be here.'

Jamie sucked his teeth, 'Yer, you can't say that. They're called travellers now!'

The Giant smiled, patting his shoulder,

'Oi' be a proper Gypsy. I knows what I means, Cacker.'

The answers worried him, 'Are you sure it's okay, me turning up?'

'Of course. Told you why you are here.'

15

Jamie groaned, 'No, you didn't.'

'Hospitality, meet the lads.'

He was apprehensive but walked behind Ginger towards the smell of hashish and the throbbing reggae music emanating from a garden strewn with sofas and picnic tables. Once inside, he was greeted with handshakes, grunts and a can of lager.

On a large armchair on the lawn, he sat back to observe while smoky embers swirled on the breeze around him. After an hour as a spectator, he realised it was both theatre and a family gathering, with each face acting as magically animated subtitles for their hard-to-follow accents. It reminded him of a school trip to the ballet, where he'd watched the orchestra pit and become enthralled by the nuances of body language as they silently communicated with each other. They were an anthropological curiosity, like a tribe of Meercats in semi-human form constantly drumming signals to each other. Non-stop they broadcasted who they were, their position within the group and what little dangers they knew of.

A tall black doorman whose muscles looked like they'd been cast in bronze approached to shake his hand and ask, 'You're a bit quiet. Ya all right mate?' then walk away without waiting for an answer. A burger later, Ginger grabbed him and made an introduction, 'Don...This is him.'

The face that greeted Jamie was a surprise. From the little he had learned from Ginger as they've driven there; he'd expected to meet a large monster. Instead, he met a short chubby man in a torn rugby top and jeans. The doorman boss had a pleasant, almost handsome face and a charming smile that radiated warmth.

Don replied, 'So you're the one that glassed that fat fuck?'

'No, it wasn't like that. It was an accident,' offered Jamie, thinking it was the right thing to say and hopeful he wasn't in trouble for what he'd done with the drug dealer. When he heard Jamie's answer, Don stared at Ginger as if he'd brought him a bag of sick and shook his head, 'He's not a boxer is he, and he's too small for the door.'

The Giant chuckled, 'Yeah, but heart, bollocks. He went for Matey calm as anything.'

Don nodded, 'Alright. I'll think about it. You'd the chilli yet? I was up at six making it.'

It felt like an interview that he'd already failed and Ginger tugged him away to a picnic table in the garden, 'Don't worry, he'll get ya some more work.'

Jamie hadn't even thought about finding a job, but before he could say that, Ginger began a conversation about going to the gym with him and why he needed powerlifting.

He declared, 'You'll need to do a bit of running too Mush. Four times a week.'

Having had so little sleep and so much alcohol since he'd arrived in England, Jamie only had the energy to pretend to listen as his eyes began flickering towards a nap. He wasn't bothered about sleeping in their company. If anything, he was relaxed when surrounded by them. Well, he was, until a six-foot-five piece of steroid abuse squeezed into a combat jacket arrived. It stomped over to a fire pit where Don was tending to some barbecue ribs to yell, 'You need to go inside!'

The new man began angrily bossing the Boss around.

'Who d'ya think you are... telling me what do?' replied Don.

Ginger tittered sarcastically and explained,

'That's our company psychopath, he is always such a calming influence. He reckons there is a bloke in the flats with a rifle.'

The man kept arguing and even pushed Don, trying to herd him into the house. Jamie tried to make sense of the scene and quietly asked Ginger, 'He a real psycho?'

'Okay, no. Not really, but his psychiatrist said it's the nearest word he has to describe him. He'd step in front of bullets for any Red-Tie, and he doesn't even like most of them. Don't fret. You can't avoid working with him, so you may as well get used to him.'

'But I don't work with you,' he replied, confused once again by Ginger.

'Pricks! So that's why you're standing around me.' Don exclaimed but relaxed again.

'We've checked,' said another, 'Nobody there.'

Don sneered, 'Think about it: anybody I have to worry about is here eating my burgers.'

'Sure Boss. If you say so,' suggested Ginger.

Don sighed at the psychotic doorman, 'Relax, go eat a protein bar or something fatty,' and the barbecue conversations switched back to issues of the city's nightlife and bars.

'What's your happy third place then?' asked a man with cauliflower ears.

'Three in the morning on my door, searching hookers,' replied another.

Don had had been up since dawn digging a fire pit for a barbecue and was now tending the flames and charred meat in the same dirty jeans he'd started the day with. As a host, he fussed over his guests more like a caring mother than a boss, but his appearance, like so much of this story, was deceiving. Listening to the savage anecdotes was educational and Jamie soon understood, nothing about Don's personality was small or rounded in any way. Anyone who knew him feared him as a sharp and disciplined leader with a massive ego unfettered by any thoughts of legality. As a man, he was regimented in all that he did, with the only problem being that most things he did, tended to involve his quixotic temper and extreme violence.

He'd once been a middleweight boxer and a reasonably prosperous drug dealer before reinventing himself as the Boss of a security firm. In that, he'd been successful too, and built a business model based on a ruthless code of conduct that had zero tolerance for failure. What he was really good at was inspiring loyalty.

The gossip was all schooling, and Jamie woke up just enough to quietly listen.

He was on his third free lager when Ginger noticed a shadow behind the garden's hedge.

'Maybe our sniper?' he said, pointing to it with a barbecued turkey leg.

Ginger ambled towards a shadow hiding behind the green boundary, leaned over the privet wall, dropped his rhino hoof of a hand on a stranger and said, 'Come with me.'

It wasn't a request, more like a kidnapping and the visitor was helped through the gate by the Giant's greasy grip on his formerly clean suit. The man followed meekly but didn't appear to be either alarmed or confused to be greeted by what looked like a garden full of muscle-bound gangsters in tracksuits.

'Have a pew mate,' said a man offering him suspicion and an orange plastic kid's chair.

'So, who are you?' Don asked as the man sat down.

'You a copper?' snorted another.

'Don't mind him mate. He thinks everyone is a cop.'

'He looks like a cop,' barked another who was strutting around like he was going to pounce on the visitor.

Hurriedly the man explained, 'Not a cop. I was in the army. Not long out, and I used to live here. It was my foster placement. Thought I'd come back and look at the place.'

One of the doormen, badge number twenty-two, stepped closer and offered him a hand to shake and words spoken as if it was obvious which unit of the army he belonged to, 'I was third battalion back in the day. My name is Crow.'

'When did you live here?' asked another, every word was heavy with suspicion.

The man looked around as if gutted and broken, 'When I was a teenager. I couldn't get out of the place quick enough. Breakfast was water and cornflakes, and they used to beat us with a cable.' Pausing he bit his lip and said, 'Haven't seen this place since I joined up.'

'Bastards,' Don growled, 'We'll find them,' and the men around nodded.

'Don't worry, we'll get 'em Mate.'

'Kill the bastards,' offered another grim-looking brute.

The man gasped, 'Bet they're dead now, mate. Old when they ran the place.'

'Suppose, suppose,' said Don, but his face was still contorted. He spoke with the snarl of an animal desperate to tear someone apart and began asking questions as if he was trying to catch the newcomer out on a lie, but he soon became engrossed by the man's story about the horrors he had endured in the former foster home. As the pair shared a few lagers, the Boss's teeth clenched, his nostrils flared and he became more agitated with rage as if torn between the need to do something and listening.

'Whatya doing now?' asked another doorman breaking up the sense of gloom.

'I work in a museum in London, watching security cameras. It's alright.'

The 'psycho,' doorman leant over him, taunting, 'Got any medals, soldier-boy?'

'Shut the fuck up! Phil,' Don commanded, 'Go get him a beer.' Then he seemed to remember his manners and told everyone, 'Hold on. How'd you feel in the middle of all this? We don't need to make him feel like he's under caution.'

'Alright Cacker, I'd shake hands,' the Giant gestured with his hands and a shrug of his massive shoulders. He now had a roast chicken in one and a can of lager in the other.

The Red-Tie boss was surrounded by what Jamie presumed was his praetorian guard and he looked proud as he pointed out his men by their characteristics.

He chuckled as he said, 'Mr. Thug over there sitting on the grass with the Alsatian puppy, that's Phil, we keep him chained up most of the time.'

'Him over there that looks like Buddha. He doesn't box. It's not that he can't box. It's just that he is too big. Even as a young lad, no promoter would risk a fighter in a ring with him. It's him that really runs the firm for me. Does all the organising.'

'Firm?' the stranger asked, pointing at a man arriving in the garden. Slung over his back was a black and white chequered guitar strap emblazoned with the word "Madness." Attached to that was a Kalashnikov assault rifle.

The visitor looked at the weapon and suggested, 'I think I can guess what you lot do.'
'Nah, that's a replica or something for paintball. He collects stuff like that. We are security. Nightclubs mostly, but we're trying to expand into other trades,' he told him.

Don carried on the narrative, 'So if you know any lads, we've got a pop festival coming up, need about a thousand bodies,' then pointing at the man who'd brought the news of sniper, he said, 'Everything from car park attendants to front-line animals like him.'

'Oh, okay,' he replied with a sincere smile and a nod of his head.

Don told him, 'We do everything except debt collecting. Like I'm not going to take the last quid from a mum on a doorstep holding a baby. Only Crow's that mercenary.'

The doorman with the Alsatian stood up, pulled a can from a brace of lagers, and walked over to the fire pit to grunt at the newcomer,

'I don't trust you, and we've too many squaddies already. We need proper old-school bouncers and not all this security event, door supervisor, celebrity-bodyguard shit.'

'I'm trying to run a business here,' barked Don, slightly irritated.

The big doorman turned and snarled at his Boss, 'Look at that useless fucker,' indicating one of the younger doormen with his thumb,

'He'll get filled in... the first place he works.'

Don chuckled, 'Maybe, but at least he passed the course.'

The doorman roared from the other side of the fire pit, 'I'm not doing the course!'

The boss stopped laughing and got up from his chair to walk towards him. Nose to nose, the two men stared at each other, until the Don found a vent for the violence building in him, want to go? Let's fucking go!' he roared.

The slab of muscle blinked first, 'All I'm saying. Can't just hire knobs, give 'em a tie.'

The Buddha-shaped man spoke. It was somehow gentle and peaceful, 'Chill. We need to pay wages, that's it. There aren't enough doors. Not all venues need cleaning out.'

The Psycho's mouth opened to say something, but he stomped indoors silently fuming.

'It is the same argument they've been having all day, every day, for years. We're their stunned observers, yet again,' chuckled Ginger.

Don sat down, once again calm as if squaring up to the man was the most soothing thing on the planet. With the entertainment over the men in the garden formed small groups of loud jokes and quiet conspiracies. Crow took ownership of the visitor's hospitality, and they walked off into a corner of the garden to chat on their own. The lager caught up with Jamie and he began to doze off.

If he had stayed awake a little longer, he'd have heard another argument erupt, and why some of them thought the incident with the drug dealer had been the student's fault. The man who'd had the Kalashnikov suggested, 'Going rate is ten grand for a hit, but matey is so cheap he'll probably get some junkie to do it for a monkey.'

Another said, 'It's not gone down well with the locals.'

'Fuck 'em,' declared Don, 'If they start on the lad, we'll finish it, once and for all.'

'So, you mean? Use him as bait,' complained Ginger, growling and annoyed.'

'Nah, don't worry about that' replied Don casually, 'He's under my protection.'

***

Crow lit a cigarette, took a deep drag to settle his nerves and quietly left Don's house to walk a few streets away with the man he'd pretended not to know. They stopped at a black Range Rover. The stranger who'd turned up asked, 'Did you like my orphan story?'

'You had me believing it. How did you know it'd been a foster home.'

'Reconnaissance mate, you know how it is. Never go into something without at least three escape plans. And yer, that tale was always gonna get me a foot in the door.'

He then exhaled as if weighing up what he wanted to say next, 'I was told you blew all your money and haven't a pot to piss in. Is that right?'

Crow shrugged apologetically, 'True. Not getting the work. If that doormen lot hadn't taken me in, I'd be sleeping in my car.'

'Well, I won't say I am embarrassed for you, but they look like a right bunch of Muppets.'

'It's a long story,' Crow mumbled, 'I am still fit though.'

'Good. That was my next question, as I've a proper job for you. Perimeter security.'

'Proper job,' Crow smiled, 'You know me. I'm ready for anything.'

'Good lad. It'll be a few weeks. We're still in the planning stage, but I can stretch to thirty for this one. Truth is, our employers are Yanks, and they're throwing money at us.'

'Lovely-jubbly, hope this is the first of many then.'

He handed Crow a mobile phone, 'I call, you answer. Day or night!' Clear?'

'Got it! Matty, I won't let you down.'

'And don't be drinking or disappearing on me.'

'Received understood!' Crow replied with a huge grin, 'Don't worry about me.'

'That's the problem. I do worry. When you're switched on, you're the best soldier I know, but when you go on the piss, you're a fucking space cadet.'

Crow grinned, 'Thirty grand is thirty grand. I'm staying sober till you call.'

'Do that Mucker,' he replied, got into his Range Rover and sped off.

Crow had first met the man when he was a young recruit to the Parachute Regiment, then later when he failed selection for the special unit Matty had moved on to. The last time they'd crossed paths was when Matty had sacked him from a close protection job in Paris. The sacking wasn't acrimonious. It was more or less expected that staff would fall asleep sooner or later with the hours they were expected to work. Matty had entered the hotel suite Crow was guarding. He'd asked, 'Who is in with the prince?'

'A couple of hookers,' he had told him.

'Yer, mate, but who is in there since you fell asleep with your Glock on your lap?'

As soon as he heard those words, Crow knew the dismissal process was coming. That day, Crow stood up, took the punch and was paid off. Matty had bought him a ticket home and even driven him to the airport. They'd parted with Crow believing that Matty was firm but fair. Now once again, Matty was his employer and once again they separated with Crow believing that the team leader would treat him well and pay him handsomely. As his black Range-Rover disappeared down the street the Red-Tie paratrooper smirked at the choice of vehicle and thought, 'With that face and that car, you may as well write "secret special forces guy" on the doors. He'd misjudged Matty though, as the plan was that when the job was finished, Crow would be too.

He didn't really want to be there. He didn't want the sweat drying into salt stains on his gaudy Hawaiian shirt, and he didn't want to be carrying a heavy bag on the hottest day of the year. Every step in his cowboy boots was a struggle against an urge to sit down in the shade until his headache went or a taxi came, but Angel Bahamonde trudged on. With his head down and hungover, he didn't see the sign to the aerodrome until after his phone's SatNav had conspired with the sleepy village to take him back in a circle, to the train station he'd arrived at. He groaned, tied back his long black hair in a ponytail and set off again. His Boss's instructions had been clear: 'Let them know you're coming,' so as he approached the main hanger, he sang loudly and off-key the wrong lyrics to a Luz Casal song.

When he finally saw Matty and his men, they were leaning against the building's wall and chatting as if oblivious to their noisy visitor. They weren't what he'd expected. His Boss had led him to believe that he'd be meeting the four horsemen of the apocalypse, but all he found were slightly overweight dad-bodies in drab fleeces, dark blue running tights and grey trainers. It sounded like one of them owned the skydiving centre they were using because as he got closer he heard one of them say, 'So how is it for you here? Think it will take off?'

'Tomorrow looks scrubbed. High winds.'

'It'll take off mate. Unlike our plane today,' said another.

Angel stopped a few feet away from them, but no one looked up and they continued to chat as if he wasn't there.

'Don't worry. We'll be back to support you,' said a man staring past him.

Angel dropped the pack at his feet and coughed, 'I'm here with braces.'

'Braces? You mean a retainer?' asked one of them, then seemingly absent-mindedly, the man rubbed his thumb vertically on his cheek as if it was a signal to his colleagues.

Angel heard the unmistakable click of a safety catch and saw one of the men's arms drop by his side, revealing he'd been holding a small Ruby.32 pistol behind his back.

'I am Matty. You are Angel, right? We expected you an hour ago.'

'Angel? Angel, my arse. He looks like holy water would boil off of him,' said the youngest of the killers who lit a cigarette.

An action which triggered a chorus of, 'Comfort blanket,' from his colleagues.

The Smoker ignored the jibes and asked, 'Why us? Don't you have your own team?'

'I am only a monkey grinder, not the big organ. I don't know anything and don't want to know anything. Here to give you this,' he replied, kneeling to open his bag.

Inside were a hundred thousand Euros, cellophane wrapped, in small denominations.

'Follow me,' said Matty while throwing him a water bottle, 'You'll have to know a little.'

Apart from the Smoker, the rest of the team offered up a hand to shake as Angel stepped over the threshold.

Inside the hanger, Matty pointed at a brightly painted Beech 99 aircraft, 'Been up twice this morning but looks like we are grounded for the rest of the day.'

'I thought we were supposed to have nice weather?' moaned a voice behind.

Angel took a drink, and a little sweat and fear vented from his pores but he kept his face relaxed and smiling. He'd read their files, seen their profile pictures and he knew technically they were on the same side, but up close they exuded primal, violent mayhem even when being welcoming. Matty spread out a map on a parachute packing table, while the others rehearsed the twists and turns of a skydiving routine. It was as if the thing they were being employed to do, was only some side gig to their primary occupation of falling out of light aircraft for fun. Moving coins around to represent his team, the team leader said, 'So this might be a possibility?'

'I'm just a liaison for resources, not planning approval.'

Then looking down, he pointed at two pennies, 'What are they for?'

'Contingency,' Matty explained, 'To make sure it happens the way we've been asked.'

The Spaniard nodded, 'Can't you do it without them? More men, means more risk.'

Matty replied, 'Told we could have whatever we need. And Us? You coming along then?'

Angel held up his hands to concede the point, 'Ah no. Sorry. It's still whatever you need. Are they from your regiment?'

Another of Matty's team interrupted, 'What regiment is that? Thought you didn't want to know too much?' Then he went back to the choreography of skydiving.

The Smoker growled from the doorway of the hanger, 'Fucking Regiment. Too many ambitious sorts these days. Can't trust nobody. They all hate each other and just want it on their CV. It's not the same as when we were in.'

Matty handed Angel a memory stick,

'I'll need this soon. As for my new recruits. Don't worry. Nobody will miss them.'

'Perfecto, I will pass it on,' Angel replied grinning, although shocked at the implication.

When the briefing was over, the Smoker was volunteered by Matty to give Angel a lift back to the train station and they drove in silence until parking outside of it. Taking a long slow drag of his cigarette and with his eyes closed in pleasure, he told Angel in a gruff voice, 'Yer okay, suppose it makes sense you lot hiring us.'

He paused, enjoying some Zen moment and a hit of nicotine to growl, 'We're really, really,' he took another drag of the cigarette, '...Really fucking good at killing people.'

***

Aboard the train, Angel was about to reach for his hipflask when he saw a woman walk towards him. She wasn't a beautiful woman but there was something about her. 'Is this seat taken,' she asked, wobbling, barely managing to stay on her heels as the train pulled out of the station. Strange, as they were the only two people in the carriage.

He grinned, 'Sure,' in response to what he felt was an overpowering throbbing sensuality drawing him in.

'I'm Tanya,' she said while unbuttoning her lightweight spring coat.

'My name is Angel.'

'So where are you going?' she asked him. Her English was perfect, but it was evident from her accent she was Eastern European.

'The end of the line,' he told her with his eyes leering at her body.

'That's where I am going. I sail!' she told him, sounding smug.

'In that outfit, oh please, what ship?'

'It's a little crumpled now. I was visiting a friend last night...' then she left the sentence hanging with a smirk to suggest she'd been doing something deliciously wicked.

Angel asked, 'What do you do?'

'Trophy wife,' she said with an unmistakable glint of naughtiness flashing in her eyes. For the rest of the journey, they chatted on every subject and found that they shared a few interests. When Angel pretended he was reading a novel, she said she'd just bought it herself. As they discussed more, it was as if the only books he'd ever read were the only ones she'd read too. It appeared they thought about things the same way and that her excitement lurked in the same random and dark places as his own.

He enjoyed the conversation and treated it like a civilised encounter from a world he missed. For Angel, a man who cat-fished on every dating app and went home with new women as an alternative to booking hotels, she seemed a kindred spirit even if a civilian. He thought perhaps it'd be good to switch off for a moment, to just be normal again.

At the end of their journey, as a statement of fact, she said, 'We will meet for drinks. Soon.'

'I'd like that very much,' Angel smiled and helped her with her coat.

As he did so, her sleeve rode up her arm, revealing a blood-speckled bandage.

She noticed his gaze and told him, 'It's RSI from my laptop. My doctor says it needs rest.'

'Oh,' he replied, wondering why she had used such a blatant lie.

She declared, 'Forget about it,' bounced back into sparkling ebullience and asked him for his phone number.

At a taxi rank outside the station, she pressed against him, kissed his cheek and said, 'You're a good friend. I'll see you soon.'

Suddenly a moment of melancholy came over him. He let his eyes wander down to her breasts and wondered what it might feel like to have a real friend again instead of organising all those he met into potential predators or prey.

As she drove away, Angel filed the encounter in his brain as, 'Pleasant, but weird.'

She'd called him, 'Friend?' as if she was following a clumsy tick list of psychological techniques designed to make a man feel protective or empathetic. Her over-eagerness seemed wrong to him, but his desire to get her into bed outweighed any caution and he thought, 'No one in my line of work is ever that stupid.'

Then Angel made a phone call to another woman,

'Hola Guapa, are you enjoying your holiday?'

The lady answered angrily in Spanish, 'Bastard! What do you want?'

He carried on in a tone as if she was happy to hear from him,

'It's just another few weeks.'

'I was on a sabbatical?' she snarled, 'And I don't want to come back!'

'The boss said you'd help,' he told her.

The woman's voice growled, 'Si, claro. I thought it was too good to be true being sent
here. I should have known you were behind this.'

Angel chuckled, 'Don't be like that. You are here anyway. And I trust you.'

'Okay. Fine,' she replied, 'But just remember. I don't trust you.'

'I'll leave a package for you. Besos Maria!' he told her and hung up.

Jamie sat waiting on a low wall outside the campus reception wondering how he'd gone from avoiding eye contact with doormen to shaking hands with them.

He disapproved of violence yet found himself at ease the company of those who were casual about it. At precisely eleven o'clock, Ginger interrupted his pacifist musings when the giant arrived with another Red-Tie doorman and erroneously told him, 'Come on. You're late!'

The doormen walked off to the admin block without waiting for Jamie, who trotted behind them only to find out that the security task he'd been hired for, was chatting, and stopping anyone from entering. He was starting to get hungry when a group arrived, it was led by a lecturer that he'd met the day before as his head of year. They were there to hand in a petition threatening a strike. His teacher had a surprise in attempting to brush the young student aside to enter the Vice-Chancellor's office, as a snarling Ginger loomed into view and said, 'Jamie says NO!'

It helped them reassess their plans for the day and they left without another word.

An hour later the admin staff set them free. In the sunshine, they all headed off campus to the gym that Ginger had repeatedly been inviting Jamie to. He'd agreed each time he'd been asked, but that day, it was as if Ginger forgot all his sentences within seconds of speaking them. The other doorman whispered, 'It's normal. He fell off a roof last year. Now he forgets sometimes.'

Jamie began processing the implications, and was just about to get into Ginger's car when a voice cried out, 'Hola Cariño!'

It was Maria, the girl he hadn't stopped thinking of since he'd first met her.

She was striding towards them dressed in tight leggings, black boots laced to the knee, a black bolero jacket with silver buttons and carrying a family bucket of fried chicken.

He stuttered, 'Hello,' then stared at her with a slack open jaw for a moment before smiling. She casually passed the fast food to Ginger and sang in her sweet musical accent, 'Hello, Mister Giant. Hello Jamie! I am pleased to meet you.'

'You too darling. You're Mary right?'

'My name is Maria de Luz de Los Amparadores Hernan-Blanco, but is too much non?'

'Nah, it's easy Mary. Good to see you?'

'I am for library today. Do you have any plans now, Jamie?'

'Think you've pulled mate,' chimed in the other doorman.

'He hesitated, and explained, 'I was going with Ginger to the gym.'

Maria sighed, 'Ah. Okay. Maybe later?'

'No offence lad, but sod the gym,' Ginger told him with a playful slap on the back of his head, 'And like. I mean like how? You are you, and look at her. So, we're off. S'laters.'

She giggled, 'Bye-bye, Ginger. Besos,' then wrapped her arm around Jamie's and sauntered off to the library with him.

As first dates go, it was perfect. Every so often, she would look up from a book and smile at him. As he pretended to read, 'Fluid Mechanics,' he let his mind wander around the pattern of events that had led him from his village to be sitting across from a truly gorgeous woman. It was a lot to process. The machine gun was probably not right and the Red-Ties seemed too a little too cheerful when discussing violence. He tried not to think about it being wrong and dismissed all of the incidents as, 'Maybe normal,' for a southern city.

At six in the evening, he was dozing in a chair with her sitting next to him flicking through the pages of a book. Neither noticed a tanned piece of handsome approaching them until he stood over them to ask, 'Alright mate. You're a Red-Tie, aren't you?'

Maria replied for him, 'Yes, yes he is!'

Jamie bit his lip, and unsure, answered, 'How can I help you?' hoping he sounded friendly. Then more students like the tanned one arrived. They were all ebullient and determinedly chatty despite the library sign that read, 'Quiet.'

'Have you asked him yet?' said another handing him an embossed card that was an invitation to a Rugby club ball.

'Asked me what?' Jamie had no clue what they wanted.

'Shouldn't be a problem, just need a guy on the door for our ball. We'll pay.'

It was something to do with Rugby in two days, and he replied, 'Aye nae bother,' only afterwards thinking that he should have asked the price first, but it all happened so fast.

'Shouldn't be more than seven hundred and not too much mayhem,' said another and Jamie's expression changed to that of someone who knew they'd made a mistake in agreeing. He gulped, 'That's a lot.'

'You can handle it. Heard you took on twenty men in a pub on your own.'

When they'd gone, noisily exiting as chaotically as their entrance, he put together what he'd agreed to. It would be anarchy, on his own, with large rugby sorts who'd all be drinking. To Maria he hesitantly murmured, 'I don't think I should have said yes.'

'Cariño, No Te preocupe. Those types are no problem,' then she got up asking,

'Do you want to walk me home?'

He nodded but was still a little puzzled about why she wanted to be with him.

It seemed too enthusiastic but he wasn't complaining. At an underpass, she feigned fear gripping his arm, didn't let go until on her doorstep where she invited him in for a coffee. Jamie managed an almost sheepish nod and stepped across her threshold to encounter a lighter, brighter home that was five stars more expensive looking than his student accommodation. Maria asked, pointing at a sumptuous sofa,

'Do you want to see a movie first? Are you hungry yet? We can have takeaway; Chinese, Indian, or Italian. Que tú quieres? Sit, sit have a seat Cariño.'

Her way of speaking varied between English and Spanish. It wasn't consistently one language or another, as if who she was depended on how she felt at the time.

'I can go get a pizza,' he replied.

'Bueno, espera un momento. I will go to change,' she said disappearing from the room.

When Maria re-entered, she said, 'We don't need to go out. Delivery will be here in twenty minutes. Do you want a drink?'

He didn't answer but gasped when he saw she'd changed into a Penguin onesie.

She wiggled towards him as if her feet were tied together, then overpowering him with cuteness, she talked non-stop in something that was almost English until the pizza arrived. First, she told him that she'd worked as a typist in Spain. It took Jamie a while to realise that she meant the checkout of a shop before explaining her father owned the chain of supermarkets. She poured them both Rioja and changed his glass for a mug after he fumbled it, spilling wine on the carpet. They watched 'Dirty Dancing,' in Spanish, and while he didn't understand a word of it, he wanted it to last forever.

Halfway through the film, she asked, 'Do you like it,' and he spilt more wine on his chest while trying to nod and gulp simultaneously.

Sniggering, she fetched a cloth and gently dabbed where his shirt was wet. She was so close he could feel her breath on his neck and turned red pulling away. It was like he was simultaneously surprised, excited by Maria's touch and drowsily happy in her company. Nothing was said for a while until she asked, 'Why do you come here to study?'

Jamie didn't have a good answer and nervously mumbled a glib, 'Better than cutting trees.' What followed was more like an interrogation, as Maria extracted information about his course, his home and Scotland before suddenly asking him, 'Can you ride a horse?'

'Nah,' He replied, 'I was like boasting to my mum about what I could do, and she gave me an attitude adjustment about my skills. Jeez, I didn't even know she'd ridden horses.'

'What do you mean you didn't know?'

'Ma maw just tellt me; aye well, until you can jump four by four foot while using a sabre or shooting from the saddle, you can't say you can ride.'

'Oh my god, she sounds funny. What does she do?' Maria asked.

'She was a nurse,' then Jamie sighed as if unwilling to divulge more.

'What's wrong? Do I ask too many questions?'

He smirked, 'Well, duh.'

'Oh, okay,' he said, then paused to gather his thoughts before asking,

'You have a boyfriend?'

'Trust me, you don't want to know about my life before,' she told him and asked in her strange grammar, 'What is motivations for you and your Red-Ties?'

That question dried up their conversation as he had no idea how to answer. As far as he could tell, doormen did what they did because they were doormen, and they were doormen because that was what they did. It wasn't that complicated for them.

The next time he reached for a slice of pizza, he slithered down to the takeaway box on the floor and rested his head next to the fluffy Penguin's feet.

'Are you sulky?' she asked in a sweet musical tone.

'No, I am just more comfortabler.'

She giggled, 'That's not proper English.'

'It is,' he told her and returned to quietly lying on the floor with Maria occasionally refilling his glass. As the film ended, she stated, 'Jamie, the wine makes you sleepy.'

This time when he spilt his wine, it was because he'd stood up suddenly to splutter, 'Thank you for dinner,' and, 'I better go home.'

'No, I not mean that silly,' tugging his sleeve to sit next to her, 'I not want you to fall asleep on the floor, be with me. Here!' she commanded, tapping the sofa next to her.

She put on another DVD, 'Mujeres en el borde de un ataque de nervios,' and tried explaining the plot to him. The last thing he remembered before his head fell backwards snoring, was Maria covering him with a duvet on the sofa.

The following day, he was woken by a surfeit of cheerfulness and the smell of breakfast. 'We will be late; breakfast is on the table. Eat, eat, I get changed,' she smiled and waddled off, pretending to be a penguin again.

Ten minutes later, she returned dressed in jeans and a white t-shirt carrying a pack of spearmint that she offered him, saying, 'Chew-chew, that breathe is so stinky.'

Jamie almost made it to his mouth with the gum but froze, blushing again.

It was obvious Maria wasn't wearing any bra. She followed his gaze, smiled, cupped his cheek with her hand and kissed his nose, 'Let's get to class.'

'You kissed me. I mean…'

'Yes Tonto, and I let you stay because I like you,' she explained.

'But…'

She interrupted him with a grin, 'And you are a friend, so I can kiss you, maybe.' With that, she bounced on her tiptoes to kiss his forehead and hugged him in her arms to tell him, 'See, I did it again stinky boy!'

Jamie looked down at the floor as if searching for a clue, his head muddled, 'I…erm….'

Maria had a smirk on her face. 'Ayee Cariño, don't over-think things.'

For the next days, they were inseparable. Each morning they walked together as far as campus and then met for lunch. Sometimes between lectures Jamie went with Ginger to the gym but always in the afternoons after class, he met with Maria.

Usually, she waited for him outside the university library from where they'd walk to her house together. Ostensibly to study.

His evenings generally ended lying on Maria's living room floor flicking through a Spanish phrasebook with some wine in a mug, and her on the sofa behind him choosing DVDs. Sometimes they'd talk for hours with Maria quizzing him about his life before he'd come to England, and sometimes it was him talking non-stop on a subject from his lectures. Every night he bought a tasteless wine that Maria made fun of, and every night he fell asleep on her sofa with her draping a duvet over him. It was relaxed, comfortable and gentle as if they'd known each other for years and a quiet relationship that never gave any clues about the fact that Maria was a captain in the military or that, almost uniquely for a female MOE officer, she was a trained sniper.

Maria was a woman on a mission. She knew how to dress, what to say, what body language to use and when to flick her hair with a coy smile to make any man do what she wanted. As she strode towards her willing prey in a short, red tartan skirt, a black vest-top and clunky military boots, she knew every figure-hugging inch of her body looked like it had been sculpted to lure men towards her curves.

In her previous employment, she'd used this look for similar targets and her ability to compartmentalise emotions, smile and ruthlessly achieve an aim had always been a simple switch to flick. This time it was perhaps different, although her objective was more accessible than most, she just plain didn't want to manipulate him.

Finding Jamie at the engineering department, she asked, 'Mi casa esta noche?'

'My house this night?' he replied.

'Si Bueno! My house tonight, you to learning. I am very please-ed.'

'I want to, but I am doing that Rugby club thing.'

'Si, but after you finish, Si or No. Que tu quieres?'

'Okay. I'll come, but I'll be late, so if a light isn't on, I won't knock.'

Maria smiled and rapidly clapped her hands in front of her face, 'Goody! I will wait up,' and perhaps for the first time in her life, her childish delight wasn't a coquettish act. She pulled a gift box from her bag and grinned, 'Wear this tonight!' Inside was a black shirt and some sort of white band wrapped in tissue paper. He looked confused and jokingly pointed at his attire to name what he was wearing, 'What's wrong with this? Black Jeans, tee-shirt, bomber jacket. I'm proper Gangsta!'

'Mira Cariño,' she told him, 'Promise me. I have seen this work.'

He made a long, happy sigh and nodded, 'Si, I not to say no, to your mangled English.'

Then she kissed him on his cheek again and explained, 'Bye Scotty-boy, I have to go to.' She didn't finish the sentence to say where, as she didn't want to lie to him.

So, with a swirl of her mini skirt, she simply turned on her long legs and strode away.

An hour later Maria ordered an espresso from a café in the city centre and sat down in a corner facing the door. She waited for five minutes until a couple walked in. When she saw them, she muttered, 'Chulo puto,' under her breath and left.

She knew someone was following her and turned towards home through a shopping centre. Occasionally, she used the reflection in a shop window to catch a glimpse of the woman mirroring her movements. It was irritating, and Maria shook her head as she thought about the woman behind her, who was dressed the almost the same and close enough in looks to be her sister. At a set of traffic lights, while waiting to cross the road, the woman caught up and from behind slid her arm around Maria's to squeal, 'Hola.'

Excitedly, the pair embraced for an air kiss on each other's cheeks and began chatting excitedly in their dialects as if they were the best of friends.

On a quiet street Maria asked, 'Qui etstuie bé que és el teu anglès?'

The new arrival replied, 'I'm a friend of yours visiting from Spain. I'm Gabriella, and I work as a PA for the boss of a travel company. Apparently, I'm a fun party girl.'

'Typical. But okay. I can work with that. What'd he tell you about me?' she asked.

'I was told that you are not officially here, and you've found a fool as a way in for me?'

Maria's nostrils flared when she heard that, but she replied calmly, 'More or less.'

'How soon can I get into a room with the target?' she asked, 'I don't need long.'

'Within forty-eight hours,' she explained, 'And the two intelligence agents walked to Maria's house discussing their mission as if two girls just giggling in the afternoon sun.

***

Jamie was yawning over a pint of coke and wishing he hadn't agreed to work that night. The ambience of the Students' Union bar was adding to his dejection. It felt like the gloomy holding cell was only there for people to gather in as a herd before escaping into the wild. The place did chips and assorted burgers but what he'd ordered was taking too long, and rather than be late, he left hungry to head out over the park towards the Rugby Club Ball. As he crossed the main road outside of the university, he recognised a girl from the art department who started yelling at him, 'That's offensive. I am a catholic, and that's out of order.' He shrugged and replied, 'Aye, probably,' and began to doubt Maria's idea, but changed his mind when he arrived at the venue and was greeted with, 'Cool, I didn't know you were a vicar.'

In the hotel, whilst collecting tickets, he sucked up the smells of perfumes, sweat, and beer. It all pulsed in rhythm to the music and boisterous laughter. Their manners were kind-natured, and despite the rugby lads advertising themselves as big and naughty, they became meek and obedient with a simple walk amongst them as a cleric.

There was only one sober enough to listen when her brain suggested a double take at the outfit, 'You're not a fucking priest!' she said grabbing his balls. Then she laughed and staggered off. Whenever he heard glasses smashing, or one of the organisers called him from the door, the effect of the vicar's outfit was amazing. Whatever was happening stopped; the women ceased dancing on tables, scuffles between drunks parted like the Red Sea, and all were obedient to their middle-class mores like scolded toddlers.

Around midnight a nod from the organiser said his work was done, Jamie pulled off his dog-collar and left the debauchery that was unravelling behind him in unzipped gowns to head back through the park. He walked, enjoying the solitude of a clear moonlight night with a growing sense of joy about seeing Maria again. Then as the last of autumn's pollen tickling his nostrils gave way to the stench of a piss-smelling under-pass, he heard the quickening pace of someone's footsteps echoing behind him.

In the dark, he glanced back and saw a man in a shiny track suit staring at him with a weird unfriendly grin. He held something behind his back and Jamie started to worry. His mind flicked through the options, a baseball bat, bottle, house brick or perhaps an iron bar. 'Whatever it is,' he concluded, 'I'll be safer under the pubs' CCTV cameras and some light.' He crossed the road towards the rear of the Leni Quintain and sighed relief when a door opened, and Ginger stepped out.

'Alright mate. Come on in,' bellowed the Giant above the noise from inside the bar. Jamie glanced back to see that the man in the tracksuit was gone, and with him all perceived threat. Then as various Red-Tie doormen greeted him with handshakes, his concerns of mugging became replaced with the thought, 'I was being paranoid.'

Inside that part of the Lenny Quintain, he was surprised to see it was a quiet shadowy place full of dark red upholstery and scuffed wooden tables lurking in gloomy recesses. It was all in sharp contrast to the adjoining bright, busy student pub.

'Whatcha up to? Where have you been?' they asked and a proud boast burst from his lips, 'Can't stay. I'm meeting Maria in a bit.'

'You shagging her?' asked one of the Red-Ties.

Jamie was at once uncomfortable and regretted saying anything about her, so told them, 'Was working tonight at rugby club thing.'

They looked surprised at the admission, 'Who ya working with?'

'Just me,' he said, and Ginger's face immediately contorted into distrust and disapproval. 'That's not right. Who didn't turn up? Don know?' it was an urgent thing and Ginger's body language shifted to indicate a sudden annoyed interest.

'No, it was a student thing. Why would he know about it?'

'Rules! Mate, and you've just broken three of them. Better get yourself a beer and tell Don before someone else does. Like me!'

He felt Ginger was upset with him, but stayed chirpy, 'Okay, I will.'

'He's at the back,' the big man told him, quite insistently, before moving his fingers in a flurry of hand signals to someone above. Jamie trudged upstairs past tables that jutted out to trip the unwary in the dark. He had never been in the pub's club area before, and it wasn't very nice. The carpet was sticky, and the beat of the DJ's noise pounded on his eardrums. It was too loud, and it just made him more eager to race to Maria's house.

As he walked past her, a barmaid pointed to a lager she'd just poured and said, 'Ginger says that's yours.' Automatically he took it and began looking around for Don in the various alcoves but stumbled into the DJ's deck, causing the music to abruptly give up.

In the silence, he heard the boss before he saw him, and everyone else in the bar now tuned into his conversation too. There was loud, 'How much?' started them giggling, but Don yelled for everyone to, 'Shut up!'

Jamie became shocked when he realised it was an argument about a young girl sitting in a group of Red-Ties. She looked like a teenager with a petite dancer's body and a doll's face. He thought she was perhaps, 'A doormen's younger sister?'

'I just took it to pay my electric bill,' she spluttered.

Mostly the lads stayed quiet but a few sniggered in their beer, stifling their laughs, which caused Don's nose to flare. He growled, 'What the fuck?' and with just those words, the men around him were suddenly silent, still and nervous. They seemed to know the tone and reacted to Don as if he was now pure darkness on the cusp of rage.

For those who knew him, it was more or less true, the boss was unpredictable, a potentially murderous menace that anything could set off. The Boss took a deep breath and tried to speak calmly in a gentle tone, 'Why didn't ya get money off of me?'

'It was an hour for £300, and it was a...,' she stuttered slightly, unsure how to phrase it. Don raised his hand in a half-hearted wave and yelled, 'Fuck it, she's family. We don't judge,' then sat beside her to say, 'Give all your bills from now on.'

The conversation was over, Don had taken on the problem, and no one sensible would mention it again except for Jamie. He muttered, '£300 an hour, I need a computer. I could do that,' without realising what, 'That' was.

Crow, standing nearby, grabbed him around the shoulder in a friendly hug to whisk him through a passageway into the empty pub next door and said, 'Mate come with me before you say something stupid. Do you need a burger? I'm starving.'

'I saw the burger van packing up. It's finished,' Jamie explained.

'Let's try anyway. Don is in a mood. Best keep out his way, eh?'

'Okay-dokey,' he agreed, sensing Crow wanted to chat about something.

The pair went down through the pub and opened the beer garden's gate onto the car park to see the van's operator using Leni Quintain's bins to dump his refuse sacks. There were still a few people scattered in the car park enjoying the greasy food, dropping chips and drinking from the glasses they'd smuggled from pubs. They were mostly older people, not students and better dressed yet seedier looking in their quiet loitering. Aided by streetlights and a full moon, he could see their faces in the bright yellow glow. They didn't look nice either. The smell of chips hit his nose and reminded his stomach that he'd not had more than a pint of lager since lunch. Stepping up to the food van, and asked, 'Could I have four cheeseburgers, please?'

'You are in luck. I've four left,' said the man as he flipped warm overcooked patties onto the hotplate and pressed them down with a fat-bladed knife.

'Okay, Mr Crow, what do you want? I'll buy.'

'We'll share those four and any chips you have left.'

'Where are you working?' Jamie asked.

'I'm up Watford mostly, but that's not enough shifts. Don says I could help him structure the company or set up a radio net for communications at big events, but I need proper work. It's okay for you. You're a student,' he moaned, holding up his wrist, 'All I got to show for my life is this twenty-quid watch.'

They sat just inside the beer garden to eat, and because their hands were full, they didn't lock up the back gate. Crow had tried to pull it closed with his foot as he stepped in, but kicked it instead, causing it to swing open even wider.

'So why is Don in a mood?' Jamie asked.

'He's always in a mood mate, don't worry about it.'

'I have to talk to him tonight.'

'What for?'

'Ginger told me to. I was working as a doorman tonight.'

'Where d'ya work? not being funny, but you're not exactly streetwise are ya?'

'At a hotel,' Jamie told him, 'Worked out about twenty quid an hour.'

Crow scratched his head, 'Well, now I'm truly baffled. Who with?'

'Huh? No, just me, not for the firm. Was a studenty thing for a few hours.'

'And Don doesn't know?'

"No, not yet. I have to tell him.'

'Don't talk to Don tonight. Phone him in the morning, okay? Working solo, undercutting prices, and moonlighting are all against the rules.'

'Oh, if I've messed up? I'd better go tell him now,' Jamie had finally put the patchwork of company rules together, but Crow grabbed him with a friendly arm around his neck and said, 'You can explain that when he's not looking for an excuse to punch someone. Just stay here, out his way.'

Jamie sat down again and looked at his burger as if he was a ravenously hungry animal. The taste touched his lips and he was about to gorge himself like a wolf tearing at intestines on wildlife show when a fast-moving shape caught his eye. Charging towards them twenty yards to his front was a grubby, curly-haired man. The same man he'd seen when he'd entered the pub. He and Crow both noticed something about him worthy of attention. The following points were clear; he was too late for admission, he looked like a bad 1980s fashion exhibit in a dirty purple shell suit, and of course, the big Japanese sword he was swinging around his head was somehow just not right.

Jumping up from the beer garden's picnic benches, Crow yelled, 'Stay here!' Then, with a tired sigh, he threw his lovely hot moist cheeseburger towards the upstairs window of the pub, where it banged against the glass. The swordsman moved forward, screaming, 'Fucking Red-Ties! Come on, let's have it!'

Crow threw his second burger. The half-pounder was on target, hitting the man on the left side of his face, and the doorman used the distraction to drive off with perfect timing. He hit the blob of angry Bampot just as he stepped up from the carpark gravel onto the decking of the beer garden. The surprise hit battered him with something halfway between a rugby tackle and a flying head butt, causing their combined weight to land in a heap. Jamie saw the man's hand search for the fallen sword hilt on the ground and then find his grip. Struggling to turn the blade's point towards Crow's unprotected ribs, the attacker yelled, Bastard!' in frustration.

Crow, who was still winded from his own impact on the ground, groggily tried to brace his knee against the shell suit's elbow and block his action. It was only then that Jamie finally came out of shock and stood on the man's hand, just in time. A wrist twisted, and he bent the attacker's arm to hold it against his thigh like a cricket bat, forcing the shell-suited man's shoulder into a painful contortion. For support, Jamie stood on his other arm, pushing the body into the shape of a chicken having its wings pulled off. But by then, a group from the car park had gathered around them. Well-wishers or the attacker's mates, he didn't know, but they all kicked what lay on the ground and Crow's head was soon booted unconscious in the scramble.

Ginger had taken Don into the back bar to break the news about Jamie just as the first burger was thrown. It was lucky for Crow, terrible news for the man with the sword, and not that nice for the rest who had preyed on the opportunity for casual violence. The giant moved surprisingly fast for a giant and arrived first, followed by Don and half a dozen Red-Ties, who began knocking out any face they didn't recognise. One of them opened his blazer like a flasher and yelled, 'Dig in,' offering his friends the tools of crowd control; CS gas, a cosh, knuckle-dusters, and a stubby machete that were all fitted into his leather waistcoat. Within seconds, no unfamiliar face was left inside the beer garden to be knocked down. Unsurprisingly, the machete in the hands of a giant was enough for the onlookers from the carpark, who evaporated as suddenly as they'd arrived.

'Stunning, isn't it?' said Ginger.

'He's a nightmare, dunno what to do with him,' Don replied, gesturing an outstretched palm at Jamie who still had the attacker in his hands.

'Stop! Get off me. Get off!' cried the shell suit.

'Gonnae no dae that,' he replied slipping back into his Scottish, 'And yir a pure fud, do you know that? Did naeb'dy tell ya violence is wrang?' he sneered sarcastically.

'Let me up, you cunt!'

'Uch don't swear at me, Ahm no even hurting you ya bam,' Jamie growled.

At that moment, Don's foot connected with the man's head. It was a well-placed thoughtful arc, precise, and measured as if he was connecting with a rugby ball for an extra point over the posts. Then the boss relaxed and said, 'Take Crow inside and check him for damage.'

Pointing at the swordsman, he told two men, 'Get his wallet. Put him in my car.'

Once back inside and upstairs, Crow was passed fit by one of the doormen, who was also a psychiatric nurse, 'He needs to go to casualty to get checked out but looks fine.'

'I'm alright mate. What happened?' asked Crow.

'Nothing, this is a student pub, never any trouble,' Ginger smiled.

'Yer, but what happened? I remember a guy with a sword running at me,' Crow was rubbing his neck where a mark had been left by a glancing blow from a high heel.

Ginger explained, 'We saw that, but Jamie had taken him out by the time we got downstairs. Funny as fuck the way he talks.'

Jamie, now staring at his lager, broke his silence to say, 'I was hungry.'

Crow laughed, 'D'ya know what's funny. I did Aikido in the army for years. Loads of sword-disarming drills, but finally, a ninja comes at me with a katana, I got nothing.'

'I just stood on him,' said Jamie, looking around like he'd done something wrong.

The ex-Para asked, 'How did I get knocked out, anybody see? I don't remember.'

'Nah, lucky you had Jamie.'

'Good lad Jamie, I'll let you put a pint for me on your bar tab,' said Crow grinning.

'Huh,' he replied, but he felt refreshed too, comfortable to have a sense of belonging.

'He - is - my - new – besty,' Crow joked with a hiss.

In the club, the Red-Ties settled back into their seats with fresh pints and Don became full of smiles as if the sudden violence had refreshed his mood. Then he giggled, 'What we gonna do with ya? Anyway, over here mate, I wanna talk to ya.'

When he sat down, Don said, 'For god's sake Mush, don't do that.'

'What did I do?' he was equally confused by why he called everyone Mush.

'For a start, you opened the back gates to the beer garden.'

'Sorry.'

'If you see a problem like that. Just shut the doors, but fuck-sake mate, you just took out a guy with a sword. What would you be like if you had muscles?'

'I didn't do much, I wouldn't have hurt him,' he promised, 'I just held him.'

Don was chuckling again. He leant over the table and pinched his arm, 'Hey, I don't know if you are on a wind-up or just fucking mental.'

'Aye well. I'm no mental,' replied a little too defensively in his Scots vernacular, 'It's just I like things in order, and by the way, that Bampot wiz oot of order.'

Don laughed again and asked, 'You do any boxing?'

'Nah, I like yoga and archery,' he said without offering any boast about all the other martial arts he'd dabbled with back home in Scotland.

'Awesome. Totally useless on a door. Ya sure you haven't done any boxing?'

'No, I never fancied it. Looks like an excellent way to lose brain cells.'

Don sniffed, 'Well, you don't have to worry about that? So, what's with the ninja shit?

'I did a bit of judo. There wasn't much else to do in my part of the world.'

'You reckon you can fight do ya?' Don asked, but it sounded so like a trap.'

'Don…' Jamie sighed, 'I don't like hurting people. If I am attacked, I can stop them, or if they are hurting someone else. That's it. And I don't really like judo, but it was something to do.'

'Weird, but fair enough, so what about the bloke that tried to slice you up?'

Jamie misunderstood the question and replied, 'Honestly, it was a bit frightening. Y'know. with a sword. I didn't know what to do. I just held him down and hoped.'

'Awesome, but what do you want to do with him?'

'Nothing Don, it's over,' he replied.

'Fine. I'll deal with him then,' Don told him sardonically, then spoke as if an order, 'I hear you're going to go to the gym with Ginger. That's a start, then we need to get you boxing. That Japanese pyjamas shit doesn't work by the way.'

He didn't want the argument and was glad he hadn't brought up his Karate, so replied, 'Erm, I'll probably go to the gym, I know you're a boxer, but I don't like boxing.'

Don snarled, 'Never asked you if you liked boxing,' then changed the subject, 'Anyway, don't worry about it, he'd have found you sooner or later.'

'What do you mean?' Jamie was puzzled.

Don pulled a picture from the man's wallet. It was of him on campus with Ginger, 'Vengeance is the most beautiful thing there is mate. It is a simple, perfect relationship with enemies. Embrace it, but next time see them coming, don't walk into it like a toddler.'

Jamie stared blankly. A lot was coming at him at once, so he returned to the start of the conversation. 'I don't think you should've kicked that man; you could've killed him.'

When Don stopped laughing, he took a sip of lager and explained the firms' rules, 'They start things, we finish things. It sends a message.'

'He won't understand if he is unconscious,' Jamie muttered but didn't go any further to explain what it was that bothered him most about the incident.

From over his shoulder, another pint of lager arrived and Don told him, 'Jamie, we are a family. Your problems are my problems. You belong to me. I belong to you. Anyone messes with you, I'll spend my last penny to put them in the grave. But let's not tempt fate, huh? We'll keep you close. Make you my driver, eh?'

Jamie began to worry about the legality of his situation. Although he was used to driving around his village on forestry roads, he'd never actually passed his test. So told him, 'Don, I don't have a licence, and I think that...'

'Fuck off Jamie. You don't needs one. I got a licence, but if I dropped it out the window, I'd still remember how to change gears, wouldn't I?'

Ginger interrupted, 'Don't think. All you need is loyalty. Everything else can be taught.'

Don leaned over, 'You're my driver. Might even teach ya to drive proper.'

Ginger smiled as if to imply it would all be okay but said, 'Don's driver, poor bastard.'

Staring at his drink, avoiding eye contact he muttered, 'Still no daeing any boxing.'

The boss just shook his head, 'Let's go. I need to see someone about a sword.'

'I can't. I promised to see Maria, and I've been drinking!'

'Well, if it's a burd, start tomorrow,' he replied, saying, 'C'mon, I'll drop you off.'

Jamie nodded with relief, 'Thanks. It's Shakespeare Avenue,'

'Alright, s'laters,' said Ginger as they left, 'I'll come find you for the gym.'

Once Don was behind the steering wheel Jamie began reconsidering the situation, 'Can I have your keys please. I don't think I should be driving; you've been drinking.'

Don exploded for a second before laughing, 'Take my keys! Yer right, I'd knock you out,' fumbling in his pockets, he found a mobile and told him, 'You can take this though.'

As they drove towards Maria's, the car bumped over a few kerbs on the corners while Don explained, 'Anyway Mush, there are no car keys for the Jag, that way fuckers like you can't lose them. It's just a push button to start and a switch for the fuel.'

Jamie was surprised, 'So hold on. If no keys, how do you lock it?'

He drove to Maria's before responding, 'I don't need to lock it. Who'd steal from me?'

Then as Jamie opened the car door he laughed and said, 'Listen. You is under my protection, but ya need to learn what's okay and what's not. Only way to see if you're okay, is to throw ya in the deep end. That's the way we train lads. Newest on firm, gets all the hard stuff.'

'So just the dangerous stuff then?' he replied sounding sulky.

'Yup. All you gotta do is your best. And remember, you're only as good as your next fight, not your last trophy. So, get yourself to the gym every day.'

'Well, thank you for the lift,' Jamie replied, unconvinced about the boss's priorities.

'Yer mate. S'laters,' said Don as he drove away. Using momentum to close the door.

***

When Maria opened the door, she was only illuminated by moonlight, and she seemed to shimmer in the hallway and everything lingering in his mind about the Red-Ties disappeared when he saw what she was wearing. Crushed white silk pyjamas that clung with static to her curves. She embraced him with the dulcet electricity of kisses on each cheek and as usual he blushed at the show of affection, 'Sorry have I woken you up?'

'No Cariño, I am to wait for you,' she replied and gently led him by the cuff of his sleeve to her living room. There she made him a cup of cocoa sprinkled with marshmallows. 'Eres lindo,' she told him, but Jamie stared back blankly not realising what she meant.

All he could think of was, 'Whatever she sees in me. It was okay,' and from that moment, all tension from his night drained away as if a plug had been suddenly pulled.

'So, was it a good night?' She asked.

'Well yes, the Rugby club lot behaved. They became like schoolboys. Red-Ties but, they are different. It'd not work on them. They like mayhem I think.'

'Ayee. Of course. Nobody ever say that criminales are logical. They are the self-destructive people. Why mention them? Que te pasa?' she asked.

'The Red-Ties are not criminals really. They are just a bit reckless.'

Then sipping his cocoa, because inside her house it felt like a sanctuary and her sofa a confessional booth where he could say anything, he explained all about the burger van.

He told her, 'This guy tried to stick me with a sword, but Ginger stepped in and stopped anything from really happening.'

Despite being there when the order was given, he forgot about the frightened man in the boot of Don's car that the boss wanted to talk to and moved on to say,

'Oh, and I've got a job as a driver.

When she heard the two statements, Maria's hands went to her hips, and she wanted every detail. And the more he spoke, the angrier she got. Deriding his colleagues she exclaimed, 'That fucking Don. You think you can trust him. He is the chameleon. Today, he thinks it is funny to go with a gillipollas with the katana. Es la mierda.' As she paused for breath, Jamie leant back stunned by her reaction.

'Oh, so is okay. You relax on the sofa. Bravo!' she told him, 'What next? Today these Don of yours act like he step in front of a bullet for it. Mañana, he throw you to wolves.'

Jamie jumped to the hood's defence, 'Uch, I don't think so. He's just a bit impulsive.'

Maria shrugged, closed her eyes and calmed down. The last piece of frustrated Spanglish grammar was, 'Your choice. I am just to say it doesn't seem so safe and you are being tonto.'

'Aye,' replied Jamie sensing it was safe to talk, 'He's obviously a Bampot, but he's okay.'

She laughed, 'Que es Bampot?'

'It means someone who is a little rowdy,' he said, bending the truth.

'I see. In Spanish, he would be called a delincuente o el gangster.'

'Aye Okay, yer but can I ask you something?' he said hoping to change the subject.

'Ask me anything?' she replied.

'How come, sometimes speak like you're just learning, sometimes speak perfectly but?'

Maria replied with a quizzical expression, 'But, what is the but.'

'What but? There is no but. I'm no complaining,' he said, sounding stressed,

'Just wanna know why sometimes your English is perfect.'

She repeated, 'You said but?'

'Aw right, yeah, yeah. Maybe Scots say but at the end of sentences. I dunno why, but.'

Maria didn't believe him and searched the internet for a reference with her phone before declaring, 'I don't understand what you say,' then cheekily asked, 'Do you need the classes?'

'Ur you evading my question?' suggested Jamie, and the mood in the room changed.

Maria smiled at him, 'I have been caught, haven't I?' Then with a comical gasp she clarified, 'I speak four languages, and I am to improve my English. But sometimes I am lazy, and it is too much hard work to speak correctly. Especially if I am flirting with a boy, no? And it is better non, if I say, me gustas más que tomar vino?'

Her accent was pure honey when she spoke in Spanish, and even though he didn't understand the words, he nodded, 'Yes. God yes.'

Maria smirked and hit him softly with a cushion, 'Do you speak any languages? Are you lazy sometimes? Did you read when are in the library or just look at me?'

'I surrender. I surrender!' he laughed, 'Okay. Keep with the lovely accent. I prefer it to your Spanglish. I like it when you purr.'

'Purr? I don't purr. I am not the cat!' she purred, and in her most sensual whisper, said, 'I like your funny accent too. When you're tired, you say things.'

'What things?'

'You say waan, not one. You sound this. Ach uch hurrruurrrrr fill-um nae noo noo!'

'No, I do not,' then with a straight face, he told her, 'Scottish people don't have an accent. It's rest of the world that hus an accent. Don't yir school teach ya anything?'

'So funny, Scotty boy,' she giggled and smacked him with a cushion again.

46

'Okay, maybe I have a little accent,' he answered, trying not to laugh, but the more he tried, the more he pursed his lips and made his dimples show. Maria smiled sweetly and told him, 'I like to study with you and to improve my English.'

'Aye, nae bother, nae bother' at awe,' he said, speaking rapidly.

'Qué dirías?' she asked, giggling, 'What language is that?'

'English,' he explained and stuck his tongue out at her.

'No, I'm studying Cambridge English proficiency. You don't speak properly.

'Oh really,' Jamie laughed, 'I to speaking English more perfecto of you.'

She scowled, 'I'm not that bad. Mono malo!'

Jamie drew an imaginary zip across his mouth and stayed quiet.

Maria took both of his hands gently in hers and asked, 'I have a question. For you! Realmente, I have the two questions.'

'Anything Maria, verbs or adjectives?' he replied, grinning.

'No tonto, I have a nice house, but I am lonely on my own.'

'Si claro que si!' he replied, mimicking her purring Alicantina pronunciation.

'You know I have spare rooms, isn't it?' she asked with a beaming smile.

'I guess. It's a big expensive house for a student…are you like really a bank robber?'

'Joder no. Okay, let me explain, I've someone coming to stay, and this might mean I spend time with them and not to meet at the campus like I do.'

When he heard that, Jamie flinched, his heart possibly cracked a little. She saw his frown and smiled some consolation, 'It won't be long. A few days.'

Jamie nodded, 'Okay, I understand,' but his face was still a picture of sadness.

'So, is that alright with you? You don't mind her being here?'

'What do you mean?' asked Jamie puzzled, 'It's your house?'

'Her being with us?' Maria said smiling, 'Me gustas aqui todos los dias. You will be doing me a favour. You can do that, can't you? Is normal for estudiantesto move in together at beginning of year, no? I like the company, and you can pay whatever you pay for this shitty student shed. Because your bed-sit is shitty. You know this!' And I can to see you every day.'

He was stunned, but his face lit up, 'It's not a shed,' and his brow furrowed as he thought of the implications, 'I'd have to give notice. What if we didn't get on?'

Maria folded her arms to put on a grumpy face, 'Are you planning to be not my friend?'

'Well no. Obs! I was just saying,' he replied.

'Okay, so not to pay until that, but move in now. Say yes?' she asked, pouting.

'This is weird, isn't it? Moving in after like just meeting you? Not complaining but.'

'Ssssh, Cariño it is late. I've spare rooms, and the house is so lonely,' she told him holding his hand and turning her bottom lip into an exaggerated pout.

Jamie grinned, 'Be honest. You're manipulating me to do what I'd love to do anyway?'

'Yes. Of course. I am manipulating you. I am good for you. You are good for me. We are students, so we are meant to share accommodation, isn't it?'

'Okay, I will talk to my landlord.'

Maria's eyes lit up like stars, saying, 'Bueno! Perfecto! Oh, one more thing!' 'But you have to promise me. Please, please. Por favor!'

'Anything, whatever you want?' Jamie asked, happy that she was now smiling.

'Can you please to speak slowly and try to learn some English? I never understand you.'

The question set them both giggling and Jamie, in a sluggish sulky tone, asked her, 'Sorry, I didn't get that. Can you repeat it without all of the funny El-o-cu-tion?'

She stuck out her tongue again and asked, 'I have the next question for you?'

'Que? Que. Di'lo,' he asked attempting to speak some Spanish.

'Why is you so sweet, but tranquil with gangsters? They is not normal, no?'

His reply, in an intentionally exaggerated Scots accent, surprised them both, 'The thing is, Ah like my gentleness. Ginger thinks I'm acting like a Labrador puppy so I kin make folk underestimate me. But it's no a façade. When I see stuff, it doesnae really bother me. Okay, I saw a sword and froze. I knew frae judo whit to dae, but at same time I didn't know and ma brain wiz just nagging me, no to hurt him. But no 'cause it was wrang. I kinda just didnae want involved.'

'I see. Well, I hope you never change. Sweet boy.'

'I won't, what about you? Why me?'

Maria replied, 'I don't question why I like having you around. I don't want to. Seeing you in day, talking about boring things is good for me. I know this.'

Then she smiled, and looking happy she wrapped her arms around Jamie's and rested her head on his shoulder. He was content too, and it was the last thing he remembered before passing out next to her. It had been a long day.

***

As he slept, Maria listened to him snore and pondered what her inner voice was telling her. The next stage of a plan, she wanted nothing to do with, was being forced upon her. The voice told her it was wrong to have him around and dangerous for her to like him, but as she weighed up her options. She let herself think of something terrible for a spy like her, 'I like him, he will be safer with me.'

Although Jamie had again fallen asleep fully clothed on Maria's sofa, he'd somehow woken up in the spare room upstairs wearing just his boxers. While yawning and pondering this, a text arrived to explain where Don had left his car and who he'd to pick up that night. It looked like he really was working as a driver.

Once he got dressed, he went downstairs and walked into the kitchen. To his astonishment, there was a brunette, a lady who was almost the clone of Maria but wearing just a short, tight tee shirt and a thong.

'Hi, I'm Jamie. Is Maria...?'

She replied him yawning to say, 'Mi Cabeza Joder, shhhshhh,' and as if on autopilot, she wandered around the kitchen making a coffee.

Jamie stood and stared at the ceiling, wondering if he should leave. Then a minute later the stranger spun enthusiastically around from a cafetière and kettle to squeal, 'Oh Jamie, Jamie, Jamie. You ese Jamie, Joder, es puta madre tio. I know you. I very please-ed to meets you! Maria, she say everything to me.'

'How ya daeing,' Jamie said offering his handshake to the new girl, but he was unable to look her in the face or indeed look at her at all.

'Encontado Guapo,' she replied with exaggerated flirtation, 'I am Gabriella.'

She kissed his cheeks and hugged her body against his. It was nothing for her, but Jamie went red and began spinning around in embarrassment, wondering how to respond to what was essentially a half-naked woman cuddling him in the kitchen. That was when Maria arrived banging through the front door with shopping bags. She paused in the hallway only to yell, 'Oyez. A comer!'

It was evident from Jamie's looking up at the lights that something had happened. There was a conversation in Valencian between the girls. He didn't understand any of it, but it ended with Maria asking, 'What's up my Jamie?'

'Nothing. I just, y'know. It was a surprise,' Then he whispered, 'She's not wearing anything.'

'Ayeee,' she replied, 'It's not Arabia Saudita,' but said then something in Valencian to Gabriella, who responded in English to chuckle, 'Okay, I remember. Esta casa es Amish.'

Maria spoke in Valencian again. It sounded serious, as if she was scolding a small child but changed into English with a softer tone to point at the table and say, 'I've been to the deli, you go sit.' Then she raced around to serve a mix of Spanish and Sicilian foods as breakfast. She was wearing a figure-hugging blend of pastel blue Lycra and black mesh; as she bent over to take something out of the fridge, Jamie stared and remarked, 'Maria, you're amazing.'

She turned and smiled, 'I like to do this. It reminds me of my mama's house. Jamie just eat. Don't to rush. Eat slowly, enjoy, enjoy!'

'I am fortunate, amn't I?' he replied.

'Jamie amn't I, is not the correct English?' Maria told him.

'Don't know, but I am very lucky to be here with your food, amn't I?' he replied as his eyes followed her while she opened the oven door for something keeping warm.

When Maria bent down, he stared again at her bum, which prompted Gabriella to kick him gently and give him a conspiratorial wink,

'We can go out another night for fiesta.'

She writhed in her seat, clicking her fingers as if using castanets in a flamenco dance, 'Party, party, party. Jamie, you come for us to pubs, please yesterday?'

Maria corrected her and sounded a little cross with, 'Not yesterday. Today!'

'Sorry,' he replied, 'I have just agreed to work tonight. I am driving.'

'Oh okay, Jamie,' she said, holding up her hands as if surrendering. She began a conversation with Maria that sounded like an argument, with Trojan-Horse being the only word he recognised. Whatever they were talking about seemed to make the new girl nervous as she kept playing with her watch, repeatedly sliding it on and off of her wrist.

Hopeful of interrupting their bickering, Jamie tapped Maria on her arm, and when she turned towards him, he looked into her eyes and started to tell her what he was thinking about tostadas she'd served up, 'I love your...'

Maria erupted angrily, 'Jamie. Please not saying this!'

He looked puzzled and avoided saying more about the food; instead, he just nodded and said, 'Okay.' It was at least 30 seconds before he realised why she'd probably reacted.

'I meant the food. I love the food. Definitely the food, not you, obviously. I'd not love...No... I didn't mean that. Well, I mean, wouldn't.'

For a moment, she looked confused. Then mockingly, she slapped her hands over her heart and stretched open her mouth as if she'd been shot, 'Jamie, how could you!' He stuttered and spluttered an apology, 'Oh no, I didn't mean. I don't, wouldn't. Obviously, but I wasn't saying that. I didn't mean… weren't…you, I mean, I would. Because you know.' Maria laughed and told him, 'Stop talking,' while vigorously shaking her head from side to side.

***

That night from eight-thirty, Jamie ferried doormen between pick-up points and pubs. He constantly redistributed staff to reinforce nightclubs until at midnight Don phoned him, 'Mush, take the car to Crow. After that, you're finished for the night.'

'Where is he,' Jamie asked.

'The pub next to the hospital,' Don told him.

'Okay boss, I'm moving,' he replied and hung up. He was relieved that it was one of the few places he knew how to get to in the city, courtesy of all the A&E signposting on the roads.

When he arrived, the doormen didn't recognise him, nor did they believe he was in their firm, even when he used Don's name. It didn't surprise Jamie; hundreds of bouncers were working for him, and he'd only met a fraction of them.

One growled, 'Mate, it's a private party. End of,' so it was a relief when Crow arrived at the doorway grinning and introduced him by using the story about the katana.

Crow explained, 'If you are stood down, mate, then look in the function room, your bird is in there by the way. Hope you're not greedy, but I'll have the other one any-when,' he said with a smile and Hampshire slang.

Jamie struggled with what he was saying above the pub's noise; he wasn't sure about half of it, but he nodded and followed inside.

Upstairs it was quieter, and he was about to ask Crow to repeat himself when another doorman greeted them, 'You should see what they're up to in there. Well out of order!'

'As long as they ain't breaking glasses, landlady says it's all okay, let him through, he is one of us, but not working tonight.'

The man blinked in disbelief but replied, 'Okay,' and let him through.

Inside was a fancy-dress party full of pirates, pharaohs, cowboys and at least three Vampires. As Jamie stepped across the threshold, it became dark and loud again with the noise assaulting him from all sides. It was music, sporadic singing and a lot of happy shrieking. Jamie could see it was only well lit at the back of the room where a man in a tuxedo wearing a black and white face mask stood. He had a wireless microphone and asked, 'Quiet, please. Ladies and gentlemen, quiet! We need quiet, or we can't continue!'

A hush descended, and whispers became silence allowing the compère to tell them, 'Our next offering is Sophia. Please welcome her. Remember, it's for charity. You all know the rules.'

A blindfolded blonde in a Wonder Woman outfit was led by a leash and collar around her neck. She was helped to stand on a circular table as the man with the microphone asked, 'Who will start the bidding?'

Someone at the back yelled out simultaneously, 'Fifty quid.'

'Fifty? Fifty for a date with her, are you sure? Where are you taking her? A burger bar, you cheapskate! Do I hear an advance on fifty?'

The offers continued with yelling and shouting, and the microphone called out insults and charm to increase the amounts offered until Sophia was finally sold to her boyfriend. It was well organised, to the extent that a card payment machine took the final bid before the slave's leash was handed over. As Jamie edged closer to the front, he saw a pair of gladiators tugging the wrists of a nun in a pretence of dragging her to auction. That was when he heard, 'Gabriella, eres loca.'

Maria too was dressed as a nun, a very sexy nun.

The compère asked, 'What am I bid?' but there was no response as if the students had lost interest in the evening to drunkenness. To the gladiator behind her, he called out, 'Go on then,' and a cheer erupted as he groped Gabriella and began to unbutton her outfit. With a smile she shimmied to let the robe fall as far as her shoulders and reveal the top of her large pert breasts.

A shout came from the crowd, 'Sixty quid.'

Maria watched on, sighing and shaking her head, and whilst her attention was drawn by the gladiator with Gabriella, another slid up behind her and curled his arm around her waist. She looked disinterested but didn't push him away either. Instead, she was trying to yell at her house guest above the noise of the bidding, 'Joder, nos Vamos. Venga!'

Gabriella dropped her outfit some more, pressed backwards against the groin of her gladiator and seductively squirmed. Maria however, looked like she had stopped having fun and her expression settled somewhere between a bored smile and annoyed.

Then as if in a hurry to leave, she called out, 'A hundred pounds.'

'Sold!' agreed the compere, who tried to flirt with them both as Maria took the leash and slapped cash in his hand . Every word was heard on his mic as Gabriella giggled, 'We have to go,' and pulled away from her gladiator. The other one suggested to Maria, 'A kiss,' and when she turned her head to walk away, he swept in to plant his lips on hers. That was the moment when Jamie got to the front. He only locked eyes with her for the second that his face drained of colour. He was lost and his lips quivered, unsure what to think.

'Oh my god Jamie, you cannot be here!' and all smiles she'd had that evening were replaced by an open, dropped jaw.'

The gladiator didn't see her elbow, it connected with his sternum, and he fell away as Maria stepped towards Jamie. Then, as she became stuck between two ninja turtles offering to buy her a drink, Jamie spun around and was gone.

That night, he went to the Leni Quintain and slept on the pool table under his blanket that smelt of dogs. He tried to switch off the tormented thoughts he was lost in, but his head only had Maria and a gladiator kissing. In the morning at seven, the pub phone rang and the cleaner yelled, 'Jamie, it's for you!'

Sleepily he picked up the receiver, 'Hello.'

'Are you okay?'

'How did you get this number?' he asked in a sulky tone.

'I want to see you,' her voice pleading slightly.

'Why?'

'You know why.'

'I don't,' he said petulantly.

'I do like you, I do. Please don't be this?'

It must have been about five minutes of them breathing on the telephone without saying a word before she sighed and asked, 'Can you come home? Please, I need to talk to you, please. It is rude if you not come.'

He didn't reply. He just bit his lip and hung up the phone instead. Then regretting what he had done, he raced around to knock on the door.

When she opened it, she pounced on him in an embrace and told him, 'Jamie, I did not sleep last night. I worry too much about you. I am sorry what you saw.'

'I am sorry too, you look terrible,' he told her, and she did.

Still in her nun outfit with her hair tangled, and her eyes red from crying, she told him, 'Don't come here and say that. Don't be mean!'

'Oh, sorry, I'll go. Sorry, sorry,' he stuttered and tried to leave, misunderstanding her.

'Cariño stay here. Stay!' she pulled on his shoulders and tried to catch his gaze, but he twisted his face and shrugged his head into his shoulders to hide. There was no escape, she held him close, and he could feel both hearts beating, thumping through his chest.

She murmured, 'I am sorry you saw.'

'Okay,' he replied, mumbling, 'I don't want to discuss it.'

The sound of footsteps disturbed them and he broke away from her grip; it was Gabriella half-sleepwalking and going upstairs, also still dressed as a nun. As she passed, she held out her hand and patted his chest while yawning to say in English, 'Mornings! Goody, you are here now, so I can to sleep. You two are crazy.'

Maria took him away by the sleeve of his shirt and led him to the front room's sofa. Soft words rolled off her tongue to say, 'Sit, we talk, okay?'

'Okay, I sit,' he replied but he sat down, staring ahead with his arms rigidly fixing his fists on his lap. She grabbed a hand, then struggled to unfurl his fingers and them entwine hers in his.

Maria took a deep breath and told him, 'I like you. You know this!'

'You don't have to tell me anything,' he said with a blank face and monotone voice. She didn't let go of him but turned to straddle his lap and grab his other hand. She sighed and smiled, 'Don't be like a silly boy,' it wasn't an angry tone, just tired.

'I have to go now. Really!' he said, still avoiding eye contact.

Her words raced like a revving engine as they left her mouth, 'Okay, no. I do not to explain, but you are like a child. It's not an excuse. I have not seen Gabriella and... I was having fun while she... Joder, okay! A boy kissed me last night. But, when I saw you, I saw your face. I didn't feel very proud because maybe we are not just friends. Maybe more than that. Happy now?!'

Jamie shrugged then asked, 'Is he your boyfriend?'

'No. I have no boyfriend, Tonto! I like boys and I have. I had the boyfriend in Spain. I had him, but he wasn't nice. So, you understand? Joder! I can't to speak English now. I saw you last night, and it made me sad.'

Then she whispered, 'I promise I don't have any boyfriends. I can't do that now.'

Jamie pursed his lips and furrowed his brow in confusion before telling her, 'I upset you. I will keep out of your way.'

'NO! You not upset me. I am to work. I can't want anything else now.'

'Work?' he asked.

'I mean to study, sorry my English.'

Stuttering he replied, 'I don't want to talk. I'm going.'

'Joder. I don't want to lose you as my friend.'

Jamie huffed and told her, 'Oh okay. The friend zone huh? Fine, but I can't do that. Every time we are alone together, I just like you too much. You don't want me like that, so I won't say what I think anything anymore. It's fine! And yer, like I said, I'll keep out your way.'

Maria's face flashed in anger for a second. Then she sighed, cupping his face in her palms as she told him, 'Sometimes I want to strangle you for being so tonto.' With that said, she leant forward to kiss his forehead. She kept smiling at him and began shaking her head to make her hair caress his face until he stopped sulking and smirked. 'I was jealous,' he told her.

'No, really?' she laughed and began tickling him.

After a long pause, he tried to get up, but Maria pressed him down with her breasts pushing into him. Her body's warmth on his crotch made him writhe and his cock started to harden. Finally, he replied, 'Okay, you have to let me up. I need a pee,' and tried to stand.

'You don't need a pee. Tell me we are okay, and I will let you go.'

'I...' Jamie tried to speak.

'Shhhhhh, no don't say it. I know I'm not fair to you, but now I need you normal for me, or everything in my life is just crazy. You are to be my safe place. My friend. Okay?'

She sighed, squinted at the bulge in his trousers, and then dragged him to the kitchen. As she laid the table for breakfast, she didn't let go of him. All the time, moving between the patio table, fridge and cupboards with her fingers tightly wrapped around his.

Maria prepared a medley of Valencian foods for him, but only use his left hand to eat. She didn't even let go of her grip when she poured him coffee from a cafetière.

Jamie sighed, 'Am I allowed to say friends and I like you, but to consider being more?'

'No, you can't say that,' she said drawing in a deep happy breath.

'Just did!' he replied, but while looking down, avoiding eye contact.

There was then a tremor in his voice as he said, 'I don't like this. I liked being with you when I could fall asleep without thinking about stuff and without my dick getting hard.'

'I know Cariño,' she sighed and told him, 'I am not fair to you. I know this, I will be better with us. Okay, but I need sleep now.'

Then tugging him upstairs to his bedroom she told him in a whisper, 'Hablar despues. Not today.'

Her hand stayed where it was in his. In the doorway, they stood in silence, until he blurted out, 'I want to be your...'

'Cariño, shhh! I know what you will to say, but don't ask these things. Just be my friend.'

Jamie made a long heavy sigh and weighed up the gamble of telling her every word of how he felt, then instead he mumbled,

'I feel like a wet cat that's turned up on your doorstep.'

To turn the door handle of his room, he tried to slip his hand from her grip, but she tightened it and told him, 'Mira Jamie. You think I am looking after you, don't you?

'Escúcha me. Is not me looking after you. It's you who is looking after me!'

To his surprise, the hint of a tear appeared in her eyes, and she bit her quivering lip. He saw he'd upset her and pulled her closer to say, 'Sorry.'

'Don't be, it is me who has the regret,' she told him, then hesitated for a moment of teeth-bared frustration before explaining, 'Okay, so you never ask me anything about who I am, why am I here or what I do before. You don't even ask about this big house. You just sit on my sofa and you talk silly things. I need that. You're my normal life.'

Jamie's face scrunched up in confusion, 'I don't understand.'

'Shhh, just be my Jamie. Just be you,' she told him and pulled him into her chest, where he melted in her arms. All the doubts seeped out of his body. They embraced with her hair tickling his nose again.

He clumsily readjusted his arms a few times, but apart from that, the only movement was their breathing and the thumping heartbeats as they hugged. After an age, Maria whispered, 'Night-night Cariño,' and they went to their separate rooms.

**

Then next afternoon Jamie moaned when a call came in from Crow asking him to drive him to Wiltshire. At first, it seemed as if he just wanted the car that he already had, but it turned out that he was too drunk to drive, and that Don had given Jamie out on loan. On the journey there, Crow snored and reeked of alcohol. The SatNav did all the work, but even if the Paratrooper had been awake to give directions, Jamie was too grumpy to want to talk to him. It became a seven-hour round trip, with Crow leaving him for three hours with the words, 'They dunno ya, best you stay in the car.'

Overall, it was a very dull, unpleasant day with his colleague. The only vaguely interesting thing to occur was the sight of Crow in the distance being shouted at by someone who looked like the man who'd turned up at Don's barbecue. When he returned, Maria greeted him with hugs and another evening of rioja and watching DVDs on the sofa. What he didn't know was, that whilst Gabriella was dressed as a nun and flirting with Crow, she'd switched his watch for one that looked the same but listened to his every word and tracked his movements.

'Good morning. Another beautiful day,' said an old man into a mic on his collar.

A woman's voice in his ear moaned, 'Boss, it's still dark. Where are you now.'

'Just on my way in. I might stop for breakfast somewhere.'

'You know I could always pick you up in the mornings,' she replied.

He ignored the suggestion and inquired, 'What's in the mail today?'

'Nothing much. Cops are bit excited about the pub you wanted me to watch, that's all.'

Boarding a bus and flashing his pensioner's pass, he asked, 'Why? What have you done? You've done something, haven't you?'

The woman chuckled, 'Nothing really bad. I called in as a concerned citizen who wanted to remain anonymous and said that I'd seen red tied men with guns doing what looked like a big naughty drug deal.'

'And you did this why?' he asked quietly.

'Boss. I can't watch everyone. It'll save us time if the local plod did a bit.'

'Fair enough. I mean. Good idea, and I guess it will keep everyone busy,' he told her.

'Thank you. Nice to get a bit of praise.'

'Do we have any reports back?'

'Yes, it's good stuff. I am pinning up on your board now,' she told him.

'Good…good. I will be there soon. Well, after breakfast,' he told her, 'Bye for now.'

The old man was called Ken. His journey to work was always by a different route and a quiet time where he could gather some thoughts and plan the complexities of his trade. No one ever spoke to the old man, and he doubted whether anyone ever noticed him en route, or would even be able to remember if he wore spectacles or not. He liked that. Once off the bus, Ken shuffled into the Admiralty and fumbled with his access badge until one of the guards helped him scan it.

He showed on their screen as the curator of declassified archives in section G.

It wasn't his real job in the security service, just a dilapidated image he'd cultivated. Everything about his manner had been crafted to encourage people in the building to see him as a benign academic that perhaps the service had kept on past retirement, rather than the terrifying creature of espionage he really was.

His actual department was Military Intelligence-11. It was a section that had been formed once and officially disbanded twice without ever ceasing its clandestine work. He didn't truly exist either. Even the name on his pass was one he'd acquired from the previous post-holder who had inherited it from theirs. He was of the security services but not in the security service, and he liked that extra layer of obfuscation.

Using a lift, he went down to a labyrinth of tunnels, an office that looked like it'd once been the furnace room of a Victorian bathhouse where his assistant was waiting for him. Her name was Petra, and she looked like an exhausted city worker who'd just woken up in the same trouser suit and blouse she had drunkenly fallen asleep in. Apart from the sport of throwing the Olympic hammer, she was only known for her attempts at running.

Whenever she attempted the motion, it was like watching a house brick roll down the street, but what her boss liked about her was her ability to do plodding police work.

'Morning Boss, I have an update on the paratrooper.'

Ken snorted, 'Oh please, they are all bloody paratroopers. Which one?'

'Crow, he contacted his former colonel. To ask if the job was all okay.'

'And?' Ken asked, 'The colonel went up the food chain? Came back to tell him he told he was good to go? Yes?'

'Yup, and just as quickly, an MI-5 officer descended on him to tell Crow to take the job, while promising him money and immunity from prosecution. You know, the usual.'

Ken shook his head slowly from side to side and suggested, 'Let me guess, it was the same MI-5 officer who'd short-listed Crow to be approached in the first place?'

'Absolutely,' she told him and handed over the dossier. He ground his teeth as he read through the files. For him, it was tired old nonsense from the book of spies; audacious deceit and some poor sod made to think he was one thing when really being groomed as a patsy. 'What else have we got today my dear?' he asked.

Petra handed him an envelope she'd been holding under her armpit, and Ken broke its seal. He pulled out the summary sheet and sighed,

'Oh, that's quite a lot. Leave it with me.'

Their morning briefing was interrupted by a flashing red light and the noise of a shutter slowly rolling down in front of what Ken called his "Murder wall."

A few minutes later, they heard the noise of scurrying rats and the echo of someone in the tunnels clip-clopping towards them. They liked the noisy vermin; they were another early warning system and added to the illusion that his office was an insignificant place.

His visitor had descended by a modern lift at Horse Guards Parade, past all the clever people, to arrive with the arrogant confusion that he'd been somehow demoted to a postman. They always looked the same. They were always rising stars of the service. Their faces always seemed unsure if anyone in the tunnels was someone important enough to defer to.

Petra met him at the threshold with, 'Hello sir, please come in.'

The officer was polite and to the point, 'I'm looking for the curator.'

I'm curator,' said Ken flicking the name tag on his coat pocket,

'How may I help?'

'Requests for file destruction. Should they come here?' he asked, handing over his paperwork.

'Yes, thank you, replied Ken.

The officer gave over a list, muttered a hasty 'Thank you,' and hurriedly left.

By noon two more MI-5 officers had arrived with more, Top Secret bureaucratic compliance. Some of it was interesting, but most were merely the receipts of espionage to cross-check the who, what and where of agents acting shamefully. Ken grumbled, 'Bloody hell,' when he saw how his assistant had organised new connections.

'What's wrong with it?' she looked confused.

'Everything, the wall is beginning to look like Whack-a-mole in various European languages.'

From the comfort of his Chesterfield, Ken pointed to a Post-it note where she'd written, "Operation Fluffy-Bunny. What's that?'

'Not a clue. Yet,' she replied.

It seemed Fluffy-Bunny wasn't the real name, but it referred to a routine RAF training flight over Scotland that had captured only pictures of empty moorland and rabbits. The photos had ended up being reviewed and flagged for an investigation, yet although no enquiry ever officially took place, the images were classified as "Top Secret." Petra had found out that the request to restrict access to the file had been made by the same MI-5 officer who'd selected Crow, which absolutely guaranteed that Ken's department would ask, 'Why?'

Suddenly tired of thinking about the problems on his wall, he told his assistant, 'Brunch,' and retrieved a bottle of whisky from his old mahogany desk. She carried on pinning notes to the wall and commented, 'No, I'm good.'

Pouring two glasses of peaty malt, he repeated, 'Brunch, this time, it's an order.'

His assistant groaned, 'Boss. I'm working,' but she accepted the drink and sat on his desk.

That was when his phone rang. On the other end of the receiver was a man he knew as a former head of MI-6. His gentle, quiet voice asked, 'Ken, are you looking at the CIA?'

He'd expected the call, 'Sir, yes. I'm afraid so. They're rebooting a tiresome version of Operation Gladio.'

'Oh, I see, but we want to be friendly. No action. Just observe, Understood?'

'Of course, sir,' he'd been told. It seemed that whatever he'd started. He was to stop. The man on the other end of the call then said, 'I'd better hear about what you've done so far? What they're up to.'

Ken replied, 'I'll write a report.'

'Yes, well, no need for that. A chat will do. Pop round to my club when you can,' he was told, and the caller hung up.

Ken drained his whisky and mused, 'Best. No checks, no balances.'

Petra asked, 'What was that about?'

He sighed and told her, 'Lunchtime now. Your shout!'

'No thanks. I'm working,' she said sarcastically.

'Well, dear. It's definitely lunchtime. We've just been taken off the job.'

That's when his assistant in her un-ironed white blouse and ill-fitting black trouser suit erupted with all the professionalism of a rabid badger, 'What the fuck?' she snarled.

He briefly switched off his guise as a frail wrinkly pensioner to stand and speak in the tone of her commanding officer, 'Lunch,' he barked, 'We need to talk about your future.'

They locked up and took a route out of the tunnels that led to the cellar of a medieval guild hall. The building was suffering some renovation, and they made their way up a stone staircase to a long oak-panelled gallery. It still had the remains of heraldic shields cobwebbed to the wall.

'This is you,' he declared, pointing at a worker's bright, battery-powered lamp. 'And this is me!' he said, indicating the remains of a delicate wall frieze.

'I'm all the centuries of mould and broken plaster, and you're the new guy that wants to rip holes in my damp walls to put in electrical sockets. But Dear Petra, I need fine art restoration from you.'

They stopped and waited in a 12th-century gatehouse next to an iron-riveted door, and Ken tilted his head up to speak to an unseen security guard, 'Yes, please.'

They heard the hiss of hydraulics that let the pair step outside onto a cobbled London Street. Then out of the building, they walked towards St. Paul's. Ken, now back in his guise as a harmless old-aged pensioner, quietly admonished her, 'You can't expect us old fuddy-duddies like us to understand the complexities of this milli-second modern world... Just because we invented it... Can you?'

'Sorry, Boss! It just. You know.'

He interrupted her, 'You were about to be critical, weren't you? Walls have ears, careless talk costs lives, and never let anyone outside the family know what you're thinking.'

'Godfather?' she asked, rolling her eyes.

'You deserved it! The service sometimes demands obedient bewilderment, not questions.'

He was smiling again. His facial expression returned to that of a tired old man.

'What are we up to, Boss? And why have I got the feeling we're about to be mugged?'

He ignored the question and asked, 'Do cops still have collators?'

She sighed, 'Nah, Boss. These days they just tap into computers. There isn't always a sergeant in stations to join the dots. It's shit, but that's the modern world.'

'It's good,' he told her, 'I need you to use the police database to tag more people.'

'Oh shit. Are we still on the job?'

'Yes and no. We've to go a bit quiet, but I'll still need to know more about their pattern of movements. Who is seen with who? What cars they're in? Nothing too clever.'

'Will I be able to look at myself in the mirror after this? If I don't get caught logging in?'

'You won't. I don't ever recommend either of those things. Use a back door,' Ken told her.

'Yer right. Our computer nerds are always changing the system. What if I do get seen?'

'Don't worry, we're exempt from prosecution these days. You'll just be locked up in an asylum and go mad with regret wondering why the matron doesn't believe your story about; how you were once a contender, tip of the spear, edge of the knife for the Crown.'

'Yer, awesome,' she replied with an insincere smile, 'I should be worried, shouldn't I?'

The old spy was on a roll, 'We've a proud tradition of obediently watching leadership make mistakes in compartmentalised structures and taking far too long to correct them.'

'What's that mean? Because y'know, I am not fluent in Eton.'

'It means we would like our allies to think they're getting unquestioned agreement and over-eager support. While we work as normal. The person on the other end of my phone call used a specific phrase. He said we want to be friends and asked if I understood.'

'Oh, I get it. Spy stuff,' Petra replied grinning, 'I like it. I like it a lot.'

In the gardens of St. Paul's, as they ambled between passers-by who might overhear them. Ken popped a dose of prednisolone into his mouth and Petra noticed, 'Erm…What are those?'

'Those dear, are your promotion prospects.'

She held her hand for the medicine bottle and read the listed side effects, depression and violent mood swings. She gasped as she read the words, "Potential suicidal thoughts."

'What's going on?' she looked concerned, 'And no bizarre answers, please.'

'Petro-dollar lasted a hundred years, so there is a struggle.'

Petra snarled, 'That was an eleven out of ten for avoiding the subject.'

He explained in a whisper, 'I am having repeated lung infections and pneumonia. I suspect I'm allergic to my work-life balance of dust, dampness and demons.'

She was irritated, 'But you are okay?'

'I find my instinctive aggression keeps me going, and whenever the familiar symptoms arrive, I take an identity to a drop-in centre and convince a doctor to prescribe what I want.'

'Bully a doctor to give you drugs you mean?' she asked, as if concerned for her mentor.

The spy shrugged, 'They smash the warning lights that say stop. The only problem is that my steroid of choice is made from female hormones, which means I might cry when I'm cleaning my Walther or doing something mundane like looking for a pen. It's been emotional.'

She shook her head, 'The service doesn't know, do they? Is this why you're falling asleep?'

'Temporarily a bit out of fizz. Not too old yet! Side effects are hilarious, aren't they?'

Petra growled, 'Erm...No!'

Ken changed the subject, 'Oh, by the way, when we return to the office, ask for a holiday. Sound annoyed with me, okay?'

'You're kidding, right?'

'Nope,' He told her, 'We'll have to pretend that we're not that interested in things. Take photographs of my wall and box everything up.'

'What's this? A holiday in the Bahamas, you say?' she asked smiling.

'Almost. I am going to sign you off on a course to learn Dutch. You will go to some friends of mine in a convent near Arnhem. Stay for a minute, sneak back through Bruges on another passport. Use Ramsgate. Avoid facial recognition it's gotten better now.'

'Not the Bahamas then?' she replied, looking like a surly teenager who had been grounded.

'No, but if you bring me back some nice chocolate, I'll get you a sunlamp.'

She scrunched up her face, 'Cheers. Anything else? Nougat perhaps?'

Ken nodded, 'Good idea. But once home, I want you working from a safe house.'

'Why?' she asked, sounding both concerned and a little excited.

He told her, 'Let's just say I am suddenly mindful that we are in the trust-building and betrayal business. We will be going after someone untouchable.'

'Who is that?' she snorted with a giggle, 'The prime minister?'

This time the old spy laughed too, 'Oh dear, how'd you ever get past vetting? And No.'

'I'll need a clue?' she replied.

He was silent momentarily while constructing precisely what he could and couldn't say, 'The service is stretched. Right now, for expedience, our government is approving every; what, when, or oh look a squirrel that our American allies suggest.

I am repeatedly told not to worry about things. Things that even our propaganda departments have no idea about how to spin.'

His assistant wasn't innocent by any means, but she seemed shocked by what he described and asked, 'We know what's going on roughly though, the service I mean?'

He shook his head, 'I think we are either being genius or making the biggest mistake since we backed a young journalist called Mussolini and his friend Hitler. I just don't know yet. What I do know is that when I joined the service, it would never have occurred to me that I'd see a day when our Prime Minister, the US president or our bureaucracies would be so openly infiltrated by foreign agents. It's like the KGB, Mossad & that butcher in Saudi have bought the lot.'

'Oh bugger,' she replied, 'So, who do I go after first?'

'Who do you think?'

'Please, straight answers today,' she grumbled, 'Can't we just take out the American?'

'God no! My little protégé, that would piss off half the US State Department.'

'We could let the ops stay open but block our guys working with them?'

'Nope, that will annoy the other half. Guess again.'

'You want them to close it down?'

'Bingo!' replied the old spy, 'You're learning. What else?

'A scandal? Pull out some dirt?' She asked. Her mentor stopped walking and used his disappointed look as he told her, 'Not this time. We can only nudge behaviours if they are taking a bribe without boasting about it on their bloody websites. Anyway, officially we are off the case, so it's only the illegitimate we can go after. That man Angel. He is her weakest link and as he's neither British nor American, he's fair game.'

What Ken didn't realise, and no one could have expected, was that it wouldn't be other agents or the technological might of an intelligence agency that would get in his way, but instead a naïve student and some semi-literate doormen.

Monday morning Jamie wasn't awake enough to do much more than moan slightly and pull the duvet back over his head, every time Maria jerked down.

'No, leave me,' he whined, but she didn't relent. In fact, she increased the level of assault on his sleep by tickling his nose with one of his discarded socks.

'Wake up. Jamie, wake up. You will be late for class,' she told him with a croaky voice.

He didn't move until his phone began blasting out a Reggae ringtone, she held it to his ear. Even then, he only groaned and attempted a half-hearted fumble to push it away.

'Okay, Cariño. I answer it for you,' she told him and held it to his ear, and the first shouty words he heard were, 'Where the fuck are you?'

'Hello, this is Jamie,' he mumbled, 'How can I help you?'

'Shut up, you knob-scratch. You were meant to pick me up.'

He didn't recognise the voice and replied, 'Who is this?'

'Get your arse over here!' he yelled and hung up.

Jamie felt disorientated, and looking around his room asked, 'What just happened?'

Maria stroked his hair and told him, 'Your phone has lots of texts.'

It didn't help that her voice was like a lullaby told with a deep hoarse tone, and it took him a few minutes to register what she'd said. He groaned and groggily yawned his way out of bed. 'You okay?' he murmured.

'Is little cold. En me nariz. Not to worry,' she replied and sneezed.

Once standing, he readjusted the morning wood with a few strokes of leisurely massage then suddenly froze in panic when he remembered she was in the room with him. Hurriedly he turned himself away, grabbing his trousers to hide the cock that had been tenting in his boxers and pointing towards her face. With his belt buckle locked in place, he twisted to peek over his shoulder and mumble with embarrassment, 'I have to go. I am late. I've gotta pick a car up.'

'Si claro que si,' Maria chuckled. With an exaggerated frown, she told him, 'I tried to wake you, but you only move when your silly Red-Ties phone you. It makes me sad.'

Then pulling down the sides of her mouth with her fingers, she said, 'See, I am sad face because you snore. I thought it was the earthquakes.'

'I don't snore,' he complained while reading the texts on his phone and made the mental calculation that he had one relatively important lecture that day, and he could get the notes from his classmates.

'Si, you do. Like this. Oh no, I am so sleepy,' she told him and threw herself down on his bed to make the noise of a comic pig snorting with her tongue hanging out.

That was the moment he properly woke up and caught sight of her black silk pyjamas that clung with static to her body. He had a physical reaction to the gorgeous woman lying on his bed, and he winced as if in pain then began to walk out the door saying, Gotta go.'

She called him back, then briefly tapped her forehead with a finger and demanded, 'Kisses, where are my kisses goodbye?'

Tentatively he pushed her hair back, gave her a peck and he rushed off to Don's car, not even stopping for a piss.

***

It was a short walk to the pub carpark where Don had left the car, then Jamie drove to the other side of the city. The person he'd been sent to pick up didn't say his name, but Jamie recognised him from the barbecue. It was the man who'd insisted a sniper had been overlooking Don's garden. He mumbled a greeting and told Jamie, 'You're driving, I'm still pissed.'

As they drove, the big doorman grunted and casually pointed with his finger which way to go at junctions. As they passed a tyre fitter the doorman asked, 'You see that blue beamer in the rear view? The one zigzagging through traffic?'

Jamie glanced in his wing mirror and saw a BMW M3 racing towards them, and replied, 'Even I know that is dangerous driving.'

'Watch them, it looks iffy! We're gonna get stuck at the lights up ahead. If they get out of the car, drive over them, okay? Just hit them with the car.'

Jamie began to fret. It was hard enough driving around a city without this sort of madness. 'Watch them!' he was told more urgently.

The car sped up and changed lanes so that the rear passenger side window was level with Jamie, and a quick sideways look revealed a large thug rising with a raised shotgun. Without waiting for orders he braked hard, and the car passed by them to be stuck between two cars in its lane of traffic as the lights turned to red. Jamie was about three car lengths behind with a clear space in front. The big doorman yelled, 'Mush if the fucker turns, ram him! Hit the back wheel. Got it?'

Jamie nodded. He wasn't sure what was going on, but obedient to his orders, he turned the wheels and edged the car forward to align with the window he'd seen the weapon in. Then just as suddenly the lights changed, and the BMW sped away.

Jamie asked, 'Whatdafuck was that?'

His passenger shrugged, 'Probably some lads having a laugh.'

Still in a little shock at the incident Jamie stalled the vehicle, and to the beeping of horns from other drivers they missed the change of lights. There was a part of him that was alarmed, and another part of his brain that thought, 'Okay, it's scary, but it's a lot more interesting than, "Sea and ship motions,' with Doctor Kim.

'Hurry up, get driving!' declared the big doorman.

They then pulled off the main road onto country lanes, where Jamie de-stressed by focusing his mind on something else. He might not know any page of the Highway Code or how to drive in a city, but he knew single-track roads. Hitting the accelerator, he threw the car around corners like a rally driver while his passenger hung on to his seat with white knuckles, albeit pretending nothing out of the ordinary was happening. When they parked up at a leisure centre and walked inside, they met an enraged Don who grumpily greeted the pair,

'Phil, you Fucker, you're late!'

The big doorman's reply was surly, 'Yer, and. Why am I here? I know all this shit.'

Don snarled, 'Yer ya do, don't ya,' and pointed at men demonstrating a self-defence drill. It involved using both hands held together to palm strike into an attacker's solar plexus. Phil moaned, 'Do I have to?'

'Yes, Smart-arse, you can show us all how it's done.'

Phil turned towards Jamie and told him, 'It's your lucky day!'

The big man took the first shot, but Jamie pivoted, and the strike slipped by as it touched. 'Stand still prick,' he told him angrily.

'I'm not moving,' he replied, sounding nervous, but flashing a grin.

Phil tried another strike to his chest, and Jamie rotated to the left. The third time he evaded getting hit, Don shouted at them, 'Stop fucking about!'

'It's not me. It's him,' Phil complained.

Don's temper exploded, 'This isn't a fucking joke. You should be setting an example. 'If ya can't do this. Just fuck off now,' then he sighed, 'Go on Jamie, show me on Phil.'

'Sorry,' Jamie said, shrugging. Without warning, he took a short step that landed with a twist of his hips as his hands connected with Phil at a point just under his sternum. He yelled, 'Key-aaaah!' and surprise took over Phil making him stagger backwards to trip.

From the ground, the doorman snorted like an enraged bull, and he puffed, 'So it's like that is it?'

'You done this before?' Don asked with a wink, putting his body between them.

'It's yoga,' replied Jamie, unwilling to be drawn into talk about other sports he'd experimented with. Don pulled a face at the apparent bending of truth and began barking orders about moving tables and chairs to make room for the next set of drills. He told the trainees, 'The lads will play the part of customers in a pub. Your job will be to assess the situation and deal with it using the techniques we learned in class this morning.'

Jamie was assigned to the first group of novices to act as doormen in the role-play. Once an area had been marked out on the floor with tape and road cones to represent a pub's entrance, Don explained, 'Phil's barred but he wants to come in. You have to stop him.'

Phil grinned and muttered, 'That means we don't have any rules.'

Don maybe overheard the remark as he yelled, 'No punching anyone. That means you, Phil!'

The big doorman rubbed his hands together with glee and looking at Jamie told him, 'You're so fucked!'

Don then yelled, 'Go!' and Phil sauntered forward to barge through their line, a struggle began immediately. One recruit lunged for his legs while another went high, but both were swatted away with casual disregard, which left Jamie standing on his own as the final line of defence.

What began as lumbering ended as a charge, as Phil closed on him like a rugby prop with the obvious intention of smashing him into the wall behind. Jamie crumpled as the weight of Phil's body hit and he was spun around. His head would have been cracked and crushed onto the ground if not for his half-remembered martial arts. Squatting momentarily with Phil's bulk still ploughing onwards, Jamie grabbed the doorman's loose arm, continued to turn and flexed his thigh muscles to lift his attacker. He had neither the agility nor skill to do it well, but Phil flew over his back to land sprawled flat on the floor, yelling with a broken ego and his ankle smashed into the wall.

'Jamie! For fucks sake, tone it down a bit,' Don shouted, then turned to the Red-Tie tasked with admin for the day and quietly told him, 'Mark him down as a three.' Jamie rolled away quickly from where he'd fallen clumsily, and Don waved forward more trainees with the order, 'Drag him out. It's not over until he's out the door!' Those selected to restrain Phil were still busy laughing, giving Phil time to rise and recover with his back against a wall and his hands clenched to make fists.

The next man sent forward was hit with an elbow to his shoulder that struck simultaneously with Phil's knee hitting the inside of his thigh. The one after that was guided by Phil's palm into a spiralling trajectory to fall at his feet. That was when Jamie was urged to engage again, and he reluctantly attempted a grab on Phil's arm for a wristlock. The move didn't go as planned, He didn't have the strength to do anything except get caught and pulled in with Phil then wrapping his forearm around Jamie's neck to make his legs dangle, which was the last he remembered until he regained consciousness.

***

As punishment for using a prohibited technique, Don volunteered Phil to stand next to a small, wiry-looking man of about five foot two, who was introduced as SF-Ben their self-defence instructor. Standing beside the big man, he looked vulnerable until he began his lecture. He coolly jogged past Phil with a smile and a relaxed wave. He said, 'This is how you stab someone,' and his right hand worked like a sewing machine to rapidly jab his target in about eight places without breaking stride. 'Main rule to remember in a knife fight,' he said, 'Is everybody bleeds.'

The little man then brushed his plastic knife with a red marker dye and gave Phil a white paper suit to wear of the kind that forensics officers use at crime scenes.

'Oh, for fucks' sake, do I have to?' Phil moaned, but Don insisted, 'Unless you aren't up to it and need a rest?'

Once Phil was zipped up in the slightly too small paper suit, the little man restarted the lesson and spoke gently, saying, 'Phil, please defend yourself.'

'I'm gonna hate this bit, ain't I?' Phil sighed while taking a wide-legged stance. SF-Ben was nimble and seemed to dance slowly with his knife hand arcing upwards. Phil lunged, tried to block the man's arm with his left and drop a punch onto the man's chest with his right, but it was to no avail. In a swift movement, the trainer side-stepped, and in a flash, he was past and behind Phil.

'Fuck!' was the gasped consensus from the class.

It was only clear what the instructor had done from the red marks on the white paper suit. One line ran from inside his thigh to his groin, another looped around Phil's wrist and a third stripe ran up to his armpit and across his chest in a zigzag cut before looping around his neck and down the length of his spine. It had been as fast as the blink of an eye.

The instructor told everyone, 'I am not particularly good with a knife, but that should have given you an idea of what might happen if you confront someone who is tooled up. Don't fuck about. Don't try to grab a sweaty wrist with some crap you saw online. Hit the arm with force and take the man to the ground. Trust in your mates to finish him.' He ended by explaining, 'You won't have time to think. You might not even see the blade.'

Don added to the advice, 'It's a lot to take in, lads. When your mate grabs the knife hand, he does not let go. Phil's gonna demonstrate, how even a big lad can be taken down.'

The lesson continued with the instructor using Phil to show how various wrist, arm and shoulder locks to restrain people, were meant to work. It wasn't pretty, Phil resisted as much as he could and did everything except bite the trainer in his attempts to struggle out of the grips.

It looked like the happily obstinate doorman wanted to prove that nothing would prevail against his strength, so let the instructor place him in a wrist lock and gradually apply force. He grinned like a poker player calling everyone's bluff and repeated, 'No, can't feel nothing,' until a loud crack was heard, followed by a leg sweep that smashed him onto the ground. Phil's stubbornness resulted in a trip to the hospital for a fracture.

The day's momentum didn't slow for casualties, and the remaining attendees were split into groups of three to repeat the techniques with degrees of distraction added to the routines. Sweaty men in torn shirts practised their drills with arms in the air as if surrendering and used a closed fist to signify which side of a target needed to be assaulted, but Don wasn't happy with anyone's efforts. In the absence of Phil, he called on Ginger to make a point. The choreography began badly, with those chosen to confront the giant draining themselves of confidence before it'd even started, and after that, it got worse. Don told them, 'Don't hesitate. Go for it! Hard and fast.'

Like Kamikaze pilots, they communicated poorly and instead of acting as a team, each individual picked their moment to attack. The first slammed into Ginger's knife arm in a forlorn hope of pulling him off balance. When that failed, the next man attacked the giant's leg, and the final man in the assault tried with his bodybuilder's physique to knock the giant down. Ginger looked unimpressed and caught him mid-stride as if catching a toddler and used the man's toned body as a ragdoll to swing from side to side. Skulls cracked as the bodies clattered off each other before being dumped on the floor as broken toys and Ginger declaring, 'This is the job. Get used to it.'

Don shook his head and called, 'Stop. That was rubbish. Start again,' then whispered to his aide, 'Mark them down as fives.'

The bodybuilder didn't get the message to halt. He seemed concussed and struggled to regain his balance by grabbing onto Ginger and attempting an arm lock. Someone cried, 'It's stopped mate!' but neither heeded.

As the man pulled down on the giant's wrist, a huge, wicked grin erupted on Ginger's face. Don yelled, 'No!' but it was too late.

He pulled the man horizontally across his stomach and bounced slightly before propelling the trainee upwards as if merely a warm-up weight in the gym. He paused only for a second with the man's torso braced across his neck before pressing him through the ceiling tiles with a roar. As debris clattered to the floor in a cloud of white dust, Don called out with a sigh, 'Down. Please?' but Ginger ignored him again. Holding his victim above his head with outstretched arms, he told everyone, 'Listen you Muppets. There is only one thing that wins a fight. It's not size or strength, speed or fekkin knife skills. It's heart and bollocks!'

'That's two things Ginge,' offered Don.

Ginger was on a roll and growled, 'When you come against a big lad, ya can't just let your mates go in while you hang back like wankers. You gotta go in hard. Together! It's teamwork, innit. Teamwork! Teamwork!'

It was more like an afterthought when Ginger lowered his victim to his shoulders, dropped him to his knees, and let the man fall to the floor. His last bellowed advice was, 'Don't lose. It hurts.'

To everyone's relief, Ginger took a break from instructing and ambled to the side of the room to chat to Jamie. He told him, 'Good lad, ya done good.'

'Cheers.'

'I see you met Phil. Oh, and don't worry about working with him.'

'Why would I work with him?' replied Jamie, slightly shocked.

Ginger didn't elaborate and simply smiled and nodded as if he couldn't hear another word. The day ended with Don in a surprisingly good mood and offering to drive Jamie back to Maria's home. As they went into the city from the suburbs, the boss surprised him by asking for an opinion, 'What you think of the training?'

'You had two walk out y'know.'

'Yer, I know, wankers. But whatcha think?

'Suppose it's realistic. No point working on the door and thinking you won't get hurt. Pretty much gave me a bit of context too, for how you think about stuff.'

'Good. Was it too dumbed down?' asked Don, for once it didn't feel like a trick question.

'Nah,' replied Jamie surprised by the affable attitude of the boss, 'The folk you had there were all big and heavy, they didn't look like they do any sorta agile techniques. But anything they hit I'll bet stays hit.'

Jamie winced as he relived being strangled, 'Phil could've killed me.'

The answer astonished him, 'Nah, think he likes ya. You're a calming influence on him.'

'Aye sure,' he replied.

Don chuckled, 'Honest, that was him controlled. Usually, if someone knocked him on his arse, he'd have been stamping on his head, and even Ginger wouldn't be able to pull him off.'

'That's him gentle?' asked Jamie.

'Yer, he stuck up for you already.'

'How, when?'

'You do something, and we all hear about it.'

'What did I do that he had to stick up for me?' Jamie asked, confused.

Don scrunched up his face in annoyance, and shouted, 'Arsehole,' at another driver that he was cutting up at traffic lights.

As a reflex, he dangerously switched lanes then said,

'And Jamie, just so you know, you can't use that bollocks you were doing. You'll kill someone. On a door, it's just arm locks, and maybe giving someone a dig in the stomach. That's it. And don't talk to people.'

'Don't talk to people? Why not.'

'You know,' Don smirked, 'That act of yours where act soft to draw people in. I know why ya do it, but it's fucking evil. So, ya can't do it.'

'Don't understand,' then stressed about what was being suggested he grumbled in his dialect, 'Dae ah huv to be acting awe hard then, can I no be a gentle person and watch chick flicks and cry at sunsets if I wanna. And y'know, not be like Phil?'

'You like chick flicks?'

'No. Not the point, is it? Should I worry what people think of me?'

Don just grinned, 'Yer well, talk less, and nobody will know what to make of you. Okay, as long as you keep Phil calm, I don't care.'

'I don't have much to do with him,' he declared as they parked up outside Maria's house.

Don still smiled, 'Well, if you really wanna work with him. I'll sort it out.'

'I don't wanna work with him!' Jamie whined, getting out of the car, 'I'm just a driver.'

'Good one mate,' he replied, 'Just the driver. Funny.'

'Bye, thanks for the lift,' Jamie told him with an exasperated sigh.

'Laters,' said Don as he drove off, giggling.

***

Jamie used a key Maria had given him and stepped inside. Immediately he knew something was wrong, everything was dark and gloomy without a light on or a blind open in the house.

'Hello,' he called out but there was no reply. Quietly he walked down the hallway and peered into the living room. It was a surprise; the place was a mess with tissues piled on the coffee table and on the sofa was a massive duvet from which a pair of bunny slippers poked out.

Maria's voice croaked from underneath the twenty-tog quilting to ask, 'Hello Jamie. Are you hungry?'

He replied, 'No, I'm fine. You okay but. You want me to do anything?' She didn't say anything else, and he presumed she'd fallen asleep so took off his shoes and began tiptoeing around, quietly tidying up.

When finished he picked up a Spanish-English dictionary and moved to his normal spot on the floor with his head resting on a cushion. That was when he felt her hand slide out from under the cover and begin casually stroking his head. She mumbled, 'Are you sure you are not hungry?'

'Aw, right. Gotcha,' he replied and sprung to his feet to scurry around the kitchen. He made her a snack within the limits of his cooking prowess; a large glass of juice, poached eggs and a warmed-up ciabatta that he buttered. Maria sat up to nibble a little and declared, 'Good drugs. I am better now.'

'Can I do anything?' Jamie asked, and despite her tangled hair, red eyes and blotchy complexion, he saw only the most beautiful woman in the world.

'Yes, tell me where you have been. What you are doing and what your plans are Carino? I've homework for my English future tenses.'

They took their familiar positions on the sofa, with her snuggling under the duvet and him lying on the floor beside her while she quizzed him about the training and all the who, what, where and when, of the doormen he knew. Jamie confided in her what he thought of the training scenarios and concluded that although violence upset him intellectually, it bothered him more that he also liked it.

He told her, 'It was almost relaxing today. Kinda soothing. As if I can see every move and reaction before it happens. For me, the way people fight is just like watching a slow-moving computer game, and like I've got all the cheat codes.

I understood that I was there, but at the same time, I'm not really there either. I'm just an observer.'

'Joder, that's deep. And you act all sweet.'

'It's not an act. I don't like violence,' Jamie replied indignantly, although some doubt had begun to creep into his image of himself.

Perhaps he was merely ambivalent about it, but he wasn't about to argue the philosophical semantics of viciousness with Maria.

She smiled, tapped the cushion next to her and told him,

'Here is more comfortabler, with me.'

'That's so not proper English,' he replied sitting next to her.

Maria wrapped the duvet around them both and said, 'I change my mind. I don't need to study English my grammar is perfects,' then handing him her mobile she asked, 'Have you phoned your mum this week?'

His look told her he hadn't, and he dialled the number. It wasn't long before his mum asked who was sneezing in the background, and Maria joined the conversation. Five minutes later it was just the two women chatting with Jamie wandering off to the kitchen to make cocoa. When Maria finally hung up, their evening ended as it usually did, with Jamie falling asleep on the sofa. Only this time when he did, it was while entwined in her soft, hot body.

Chapter 10 - Embracing diversity.

After a late breakfast of painkillers washed down with orange juice, Angel drove his Prius to a desolate industrial estate within a clutter of identical flat-roofed buildings. He parked in a blind spot beside some storage silos where the CCTV cameras couldn't see. He always did. The downside of the location was that it was at the hub of a system of air blasts used to push rattling green coffee beans along pipelines. His hangovers had never really gotten used to the noise of the place, but at least the smell of freshly roasted coffee was pleasant. He was greeted by a young girl beeping a forklift horn as she drove past him and recognised her as one of the more interesting characters in the place. Only a few like her and Angel had any colour in the company; he had his boots and Hawaiian shirts, and she had her bright green hair. Overall, he saw his colleagues there, as a drab, soulless bunch of coffee snobs in tan chinos and company logos masquerading as professionals. It was one of the things that tired him about the place. Strolling into the packaging part of the factory, he was met by the production manager having a cigarette, who asked him jokingly, 'Whatcha doing here so early? It's not even noon?'

Angel sagged, groaning, 'Very funny. New product launch, I've a big presentation to do.'

'Thought you just did the trade shows?' he asked, flicking away his cigarette.

'I do all that stuff. My job title is Quality control negotiations coordinator and corporate green partnering associate with the assets management team,' he replied sounding weary.

'Oh, that's nice,' he chuckled with a hint of a sneer.

'Si, pero no es culpa mio. I've been asked to show the visitors the process from green coffee to steam in the cup.'

'Lucky boy, I only get to enforce the daily grind, one shift at a time.'

'How long did it take you to memorise that one?' Angel asked.

'I'm putting it on my email signature. Some visitors are here, by the way. Are they yours? I've a foody journalist upstairs in the blue room, staff training for some coffee shop, and a lot running about in a panic looking for a delivery that was never ordered.'

'Ah, that is nothing to do with me. Mine are with the charity lady.'

'She's not here yet, let's get ourselves a coffee,' the manager suggested, and the pair sauntered through the factory's pulsating hum of machines.

A worker approached to whisper to the manager with a moan, 'Look?' indicating a suited man lurking near a roasting machine, 'D'you know what he's doing now?'

The manager shrugged, 'What? Is it building spaghetti towers as a teambuilding bollocks or do we now have to do Tai Chi or something?'

'He told me to not drive the forklift so fast when I go up the ramp.'

The manager threw his hands in the air in despair, 'Idiots, everywhere idiots!' and turning to Angel explained, 'They won't pay for a proper ramp, so we need speed to get up it.'

He told his worker, 'Just pretend you can't speak American and carry-on shifting coffee, or we will run out of something to roast.'

'Who is he?' asked Angel pointing a man wearing a suit. He'd never seen him before. New faces were always passing through the coffee plant, but he was always suspicious.

'Another drone, it's like we get a new VP every month who thinks this place is his cost centre. They never seem to have a clue, but luckily they don't last long. I didn't bother reading the email. I think this one is looking into Health and Safety, so you better not let him see your shirt, or he'll get you for noise pollution.'

'Alright Angel,' said another worker who stopped to moan with a description of his world, 'Welcome to the dumb-fuck coffee corporation. Every time we have a visitor, nobody tells production until half an hour after they turn up, when we're supposed to stop production, to look more like we are in fucking production. Today, I shall be mostly packing air into empty bags for a fucking journalist.'

The manager yawned and told him, 'Yeah okay, I heard. Start peeling folk off from the directors, or else we'll be here all night. Send a few lads on break and use the storage hoppers till they piss off. I'll go find my magic hat to pull out four hours of production.'

'Have we even got what they wanted for that tasting?' the worker asked.

The manager shook his head, 'Nope, use a Guatemala instead. It's what they should have asked for anyway. Fuck! No idea how we make a profit, as all we do is waste time and money!'

Angel knew where they got the money to waste, but of course, he said nothing and kept looking vacant until the worker cantered off to pass on the manager's message, then he asked, 'You like your job?'

'Yeah, sure. It's great fun. I've two plant managers from Colorado today. Halfwit One obviously understands things but is clinically unable to voice a decision. His teammate is Halfwit number Two, knows nowt about anything, but bangs out orders on everything.'

'Hey, don't be like that. It is a great place to work,' Angel told him in an attempt to commit to his cover story, 'There are worse places to work, here we're ethical, diverse, and everybody is happy.'

'Yer whatever. My guys pack at twenty-two bags a minute, eight hours a shift. It's alright doing some little induction, but forty hours a week, every week of the year is a different life. They talk about embracing whatever and cultural change where they so love us workers so very, very much. But that's only okay for you suits who stroll in whenever you like and watch porn at work all day,' the manager was laughing now, 'But for all of my boys, it's a race and they can't even stop for a piss.'

He then pressed a walkie-talkie mic on his collar and began chatting. For Angel, it was like observing a battlefield commander push the momentum of an attack and bark orders to his team. Angel felt all the manufacturing workers were similarly cynical, surly and grim. They acted like they saw their executives as the enemy, and he liked them for that. Suddenly the manager grabbed Angel and pulled him backwards. A forklift carrying a tonne of green coffee beans braked hard, and the driver scowled.

'I shouldn't have let you through here,' he told Angel leading him through a set of swing doors and into quiet, 'You belong in the nice places, not here.'

Past the entrance was what looked like the lounge bar of a pub.

It was set up with trendy wooden furnishings made from the recycled wood of tea chests and covered in coffee sacks. The production manager pointed to a set warehouse pallet that had been reimagined as a bench, 'Have a seat. The charity burd will probably end up here,' then into his mic he said,

'Little one, coffee for parrot shirt in cold brew room over.'

'You mean please, over,' crackled a reply.

'Please and find out why some moron of a sales rep has put two nitrogen bottles out here. They're connected to a drinks machine without a stand. They want to kill us! Over.'

'Okay, biscuits, halfwits, get a stand. Received out.'

'Were you in the military?' Angel asked.

'Hmmm, I was definitely in the Boy Scouts,' he sighed, 'I seem to remember a few years eating food outta tins in the rain. Anyway, I'm off to do some shouting for a bit.'

He replied, 'Thanks, they might not need me, but I made a PowerPoint just in case.'

'Whatever turns you on,' he told Angel as an enthusiastic teenager arrived and began making espressos at the bar. He poured out four before being satisfied with the quality. Handing one to Angel he said, 'Try this and tell me what you think. Oh, and don't listen to him,' chuckling at the departing manager, 'Could be nuts and bolts for all he cares.'

'Oh behave. You care, so I don't have to,' the manager chortled as he walked away.

Angel was then left on his own with a large Americano and a plate of brownies in the hip-looking room they used for sales. On the table before him were ring binders with the company history, induction documents and a book of stories about different 'Origin-coffees'.

Anyone reading could see how big the company had grown, how profitable it was, and how it was such a great corporation to work for. There was also a clutter of sweets, whisky samples and a box of cigars left over from another meeting, so he began gorging on Madagascar chocolate and pocketing Cuban Churchills for later.

A face peeked around the door; she was another dress-code dodger in bright tie-dyed clothing with a face full of piercings and enthusiasm, 'Hi, we are having a tasting in the fruit room with some excellent varietals. Oh, you must come. It is my birthday!'

'Hey that's great, happy birthday. I'm coming. Hope there are muffins!'

She smiled, 'Oh lots,' and bounced out of the room as quickly as she'd arrived. From his jeans pocket, Angel pulled out his phone and checked his emails which were mostly about nothing at all. It was irritating to be copied into so much nonsense, but he knew it was essential to respond to everything, as one of them might relate to his real job.

He scrolled through until he found the meeting he wanted and groaned. It had been switched to a rendezvous with someone else, with a note explaining that he needed to wait for a delivery of coffee samples sent to his home before attending.

In place of his original appointment, he'd now been invited to a beanbag-strewn room with no tables called the 'Creative Zone,' to endure a discussion on Ethical Sustainability. Once there, the organiser waffled about, 'Really looking forward to your input on recycling issues,' then never brought the subject up again. Instead, they talked about the 'Ticket prices,' of the coffee shop check-outs and how to get customers to buy more non-coffee items in stores. It went on for hours, and although he pretended to be interested, it was torture for the Spanish spy.

After work and the arrival of a courier, he went to a Tapas bar in the marina near his flat and listened to the chink-chink of lines slapping on their masts. He'd just ordered his second lager when Matty, dressed in the camouflage of a Yachtie, sat down next to him and said with a hand cupped over his mouth, 'Hi Mate, did ya get it?

'It's under the napkin,' replied the Spaniard sipping his beer.

'Have they supplied everything on the list?' asked Matty, scooping it up and putting the memory stick it hid in his pocket.'

'Si, claro. They only questioned some of the electrical kits as they wanted 120volts.'

After waiting in silence while a waitress walked by, Matty answered, 'What?' with his face scrunched up in incredulity.

'It's a double-blind, the supplier thinks you're based in Fort Liberty.'

'Ah, right, no delay then?' Matty whispered from behind his palm.

Angel told him, 'We are only waiting for the final approval. But, if you ask me, this whole job feels wrong.'

Matty shrugged, 'Mate, we're in the outlier business. Our orders never mention morality.'

'I guess,' Angel smiled and quoted his favourite political theorist, 'I suppose if he hadn't committed great sins, God wouldn't have sent you as a punishment.'

Matty nodded and stood up to leave, 'Well, mate if government say it's okay, then it must be okay,' then he sighed and added, 'I'll be off unless you wanna chat about sailing?'

Once Angel was home and behind his locked door, his calm exterior submitted to the suppressed fear he carried each day, and he raced for his toilet to throw up. His panic attacks were becoming more frequent. In Afghanistan, he'd been decorated for valour, but now fear was jumping out at him on a daily basis.

A week previously, he'd become suddenly frightened driving past a group of school children. It made no sense to him, they weren't doing more than jostling each other, but he freaked out.

Later with half a bottle of whisky in him, he tried to rationalise the incident and accept his new reality of terror. Every day it was becoming more and more of a struggle to hold in his anxiety and the hope that he wouldn't let slip what he was really doing. An hour after locking the door to his flat and placing a wedge under the door, Angel finished another bottle of whisky in his bath. Between swigs, he tried to focus on what he was supposed to be doing and who he was meant to be. It was all part of a process he had been prepared for by the army, but the memory of one day frequently came back as a waking panic. Even in a warm bath, cold fear ran down his spine as he relived the moment when masked men in black tactical gear followed a flash-bang grenade through his door. No one had spoken, but they convinced him to change his plans for the day. One military-grade lump placed a pistol in his mouth as another helped him into some handcuffs and a thick black hood.

That day he caught a glimpse of a Guardia Civil emblem on a lapel, and that was the last thing he remembered until waking up with a headache 24 hours later smelling of piss. The next stage of his nightmare, he recalled, was lying naked on a prison bed in a bare prison cell with a bottle of water and the clothes from his bedroom floor. There was no underwear or socks, but they'd brought his cowboy boots, jeans and a shirt still marked with crusty sweat stains. He was surprised they'd let him keep his belt with its large silver buckle, and he noticed his watch and wallet were there too.

Looking around, he saw it was a small brick room decorated with brick dust and flecks of mould. Above the dilapidated whitewashed wall, high above his head was a narrow iron grate, through which he could hear peacocks screeching at dawn and the bugles of a garrison waking. Angel had to stand on the bed first to jump for the window and use his tight muscles to pull his eyes level with a courtyard outside. There he saw ankles slowly marching past. He knew the regiment and muttered, 'Joder,' realising he had woken up on another continent. Then sagging on his prison bed, drank the water and sunk into self-pity.

At noon his cell door clattered open and a Legionnaire of the Tercios appeared to flick his head to the side, meaning for him to follow. In the corridor outside, two more waited. One led him by his shirt cuff, but none seemed eager or insistent about where they were going. They walked to the end of the passageway, through a steel barred door, and into a place where the architecture became medieval. Then as they descended, he heard someone's humming become louder. In a dank stone-spiralling stairwell, the guards hesitated. The closer to the noise the soldiers got, the slower they moved. In the shadows, they looked haunted with a thin layer of personal despair on their faces. It was as if they were trudging towards some madness that they'd been sentenced to feed every day in an underground lair.

They entered a room that looked like a dungeon cluttered with ammunition boxes and old wine barrels. Brutal meat hooks hung from oaken beams, and solid wrought iron manacles were chained to the walls like a shrine to Franco's torturers. Angel's eyes still had not adjusted to the gloom from the white cell above, but on the far side, he could make out the shape of the large man making the noise. Only it wasn't humming. It was a moaning, grumbling growl and a man slowly running his fingers through his hair, staring at the ceiling.

A lone light bulb revealed he wore a crisp white shirt, a crumpled olive-green suit with his striped tie pulled out of the folds of his jacket and caught dangling from a pocket handkerchief. Strangely the man's head was tilting from side to side as he groaned. Angel twisted to look at the soldiers guarding him. He saw their faces rippled with sympathy as they snapped to attention, one barked, 'Sergeant Rivera. The prisoner!'

The man in the suit whispered, 'Lock it to that,' and pointed to a shadow of a desk in the dark. Angel had been through training for capture and interrogation, but the words softly spoken, still sent him into a panic that he'd never felt before. The Tercios

84

pushed him and rushed to handcuff his wrists to a long chain fixed to a ring, then stood at attention with their eyes and chins raised to the roof. They appeared frightened, eager to dump their baggage and get away from the decor of fear back to their routine joy of fresh air and sunshine above.

Near the desk, Angel could see why. Another man hung from the wall, naked and entangled in a coil of bloodstained rope.

He gasped when he recognised him as a Galician mafia captain that he'd been partying with only a week before. In pain, the crook was babbling, 'No,' repeatedly. Words that drew the attention of Rivera.

The psychotic gorilla screamed, 'No, no, what do you mean no!' Rivera began shouting in guttural Spanish mixed with French and Arabic words with an occasional English curse. The sergeant walked over to him and pummelled his victim with his fists, ribs cracked, and Angel's suspended former accomplice sagged in the ropes, unconscious. The sergeant finished the conversation by calmly pulling a .22 pistol from his waistband and shooting the man in the head.

What frightened Angel most was when the torturer turned and calmly asked, 'Would you like a cup of tea?'

'Sir. Yes sir,' Angel replied, feeling like one wet, lost shoe on some waste ground. He knew that whatever the man wanted to know, he would tell him. He didn't need any lesson in interrogation. His training may have prepared him, but this reality petrified him. 'Don't call me sir. Sergeant Rivera to you,' then he barked, 'Tea and take this body away!'

Angel felt a tiny dribble of warm urine dampen his jeans and tried to push thoughts of what the Rivera might do to him away, but it wasn't working. The man in front of him was not just a sergeant. He guessed even generals feared anyone with the power to take him from the Guardia Civil, kill a man one moment and speak with a delicate lover's voice the next.

Rivera smiled, 'Ah, don't be alarmed. That is not for you. I think we will have a nice chat instead. Let's talk about loyalty, shall we?' My loyalty is my honour. Our friend didn't know that. He was just a criminal, and I needed to teach him a little lesson. ¿Are you loyal?'

'Todo por la Patria!' Angel replied. He was not that interested in being taught by Rivera. The death of the day's floor show looked like a mercy. The mafia captain had not even flinched to protect himself.

Into the empty corridor, he yelled, 'TEA!' again and asked,

'He was your friend that I was chatting to, non? Oh, and you like tea?'

Angel nodded and for minutes that seemed years, they were in silence as the maniacal gorilla stared at him before producing a pack of Habanos. He lit two with a skull motif Zippo before pressing one into Angel's lips. Then the mint tea arrived with a different legionnaire, crushed leaves in tall, sugar-crusted glasses.

'We've had our eye on you for a long time, so how do you see your future after prison, Sir?'

Angel's jaw hung slack for a few seconds before saying, 'Sergeant, I'm in your hands.'

Still terrified, he sipped his mint tea, scalding his lips.

Rivera shook his head and began reading from a report, 'Stop me if I have anything wrong: Commissioned as a lieutenant. Lying in the fields of the train link between Seville and Madrid under an unforgiving sun was hard for the boy. He was relieved when his battalion was tasked to guard a prison in the cooler north, but then he was caught moving drugs inside for the local mafia.'

Angel nodded, and Rivera continued, 'My options are prison or that you slowly die in a training accident, perhaps with chemicals burning your flesh from an accident on a tank range? Don't be frightened. You were silly. I can fix things. Work for me and all is forgiven. I can change your life…with…just a few phone calls.'

Panic burst in Angel's brain like a headache and he tried to recover his wits,

'It sounds better than prison, sergeant.'

Rivera told him, 'What if the work is to find separatists, kill them, bury them, and not ask questions? What if I said live in the mountains for months at a time, and for each new month, the supply drops might even arrive.'

Still struggling to compose himself his words sounded flippant yet nervous,

'Well, I might enjoy life away from the parades.'

The psychotic gorilla shook his head in mock pity, 'Sadly, this job is not in Spain. Officially you will be in Oklahoma on a research project at an artillery school.

'Americans?' Angel replied, 'Joder, I'd prefer E.T.A and the mountains.'

Rivera laughed but then his tone became grim, 'You are still a soldier, and you will stay loyal to Spain. If you are tempted in any way, know that I don't use euphemisms. I don't say removed or erased; when I say killed, I mean kept alive with an IV stuck up your arse as I torture you to death. So don't betray me!'

Angel gulped, 'I am still a soldier and I'll be loyal.'

Someone lit a cigarette and appeared in a dark corner of the room answering for him, 'Of course he will,' Angel turned, but saw only a puff of smoke and part of a woman's face. Whoever she was, she spoke in a slurred American accent, 'Yup, I'll buy him.'

As the voice came closer with the sound of high heels clattering across the floor, she told the Rivera, 'But don't bother gift wrapping him, he's fine as is.'

The woman stepped into the light to stand in front of Angel, and she licked her lips, 'I'm Jessica and I'm a looking for a criminal, someone capable. Your military record was wickedly impressive for what I got in mind, even before you became a naughty boy.'

Rivera grinned, produced a bottle of whisky and glasses from the desk and said, 'No one will miss a loner with no friends, a Puto Chulo making too much time for other men's wives and seedy bars. Try to imagine the shit holes you could be sent to.'

Jessica reached forward to shake hands, her perfectly manicured nails scratching his skin in a flirty way, 'Y'all will be a lot happier with me and out of prison, Honey.'

He betrayed an honest emotion by happily raising his glass and saying,

'Ma'am, yes ma'am.'

'Oh, that sounds so sweet when y'all say that. We are gonna get along just fine,' she drawled in a sexy Southern accent. Angel didn't know it, but it was the one she used to lure the unsuspecting to believe she was a simple country girl instead of a senior CIA officer. He drained his whisky in a gulp and put the glass on the table.

The woman sat down on the desk with the face of an innocent and began tugging at the silky material that was rising up her thigh to reveal her stocking tops.

'Oh, call me ma'am again,' she refilled their glasses, 'Your accent sure makes me tingle.'

'Yes, ma'am,' he replied and straightening up, placed his hands on his knees.

The rest of the meeting was not unfriendly. Angel walked with Rivera out of handcuffs and into a shower at Jessica's hotel room with a promotion to Captain. Rivera had repeatedly reminded him that he'd report what the Americans had him do or that the best he could expect was Prison for the full twenty years under Article 344 of the penal code. His deal was simple: he would serve in a specialist unit with his criminal activities never having existed.

The sergeant's last words to him as he left were, 'You will be under constant observation and assessment,' he pointed skyward, 'Satellites.'

Once alone with Jessica, she'd poured him more whisky, 'I am technically a General, y'know. But I've never even got into an officer's blouse. Can you imagine me in a uniform?'

He smiled, 'Yes, ma'am.'

Apart from the relief of being out of handcuffs, Angel was enjoying the view of pure sex in a figure-smoothing outfit. As he went along for the ride, the cynical part of his brain shut down, leaving the rest to concentrate on her cleavage.

'Anyhoo, let's get to business,' she told him. Jessica pulled a thick envelope from a handbag and handed it to him, 'This is your cover and instructions for the next week. After that, watch out for emails from Denver. You work for a coffee company.'

Jumping to conclusions he asked, 'Really coffee? or is it drugs?'

Jessica giggled, 'Don't you worry now. I'm starting you off slow on all that. The murder, and torture y'all must be imagining I've in mind will be later. The job is do as you are told to do without question, hesitation or, more importantly, getting caught. It's all in the starter pack honey, get studying.'

Angel knew better than to flinch about the implications, hoping that he gave his new employer no reason to doubt him, 'I prefer blackmail, betrayal and bribery ma'am, but you're the boss.'

'Good boy, I just know you are going to do fine under me.'

Jessica was intoxicating. Her constant, confident flirting was an overpowering, mesmerising barrage, and he loved it. Then she told him, 'The office will work out the rest once I tell them how cute y'all are.'

'Yes ma'am. Thank you, ma'am,' Angel replied.

The thought, 'She is a general,' continued to bang around his brain repeatedly with an image of her with a pistol in one hand and a glass of whisky in the other. In his mind, she stroked a large white cat saying, 'Kill Bond now!'

'Are you my handler?' he asked.

'No honey. Think of me as someone interested in your welfare that's gonna look in on you from time to time. I've always believed a leader's role is to look after the horses, troopers and officers in that order. And honey, you are the new stallion in my stable.'

She was charming. He almost wanted to believe her, 'Yes ma'am, what's your cover?'

'I don't have one. I'm just a southern gal who consults on things like this when not advising on humanitarian projects. But don't you worry none about that. I want y'all settled in first.

**

The reality Angel had found out later was terrifying. She often said, 'The movie JFK is a blueprint for how not to run an operation,' and had a motto of, 'Delete all loose ends.' That blinkered mentality scared him a lot more than Rivera's ruthless cunning.

'Joder, how can you be so Tonto!' Maria shrieked as she parked at Jamie's campus.

'Is not what you think. You don't know everything!' he told her.

Maria leant forward onto her steering wheel and gently tapped her forehead on it as she declared in frustration, 'They're gangsters. You're not!'

'Not listening. I am who I am!' Jamie replied and reached between his feet for his backpack.

Exasperated, through gritted teeth and now pulling her auburn hair, Maria peeked out from behind her forearms to tell Jamie, 'You have two worlds, don't take the gamberro of Red-Ties into class. They won't understand.'

It was almost an argument. He knew what she meant but stuck out his tongue in playful defiance at her advice, then gave her a platonic hug goodbye.

Struggling to get his tall frame out of her low-riding Audi TT, he parted with a defensive explanation, 'I know, I know, but y'know. I am a student and it's all educational innit.'

Maria replied shaking her head, 'Oh, Dios mia! Please don't start talking like them too!'

She drove off, leaving him waving goodbye to her at the entrance to the campus with a grin on his face. He knew she was probably right. He was changing, evolving and becoming at ease with gangland etiquette. In a very short time, he'd absorbed the nuances of how to act or talk around hoodlums, instinctively knowing the line between sticking up for himself and not sticking his neck out too far. His evenings after university had become a roller-coaster that sped between strip clubs and dive bars as he collected shady anecdotal criminal lore.

The influences on him that reinforced what was and what wasn't acceptable behaviour, were already affecting how he viewed the student world around him. So far, he'd restrained the impulses to yell, 'Who da fuck ya think ya are?' at an arrogant professor, who was explaining how he'd once lived in Scotland but had left because he didn't want, 'His children growing up with the Scots' atrocious accent.'

It was that class Jamie was heading to. As he shuffled into the engineering department. He expected it to be another word-for-word repeat of the materials sermon he'd previously been given and at least half an hour of a monologue on how wondrous the lecturer's cricket-playing son was. After that bore had gone on as expected, Jamie was treated to, "An introduction to beam theory," by a no-nonsense Doctor of Engineering, who cut a swath through the syllabus by loading up the year's total stress into one diagram on his whiteboard, then showing how the mass of information was just a series of small manageable moments of study.

That class was also quite fascinating because the room was shared with the students from another course, who'd all turned up in wet weather sailing clothes as if they were about to cross the Atlantic. In that lot, there were four Spanish, two Italians, an Argentinean, an Irish lad, a blonde girl from Hamburg who never smiled, and an ever-ebullient French student who balanced out the German's grim persona by constantly joking. When lunchtime arrived, with no more lectures in the afternoon, Jamie wandered with them down to the docks to see a luxurious hull that was parked there. It felt like a perfect day, warm sunshine, a cooling sea breeze, and friendly conversation.

At the main marina bar, they plonked themselves down at a few tables overlooking the vessel and ordered lagers. Out of courtesy, his classmates began chatting about its design features in English, even though it was clear most of them found Spanish easier. It was a gentle pause in his life listening to their middle-class politeness and the rhythmic chink lines on masts. Even as the students argued about technical points, they did it with civility and calm voices. One said that he had briefly been employed in a yard laying down the ship's hull, and as they discussed the thickness of keels. It impressed him how pure their enthusiasm for flimsy racing boats was explained.

Their behaviour even made Jamie restrain himself from giving his own opinions on what he saw as a gaudy piece of fragile red plastic cluttered up with ropes and deck furniture. As he listened, he learned that most of them had sailed from a very young age and won races and that their whole lives revolved around a pursuit of speed on the water by way of high-tech innovation. It was a massive eye-opener for him as whilst his classmates had all lived on boats, his nautical connection had only been stepping onto the Clyde ferry. While the group hinted and named dropped, Jamie realised his mum had been right; living in a new city and the people in his class were as much an education as lectures. They all had exotic back stories from worlds he had never imagined while living in his little village, with only a few indications from the group that it wasn't all drinking beers at regattas in the sunshine.

One of them, whose father was a naval architect, explained that the job was mostly a life hunched over a drawing board. As for his descriptions of his dad's demanding clients, Jamie struggled to comprehend that such people or such wealth even existed. It was interesting, bright and passionate how they talked about boats, but simultaneously in that moment, he doubted a life of creating deck plans in an office was for ever going to be for him. It wasn't a career choice about where he was heading, it was more like accepting the inevitability of where he wasn't. He wasn't them.

That was when the glass broke on Jamie's campus life to reinforce the notion, and Crow turned up at his bar with the large brick-shaped doorman he'd seen at the barbecue carrying the Kalashnikov.

'Oi-oi, Savaloy,' he said, tapping Jamie on the shoulder, 'What are you doing here?' The ex-Para was in a regimental rugby shirt and looked like he had been drinking all day.

I am...' Jamie began, but Crow cut him off.

'No worries, Mush, you are allowed out. What're ya having to drink?'

The other scarier-looking man grumpily shoved past the shoulder of the Irish lad sitting next to him and pressed a driving licence towards him 'Been looking for you, Mush.'

Crow added, 'Yer Don said you were crying about not having one.'

The two Red-ties seemed oblivious to the people Jamie was with as if they weren't there, so he began introducing them. 'This is...' he began but was again interrupted by Crow, whose attention was now drawn to the Argentinean flag on the polo shirt of his classmate.

'You an Argie then,' he asked, his face scrunched up in a gurning expression.

Jamie guessed what was coming next and stood up to pull him away from Juan. Tugging his sleeve, he said his goodbyes to those he'd arrived with and led the Red-Ties out of the bar.

Crow followed smirking and laughing as he told him, 'Was only gonna wind him up a bit.'

'You were being rude,' he was annoyed and began lecturing Crow, but his doorman friend was in too good a mood and giggled drunkenly without taking anything Jamie said seriously. That was when Jamie's phone pinged a new message. It read, 'You're working the RRF.'

He replied to say, 'Don said I'm only a driver.'

A brutal answer came back, 'This is fucking Don! Car at your pub. 8.30 and don't be late.'

Jamie was unsure what options he had available to tell a man like Don, 'No,' so he chose the line of least resistance replying, 'Okay,' and asked Crow how to interpret the message. The ex-paratrooper grinned as he explained, 'RRF means rapid reaction fuckers. Just follow orders, and you'll be fine. If ya want my advice. Stay in the car.'

***

Jamie was in and out of the house without seeing Maria but left her a note to say he'd be working. He did his best to be in a Red-Tie uniform by wearing black jeans, a white shirt and the black mountain boots he previously used in the woods as a lumberjack. It wasn't exactly right as attire, but it was the best he was able to do for the job. Don texted again as he left the house, reiterating his orders, 'It's a cushy number. Stay in the car. Don't start anything. Don't let Phil do anything mental. Minimum force tonight. Okay?'

All he could think of was, 'How would I stop Phil?'

That night as he waited in the Lenny Quintain pub, he heard the same instruction from a doorman who arrived with the build of a bull to growl, 'You stay in the car. Right!'

After him, a heavily muscled mass arrived. Another without a distinct neck or waist, and whose clothes were so tight that it looked like every seam of his jacket was bursting. He also said, 'Stay in the car. Yeah?' which was as friendly as it got.

Without being asked, a bartender brought over three glasses of soda water and lime, and they sat quietly until Phil arrived with his broken arm in plaster to say, 'Let's go!'

Walking to the car, the doormen clipped on their red ties and their self-appointed leader barked, 'Docks. Let's go! And you, fucking new guy. Stay in the car.'

The plan was evidently to travel the busiest part of the city for nightlife and wait to be called, but ten minutes later, parked up under a tree near some flats watching a line of pubs, Phil spotted something and decided to start the trouble. He declared, 'There!'

'What?' asked Jamie, and the others, already leaving the car told him, 'Stay!'

The three doormen launched themselves as rabid berserkers at two equally large brutes walking across the street. Jamie recognised one of them as the ringleader from the beer garden that he'd stumbled into with a glass. The targets looked to their left, just in time to see Phil's one good arm work like a piston and knock them to the ground. The Red-Ties, full of malice, continued stomping on the bodies of their victims. Those ambushed had no time to defend themselves, and it looked more like bears crushing empty boxes with their paws than a fight.

It was sickening, and enough of a worry for Jamie to cross the thirty metres to the crime scene and grab Phil from behind and whine, 'Stop, you'll kill him!'

Phil roared, 'Get off me! You melt,' and pushed Jamie away, but that was it.

It stopped. Instead of rage or assault from the alleged psycho, all was calm, and the Red-Ties ambled back to the car. Only then did Jamie see the blade of a short knife stuck with force into Phil's plaster cast.

The big doorman mumbled, 'Oh, how about that,' pulled it free, and in an irritated tone asked, 'Why get out of the car, why?'

There wasn't time to answer as another Red-Tie yelled, 'I hear sirens. Drive!'

As blue flashing lights coloured the walls at the end of the street, Jamie added a new talent to his resume, and he became a reluctant getaway driver. His skills were not textbook though. His three-point turn was perfect and his gear changes smooth, but when he reached a junction with an exit left that took him quickly from the scene, Jamie chose the right that took them down a short cul-de-sac.

'Lights off, switch the fucking lights off!' The doormen yelled. Jamie managed to flick them off a moment before the police car sped past, only twenty metres from their rear bumper.

'What was that for?' Jamie asked, 'As, by the way. None of that was a rapid reaction to problems on the door.'

His Scots accent must have leaked out as Phil replied with a pretence of misunderstanding, 'Yer it's about nine o'clock, Sweaty.'

'Sweaty?' chorused the other doormen who began giggling as if to release the tension.

'Sweaty-Sock, Jock innit. But yer you is correct. Not very rapid, was it? But it had to be done. He was giving it large. So, it was our civic duty. Any other stupid questions?'

Jamie processed the words and sulked, 'It's not okay.'

That was when Don phoned to speak via the car's speakers, 'Phil, you there Mate?'

'Yer boss.'

'Everything okay?'

'So far.'

'Can you get over to the Irish pub in the valley? It's a bit iffy.'

'No worries,' he replied, signalling Jamie with a slap on his shoulder and a spinning his finger to indicate he should turn the car around.

'How iffy, who we got there?'

'Stag-night. Pikeys. Nothing happened yet, but y'know.'

Phil groaned, 'Yer we're moving,' and slumped back in his seat as if drugged up in a dentist's chair. His only movement was pointing, and occasionally moaning directions, 'Right turn at the next junction. Stop. And yer, don't get out the car.'

This time Jamie didn't, but five minutes later, Phil came out of the pub alone and ordered, 'Get out the car! You're on the door. Just let people out. Got it?'

Jamie thought he meant to do it alone, but Phil stayed with him and told the original two doormen and the extra Red-Ties they'd arrived with to, 'Spread out, L. O. S.'

Phil lit two cigarettes, and much to Jamie's surprise, he began chatting intelligently, nicely. His tone almost sounded a little friendly,

'L. O. S., in case you was wondering, is line-of-sight.'

While handing him a fag he said, 'We can have a smoke here Mush, but hide it from the landlord okay,' then clarified what he meant,

'Line of sight means we never go anywhere another doorman can't see us, that way if it kicks off, there is chain-reaction. Always be a maximum of about ten seconds apart.'

Then Phil explained, 'Mate, we don't search anyone. It's a pub. But if anyone turns up that looks like scum. Give 'em a quick check anyway, or knock 'em back for something.'

Jamie didn't smoke. He'd perhaps stuck burning lung damage in his mouth only twice before, but without thinking, he replied, 'Understood. Phil,' and took a tentative nicotine drag. He began wondering if the big doorman's savagery might be an act, as he watched him use hand signals to communicate with the other doormen and direct eyes around the pub.

Phil asked, 'Do you know why we is here? What's wrong with this picture? What corners have wrong 'uns? When to check toilets for drug use? You know anything?'

'It's a stag night, isn't it?' said Jamie, now feeling more relaxed with the thug.

'True. Travellers most of 'em, and they is on the piss, but they ain't the problem. What is a problem New-Bloke?' he said, pointing at a small group next to the bar.

Jamie spied three students he knew from the engineering department. They were bumping into people, spilling drinks and two of them looked like they were trying to play, 'Hide and Seek,' behind a slot machine.

Phil turned to Jamie and insisted, 'They are pissing off the Pikeys. Sort them out, will ya?'

'Oh fuck, no!' Jamie moaned, 'I know them.'

'I don't speak student, so you have to go.' Phil leant into his ear and told him, 'I am a bit nervous that two dozen Gypsy lads who don't mind a fight have surrounded us. And your prick mates are about to kick them off. So y'know. If you don't mind. Pretty please with sugar on top. Do your fucking job!'

Jamie walked over and tried talking to them again and again, but they only had sneering conceit for the suggestion to calm down. Drunk as farts, they obviously knew everything and so their fate was sealed. For ten minutes he'd tried patience. But finally, an exasperated Phil came over and began pushing them to the door. The students struggled like half inflated sex-dolls until, from the pavement, they informed Jamie that he, 'Was a prick.'

Jamie had to press against Phil backwards and use both hands on the doorframe to keep his colleague from expressing his counter-argument. That's when one of the students, who fancied himself as a boxer, took the opportunity to punch Jamie.

In response, he growled, 'Gonnae no dae that!'

Then, desperate to stop the inevitability of Phil being Phil, he used what he felt was his only reasonable option and closed the door. His fellow doorman was furious.

His position was that if Jamie let them act with impunity, it put them all in danger, 'Fucking pacifist doorman they put me with. Fucks sake!'

Jamie whined in protest, 'I can't. They're students,' but he knew Phil was right. A few minutes later, they came back to swear at Phil and demand that he phone them a taxi. This time he couldn't stop his colleague from rushing out, and with strikes from his one good arm, he laid all three out on the pavement like a line of flapping fishes. Phil laughed. To him, it was nothing. As he walked back inside, he lit another two cigarettes and handed one to Jamie, 'You'll probably get nicked for having a word, but it had to be said.'

'Brill-yint. I'm a pariah now,' Jamie replied, inhaling deeply.

He had already heard some exaggerated rumours about himself on campus since the incident at the beer garden. This would be worse. His reputation would be that of a vicious bully, and the chances of the entitled drunks being objective about their part in the incident he knew were zero.

That was when Phil decided to explain his profound philosophy about door work, 'Listen Mush. No point in being all appeasing and shit. Fear is what keeps people in line. Stops us having to hurt 'em more. So do me a favour. Don't show weakness. It's a criminal offence. He who hesitates is a cunt and all that. Anyway, if they'd worried more about getting a slap, they'd still be in here.'

'I know you aren't mad, but did you need to be so heavy?'

'Not as bad as what the gypsies would've done. I did them a favour really.'

Jamie snorted in annoyance, 'Sure ya did, Phil.'

'Oh, fuck you. Don't give me your high and mighty condemnation. You know fuck all. All you got is an innocent act. You call everyone sir or ma'am 'cause you wanna pretend to be a sweet cunt, but you're just like the rest of us except ya make out you're better than us.'

'Bollocks,' was his carefully weighed retort.

Jamie knew why he was obsequious to everyone; it wasn't really fear and it wasn't delusion either. It was a firm, absolute trust, that if behaving politely and Mike Tyson was about to throw a punch at him, then the boxer would be struck by lightning. Conversely, he knew that if he was conceited in any way, then any eighty-year-old granny could beat him to a pulp without breaking a sweat. For Jamie, it was a certainty, not a superstitious belief.

Phil replied. 'Yer, whateva. You've got selective autism you have cunt. I'm going walkabout. When I get back, we'll have to kick out the gypsies. They're head butting people again, and that's probably wrong.'

As Phil snaked his way through the pub, passing on his plan to the other doormen, a surprise arrived in the form of Maria's pretty smile, 'Hola!'

'You can't come in,' he told her with what he hoped was a serious tone, but then felt embarrassed, and his face ended up with a deadpan expression looking out into nothingness. Fumbling with his hands, he looped his thumbs in his belt buckle, just as another doorman turned up at his side to reiterate, 'No more...'

Maria gasped, froze, and her face dropped as if she was going to cry. She didn't wait for him to finish his sentence. Her nostrils flared, and the woman Jamie lived with spun on her heels and rushed away.

It was just seconds before the pub erupted in violence.

Chapter 13 - Mission Statement.

Later, after he had unclipped his tie and drunk a lager, Jamie left Don's car with Phil and shuffled, shell-shocked, back to Maria's house. At three in the morning, he had no physical tiredness. It was more like a mental fatigue that'd left him exhausted and stressed. With twitching muscular spasms and sudden cold shudders, he relived what he had seen with every step towards the sanctuary that was Maria's house.

On her doorstep, he took out the key she'd given him, then abruptly changed his mind. He was about to walk away when she opened the door to greet him with a barrage of rapid, angry Andalusian. Jamie's jaw hung open, and he offered only the faintest of nods in response to her tirade. In the hallway light, he stopped listening and became engrossed in the vision of her tanned, taut body in the white silk camisole pyjamas in front of him.

Suddenly, she stopped snarling, tugged his sleeve and turned around to drag him across the threshold with the quiet, slowly delivered words, 'La que tu me haces.'

Although mostly sober, he staggered behind her to the living room. There she paced around, looking him up and down with her hands on her hips, glowering at him with gritted teeth. Jamie tried his best dimpled smile to calm her mood, but as he leant to the side to catch her eye line, he felt pain from a newly cracked rib.

Maria noticed and gasped, 'Joder! What have you done?'

'Nothing,' he replied and not for the first time, his mind tried again to reconnect the scattered pieces of trauma he'd seen since he'd sent her away from the pub.

She hauled him to the sofa and unbuttoned his shirt; there she saw a long thin red mark across his ribs and belly, 'What is that?'

'I don't know. I think someone tried to stab me. It was just after you came to the door. Sorry you couldn't come in, but it was too dangerous. Was about to be bad and I had to be a doorman. And y'know not all yeaaaah Maria is here. Love her to bits and stuff.'

'Stop!' she barked at him, then mellowed her tone, 'Oh Cariño, what do you mean you not know? What happened, are you hurt?'

'Honest, I don't remember. I had to keep an eye on Phil in case he hurt someone. And it went on and on. As soon as we sorted one fight and had a cigarette, another one started.'

'You were in a fight?' her face was full of fright, and she looked to be struggling with the incongruity of Jamie's calmness.

'It's okay. I've no got cut. Only my shirt. See?' he said, taking it off to show her.

Maria began examining the developing bruises on his torso, 'Where did you get these?'

'Oh, from tonight.' She wasn't angry anymore, but she kept muttering something in her dialect and rushed to the freezer to wrap a pack of ice in a tea towel. She pressed it onto a red mark that looked like it was throbbing out of his side. He winced as she pushed it onto his skin and asked her, 'You forgive me, right?'

She continued to cool his wounds with her soothing touch, sighed as if gathering her thoughts, then smiled, tousling his hair, 'I'm still annoyed with you, but M'importa. No em vaig adonar que eres important per a mi, fins que et facis mal.'

'Sorry, okay.' he replied, 'But I've no idea what you're saying when you're all Spanish.'

'Is Valencian, not Spanish,' she told him, 'And stop apologising for everything. Vale?'

Jamie leant backwards onto the sofa and melted into its cushions, and as a confession, he told her about everything that had happened. As he began, she nodded and went to the kitchen to make them both something to drink, but he couldn't stop talking whether she was in the room or not. He was desperate to download his experiences, say them out loud, and try to make sense of them.

He stuttered a little, 'It's not even that I disapprove. I get it, as there isn't another way sometimes. Especially tonight. What's hard is how ordinary it is to them.'

'Okay, so did you get knocked out, even for a second,' Maria asked walking back into the room with two cocoas.

'No, but I did something stupid. I think maybe caused Phil a problem.'

'Que? What did you do?'

'Okay so, on the door. After the first fight. Phil told me to knock a guy back. He was a drug dealer type. Y'know a weasel on a warm evening wearing a big winter puffer jacket, and he had this bag of drugs on him. Like Lots. And I don't really approve of that. So, you know.'

'You beat him up, no?' asked Maria looking slightly concerned.

'No. God no! I just ripped the bag of gear and threw it into the street.'

Maria burst out laughing, 'What? Really. Joder. That's worse.'

'Yer, Phil wasn't happy. But all he said was, I wish you hadn't done that. Then after we finished the night. He was on the pub phone talking to someone about it, and I think he was worried.'

Maria then looked confused and asked, 'What did he say?'

Jamie shrugged, 'He just kept repeating, you gotta do what you gotta do.'

'Ah, you had a call from whoever the dealer worked for,' she declared as a matter of fact.

'How did you know?' Jamie asked.

Her reply sounded annoyed with him, 'Don't you have a brain? Mira. Tonto. ¡Be care-e-ful!' Y no trates de ser amable. Eres stupido Tambien.'

'I don't know what you are saying,' he replied, 'Except that you think I am stupid,' then looking at his cocoa mug he slumped ashen faced with tiredness and told her, 'I don't understand any of this.'

'I know you don't. We can talk in the morning,' Maria told him, tugging on the waistband of his trousers, she dragged him from the sofa and ushered him upstairs. On the threshold of his room, she told him, 'Jamie! Eres stupido, muy stupido. You make everything so complicated,' then pushed him gently into his room and closed the door.

The next day, over breakfast, neither of them brought up the subject of doorwork but at lunch, when Maria and Jamie met in the university refectory, Phil turned up. Without even saying hello, he asked brusquely, 'Can you work Park Corner tonight?' Jamie turned to Maria with a look as if he'd just run over her cat, but she waved him away, saying, 'It's fine.'

'I suppose so,' he replied to Phil, 'What time?'

'Nine, but don't worry, you're just making up the numbers. Nobody expects you to do anything. If it kicks off, hide behind something and be all small and skinny.'

A few more friendly insults later, they said their goodbyes, and at half-past eight that night, Maria dropped Jamie off at the pub next to the docks. Opening the door, he told her, 'I'll probably be quite late.'

'Don't worry, I still pick you up,' she said, kissing his cheek goodbye.

That night inside, he met the regular doorman of the pub, a lad called Jonas.

He was amiable and straight forward in his expectations of Jamie when he said,
'If you run, I'll wet ya!'

Jamie didn't understand the vernacular until the doorman opened his jacket to reveal a machete hung under his armpit. Which prompted him to focus on a positive, 'Where's Don?'

'He said he'll go around all the doors for audit standards. You've got his spot.'

'Oh,' Jamie replied, 'An audit?'

'Yer he's on the piss and going to tax everyone he meets,' he replied, referencing Don's system where he arrived at a door and fined workers for things like unpolished shoes, parking nose into a space or anything else that contravened his long list of quixotic prejudices. The fines imposed were always a few pints of lager and a lecture on security. It was Don's way, his method of building the foundations of his firm. There was always an opportunity for staff development with the Red-Ties. There was always more to learn, and in that place, it meant the doormen explaining the pub's key features to Jamie.

With a bit of finger-pointing, Jonas told him, 'Toilets. There is a dry-cleaning bag hanging in the office with a sawn-off at the bottom. If anything naughty happens, grab that.'

'What?' Jamie was shocked.

'I just mean if someone tries to rob the place.'

Jamie began wondering about how many years in prison went with the possession of a firearm when another doorman turned up. He was a broad build with a fair complexion, acted like an archetypical dodgy geezer and spoke as if he knew every mugger and burglar in the city. The strangest thing about him was that he was compulsively licking his lips and sweating, even in the cool evening breeze.

Then Crow arrived in some home improvement version of a rally car, he complained that he was losing his fitness to the sport of driving everywhere instead of using the legs and lungs he had developed in the army.

The three of them chatted with Crow telling an anecdote about his time in the parachute regiment, and Jamie's mind wandered off on a tangent about weapon design. He ended up using Crow as a sounding board, not realising he was boring him with outlandish ideas, 'How about you made a subsonic round for a rifle, or would it not work with it having a straight trajectory?'

'Really don't know.'

'So, can you use powder metallurgy to make rifle barrels?'

'Fuck knows Jamie.'

'How about using smooth-bore titanium and rifling the rounds using plastic explosives as the propellant?'

Crow groaned, 'It's going to be a long night, ain't it mate?'

'You could make the rounds like chocolate sweets and pour the charge into a rifled mould, right?'

'Erm... I dunno.'

'Suppose you had three barrels on a bullpup rifle, with their magazines feeding the wee rounds parallel to the ground?'

'Mate, I am off for a piss,' Crow told him as he disappeared from the conversation, leaving Jamie and the lip-licker alone at the entrance.

At nine pm precisely, they all put on their Red-Ties, to signal work starting in earnest. A minute later, a minivan mounted the pavement, and sudden violence poured out. 'Close the doors, close the doors!' shouted Jonas from inside.

The order was clear, loud and urgent, but Jamie hesitated.

'Shut the doors, shut the doors,' another yelled, but it was no use.

Jamie saw the lip-licker grabbed, prostrated on the pavement and kicked in the head. That was when his village sensibilities took over. 'Fuck that!' he said, and he moved forward. He didn't know how many men there were, but it was more than seats on the minibus. One man he knew from the gym was still sitting in the vehicle on a barstool. The lump was not built for speed and was too big to get out of the doors easily, so he sat, looking on, disapproving.

Jamie never made it too far either. By stepping off the door, he had allowed the visiting thugs to surround him, and rain hits on his head and shoulders. Luckily, the men were about twice his size, and their press of bodies kept him from falling. Blackness came over him for half a moment, but adrenalin brought him back into the fight.

With his hands pressed against his chest like a praying mantis, he had only one option: the eyeballs of the man directly in front of him. Jamie squeezed his fingers into the sockets and tried to remove his attacker's vision. As the man screamed, the momentum of his mates wavered. On the street was one of them was full of himself and shouting, 'I box for England! I box for England!' It drew just enough attention away from Jamie for him to stagger backwards and out of the way.

The crowd moved into the pub like a pack of dogs that had just sniffed fresh meat, and without thinking it through, Jamie followed. Inside he saw the diminutive landlady. She was a tight-bodied hard-faced twenty-something who told them all to, 'Fuck off,' which they did after helping themselves to a pint of lager or two and briefly searching for Don. Jamie was still trying to focus on what he should do and moved forward like a sleepwalker into the path of a bulldog in the shape of a man, 'Come on then!' it yelled.

The boy's foot was sent the signal from his brain to move forward, but it got lost somewhere around his knee. His legs buckled, and he staggered around ninety degrees just in time to meet the main body of thugs on their way out. 'Fair play to you,' one of them said with a pint in his hand whilst offering the other for him to shake. He'd slowly begun to think about being glassed in the face, but his palm was already reaching forward. As the hands clasped, another man's punch sent Jamie backwards to leave two neat tram lines cut in his back where it connected with the door frame. The next thing he remembered was the landlady putting stools upright and giving some leadership to her shaken staff. 'Start cleaning up,' she told them all.

Jamie wobbled in a daze towards her, and she told him with a smile, 'Don't worry honey, it doesn't happen every night. Looks like nobody likes how Don sorted things.' He wondered how often men came in armed with bats and iron bars, beat up the doormen and wandered off again. Then his body began to shut down; his head throbbed, ears rang, and random parts began to judder. The lip-licker lurched in, and his voice trailed off while asking, 'What happened?'

He and Jamie walked in hesitant circles around the pub like a pair of concussed toddler twins lighting cigarettes and breaking them in their shaking hands. When finally, one stayed in his mouth. It was so soaked in blood along its length that half stayed un-smoked.

'Go get cleaned up,' yelled the landlady, and they followed the order.

In the toilet, they both checked their broken noses and ripped shirts, and Jamie splashed water on his face while trying to suck in his first lungful of cigarette. The lip-licker mumbled, 'They are after Don. They'll go to the marina next.'

'Okay,' replied Jamie.

Then the doorman, despite his beating, became alive again and asked, 'You coming?'

At that moment, Jamie was lost: if you'd asked him how many fingers he had, he would have needed a very long time and a calculator to work out the answer, but he followed the lip-licker outside into a taxi. The pair stumbled into the night, and as pride surged through them, they both became possessed robots looking for revenge. 'Marina mate, you got any fags?' he asked the driver, 'Any tools?'

It wasn't a brilliant. Whatever was underway would be of interest to the old-Bill sooner or later, and chatting to a taxi driver about procuring weapons was definitely not clever.

By the time they arrived, the minibus had already been and gone after throwing paving slabs through the theoretically bullet-proof glass doors. The visitors had exchanged injuries and left before the sound of the police sirens arrived. Half an hour later, Jamie was back at Park Corner to finish his shift without a clue what he was doing or where he was. Crow explained that he had seen team arrive and had raced off to the next pub on the block to get help. The landlady interrupted with a sneer, 'Ah...discretion was the better part of valour, was it?'

Then an old police Sergeant knocked on the door to ask about the incident. With blood stains on the collar of his shirt, Jamie said, 'I'll have to ask Don what happened.'

When he heard that, the copper's ears pricked up, and he asked, 'Why, was Don here?'

Jamie knew what was expected protocol. From Don's commentary at the training session, he understood the law and replied, 'No, but I'll have to ask him what I can say to the police.'

The cop laughed and said, 'Fair enough,' accepting that the firm had its own rules. His last words before ambling down the street were,

'You should get yourself to hospital.'

By midnight, the pub was packed with two dozen doormen from other venues, but it was only when Phil arrived that Jamie was put in another taxi. The big psycho had put it succinctly, 'Go to casualty now, or I will kick your heads in!' and he pushed him and the other damaged Red-Tie out the door into a waiting car.

At the hospital, a few men from the minibus were in the waiting room, but the lip-licker greeted them like old friends. He asked, 'Got a cigarette?' and they shook hands.

Jamie stayed insolent in silence to the friendliness as they said why they'd been there, 'We've just had enough of Don.'

When discussing Park Corner, they suggested, 'Just in the wrong place at the wrong time,' and that the trigger had been an attack on another local drug dealer; two dozen men had smashed him, his house and his brand-new Range Rover. They blamed Don.

By two in the morning, Jamie had been sewn up and returned to Park Corner to sit curled up in a corner. He had a total of eighteen stitches on his lip and around his head. Crow came over to his table and began with excuses, then Phil joined them with a huge grin and two pints of lager, 'There you go Jamie, have that, good lad.'

'Didn't get you one Crow as obviously you are a bullock-less Muppet, but I don't blame ya mate after all, you are only an elite English soldier and pretend doorman.'

'It wasn't like that Phil. I went to get help.'

'Yer right, you ran away like a pussy. Jamie stood. You fucked up, and you know it.'

Crow looked embarrassed and suggested, 'It was over as soon as it started. There was nothing I could do.'

Phil repeated, 'Yer whatever, mate. You ran,' then he strolled off to taunt someone else.

Crow mumbled apologetically, 'Getting my head kicked in for a few quid. It's not for me.' Then he changed the subject to hints of mercenary work that he said was coming up shortly. Jamie believed only the latter from Crow, not the nonsense about why he'd disappeared.

When Don arrived, a meeting was called, and Jamie was asked, 'Alright Mush, you stood your ground. So, you get an opinion.'

'We should make statements to the police,' he suggested. The room erupted angrily, 'Fucking grass! He's the fucking reason they did it.'

'Let the boy speak. He took a kicking, and so fuck, we don't have drugs in the clubs. Maybe we should all be having a word with dealers!'

Phil closed in and stood next to him in silence. The big man lit two cigarettes and handed one to Jamie, who continued with his idea, 'Right now, these fucks are standing behind their front doors with a bat, right? Expect us to hit them, right?'

He took a long deep drag. The cigarette stuck to the dried blood on his lips, and he spoke with it dangling from his mouth. 'So, if we go to cops and make statements, they'll think we are going that way, they'll drop their guard. Then we hit them!'

It was as coherent a thought as he could muster. The mood calmed a little, and it was easier to speak with Don and Phil standing beside him, holding their hands out to calm the lads after the blasphemy of suggesting police. A commotion on the side door interrupted him. It was Maria angrily arguing with another doorman he didn't recognise. Someone shouted, 'Let her in! She's with Jamie.'

The room was shocked when she entered, oblivious to the calls of, 'How did he pull her?' and, 'Fuck' sake, I didn't know Jamie had a bird.'

Ignoring everyone else, she strode over to Jamie's bloodied face and tenderly cupped it in her hands to say, 'You're with me all night, okay?'

The pub erupted in jeers and a mocking, 'Awwwwww!'

Don rested his arm on Jamie's shoulder and shouted above the chatter, 'We'll talk about this later. I know what lads I can rely on. You know who you are. So, my house tomorrow at one!'

The Boss had made his opinion clear. Jamie had done well, and to reiterate that belief he went around the lads in the pub, checking what faces they'd seen in the fight and having a private word as if he was a herald compiling the details of his knight's valour after a battle. Don ended up sitting next to Maria and Jamie; she was wiping away some dried blood from his ear and neck while he smoked another cigarette with trembling hands. Jamie was sliding into the reality of shock, and as the full adrenalin dump caught up with him, his energy and the last of his ability to think leached away.

Maria told him, 'Cariño, come with me. Home. You understand?'

Don nudged her with a smile, 'Boy done good, don't worry. As long as he's not walking around town for the next few weeks, it'll be alright.'

'Huh?' Jamie was struggling to follow any conversation now. His head was banging.

'You have to go home,' Don told him, 'Mary will take you.'

Jamie looked around, his jaw hanging slack, and muttered something incoherent. Phil grunted, 'Your mum says it's past your bedtime,' and pulled him up roughly to march him to Maria's car, where he was stuffed into the passenger seat with the words, 'Keep him out of sight.'

In the car, she drove him in silence, her mood slowly changing from the tender affection she'd shown him in the pub to one of flaring nostrils and repeated angry sighs. She tried helping him upstairs with her arm around his waist at her house, but he whimpered in pain with every step. She turned him around to slowly stagger towards the sofa, where he stumbled and fell to the floor. Once on the ground, he didn't want to move again. Maria fluffed up a cushion for his head, covered him with a duvet and turned out the light so he could sleep, but less than ten minutes later, she stomped back down and yelled at him, 'Fucking Red-Ties.'

Then she quietly knelt beside him, slid under the cover, and wrapped herself around his body. He flinched as her arm draped across his, and she kissed his neck, but he didn't care about that or his head being so fuzzy. Jamie felt Maria's arms around him, and that meant everything was okay.

'Lot of space on my sofas,' declared Don while scratching his neck and looking around the room. What he meant was that out of the two hundred doormen he had working for him, there were less than a dozen at his house. Jamie had turned up, but those with fear, or friends and family on the other side of the feud were absent.

Walker asked, 'What about Crow?' and tapped the ex-paratrooper on the shoulder.

'I like him for the walkie-talkie stuff at festivals and y'know, shit jobs,' said Don, and all laughed as Crow shifted uncomfortably in his seat.

Walker grinned and winked, 'Dunno Don, he ran, by rights, we should fuck him off, but we haven't enough good lads to cover the doors. So, we might have to keep using him.'

Crow gritted his teeth when he heard that mocking indictment but said nothing. Don had been drinking that morning, and although annoyed, was more sympathetic, 'He says he went for help, probably how squaddies think innit?'

Walked shrugged, 'Yer... Well, all that shit he was talking about bodyguard work?'

'And okay, he's full of shit,' said Don cutting him off mid-sentence, 'But a shit boss will always go looking to blame his workers. Crow can stay, and the sooner we un-train him from all that army bollocks, the better. We're only as strong as our weakest link, and all that.'

Ginger spoke, 'Jamie still keeps out of sight, right?'

It took Don a very long time to answer that question, and he took the moments to scratch his head as if still deliberating, 'I know what lads I can trust for this. The rest of you just know we will be stretched for a while.'

Then he turned to Jamie, 'You didn't need to come today, just go home and get some rest. You look like shit.'

'I'm okay,' he replied as Ginger handed him a pint of lager.

'Didn't ask that, did I?' said Don with his notorious temper flaring for a second, then pausing he added with a calmer tone, 'But, as you're here I've an idea. Stick around for a bit.'

***

Jamie did. He lounged on a large armchair until an hour later, Ginger tapped him on his shoulder to ask, 'You been drinking much?'

He yawned and replied, 'A bit.'

'Need you to drive.'

'Well, I do have a licence now.'

Don bounded up to them, 'Ready?' Jamie stared back at the face of a now clean-shaven and showered Don in a suit and tie. In company director mode, he explained, 'New guys always get thrown in at the deep end, it's how we train ya up. Today, you're the face of the firm at a meeting. So, you are driving to meet a copper.'

Jamie looked worried, 'I still don't have a licence. A real one, I mean.'

'Don's reply was succinct, 'What the fuck do I care,' then lost in thought with his rage rising again, he barked at no one in particular, 'He can't go like that. Anything in his size?' Doormen immediately raced to Jamie to put their bodies between him and their temperamental boss. One of the lads, an ex-Marine, said in a companionate tone, 'Come with me,' and he was hustled into the pub's office as Don snarled a sweary monologue about being late.

Five minutes later, he was back out in blazer, white shirt, and grey trousers. Nothing fitted, and every item was slightly too big. At the car, Don slurred, 'I'm pissed, so you'll do the driving and the talking!'

The boss's unconventional navigation was him pointing at the last moment for a turn and there was a brief period of him insisting he stay in the middle lane as much as possible until Jamie met his first roundabout and just stopped in the middle of it. Don glared at silence as he walked around the vehicle to change seats before growling through gritted teeth, 'Get out. I am driving! Have you never seen a roundabout before. Sweaty sock bastard, you can't just stop in the middle of the fucking road!'

'Don't have them where I'm from. I didn't know what to do,' replied Jamie quietly.

'Can't take my eye off you for a fucking second,' said Don with his face gradually returning to a normal pallor from beetroot-red wrath.

Lowering his window, he called to another driver who was beeping his horn.

'Oi mate, mate, oi mate, mate, mate,' he cooed, smiling at the driver with a friendly wave, 'Oi mate, mate...Mate!'

'Yes,' the man answered.

'Oi mate, mate! Oi Mate,' Don yelled with a smile. Then shouted, 'Wanker!' and drove on.

'Where are we going?' Jamie grunted.

'Council meeting.'

'On a weekend?'

'Councillors get extra money if they meet at weekends. You get nothing. It's those licensing morons. Walker usually talks to them, but you're doing it. Don't worry, I'll tell you what to say. Just remember the firm is our family, and they ain't. They won't ask about last night, not yet. They wanna talk about some other bollocks.'

'Oh, okay. I can do that, but why are we going?'

'Long before the council, when I first worked doors, I had the idea of licensing doormen in the city and properly training them. I tell you what Mush, I didn't sell my drug business for these pricks to nick my scheme and tell me who can work.'

'You are a drug dealer?'

'Not anymore. Now I'm more like a job centre,' Don said with a chuckle.

For the rest of the journey, he clarified Jamie's role. What he was to say, and how he was to say it. As the pair parked up and walked to the appointment at the town hall. Don made him repeat all the answers he was meant to give. He explained who they were going to meet by saying, 'You'll be talking to an arrogant prick. A new one from their Direct Entry Scheme. He'll assume that he is in charge. Points to note though, he used to be an IT manager at a merchant bank. So, not a real copper, just a suit and tie with a warrant card.'

Once in the meeting, Jamie began to feel unwell as the room's air-conditioning pumped out a dry dusty air that made his throat sore. It must have affected Don too as he began to cough, and his mood shifted from a bit irritable, through cantankerous and on to bloody grumpy. He made it obvious that he didn't want to be there with his body language sagging onto a cheap wooden chair. It creaked as he fidgeted with palpable irritation.

Opposite, at a long, polished table was a police inspector who suggested, 'Shall we start?' The officer was a wiry man with a kindly face, wearing a blindingly white shirt under the blue-black of a brand-new uniform jacket. Don grunted in response, 'Yer,' and managed to slouch a little bit more.

The copper ignored the surliness and with a smile said, 'Don, thank you for coming. We had an opportunity to discuss this before you arrived. I think we are all in agreement.' Don responded with a yawn and, 'Alright, what is it?'

The officer spoke hesitantly, as if he hadn't prepared for the meeting and told them, 'First order of business is Paul Gantt.'

'And..?' said Don, his face stayed emotionless while his left hand began to rub his neck with his eyes staring coldly into those of the copper.

'First, let me say how very happy we are, how we all are, with the way your company runs the doors,' he looked around the room at the councillors, who all murmured agreement.

'And. Well. It's just Paul, I am afraid,' the inspector forced a weird smiling and puffing of his cheeks to show how it was a sensitive subject for him to address.

'Well, Paul was caught on camera you see,' offered one of the councillors.

The Red-Tie boss snarled, 'I know what he did. Jamie, whatcha think?'

Don had explained that protection for his staff was the reputation of their firm. Wearing a Red-Tie signified that if you caused its wearer any trouble, you'd have the unlimited vengeful retribution. Even if vastly outnumbered in manpower, on matters of principle the boss of the Red-Ties was known as one who would happily and suicidally go down fighting. The problem was that one nightclub in the city had taken to wearing Red-Ties, although there's also had a little bat emblem too. Paul had been out drinking on his birthday, and when he walked past their venue, he'd noticed. For him, it was brand infringement and stealing Don's protection.

Jamie was struggling to remember the words he was supposed to say when he was interrupted by the officer telling them,

'We are insisting that Manhattan Club press charges.'

'I know,' said Jamie stuttering, 'You're saying you've to take his licence?'

'Well, that's it. He can't work on the doors without one.'

'Okay,' said Jamie.

The cop leaned back in his chair, and looking at Don said, 'We hoped you'd understand.'

Jamie lost his anxiety about forgetting what to say, and annoyed about being bypassed, took his cue to jump in, 'My boss. Who is going to work the doors now?'

The lead councillor for licensing responded with some well-meaning patronisation, 'No, no, I don't think you understand. As we said, we are perfectly happy with your company. It's just that Paul Gantt can't work anymore.'

Don yawned again and stretched as Jamie answered for him,

'Aye well, I don't think youse understand. If Paul doesnae work, nae doormen in this toun works, nae wan.'

All eyes were now on Jamie, as Don quietly asked, 'And why is that?'

'Well, my boss,' he replied in his West of Scotland accent, 'Without Paul, all they bad yins wull be back in toun and all they young coppers wull be oot Friday nights dealing wi' them. Instead of us.'

Don smirked as he said 'Come on Jamie, we ain't needed. They know what they're doing.'

Getting back into the car, Don took a moment to reflect on what had happened, 'That went well. The cops won't like it, they'll have some revenge, but Paul will work.'

Jamie looked worried and asked, 'What do you mean? They ain't said a word yet.'

'They'll come around. Anyway Mush, your pub and try not to get lost.'

'My pub?'

'Yer, the studenty place,' Don said, and Jamie pressed the button to start the car.

The boss now seemed happy and relaxed. He began chatting at speed, giving him what he called, 'Proper driving lessons.'

En route, there was very little on; mirror, signal, manoeuvre and a lot about ramming vehicles, evading police and how to repair car engines with things from his pockets, but it was all fascinating. He also gave his views on management and offered an enigmatic maxim to deal with every problem: 'You can be lazy, greedy, or stupid to be successful. Just don't ever be more than two of those, at any one time.'

As Jamie got out of the car, Don asked, 'How ya feel about working with Phil some more?'

Jamie gulped, 'Ah! I have to go now,' was all he could think of to say.

Don chuckled, shaking his head as he drove off.

Maria must have been waiting for him because she greeted him with kisses that stung his wounds as he opened the door,

'Are you okay? Where did you go? I have worried?'

'I'm okay,' he replied, 'Ginger picked me up for a meeting; I didn't want to wake you.'

She hugged him and said, 'You is stinky. You need to have a shower and go to sleep.'

He didn't want to sleep. He was hoping for another lazy day watching a Spanish TV crime drama with Maria, nibbling tapas, and emptying a bottle of Rioja while wrapped in a duvet with her. But she was adamant, 'Bed for you! You are still hurt. You need rest!'

So, ten minutes later, instead of episode five of a sexy Madrid detective, Jamie traipsed from a quick shower to his bedroom, then as he turned the door handle, she called him, 'Not that way, in here Cariño.'

It wasn't unusual for her to kiss him on his forehead and say goodnight, but she usually came into his room to do it. Expecting just a peck on the cheek, he ambled through her open door. He couldn't see where she was, as the bedroom was only lit by a few flickering candles, so he asked, 'Will I turn the light on?'

'Non. A la cama,' she murmured.

'Oh okay, night,' he replied and turned around to go back to his room.

Maria's voice was louder this time, 'My bed Tonto, come to my bed!'

Muddled, disorientated, he stood motionless in the doorway, unsure of what she meant.

'Are you concussed?' she asked, then sounding exasperated told him, 'Come here!'

Jamie still didn't move. It was like he was in a trance as he caught sight of her in the shadows and what she was wearing. Her black silk pyjama jacket covered only the top of her tanned thighs, and it looked like the buttons across her breasts were all still straining to burst.

Softly she said, 'I don't like when I wake up, and you're not with me!'

'Really?'

'Si, but if you get hurt again...Back to your room!'

Getting into bed beside her, with a huge grin, he told her, 'You know I like you a lot.'

'Si, claro que si,' she replied and cuddled him from behind, pressing her breasts into him.

Jamie was confused, and asked, 'So are we like boyfriend and girlfriend now?'

'No, you are my friend. My friend and I trust you to be in my bed.' She told him.

'Is that fair, like…y'know…and like I am sleeping with you.'

'Shhhh, Jamie. I can hear you frowning.'

'You know I want to be more than, like just friends. Right?'

Maria pulled herself closer to him and breathing in his ear said, 'Joder! I know, you have told me every day since I met you. Every time you look at me. But, for now, just be my friend.'

For the hour before he drifted off to sleep, Jamie was in turmoil and trying to weigh up the dichotomy of his relationship with her. In the end, he consoled himself with the thoughts, 'I care about her, I like her. I don't want to lose her as my friend just for a fuck.'

The next morning Maria must have heard him stirring awake, as she bounded into the room like an excited toddler, screeching with something in her hands, 'Do you like it? Do you like it?'

Jamie rubbed his eye and focused, he saw what she was talking about.

It was a gift box wrapped in a thick white ribbon. Inside was a chainmail shirt and a slim line bulletproof vest. As he opened the package and picked it up, it made a metal slithering sound. It took him a while to respond, as she was still only wearing her black silk pyjamas, and his mind filled with the curves of her body as she jiggled to his side on his bed.

'I love it. What is it for? I mean, thank you. Where did you get it?'

Maria grinned, 'I got it online. It's for you when you work.'

'Kinda fast delivery innit?' Jamie asked, with suspicion in his eyes.

She asked, 'You not like?' and made him promise to wear it for work.

After breakfast, holding hands, they walked to the university where Jamie had a lecture about the nomenclature of ship design, followed by an assessment of his class's mathematical abilities conducted by an old man in a cardigan. This new professor explained a formula for foxes eating rabbits that looked at their relative birth and death rates depending on food supply. It was riveting, especially as the man often mentally wandered off and began talking in long sentences of Latin. After that, he gave everyone a question paper and sauntered around their desks, offering only warm praise and advice on answering questions. The old lecturer stimulated conversations between students and acted like the double maths period could go on for days without a time limit. It was the first moment he'd had as a student where Jamie could see himself as a designer or analyst, instead of him just being there for a general education. At the end of the inspirational hours, some of Jamie wanted to hang out with the people in his class and talk about maths, but he left because Maria wanted to meet her in town at a burger bar and go shopping.

When he arrived, she greeted him with her customary kisses on each cheek, fries and a double cheeseburger. After eating at a table, Jamie noticed two men he'd seen at the attack on the pub walking through the entrance. In alarm he said, 'We gotta go. Sorry.' Full of haste, he led Maria through the wanna-be restaurant towards the rear exit, but as Jamie opened the back door onto the park, four large men exited a car. Men he'd also seen fighting at the Park Place pub.

They looked at him as if he was prey, and in fear, Jamie slid the push bar out of the fire escape to hold it like a club and snarl in his Scots, 'Youse here fir me?'

The looks on their faces were grim and confident as they strode towards him with menace.

'Can you see any cameras?' Maria asked as she stepped to his side, and with her left arm pushed Jamie behind her and down. She shook her head and said, 'Fuck off!' and to Jamie's astonishment, they did, running back to their car. With a wheelspin, they raced off.

What Jamie hadn't seen, was that as her left hand outstretched protecting him, her right slid out her LCR Ruger pistol from under her armpit and pointed it forward from where she braced it against her hip. Gathering his wits as he got up, he was flustered and apologetic, 'Sorry about that. It's, erm. I don't know what happened.'

Maria shook her head and said, 'Que le paso a mi dulce novio? You are my Jamie. You can't be this guardaespaldas asertivo? No mi gusta.'

'I didn't know what else to do. It's no like I could run and leave ya, is it?

'What were you going to do?' she asked.

'I was aiming for maybe not looking like a weakling,' he said smiling.

'Four on one is stupid,' she declared holding his hand again, 'You don't fight like this.'

An indignant Jamie grumbled, 'It's not like my village down here. I've to toughen up and do the right thing, innit. And by the way, how the hell did you knock me over like that?'

Maria avoided answering by asking, 'Why do gamberros look for you?'

Then she began questioning him again about the Red-Ties, and what he did for them, but as they walked across the park it was as if both of them were embarrassed somehow by the incident, and neither one of them wanted to keep talking about it.

Chapter 15 – Research.

'Fancy meeting you here?' asked Petra stepping onto an escalator behind her boss.

'Did you bring me my chocolates?' Ken said as he turned around.

'Maybe, at least pretend to be impressed that I got behind you.'

He moved up a step to stand next to her, 'Took you long enough, I tried waving to you at Sloane Square. Dear, you do know that I am on my way to meet you. So no need to try following someone like that is there?'

'Nope, not buying it. I got you. You didn't see me,' she replied, smirking.

'Dear, dear, dear,' he told her sighing.

'Can I make a complaint about you calling me Dear?' she joked, 'It's a bit…erm…belittling.'

'Not unless I can complain about my lack of chocolates,' replied Ken tugging at her bag. He was to be in a mercurial mood as if he didn't have a care in the world.

'None in there. Told you I didn't get any.'

Ken tried peering in her bag, asking her, 'I thought you were just too busy to unpack.'

'Why would you think that?' she replied, pulling the bag away.

He tilted his head to one side and contorted his face to ask, 'You really didn't get me any?'

'Sorry, no,' and then the pair walked, ten feet apart, as if strangers until they reached a wine bar.

Inside, Ken ordered a bottle of claret, and they sat in a curtained booth waiting for the waiter to deliver it and depart before discussing their plans.

Petra smiled at her mentor, 'I've always loved this building of suspense and intrigue thing you do?'

'I'm telling you nothing until you hand over the chocolates,' he said, grinning.

Petra put her oversized bag on the table and opened it to reveal a gift box wrapped up in a T-shirt that read, "I love Brugge," and asked, 'So what's going on?'

Lifting his palms as if surrendering he said, 'I've only a little more that I can say.'

After a long silence, she rolled her eyes and sighed, 'So what's the plan?'

'Well now that you're back. I need you to install some things in that flat in Vauxhall, then do that place they meet,' the old spy explained.

'Okay,' she said, snatching a chocolate for herself, 'I can do that.'

'And I've got a list. You need to move some files.'

'Why?' she asked, her expression changing to worry.

Ken looked muddled for a second before deciding what to say, 'I had a brief chat with someone that is above both our pay grades. I've been reminded of the words of Field Marshall Lord Slim, and after all we are not glass bottle manufacturers, are we?'

'Brilliant, not a fucking clue what you're talking about?' she replied sarcastically while filling their glasses with claret.

Ken grinned, 'It was good news. I was told that while we can't do anything, I could recruit extra manpower to not do anything. It was very good news, but I'd rather we didn't have anyone back in my lair.'

'Fuck's sake Boss. Really!' Exasperated, Petra rolled her eyes at him, 'Riddles, always the bloody riddles. But okay. If we are hiring, how about Barty?'

'Who?' he asked, reaching for his wine and another chocolate.

'You remember, he did ten years as a dodgy fucker with GCHQ before doing that TV show,' then nudging him she said, 'We know each other.'

'Oh yes, I remember, and after I last met him, I checked my wallet was still there. Next?'

'Yes, but he came across as an honest criminal,' she shrugged and leant over to whisper in his ear, 'It's all I can think of for now. It's not like we can ask around too much. Bit hard being the secret police within the secret police. Everything is so bloody secret.'

He grinned, 'Shhh, don't say that out loud, it's a secret,' then closed his eyes and whispered to her, 'You also need to source some untraceable protection you won't mind losing.'

'So does that mean we can start picking them up?' she pleaded with her police sensibilities showing.

He knew what she meant and exhaled, 'Don't be naughty. We aren't going to stop them. Just tip the balance of things. It's not like anyone is doing anything wrong.'

'Oh, for fucks sake! Nothing wrong,' she whined, her face became a disapproving scowl.

'This is serious, dear. We can't just go about doing things. Doing things is always trouble. In the long-term, schoolboy morality has no place in what we do, and you know this. It's much better if other people do things for us, coincidentally,' he told her, munching on a chocolate-coated cherry.

Holding her glass to her lips, Petra shrugged, 'So, I won't go to jail for any of this?'

'Sadly, no. Neither of us will ever be that lucky,' he told her.

'Just out of interest. What is my pay grade, boss? What's the chain of command.'

'Well, that stuff is easy to answer,' he replied, sipping his wine.

After a long pause, she asked, 'Well, are you ever going to tell me?'

He ignored her and said, 'Right now, we need that chap who looked at the pictures.'

She scrunched her face up, still puzzled, 'You think he is involved?'

'No, but I read his file,' he said, yawning and closing his eyes.

Petra was confused, 'Why are the photos so important? Can't I just accident the Angel?'

The old spy was struggling to stay awake and said, 'No. You'll get spotted.'

'What can we do?' she asked.

'Follow our hunches about how the bureaucracy works in our place, the way activities wobble along a timeline,' he replied drowsily and fell asleep for a few seconds.

She nipped his wrist with her nails, 'Okay, a bit lost, but I'll sort the flat. What else?'

Ken took a deep breath, forcing himself awake, yawned again, and told her, 'Sorry, I am a dead horse still pulling the plough.'

Petra shook her head, 'Always with the cryptic language?'

He sighed, 'When you replace me, you need to remember this. We can only do our little bits, and even then, with the lightest touch. And Little steps, always little steps. Alliances always change.'

'I'm not ready,' she replied gloomily, referring to the burden he often threatened her with.

Ken smiled, 'We'll you need to be, and put your drink down. You're driving.'

***

Three hours later at a set of red traffic lights, Petra drew level with car and Ken leaned out to tap another driver's window with a chief superintendent's warrant card. As the window rolled down, he asked, 'Paddy, be a dear and pull into the next services, please?'

The lights changed and without waiting for an answer, Petra sped off to a petrol station half a mile ahead. As predicted, the man followed and parked next to them. With a smile, Ken suggested, 'Can you get in our car so we can talk? Sit in the back if it makes you feel any safer with an old man like me. Oh, and don't worry about the cameras.'

The man looked around to see the staff rushing around between tills. It looked like someone had shut down all their pumps and electrical equipment.

The old spy told him, 'Jump in,' and held up a jamming device.

Paddy sighed, 'You two spooks then?' Then casually slipping a 1911 Browning pistol into his hand, he got in behind them and asked, 'What do you want?'

'Maybe nothing, but I have seen your file and think you can help me.'

'Bollocks you have mate. Nobody's had my file.'

The old spy sighed, 'You stole a Mercedes using a Chinook at Bagram air base.'

'Oh,' replied Paddy with his jaw dropping slightly before recovering a smiling composure, 'What are you trying to say? Things are allowed in the Legion, as long as officers get a cut?'

'That's not what interested me in you,' he replied, 'I've got a few work-related questions.'

Paddy, still with his pistol in hand, asked, 'Who are you?'

'Call me Ken, and my colleague is called Petra,' he replied, 'We have questions. I hope you'll want to answer.'

Ken's tone was calming, and Paddy seemed to relax as the old spy asked, 'You were looking at some photographs for NATO and identifying suspicious mounds and shadows in the fog of war?'

'That's right,' he replied, 'Satellite images mostly. Clumps of grass. Holes in roof. Trying to identify mortar positions or an inch of barrel belonging to a sniper, nothing too clever.'

'Was it just Iraq and Afghan?'

The former soldier puffed up his chest to reply, 'Mostly. Sometimes a staged scene in Arizona might be slipped in to monitor my due diligence, but mate, I did my job as if my life depended on it because someone once done the same for me.'

'So sometimes it wasn't just a combat zone?' Ken asked.

Paddy explained how he didn't really know and that he only ever saw a picture and its reference code. He usually swiped NO RISK, and they disappeared like an unwanted dating profile. He saw hundreds per day, and if he spotted an anomaly, whoever he sent it to would take over and escalate it for review. Then grumpily he said, 'Mate, get to the point!'

Ken pulled out a folder with photographs. He handed them over and said, 'I'm not the only person looking for you, am I? And I think you are in danger!'

'No shit,' Paddy replied, tapping his weapon, 'There's been some hardmen around already.'

'Can you describe the visitors; Did you get a number plate?' asked Petra.

Paddy gestured with the pistol, as if it was a rifle at high port across his chest, 'Not old bill but maybe old hoods, if y'know what I mean.'

Ken nodded, 'I think I know who they are, but I need more answers. I need some help. It's for King and country.'

Paddy said, 'I only like the Ginger Royal,' then rubbed two fingers together, 'How much?'

Petra interrupted, 'Maybe nothing. It's just a few bloody questions,' she told him, 'And if you don't answer, how about I show you my warrant card and arrest you for discharging a firearm at a police officer.'

She pressed herself backwards to show him a pistol flat against her belly pointing at him. Paddy looked down at his weapon and replied, 'I didn't fire at you, Luv. You'd have noticed.'

She snarled, 'Tell that to a jury after the prosecution reads out my forensics report.'

'Please, no bickering, children,' demanded Ken.

'What do you want?' Paddy asked again.

Ken tapped the wallet of photos, 'We've the same problem, I think it's about these.'

'First, point me to whoever's been at my door,' he said flicking through the photos.

'We can't do that,' Ken paused, 'Yet! As I need your help to find them.'

'Deal and by the way. I remember this lot, state-of-the-art camouflage,' he told them, relaxing more to Ken's criminal attitudes than Petra's police ones.

'Part of a military exercise?' asked Ken.

'No. You won't get that on a typical exercise. Only two types of people have that kind of kit; Special Forces officially working with spooks or Special Forces who stole something shiny last time they worked with spooks.'

Ken thought about what was unfolding, 'Yes, I came up with that too.'

Paddy grinned, 'What do you think it's all about then?'

'We are asking the questions,' said Petra.

Ken shook his head and used his kindly old man voice, 'Would you like to come in for a chat? I will, of course, pay your rate, but it might make more sense if you worked for me full time?'

'Now we are talking. I can tell you exactly what I saw and why someone might be concerned!' Grinning, he blew Petra a kiss, 'BLT with a diet coke, love.'

'Piss off,' she replied, 'As far as I'm concerned, you're perverting the course of justice.'

'Oh, pervert! So, you've seen my service record too?' he replied, grinning, taunting her.

Ken ploughed on, enquiring, 'These photos, do you know the location?'

'Nope, but I can find it. You are missing some pics. But there was a building with Loch Lomond painted on its roof, and some Gaelic spelling that was all over the place. I can't remember the name, but I'll recognise it if I look at maps. I know the general area?'

Ken nodded, 'You'll start on a grand a day. It's a big firm, we can afford it.'

'Sold,' replied Paddy, and smiling at Petra, told her, 'You fancy me don't you love?'

'What!' Petra gasped, 'Why pay him? How about he just tells us what he knows?'

'So how would you do it…If it was a hit?' Ken asked ignoring his assistant.

Paddy took a long deep breath, 'Hold on Mate, I've seen that movie.'

Ken laughed, 'Relax. You won't pull any triggers. I just want a second opinion from you.'

'As long as we are clear Mate!' he replied, 'I've no interest in being famous.'

'Mate? It's fucking sir to you,' said Petra, but it sounded like banter not anger.

They left Paddy's car at the petrol station. En route to the safe-house, he explained that what he'd seen wasn't something he suspected as an enemy position. 'I clicked RISK anyway. And for my own amusement, I typed, they needed to harden their routine and thought no more about it. An hour later, my phone rang, calling me in for a security check.'

'Where did they take you?' asked Petra.

'NATO,' he told them, 'Things started getting strange before that, though! Tickets arrived by bike messenger, and I thought, "First Class Eurostar? not for someone my grade?" Weirder still was who I was meeting. Five perfectly tailored General uniforms. Straight away they pressed a button on a remote. The picture appeared and they asked me why I'd marked it up. Took a while to remember what I was looking at. But told 'em what was wrong with it.'

Ken said, 'That's what we want to know too. It just looks like a set of pictures about nothing to us.'

'You've nothing. On the originals, the hillside had scrub that was all wrong.'

'What do you mean?' asked Petra.

Paddy told them, 'The foliage looked like it was electronic camouflage, and someone had pissed out of it from inside. I saw a random patch of green suddenly darker with a perfectly straight edge. Security check. My arse, too much effort was put into pretending it was a routine meeting and telling me to forget what I saw.'

'Then what happened?'

'Two weeks, my contract was terminated, and someone turned up at my local pub looking for me. Not a nice someone.'

'We need to get you looking at maps,' Ken told him, 'If you can find it. I'll need you to dig in and watch the place.'

'For a grand a day...I'll even call you sir.'

Chapter 16 - Human Resources.

The following day, when walking back from lectures with Maria, Jamie asked, 'Want to go for a drink?'

'A date? You mean a date?' she giggled, teasing him.

'No,' he replied, 'To prove you're not barred anymore.'

She nodded and the pair stopped at the Leni Quintain.

Don greeted them outside and said, 'Pay the lads, will ya?' and handed Jamie a large cash-stuffed envelope before driving off.

Confusion creased Maria's face when Jamie stuffed some of the money into his pocket. She gripped his arm as they entered the pub and asked, 'Joder! What are you doing?'

'It's okay,' he told her and passed the money to another who did the same, 'You just take what you are owed and give it to the next guy. It's a good system.'

Inside, amidst tracksuit-clad doormen and two Alsatian puppies running around in circles, they sat down next to Phil who grunted, 'Alright Mush. How's you Mary?' Crow arrived with drinks and said, 'She must drink wine. You put it on your tab.'

Other colleagues wandered past, each with, 'Alright mate,' which Phil and Crow mostly ignored as they were finishing an argument about the veteran paratrooper's inexperience.

'You need fixing, you're too army,' he told the Para in a lecturing tone.

'Urgh? I likes my army ways, Mucker.'

'Forget them. First thing to remember is that you are a target twenty-four hours a day because you are a Red-Tie. So, if going for a piss, lock the door but expect it to be kicked in by someone you've upset. Even Jamie knows that, and he's only been on the firm a heartbeat.'

'Yer, make sure somebody's got eyes on ya at all times,' said a passing Red-Tie.

To which Phil replied, 'Fuck off wanker.'

Jamie interrupted, 'Phil, please! Can you no be civilised in front of Maria.'

'Yer sorry, Mary,' he replied.

'Is okay I do not understand him,' she told him, guzzling her wine.

Jamie noticed Maria's jaw clench and nervousness on her face, so said, 'Phil can behave nicely around women. He's semi-tame once you know him.'

Then raising his glass to her, he explained, 'We had a chat. Apparently, there's only one way to impress him, and that's if ya take a beating for the firm. Yer, mad, right?'

They bought more drinks, and Jamie tried to explain who the different people were around the pub, but Phil suddenly pulled a red tie from his pocket and held it against his neck. All conversations abruptly stopped. The doormen in the pub followed Phil's gaze and began to rise from their chairs. 'Local,' said Phil nodding to Crow.

The pair lumbered to the door slightly behind a faster Jamie, who approached a man in the entrance to say, 'Not today, Mate.'

'Don't call me Mate!' snarled the man, a known drug dealer and mugger.

Phil stopped behind Jamie, and told him, 'You never signalled,' and lightly slapped the back of his head, just as the dealer stepped forward with a small kitchen knife in his hand. The man snarled, 'Come on then!' then flexed his head and shoulders as a challenge. Jamie was torn between not looking like a wimp in front of Maria and the Red-Tie protocols. An idea popped into his head. Grinning, he raised his hands and wiggling fingers into the air as if surrendering while asking an intentionally distracting question, 'How many light-years in a parsec?'

The diversion gave Jamie enough time to kick the man's sternum thrusting him back onto the street and lock the door. He turned and stood nose to nose with Phil while trying to push his colleague back with his skinny arms, 'Don said no Phil-ing people in unless he says!'

'NO!' Phil raged, annoyed by the loss of a target, 'Out the fucking way.'

'Nope!'

Crow ranted, taking a weapon from the waistband at his lower back, 'He pulled a knife. I'm gonna stick my fucking Kukri in his head.'

'Move!' Phil bellowed.

'Nope,' repeated Jamie and, with a dimpled smile, waved to Maria as if nothing unusual was happening, 'Follow orders. No Phil-ing anybody in.'

Phil grabbed Jamie's throat and tightened his grip to snarl, 'Don't get in my way,' then, just as quickly let go, and they sat down again.

Jamie smiled at Maria, 'Phil can't hurt me. It is against the law. He wants to punch me right now but knows he has to look after me. It's a Red-Tie thingy. Yer, we talked.'

The big angry doorman took the comment as an invitation to flick Jamie's ear with a finger and say, 'Arse.'

Maria watched with her jaw hanging open in shock, and when Jamie saw the expression on her face, he asked, 'We can go home if you want?'

She drained her wine, prompting Jamie to get up to leave, but she touched his arm and said, 'Is okay, these are your friends. Is interesting to watch, and I'm only a little scared.'

'So, we stay?'

Maria leaned towards his ear to whisper, 'Si, but are psicologico, no?'

'Claro,' Jamie replied and shrugged while Phil went back to his favourite sport of taunting, 'Oi, mate, what did the army sack you for? You never told us.'

'You've no idea, have you, Phil.'

'How many people have you killed then?'

'One less than I want to at the moment,' Crow answered with a grin.

'Go on, how many?' Phil asked again.

'Not really what the army is about. It's more of a humanitarian organisation. What I did is all in my red book,' he replied, 'Mostly, I helped little old ladies across the road, honest.'

'I've never heard of the Parachute Regiment, are they like logistics or something?' said a Red-Tie at the bar. Crow ignored him.

'What's a red book,' asked Maria draining another wine.

'Basically, doll, it's a list of all the places I worked in the army. I take it to interviews, it's like an incident book, but because I was a Superman, all my pages just say classified.'

Maria smiled at the admission and asked a more reasonable,

'What do you do now?'

'Doll-face, this is it, door-work! Wish I'd never left the army 'cause, y'know, I'm only good at one thing! Slotting people at the end of my scope. These days, my longest job was as a guard on a security van. Something happened, and the boss asked me to step out the back for a word. Well, I thought he meant what it means in the army, didn't I? So, I hit him first.'

'Don't worry mate, he deserved it,' Phil told him, then asked another intentionally annoying question, 'Tell us about that parachuting Mush. Ya know anybody who did it?'

'Oh, fuck off Phil, I am not biting.'

'Do you like to parachuting?' Maria asked in her version of grammar, and a memory floated out of Crow's mouth with a proud smile as he rolled up his t-shirt sleeve to display a tattoo.

'Tell you this; I was on the hurry up to get all my jumps in at Brize, or I'd lose my SF pay. I couldn't find a reserve chute and wobbled in line towards the RAF lad. Luckily, he tapped me on the shoulder to proceed with my imaginary reserve and my arms folded over thin air.'

Phil beamed a smile, 'You is mad Mate. I like that.'

'It's forty-six, by the way, Mucker.'

'What is?'

'My confirmed kills.'

'Fuuuuuuuuck off, bollocks it is.'

'Yer mate, enemy were sitting down to breakfast all grouped together like amateurs in some sorta mess tent. It hit bang-on with the first round. No correction. Fire for effect!'

'Mortar?' Maria asked and Crow nodded. It looked like a happy memory to Crow, but his expression changed to pain, and his mouth became a shivering hole as his eyes welled up. Jamie didn't notice her sudden understanding of military matters as she held his hand, and they both watched. Nobody moved or spoke as the paratrooper began to break down, slowly in front of them. A monologue of horror was regurgitated. Crow lit a cigarette and nervously puffed on it. He looked down and saw his hand shaking. With a long drag, he began talking in fragments of sentences. A barmaid shouted, 'Oi, it's no smoking,' but he ignored her.

Crow was no longer with them, instead, he was talking to a memory hanging in front of him. 'He was the best killer money couldn't buy...I had to push his brains back into his skull...I ask my mates about stress. How they deal with it, but they say it doesn't bother them.'

'Don't worry about it, Mate,' said Phil, getting up for a piss. Crow didn't even notice him leave and carried on muttering about an officer bringing him a mug of tea and dying an hour later. That was when Crow started sobbing and the doormen around them became quiet, stunned into sympathetic silence.

Maria asked again, 'What do we do?'

Jamie shrugged and told her, 'He's done it before. When I was driving him to a pub. I think it is okay. He just has memories.'

Crow continued to babble, 'It makes me shudder, but it's a solution, isn't it?' He continued with his jumbled mosaics of cruel flashbacks as his fragile mind spewed out words about mud and a tracer-round hitting his bulletproof in West Africa. He laughed insanely about seeing his old mates as if they were there in uniform with their wounds seeping, beckoning him for a drink to the bar.

Phil returned and looked down at Crow weeping, and helped himself to one of the paratrooper's cigarettes just as a lecturer Jamie knew from the university's art department appeared at his shoulder, 'I'm a counsellor. Would you like to talk? We can find a safe space.'

'Fuck off, yoghurt knitter,' Crow growled, and she backed off.

Phil looked over to the Buddha-shaped man from the barbecue, that Jamie now knew as Mister Walker. With plaintive despair on his face, he drained the dregs of his pint then outstretched his hands in a gesture of, 'I dunno what to do.'

Mr Walker signalled the appropriate action by putting his hand around his own neck. Jamie guessed what was to happen, winced and asked Maria to, 'Look. The window.'

She turned her head away from Crow and Phil gently held out his hand. Automatically, the paratrooper put out his own to shake it.

In a flash of violence, Phil pulled him up and smashed his head off a nearby brick pillar, 'Crow! Get it together. You're embarrassing us.'

'Sorry, Phil. I'm alright now,' he replied and sat down, taking a deep breath, 'Sorry Mary, sorry Jamie, I'm okay, it's done now.'

Mr Walker passed by on the way to the toilets and grumbled at them all, 'That's all that was needed! You should've done that ten minutes ago. For fuck's sake!'

Another round of drinks was bought, and the incident was forgotten. Jamie had spoken to Crow before. He'd talked of how he was depressed, a failure in life and saw that his only self-confidence was in the moments of violence where he knew his role. Maria whispered in Jamie's ear, 'I don't understand everything, but is too much non?'

'We are who we are,' he replied.

'We?' she asked and furrowed her brow slightly.

Suddenly Mr Walker whistled. Half of the pub stood, raced to their cars and sped off.

'You stay. We don't need a fucking pacifist today,' Phil told him as they left.

Jamie smiled at her, 'We can go. They're off doing something horrible.'

'Where, what do they do?'

'Ah, they've not invited me,' he explained, 'But, I'm sure it's something I won't approve of.'

'What do they do?'

'I told you. It'll be something horrible. I couldnae say even if I knew,' he replied again, his teeth clenched, and he stared forward and stated a mantra, 'I'm allowed to defend myself. Law says I can make pre-emptive strikes if I've no reasonable avenue of retreat, but that's it.'

Maria smiled, 'Okay, I know that look on your face. I not ask. I already know you are senseless with them,' then she whispered, 'I don't know why you are okay with them, but is fine.'

Jamie couldn't explain why either, but he knew he had found a home in a group of happy misfits like himself. They were sociopathic, self-destructive, paranoid, and often kleptomaniac violent men with no hopes for any future, but they were a family. They wore hubris as a badge of honour and joked about the horror stories of their upbringing. Individually they might be weak, but as a group, regardless of their history, they were reborn as an unbeatable praetorian guard that seemed to fear nothing. In the short time he'd been with them, he understood that he was part of something, and whatever it was, he was in.

He hadn't gone with them. He knew it was because gangland was a binary world where you were either a hundred per cent for a job or you didn't get told it existed. The other thing Jamie knew, was that having two hundred men behind him wasn't a blessing, it was a burden. He now knew that if he complained about a situation, he could very quickly have fifty animals kicking down doors and unloading brutality on anything he mentioned. As such, he had been very cautious about bringing up even an unkind comment lest it unleashed his doorman world on his student life. Walking home with Maria, they nearly argued when she declared the obvious, 'You know they're criminals, right?

'Such a thicky?' Petra mumbled under her breath while wondering why Tanya always used the same seat in the same pub when she met Angel. She nearly laughed out loud watching the bizarre date unfold and the Russian greet her mark with tears in her eyes and pathetic soft murmurs.

In her earpiece, Petra heard her say, 'You'll look after me, won't you?'

He replied, 'Of course, little one,' but the look on his face was priceless, a confused awkwardness as she threw herself into his arms like a desperately needy Teddy-bear.

The couple drained a cabernet sauvignon and picked at a plate of whitebait and onion rings while telling each other entirely fabricated tales about their day. Tanya led with a tale about a banking report, and he talked about how hard it was to source the exact shade of copper for a marketing project. Then her phone beeped, and she read the message as if it was terrible news. Her eyes welled up as she sucked in a lungful of air to say, 'I am so glad you're here. I've done enough crying into my champagne.'

Unseen in an alcove, Petra switched on the camera she had positioned to watch them and complimented herself on a job well done. As a backup to Tanya's cloned phone, it'd been a simple task to replace a corkscrew decorating the wall with a matching electronic device. She smirked when she saw what the text really said, it was a spa appointment confirmation.

Tanya's voice quivered as she spoke, 'I need to finish this.'

'The wine or the whitebait?' Angel answered, trying to make her laugh, but it caused her to erupt in a half-second flicker of tearful anger.

'You don't understand. I'm getting a fucking divorce!'

Then, she was calm again and fell back into a pattern of self-effacing chat and flattering Angel about characteristics he never had. As she spoke, he looked uncomfortable as if he wanted to leave, but his cock was obviously making the decisions for him. Petra grinned as she watched Tanya on her screen hesitate and murmur the words that were her plan all along, 'Can you make sure I get home safely? I don't want to be alone.'

'Sure,' he replied.

'My husband is away on business,' she said, reaching out to rest her hand on his.

Petra's mind reeled as she tried to collate the lies Tanya had told Angel in her previous texts. She recalled that when she'd planted hidden cameras in the redhead's flat, she had not seen a single item that could have belonged to a husband, and she sneered at the amateurishness of Tanya's honey trap stories.

When they finished, it was easy following them. They never looked her way once. Ken brought a takeaway when he joined the surveillance in the street next to the Russian's flat, and the pair of spies began viewing from behind the blacked-out window of a Lexus, with chips. The camera in her hallway had a slight echo, but they could still hear Tanya when she placed her hand on Angel's chest and whispered, 'Like a coffee?'

In the small, sparsely furnished set of rooms, Petra only needed to switch cameras to keep up with the Russian spy bouncing around her home.

'Sit. I am just going to get out of my work clothes,' she said and scampered away to her bedroom.

Ken and Petra watched as Angel checked the same things they'd been interested in, her collection of sailing textbooks neatly arranged on a small shelf. Tanya called out to him, 'Shut your eyes.'

The words drew his attention to Tanya bending in the doorway of her room to pull on designer ripped jeans. They had more holes than denim over a pair of black silk panties.

'That was strange,' Ken said, 'Did you see how he looked away there?'

'I know this one, 'she explained, 'I know this one better than I know myself. He is falling for her. I watch him when he texts her. He spends ages writing and rewriting stuff before he sends a message. He likes her. Bet he's begun thinking of her as more than a bedtime squeeze.'

'Dear, are you sure? If true, then he is in for a nasty surprise?'

'I know his mind Boss, I am pretty sure.'

Tanya smiled and asked, 'Drink?' as she walked barefoot back into the room and her tiny kitchen, 'Of course,' he replied. She poured a glass of wine for herself and filled a tumbler with rum for him.

Standing beside him, with her denim-clad crotch inches from his face, she handed him the drink and declared, 'You are a good friend!'

When he put the rum to his lips, her hand touched under his chin to make his head tilt back, and their eyes locked together.

'She is good at the seduction game, isn't she?' Ken declared. Petra nodded and zoomed in. The Russian began to run her fingers over his head, stroking him like a cat. Gently wrapping his hair in her hand and asked, 'What do you think about me?'

His response didn't surprise the watching spies, 'I like you. When I first met you, I just wanted you in bed, but now, I want to think of you differently. You are something new in my life, pure, not corrupted by things,' he hesitated, and blurted out, 'You're probably my friend now, and I worry about you.'

They watched as Tanya's face froze with a sudden panic, 'Hey, look at that. Perhaps an honest emotion there,' Ken suggested pointing at the screen.

'Told you! Told you, Boss,' Petra yelped, clapping her hands together, 'He's just met her and already smitten! It's the one bit of spy-craft the bitch is good at.'

He sighed, 'Poor bastard. Feel sorry for him. Unless he's working her too?

She laughed, 'Men huh, you just want him to be a player. He's lost it.'

Back on the video feed, they watched as Tanya placed her fingers linger on his lips; Angel kissed them.

'I think she's sobbing again,' said Ken, 'A weird seduction technique.'

'Nah boss, it's cock twitching o'clock. She is just breathing real heavy. Betcha they are fucking in seconds.'

'Dear, please don't spoil the moment. It is so very tender,' Ken replied.

'I give them a minute max before his cock is slamming into her. We should have got some popcorn for this movie.'

Their laptop crackled, and the video feed flickered for a few seconds as Tanya took the last sip from her glass and placed it on the floor. Then slowly removing her top, the curves of her firm stomach and then the beauty of her heavy breasts were revealed. She licked her lips seductively, 'You can do anything you want. I won't say no.'

Angel made a feral grunting, 'Yes.'

She replied with a demure, 'And if I do say no, ignore me.'

133

The two voyeurs watched as Angel's eyes were drawn to her nipples poking out over the top of a black demi-cup bra as he asked, 'What game shall we play?'

Tanya smiled and said, 'I am your slave,' then she turned around, knelt on the floor and bowed her head, 'My master can do as he wishes.'

A grin spread across Angel's face, and he looked around for something to tie her wrists with, Tanya seemed to read his mind when she said, 'Sorry, I left my cuffs in my bedroom.'

Angel glanced towards the open door, leaned over Tanya, and let his right hand caress her neck and shoulder. It came to rest on her warm, inviting breast.

'Master,' he whispered, 'You will address me as Master,' and punctuated the order by pinching her nipple. Tanya moaned, arching her back in pain, but he kept squeezing and told her, 'You need to learn slave. Punishment will teach you to obey?'

'No Master, sorry Master. I won't forget again Master,' she gasped in painful pleasure.

'Good slave,' he told her and let go of her nipple, 'Close your eyes, slave.'

'Yes, Master.'

'Don't open them until I tell you!' he commanded, walking into her room to find her cuffs.

If Angel had been in any doubt about what Tanya liked in bed, it was now cleared up. Her open wardrobe and dressing table had on display every kind of whip, collar, and toy, as well as a selection of bondage outfits and uniforms.

'Remember, do not open your eyes,' Angel chuckled, happily jumping into the role-play. From what was laid out, he took a thick red cord and a thin chain with nipple clamps. The choice prompted Petra to almost scream at her monitor, 'No! The whip, take the whip!'

Back in the room Angel told Tanya, 'Stand up. Do you like being at my mercy?' She obeyed with a grin on her lips, crossed her hands and blurted out excitedly,

'Yes Master, I do. It turns me on that you will force me to do anything you want, no matter how slutty. I want to be a slutty, naughty slave.'

He tied her wrists tight with cord and said, 'Yes or No answers only slut. Open your legs.'

Tanya wriggled her bum teasingly as she moved her feet wider.

She was rewarded with a hard slap to her behind, 'Slut, you want my cock in your mouth?'

'Yes, Master.' She murmured and knelt again, flicking her hair away from her face.

'Did I tell you to kneel slut.'

'No. Sorry, Master.'

'You need a lesson in obedience slave, open your mouth' he told her, producing a red bandana from his pocket that he tied around her eyes.

The Spaniard smiled and walked around to where Tanya's tongue was waiting, her face tilted upwards.

With a smile, he connected little clamps to her nipples, and she winced in sudden pain. Angel chuckled and said, 'I feel generous. If you make me come before I finish my rum, I may reward you.'

'Please Master,' she whimpered as she tugged gently on the chain and struggled to keep her balance, 'Let me taste it. I'll be a good slut.'

'No. You may not touch my cock until I tell you to. No touching. Understood,' he explained while slapping her face with his cock and tapping it on her tongue.

Angel didn't give her time to respond before sliding it into her mouth, where she gobbled the head and shaft greedily. Just as suddenly, he pulled back and twisted the nearest clamp and reminded her of the rules, 'Slut, did I say you could start?'

'No Master,' she squealed.

Angel gulped the rum and sighed, 'I've nearly finished.'

'Please, Master. I can make you come. Please!' she begged while squirming in pain.

Angel placed his cock on her tongue for a few more seconds before declaring, 'Too late.'

Only then did he remove the clips from her breasts and stoop to gently kiss her where it hurt. He untied her, but only for the time it took to lead her, still blindfolded, to her room. There he pulled off her panties and secured her limbs to the four corners of her bed. Lying face upwards, she begged, 'Please fuck me.'

Angel ignored her pleas. Instead, he told her, 'Punishment. Make a sound and it'll be worse.'

'No, I need your cock. Please, Master! Just fuck me!'

'Not yet sub,' he replied, stuffing her wet silk underwear into her mouth.

He began teasing her with a long thick vibrator she'd left on her bedside table, and comfortable in the role-play. He selected the lowest setting of hum for her pussy lips.

She struggled, and he teased. Slowly the Spaniard pushed and withdrew. Repeating the action, leaving her untouched for a minute while gently kissing her breasts.

Then the Master-Tease slid the vibrator inside his submissive lover and told her, 'Don't lose those panties slut, or I'll make it bad for you.'

Angel went to pour himself another drink, and for ten minutes, he left her squirming on the bed. She moaned in ecstasy but never let go of the lingerie between her teeth. He watched Tanya panting and spasming on the bed, her whole body twitching in ecstasy.

Angel knew this role well and whispered in her ear to ask her,

'Did I say you could come slut?'

She spat out her panties to declare, 'I need your cock inside me. Please!'

This time when she begged. Angel obliged. It wasn't lovemaking. It was primeval humping, ravenous sex as he thrust into her pussy. Climaxing simultaneously, she yelled something unintelligible while Angel pulled out his cock and spurted the last jizz onto her belly and face.

'I told you not to lose these,' he said as he used her panties to wipe up his mess and stuff them back in her mouth. Tanya wanted more and giggled, 'Can I be punished again, Master?'

Angel smiled, yawned, told her, 'In a minute,' and fell asleep on his back snoring.

Petra, glued to the monitor, said, 'She must've drugged him. He went out like a light.'

'Yup, looks like,' replied Ken.

They continued watching until Tanya curled up next to Angel and fell asleep herself. After half an hour Petra asked, 'Pick it up in the morning?'

'Yes, we can keep recording, but that's it for today,' Ken told her.

If they'd stayed observing, they'd have seen something strange and interesting. While her lover slept, Tanya slipped out of her bonds and got dressed. She placed something in the collar of Angel's shabby leather jacket and used a silent drill to insert a small metal cylinder in the heel of his boot. It wasn't until that afternoon when Petra checked Tanya's electronic records, that she realised the Russian had also been through his pockets and taken pictures of everything she'd found. Then she saw Tanya do something naughty before she left her lover alone in the flat.

When Ken called for an update, she told him all that she'd observed, 'Both gone now. She tried cloning his phone, but like us she couldn't manage. Then she left him a note, breakfast and locked up his bits.'

'What?' he replied, 'Speak English please.'

'Okay boss, to be clear. She has his cock in a chastity cage.'

'Excuse me?' Ken was laughing.

'Oh, that's not the best bit. She's sexting non-stop since then, sending him pictures of her in kinky outfits and telling him that if he wants unlocked, to come back and fuck her properly.'

'That's one way to keep him interested, I suppose,' concluded Ken, 'Anything else?'

'Yes,' she explained, 'This morning, she left about an hour before he did. I think she must've watched for him to go, 'cause a minute later she was back in the flat and having a meltdown.'

'In what way?' Ken asked.

'Yer well, our terrible spy sat on the sofa and bit into a cushion. Then she started rocking back and forth crying. It was uncontrollable. Then just before lunch time she medicated with a pint of wine.'

'That's normal for an asset on the edge. Crazy creeps up on them all. The good ones just last longer. What else,' he replied as if it wasn't a shock for him.

Petra then told him, 'Nah that was it. Just seemed a bit weird. Now she's in an online strategy game. Fuck. She's just sent a message to another player that reads, 'I have begun.'

Ken chuckled, 'Okay, got it. Totally rubbish spy-craft, isn't it?'

'Yes, I'm beginning to feel sorry for her,' Petra suggested disingenuously.

'Sure you do,' he told her, 'Keep watch Dear, keep me informed.'

Chapter 18 - Work life balance.

Angel spotted the long lens camera twitching behind the curtains and waved. He'd expected nosey neighbours as soon as Matty had told him the location of the manor house, which was about twenty metres from the entrance to his former barracks. They probably monitored everyone who came in and out of the street, including the postman. Angel had got slightly lost again, but with the rest of the scene, he guessed it was the right place. An Elizabethan-style building that had a blacked-out Range Rover in the drive. As usual, he was late, and as usual, he went easy on himself and blamed it on his hangover. He yawned and crunched over the gravel in his cowboy boots to the rear of the building and found a large marquee set up between a long stone barn and an apple orchard. From the party debris, boxes of champagne and bunting, it all looked as if he'd arrived the day after someone's fiftieth wedding anniversary. The scene of other people celebrating life made him pause and switch off for a moment of hot sunshine in the fresh country air.

He was unsure how long he sat there, but the respite was disturbed by a text beeping. Angel didn't look, he knew who it was, and it prompted him to get to his feet again. With a slovenly gait, he walked a little further on and found a thick oaken door hiding between overgrown ivy and potted plants. Across the threshold, what little of the floorboards he could see were warped were raised and ready to trip him. Entering a low-ceilinged kitchen, he smiled when he saw that every other bit of floor space was piled with champagne and boxes of Pimms. There wasn't a straight edge anywhere he looked, just twisted beams and sagging walls, but a house of alcohol made him feel at home.

'Hey Angel, in here!' called a voice.

'Hello?' he called back and walked upstairs to find a familiar piece of muscle sitting in a finely tailored black suit, reading a report.

'Hola Matty, I am here?'

The mercenary pointed to an old four-poster bed loaded with box files and crates of lager, 'Yer and you're late. Grab a bottle mate, and we'll go to the Ops room.'

Angel grabbed two, and the pair made their way back outside to the barn. He tried to follow Matty inside, but the Smoker greeted him with an outstretched palm that was telling him to stop and be searched.

The Smoker said, 'Alright, you,' and reached for an electronic, paddle-shaped device. When he switched it on, it emitted a short beep and lit up with bright green.

'Joder,' said Angel with a heavy sigh, 'I didn't know you'd have this. Is new protocol?'

'Nope, it's only you I don't trust,' he told him as a matter of fact and began passing the electronic bug detector over his body.

It lit up like a Christmas tree with red flashing diodes and an undulating screech. Angel stepped forward with his hands in the air and a look on his face that was somewhere between forlorn and embarrassment. The other old soldiers in the building all stopped what they were doing, and he could feel their eyes burning into him.

The Smoker growled, 'Strip,' and his eyes were a determined ugly urgency.

As he unbuckled his belt, Angel said, 'It's not what it looks like,' and dropped his jeans around his thighs. Thus, the shiny steel and black plastic chastity cage fitted around his cock was revealed. One that caused the room to erupt in raucous laughter.

Matty asked with tears of mirth in his eyes, 'So what does it look like?'

Angel snorted indignantly, 'Okay. Okay. You have fun. I woke. It was on, the chica keeps sending me pictures and telling me what she wants to do when we meet next.'

The Smoker wasn't laughing and shook his head, 'It's got a signal. What's that about?'

While the room sniggered, Angel pulled up his jeans and buttoned his flies as he replied, 'She sends me electric shocks. It's controlled by an app on her phone. She texts.'

'Really,' asked Matty, spluttering words between chuckles, 'What'll they think of next.'

'We could cut it off?' said the Smoker, putting away his detector.

One of the soldiers in the room, trying his best to keep a straight face suggested, 'I've got an angle-grinder here somewhere. I'll have all your bits off ya in seconds.'

Angel lit a cigarette, and declared, 'Joder, no. Is not funny. Is no way you is going near mi polla con eso. Anyway, I'm meeting her tomorrow. She is to take it off.'

As the laughter faded, Matty settled Angel down with a mug of lager and a chair at an array of computers and monitors. It was ironic, that while they watched their target, they were unaware the cock cage listened to them and sent to Tanya their voices. Matty told him, 'It's good kit, mate. GCHQ arrived one day and plugged it in. We have cameras recording every sound and view from the driveway to the bedrooms. There is a similar set-up at the target's workplace.'

He winced, 'Oh, we're at this stage already? I thought this was the last bit?'

'Nah, mate. This ain't a battlefield with tanks. Standard ops is to observe for weeks before taking any actions. Hurry up and wait should be the motto for our business.'

'And the man inside?' Angel asked.

'He knows sod all, just an ambitious colleague with no clue of the deal.'

Their intended victim was Doctor Justin Kraus, a mousy, quiet, sensitive man who was painfully polite and caring about everyone he met. He had worked for the United Kingdom's government for three decades and was primarily involved in auditing nuclear power plants.

'You can read up on him if you want,' Matty told him pointing at a stack of files, 'Background says he lectures on system vibrations and mechanical structures, but he's a clever sod. He's written papers on everything.'

Angel picked up a folder entitled, "Transport Logistics for the Modern Army," and asked, 'He military then?"

'Nah, just a boffin,' then reading from a post-it note on a terminal, he explained, 'Today he is on, *Seal failure of ballistic casings at very low temperatures. For submarines.*'

Glugging their lager, Angel and Matty listened in to Kraus on a phone call. On the other end of the discussion with an enthusiastic political intern whose tone wasn't one of respect. It sounded more like an entitled ass talking down to a servant about cleaning. The woman harangued Doctor Kraus as if she didn't understand the technical terms but had been told to talk about it.

'It is not right,' the Doctor told her.

'Can you confirm that the fire control computer upgrade is not part of your report?'

'I cannot discuss the report.'

'The upgrade isn't scheduled for this financial year; you agree it shouldn't be included.'

'I cannot discuss the report,' he said again.

The woman on the phone constantly probed and snaked around the conversation with veiled threats and posturing about the importance of her minister. The nagging was a barrage of, 'But surely you can see,' and 'You are not being open-minded.' Finally, he told her, 'Sorry, I have to go,' and hung up.

The call log showed it had been a day of phone struggles like that. All had been interrogating him and demanding compromises.

The harassment was constant. Every day, every hour. They should not know any of what was in his reports, but they constantly cited details. They referred to safety breaches and made veiled threats to him about manslaughter. It wasn't normal. Politicians usually wanted a positive spin, but these calls encouraged him to elaborate on failures. Through a video feed, Matty saw him call out, 'I am going home,' to no one in particular and leave his office. Half an hour later, when he clicked on a camera feed labelled Wiltshire2, the screen showed an old, thatched cottage and the Doctor in his unfashionable overcoat as he got out of his car. Clicking to Wiltshire3, they saw Dr. Kraus walking up to his front door.

'You will love the next bit,' Matty said, and Wiltshire5 came into view.

Angel laughed, 'What is a crumpled old suit like him doing with that?'

Kraus's wife Annabelle had appeared.

'Joder, she has a perfect body. She is gorgeous, a porn star.'

'I know right? Even in that frumpy cardigan, she is stunning,' Matty switched between screens with his remote while saying, 'Fit bird, old man, fit bird, old man.'

On camera, Kraus fumbled with his keys and stepped into the hallway, where he met his wife just behind the door waiting for him. She had been baking, and her hands were covered in flour. He smiled and hugged her, letting his briefcase clatter to the floor.

'How much do you love me?' she asked, causing him to straighten up and breathe deeply.

'What have you done?'

'Oh, baby, you look tired.'

'What have you done?' he sighed.

Just then, two kittens appeared at her feet, their heads poking up above the shallow step leading down to the kitchen, 'Darling, but!' replied Justin shaking his head.

'What are we naming them?' Annabelle asked.

Justin turned to his left, on the kitchen wall, mounted eye level, and five inches from his face was the wine rack, 'Claret and Muscadet...erm, Claret and Musket?' he told her.

'Musket is the smallest, and Claret is the black one,' he suggested.

Annabelle, beamed, 'Say hi to them, don't upset them. They want you to say hello.'

Justin did as she asked and picked up the two fluff balls while they writhed around each other in a sleepy slow-motion fight until, within seconds, they fell asleep in his arms. 'Oh, they like you,' she told him and pulled the pets from his grasp, leaving flour on his suit.

'Yes darling,' he replied with a weary sigh.

'You do the dishes, I'll grab a shower,' she told him, bending to put them in a prison bed, an upturned cage lined with towels. 'They live in the corner. It's so snugly warm.'

Both men, spying on her, moaned in voyeuristic pleasure, 'Nice ass.'

The Spaniard grinned, 'I would.'

'Yer me too mate,' replied Matty pouring out another two mugs of lager from large bottles brewed in a Belgian monastery.

Annabelle banged a cupboard door shut with her hips and told Justin, 'Well, get moving and Darling, please. After supper, we'll watch TV.'

'Sorry, I can't. They just keep pestering me to change things. They send me notes, phone me, make me explain things so much I can't get any work done during the day.'

'You're worn out. You can't work tonight, sorry,' and left him in the kitchen.

He groaned, 'Love you too, darling,' as he looked around at the piles of clean and dirty utensils muddled together, pots, trays, wrappers, with ingredients spilt on every surface.

When Matty went to the local village for takeaways, he began reading through transcripts of Doctor Kraus's messages and a study on his wife. The Doctor was simple, a workaholic, quiet and timid with no known vices, whereas his wife was a force of nature who got her way every day with everyone by the indiscriminate use of killer hugs, cheerfulness, and smiles that ambushed with charm.

Her notes from GCHQ indicated that she was past the stage of sexting, ready for a meeting but perhaps not quite ready for an affair. Angel looked at the trend, the phrases and how her online chats on dating sites had changed over time. She was slowly being walked into a tryst using supporting narratives to constantly remind her that she had one life, and as a neglected wife, she might try forbidden fruit.

One of Matty's team online pushed the idea that modern life was not suited to years of marriage, another used a dialogue that encouraged her to think of herself as sexy and available. The character they'd created was a retired teacher in Syracuse, New York, a lady who always offered safe, kindly advice. It was an excellent identity; they only had to remember the proper spellings and American syntax, while their main ruse groomed her with pictures some clever person in MI-5 had concluded to be her most likely lust. The conversations with that identity were meant to be slowly building titillation with an identity purporting to be a few miles away and the perfect balance of her likes.

When Matty came back, Angel had questions.

'The file says she is his loving wife, and yup, I can see that she manipulates him for his own good. Bit naughty, but that's it. Sure she'll do it?' he asked.

'Yes, it's working. We're pushing from one side, she pushes from the other.'

'Are you all set if she gets him the go?' Angel asked.

'Honestly, mate, it was a good off-the-shelf plan. Do it tomorrow if needed.'

Angel looked at the transcripts, 'A perfect marriage. Do they ever argue?

'We've tried,' replied Matty, 'They've never had a cross word. He was adamant he didn't want any pets. His medical records say he is allergic to cats. But look, she bought two of them, and he just smiled. He caught her sexting too and never raised an eyebrow. So, we're moving down the promiscuity route now and giving her an affair.'

Angel nodded, he'd read how the Doctor had reacted to one set of texts he'd seen. GCHQ had remotely switched off the screen lock and sent a dick pic and an intentionally explicit text about cumming on Annabelle's tits when the Doctor was beside her phone. Instead of the marital distress they'd wanted, the Doctor walked through to the kitchen with the mobile and casually mentioned, 'You've a message,' then apologised for accidentally looking at her phone. Angel laughed, 'It is almost a shame what we are doing to him.'

Matty shrugged, 'I'm gonna stay with, I was just following orders, as my excuse.'

**

After supper, Annabelle and Justin sat on the different sofas watching a film. He seemed agitated as if he couldn't switch off from work, and within half an hour he'd picked up his laptop and declared, 'I just a few more emails.'

Annabelle rolled her eyes, poured them both a glass of wine and took hers upstairs. Her husband didn't even seem to notice her leave the room.

On one of Matty's monitors was a feed showing her phone's screen and on another was Annabelle lying on her bed and clicking open a dating site. Little did she know that the men she was chatting to online were also watching her on camera while sitting next to a wall covered with pinned notes, keywords, and charts to remind them of the lies they'd previously told her. Matty typed into his keyboard, 'Hey,' and a message appeared on multiple screens.

Annabelle immediately replied, 'What are you doing?'

-Just chatting with you.

-Husband there?

-He's downstairs working. Ignoring me.

-I wouldn't ignore you. Might tease you though.

-Mmmmmmm, but stop. I am married.

-Have ya promised your husband not to suck my cock, specifically?

-I will stop chatting with you if you keep asking to meet me for sex! Tell me about you.

Then Annabelle switched to another dating site and picked up a chat where a man had asked her to meet her for a drink.

-Hi, Annabelle. Have you decided?

-I am not sure my husband would approve LOL.

-Don't tell him.

She giggled and went downstairs again, for more wine and to ask Justin, 'Have you thought any more about that trip?'

Not listening properly or looking up from his laptop, Justin said, 'In a minute.'

She looked sad and hurt, 'You never hear a word I say!'

He managed a nod, and Annabelle walked over to press down the lid of his laptop and say, 'Honey - let's go for a drink - a night out, you and me?'

'Yes, okay,' he replied absentmindedly.

Pouting she said, 'You told me it was finished months ago.'

This time he heard, 'I've to tidy up some of the data in the findings,' he bleated.

'You promised! We are supposed to have me-time, and you're still obsessed with work.'

Justin looked up, sighed but said nothing which prompted Annabelle to grumpily sit on the sofa opposite him and open up a third dating site.

Matty at once sent her a message, 'Hey sexy, what're you doing?'

She smirked as she wrote, 'Sitting across from my boring husband. He can probably see that I'm on this naughty site from the reflection in my reading glasses, but he doesn't care.'

'Forget him, you have me.'

For an hour of voyeurism, Angel watched her conversations change from salacious flirting to fantasy sex and back again, then onto a discussion about the new kittens. At one point she touched herself and moaned as she told a man online, who wasn't one of Matty's team, how her nipples were hardening. She surreptitiously took a picture and sent it to him. Justin didn't notice. Not once did he look up from his laptop.

Eventually, Annabelle, bored with online chat, asked her husband, 'Bedtime?'

'Darling, I promise. Just one hour, and I'm finished for tonight.'

Her voice was tired with a sad tone, 'You need a break. Is Hector still going on that trip?'

He replied, 'I'm coming upstairs soon, I've just got to finish this.'

She erupted in anger, 'Don't FUCKING bother!' slamming the door on her way upstairs.

Justin texted her from the living room, 'Sorry.'

-You should be. You are killing yourself. I want you to take a break, so does your boss!

- I will think about it.

- DON'T LIE TO ME! It's tearing us apart.

Annabelle came downstairs again and began shouting at him. All her anxieties and fears poured out, including the idea of a trial separation that had been suggested by her online friend in Syracuse. Then she asked, 'What about Hector's idea.'

'I already said no. I'm worried about you alone Darling. You know. The robbery.'

'Are you sure there was one, and you didn't just lose your laptop?'

Her husband grumbled an uncharacteristic 'Hurumph.'

Annabelle was unrelenting, 'Either take a break, or I will. We can't go on like this!'

'I can't go with Hector. You can't go after October.'

'Why not?'

'You just don't. Weather is too bad,' he replied.

'Oh, don't be a wuss. That means it won't be crowded,' she said scolding.

And Justin agreed, 'Okay, I'll ask work for the dates, then bed. I promise.'

Annabelle smiled but stood over him as the doctor wrote an email to his work colleague. 'Hi Hector, West Highland Way. Just want to confirm that I can go after all. Let me know if it's still okay for me to tag along.'

Cuddling her husband, she told him, 'I am going to bed, don't fall asleep again.'

Justin promised, 'Yes, no, erm, I am nearly finished, night baby.'

'Okay, you've half an hour, then I want you in bed with me.'

Upstairs she undressed for bed and messaged a cleverly constructed identity she knew as Richard, 'My husband is going away soon. We can meet.'

'Perfect, I can't wait,' Matty replied in the guise of a twenty-eight-year-old lawyer. He added to his message a picture of a young man holding a bunch of Annabelle's favourite flowers. She was still awake and horny from chatting online when Justin finally crept into bed at midnight, 'You finally made it. Are you tired?' she asked and rolled over to cuddle him with a feel for his cock through his pyjamas.

'Yes darling,' he replied, and within seconds, he was asleep and snoring.

Matty looked from the monitors to ask, 'What's this guy done to get hit?'

'It's above my pay grade,' said Angel feigning ignorance but his mind flashed to what Jessica had said about the scientist and a report about the safety of the UK's nuclear deterrent. His unwillingness to write unfavourably about something she wanted to leak to the press, was the reason for his imminent demise. Perhaps the pressure on him wasn't enough, or maybe he just couldn't bring himself to write a work that'd destroy something that he'd spent his whole life covering up. Either way, he stood in the way of Jessica making a profit. Angel's boss had justified her murderous plans by explaining it was for a strategic benefit and said, 'Honey, NATO needs to be watching China. Russia is our friend now.' However, he didn't believe a word she said about global politics. If the sub fleet stayed, she'd make money off the weapons contracts, if it left, she'd make money off the oil licences.

Chapter 19 - Delegation.

Tanya flew to Domodedovo airport on an early morning flight. Once there, security took her aside, down a corridor ostensibly to search her luggage.

A couple of square-jawed thugs in grimy parkas greeted her with, 'Welcome back, sergeant,' and grabbed her bags from her. Despite the no smoking signs, one had a cigarette hanging from his lips and they walked to a black Lexus 4x4 waiting in a no-parking zone. It was getting a ticket from two uniformed police officers and one of the Parkas yelled at them, 'What are you doing Kalhoznik,' waving them away with the flask of Spiritus he was drinking from. They didn't show ID. The police recognised the type.

For the three-hour drive, she sat in silence. Only when they drove through a military checkpoint at a village just north of Budennovets did she become even a little chatty. Past sentries, guard dogs and electric fences, they entered what looked like a forest holiday retreat and parked up at the dacha of Colonel Mishka Bruyevich. Tanya's boss was a man to be feared. He'd begun his career in the KGB reporting on the military effectiveness of tank squadrons in the Trans-Baikal region and ended it in the First Chief Directorate, where he'd stayed happily plotting.

A guard opened the front door for her, and she entered to see Mishka stripped to the waist and practising with a Cossack sabre, swirling it around his head in figures of eight. 'Da-vai, davai. Come, relax, relax!' he bellowed, welcoming her in with warm smiles. She kissed him on both cheeks, 'Happy to be home, Mishka.'
'Good to see you,' he replied.
'Who is watching me in London?'
'Sometimes us and maybe the English, don't worry, we can talk. Get settled in first.'

An hour later, she was escorted by a young officer to a large wooden lodge containing a sauna room. It was next to a jetty that protruded onto a lake. Outside, a guard appeared to be sleeping in a chair beside the entrance while cradling a Kalashnikov in his arms. He only stirred to open one eye and knock on the door. Inside, Mishka was sitting at a table laden with fruit, blinis, kubans, vodka and small bottles of kvass.

He gestured to them both to sit and eat, but the young officer stood to attention. He saluted Mishka, who winked at him in return, 'Don't do that, son. It draws attention. If you don't want to eat, bring Ivan.'

The colonel poured two glasses of vodka and raised his to toast,

'Once KGB, always KGB!'

Tanta replied with a smile and, 'Segda gatov.'

Mishka replied with a joke, 'Inagda gatov,' and in English repeated, 'Sometimes ready.' With a bayonet, she picked up a large piece of pineapple and asked, 'What've you bought me?'

Passing her the file of a man called Ivan Etylin, he told her, 'Read this. It is hilarious. In the past, if I wanted to get someone into Britain, it would have been hard. Now I have my pick of thousands who live there. I can even pay to have lunch with the men in their Duma.'

Ivan was not what Tanya had expected, but he covered the basics. Most of his time in uniform as a skier on the Olympic biathlon team and had some proficiency as a sniper. He'd done a six-month bodyguard course in the Crimea, a year on the seventh army group general's staff as his driver before becoming a minor enforcer for the Leningrad mafia.

There he was involved in a kidnapping racket where he'd guarded a pit for victims in the basement of a cottage. But he wasn't important, and one night, when he said the wrong thing to the wrong man in a nightclub, Ivan fled to England in the clothes he stood up in.

'A Chukotkan?' Tanya exclaimed, 'Aren't they too nice for this life?'

'We all are!' Mishka laughed, 'He was slapped around a little at the airport, so you can be his saviour, 'He doesn't know why he is here yet.'

They ate and drank in silence as she read Ivan's file. He was a taxi driver in London. His mother had been visiting him when a stranger approached them both in Trafalgar Square and handed her a picture of her son as a conscript in the uniform of the KGB's transport police. The man only said, 'Home to Moscow.'

When Ivan was brought to the lodge, Mishka told him,

'Sit, eat, eat, don't be shy!'

Tanya was even more inviting, 'Ivan, I'm delighted you came at such short notice,' she told him in English extending her arms and offering a hug, 'Please call me Tanya.'

He was startled by the embrace, 'I don't know why I am here.'

She lied and said, 'I do. I picked you. Don't worry. It will be fine. I know how long you have been away and why you left, but your country needs you.'

Ivan cowered slightly, and his eyes darted around. He was a frightened lump of muscle in a "RUSSIA" tracksuit, and wearing the face of a man who had just realised that he wasn't going to prison. Mishka saw his mood and said, 'Relax, relax, I can explain everything. Don't worry, if bad things were to happen to you. They'd already have been done. Sit comrade,' and waved the escorting officer away.

Tanya offered him tea and explained, 'You are just the right man, in the right place at the right time. And at this moment, you are important enough that we can wash away your sins in Sankt Petersburg.'

The Chukotkan man sat, but at attention, rigid with his fists closed on his knees. His mouth managed to open slightly, but he stayed silent. Perhaps he gasped. Tanya licked her lips, 'What caught my attention was your time on bullion shipments. You were injured when your convoy was attacked by brigands. Your vehicle was hit by RPGs?'

'Yes, I was wounded, but we fought them off in the end.'

Tanya giggled, 'I read a helicopter gunship was called for support, but what kind of man performs a tracheotomy on himself when medics are around?'

'I wanted to use my training,' he replied a little sheepishly.

What she didn't say was what she thought of him; he was a disposable piece of meat from Chukotka and just smart enough to follow her orders.

'Sauna?' Mishka suggested, and the three of them soon undressed to enter the searing heat. Tanya neatly folded a towel on the lowest tier of three benches along a wall to sit down on, while the colonel walked to the far end of the room and what looked like a pizza oven. He opened its door with charred wooden tongs, threw a fresh log into the fire, and doused the walls with a ladle from a water bucket, making them hiss with steam. She sighed; it was already too hot for her, but it was where Mishka always conducted business. He maintained there was no better place for confidential chats than in heat, moisture and nakedness, an environment that was too hard to bug.

For the next three hours, they discussed the plan they would enact while rotating between the sauna, ice showers and sitting outside drinking tea. Tanya talked as if it was a social event. She was ebullient and flippant, whether taking a break from the heat or beating Ivan with soggy oak leaves, but she only wanted to assess the character of the man she'd work within the unknowns ahead. After Ivan was dismissed and escorted away, Mishka lit a small fire pit next to the lake and sat with his protégé on railway sleepers wrapped in blankets, watching the stars. He told her, 'Keep an eye on him. He's been on his own a long time.'

Tanya raised a glass of vodka in a toast, 'Palkovnik, we will follow our orders, we will be ruthless, we will be successful.'

He replied, 'And most importantly, you will be rewarded. After all, we're not communists.' They drank until midnight, with his tone changing to that of a kindly mentor to say, 'Women have a hard burden in our life. Can you carry on? Are you better, you're well?'

'I'll carry on. You lead, I follow,' she answered, 'I'll do what must be done.'

'A soldier must say when too injured to march, that also is a duty. Agreed?'

'Palkovnik, I am fine. Sergeant Kozel-Phillipovna reports she's well and fit for duty.'

'It wasn't decided, but it is now. You can go ahead with this Ivan,' he told her and handed her a small box with a military insignia in it. She was no longer a Starshiina. He had promoted her to Praporshchik,

'A hundred grams for each star,' he told her, and toasted again.

In the morning, Ivan, who'd been drinking with his guards all night, was carried like luggage by two soldiers and dumped in the boot of the 4x4 taking them to the airport. The colonel looked as if he'd had a long, restful sleep instead of being up late drinking. Tanya appeared drunk and as if she'd just fallen out of the bed of a Special Forces soldier, and it was that trooper that was to drive them. He smiled at her and made the mistake of whispering, 'Darling, we better get moving.'

She replied like a cold Siberian wind, 'I am Starshiina Kozel, not fucking Darling and you...You're a mistake that has haunted me long enough...Please just drive. I don't know you.'

His face paled white, and the vehicle travelled in silence back to the airport. The young man only spoke again when he carried Ivan's alcohol-reeking bulk onto the flight and dumped him across three seats.

'Don't wake him,' he barked at the cabin crew, flashing his ID.

She and her new agent slept on the flight and then stood separately in the customs lanes when they left the plane in London. Tanya watched him fumble with his passport and pass security successfully, then she headed straight to a wine bar to drink her hangover away. While sipping a glass of cabernet sauvignon, she texted the man she'd just been ordered to kill, and asked, 'Meet me for a drink'.

***

Ken had been waiting at the airport, casually flicking through Tanya's private messages on her social media when she walked out of the departure lounge. Instead of her supposed cover as a bright-eyed and smartly dressed city professional, he saw a haggard, limp-haired scruff in a woollen dress and oversized sunglasses. Her only baggage was an iPhone, but there was no mistaking her when she went straight to the bar. After the Russian topped up with wine for lunch, Ken followed her into the city, watching her fidget, text, and yawn until she got off at Waterloo. That was where Petra took over the surveillance. Later she phoned her boss with an update, 'Nothing happening. Just sitting in my car. Want me to explain that new eavesdropping kit?'

'Oh please, I was using wires before you were born, and what does nothing happening mean? What is my busty brunette specifically doing?' he sounded irritated.

'Red-head boss, she'd an appointment with a hair studio stylist. I'll forward the pics.'

'Hair studio? Stylist? The world has gone mad,' Ken replied.

'Oh, hold on, she's calling Angel,' Petra switched the surveillance to speaker so Ken could hear. It was mostly incoherent babbling punctuated with an occasional spluttering of grief. Tanya talked about her husband with panic and sadness quivering in her voice, and the Spaniard replied with what sounded like sympathy. She chuckled, 'Wow! Even I'm starting to believe she has a husband.'

Ken used his serious tone, 'Yes well, I'll meet you back at the office.'

***

Alone at home, Tanya looked around and felt a wave of cold depression sweep over her. She didn't like the place anymore. It was a cold room of wooden floors and exposed brickwork that reminded her of a childhood in Moscow and a grubby shared apartment block. On her sofa, Tanya bit on her arm and listened to the ticking of an antique carriage clock as tears rolled down her cheeks. She began texting Angel again, hinting at suicide and some tragedy she said she couldn't express properly by text. Then she soaked in hot bubbles with her old friends, self-pity and cabernet sauvignon.

For a while, she stared into a make-up mirror, experimenting with smiles, looking for happiness, but her reflection simply offered misery and numbness. She reached for a small razor and tore at the flesh above her wrists on the back of her arm. Shallow cuts, only enough to scar. 'Why,' she asked herself, then cut herself some more. She liked Angel, but she knew what was going to happen, was out of her hands. It took a panicked Angel three hours of traffic congestion, road works and diversions to drive to London and meet Tanya in their usual place, she didn't mention anything about her texts or suicide, only that she was happy to see him.

They had whitebait, something to drink and then went back to her flat to fuck until dawn. Whilst he was in the shower, she downloaded the latest instalment from the planted electronics in his collar and boots. After another fuck she kissed him goodbye.

Chapter 20 - Conflict Management.

For five days, Jamie had been sleeping in Maria's room. Whenever he woke, she was lying next to him, tussling his hair. When he went to university with her in the mornings, he had a smile that would have needed an angle grinder to remove. But it all changed on Friday evening when she went shopping. She'd only been gone five minutes, when an estate car full of muscles in blue blazers, parked up at her house. Crow got out and knocked on the door. When it opened, he asked,

'Walker was wanting to know if you can work tonight. We are a bit stuck!'

Jamie groaned, 'I'm meant to stay out of sight?'

He replied, 'You are. It's Watford. But get some food in ya, it'll be a long night.'

A quick scan of the car revealed a new crew dynamic. The standard-bearer of the company, a man called Paul, was half asleep and reeking of lager on the back seat next to badge number eighty-seven. In the passenger seat was a Geordie bodybuilder type he'd seen around the office, who growled, 'Hurry up sweaty,' as if he was an old mate.

Jamie knew the Watford pub was far from quiet with a reputation for unrelenting violence but said, 'Okay.'

It all made sense, and it was only a little earlier than he'd typically leave the house on a Friday, so he thought, 'Maria will understand.'

'So where is forty-two? He normally works there?'

'He's off being horrible somewhere. Don't ask,' Crow beamed a smile.

'So, I don't have to search the car for tools then?' Asked Jamie, hoping there wasn't.

'Hurry up, for fuck's sake,' was the suggestion from the Geordie.

Jamie wasn't excited, but neither was he comfortable with hiding so replied, 'Okay, I'm moving,' and trotted indoors to get ready.

Twelve minutes later, he'd showered, dumped some pasta in a pot and made a large cafetière of coffee to take with him in a flask. Not wanting to worry Maria, he weighed every word as he wrote a note, 'I'm needed to work in a quiet London pub. I don't think I'll be too late,' then he drew a smiley face and stuck the message on the fridge.

His transformation from a student to a doorman was exact.

He dressed upward from left to right beginning with his groin protector and a pewter bracer he'd fashioned from an old ashtray. Then he strapped on his ballistic vest and chainmail. Maria had told him that the steel links should be tucked under his belt as a precaution against someone holding the bottom of his bulletproof and sliding a weapon up inside it. He wondered how she knew such things.

Once dressed in his polished German Para boots and Don's heavy woollen Crombie, he looked four stones heavier and taller, almost like a real doorman. He decanted the coffee into a flask and drained his over-cooked pasta. Into the pot, he quickly dumped, a tin of tuna, spinach, olive oil, lumps of cheddar, dried garlic and a vitamin tablet with a squirt of tomato puree. Then walked to the car, stirring it with a wooden spoon. The new Geordie barked at Jamie, 'Hurry up!'

Crow grinned and crossed his eyes in pretend fright, contorting his face and bringing his top teeth over his bottom lip to say sarcastically, 'You'd better do what the Wayne says.'

Jamie ignored it all and climbed into the car boot of the car. There he curled up in a corner and began guzzling his supper from the pot, while Wayne occupied himself with jokes at his expense, as if he'd gotten the impression that the student was the lowest in the pecking order. With his feed, he stayed silent. He wanted no part of what he knew was coming. Most doormen refused to work with the Watford crew, because of their antics on the journey there. He'd heard they often fought in the car as a way of psyching themselves up and had sometimes arrived for their shift with torn uniforms and blood on their faces like war paint.

Ginger had explained why they acted that way, with the story of a night when men had been waiting for the door crew in ambush. Their would-be attackers were surprised by five Red-Ties already in a high state of alert, who burst from their car before its wheels stopped rolling and tore into them like savages in berserker mode. When they joined the motorway, as anticipated, Paul leant over the rear seat and tried to pull Jamie's leg to bite it, 'No sleep in this car,' he said but wasn't fast enough. 'I'm trying to rest! I don't get this shit,' he told him cocking his leg ready to kick.

'Oh, how is Ginger by the way?'

'He is still the same...'

'You two going to the gym.? You boxing yet?'

'Just powerlifting with him, lots of deadlifts. Boxing is meant to be with Phil. I don't go.'

'Don't blame you. How's the gym with Ginger?' asked Paul.

'It's good, but he doesn't get it that I am half his size, and he forgets stuff. He said it was deadlift-day, three days in a row. Only change to that, is when he wants me to show him Judo.'

'He just forgets,' added Paul, 'Other days, he's a chess grandmaster on Billy-whizz.'

'Yer, I knows, he's not always been like that?' asked Jamie, 'He fell off scaffolding?' Nobody answered. The lads paused and kept silent for a while. There was some secret they weren't about to tell.

Ten minutes later, Paul suddenly asked, 'So how come Ginger can go into your house and we can't?'

'Cause you're all fucking psychos, and Maria thinks Ginge is a big sweet, cuddly dad.'

'Fuck off!' they replied in genuine surprise.

'True. Right, youz geez peace, I wanna sleep,' he said, slipping back into his Scots accent. As they drove along the M3, Jamie tried to doze off but found that he was half listening to the conversations in the front, and this new oxygen thief Wayne, was messing with karma. He'd continued with insults directed at Jamie, without understanding that in-car abuse of no one in particular was okay, but a continual targeting of one of them was not.

While the doormen in the front taxed cigarettes from Wayne for the crime of being new and stupid, the Geordie continued bragging and puffing up his chest to tell arrogant stories until there was constant, self-aggrandising whining above the noise of the engine. He used the word bodyguard in every other sentence, irritating everyone in the car. Jamie opened his coffee flask and poured out half a cup, carefully re-screwing it back on as he savoured the rich, chocolate caramel smell wafting through the air. 'Oh, that smells good,' said Wayne, 'Pass it over.'

'No,' was Jamie's terse reply.

The Geordie growled, 'Oi, you!' but his voice trailed off sounding unsure about the little doorman's defiance.

That was the moment Jamie's opinion solidified into a conclusion that the new lad was a lump of steroid abuse with a fragile ego, fake tan, and bad haircut. He did not like him, and he leant forward to tap the back of Paul's seat and say, 'He is being unlucky.'

One by one, the Red-Ties stopped responding to Wayne. Even Paul, who was usually tolerant of stupid conversions, leaned against the window and shut his eyes. In the quiet, Wayne couldn't resist questioning with a sneering tone dripping from every syllable, 'Oi Jamie, would you want to be a bodyguard?'

'No,' Jamie's answer was gruff and the regular lads in the car recognised the change of tone and perked up a little.

'Why not? Not up for the danger,' asked the Geordie.

'I don't believe in violence or going looking for it.'

Crow interrupted, 'Hey Wayne, Don's always looking for a bodyguard!' The lads in the car knew what that meant. The doors were constantly stripped of Red-Ties to follow Don around town when he was drunk. They'd all done it on foot or following the boss in a car. It was a horrible task. Don didn't want the protection and woe betide anyone caught doing it.

Paul smiled, 'We need someone like you on our team, bodyguard, eh? That's very special when you get to guard a celebrity, crème de la crème that is, mate.'

'You probably not got what it takes Jamie,' said the Geordie.

There was a sharp mocking intake of breath, and 87 exclaimed, 'Jamie, how long you have been Don's driver?'

'I don't really drive him much as it goes,' the student ventured.

87 added, 'He's lasted longest. The previous record was three days, and given the number of people trying to shoot, set fire to, or stab the suicidal maniac, he's done well keeping Don out of trouble. He just needs to learn to drive now without getting lost and heading to Scotland!'

Paul asked sarcastically, 'Hey Wayne, tell us another war story! Please!'

The newcomer must have sensed a change in attitude, as for a while, there was a bit of silence until Paul remembered a desire for cigarettes and demanded they stop at a service station, despite Crow complaining that they were running late.

'Fuck the time, stop for fags,' Paul lunged forward to bite Crow on the shoulder, who cuffed him with an impromptu backward head butt. The pair settled into a slapstick routine of puerile violence, simultaneously trying to fend off and land punches on each other until Paul leant forward to strangle the driver and convince him to pull off the motorway. 'Okay, okay. We'll get fags,' coughed Crow.

On the slip road to the petrol station, Paul put his hands over Crow's eyes for a moment, and they nearly collided with a little Renault Five. The car beeped its horn, and the occupants wound down their window to shout something. It wasn't a major incident, but when they both ended up on the same petrol station forecourt, the Geordie took it as an opportunity to usurp some sort of position in the group. It was a car full of what looked like young A' level students, all girls, but despite everyone in the car calling him back, Wayne lumbered out with his 20-stone of bodybuilder mass and thumped on their roof, sending those inside into panic.

For full-on effective bullying, he began rocking the car and threatening to up-end it. The new doorman's behaviour was a final straw for Jamie, and he growled at his colleagues, 'He's no good, I'll have to have a word with the cunt.'
On his return to the car, the Geordie's smirk assumed the occupants would somehow be impressed with this swagger and give him a pat on the back, but the car was silent for the rest of the journey.

Paul lit two cigarettes and handed one to Jamie, who was now grinding his teeth in the back, considering his anger. To Jamie, the newcomer was an embarrassment whose actions would inevitably bring problems down on them, and the more Jamie thought about it, the angrier he got. Soon he was weighing the size of the man and how he'd, 'Have a word.'

When they arrived at the pub in Watford, they parked in the usual spot and squeezed down a narrow corridor past some toilets while putting on their red clip-on ties to start work. The Geordie tilted back his head, 'I'll take the front door.'
Jamie asked, 'What are you putting a tie on for?'
'I'm working,' he replied, but with a bit of puzzlement creeping across his face.
'Are you fuck, ya piece of shit,' the words landed simultaneously as Jamie's elbow connected with the bodybuilder's solar plexus after deciding against his throat.
The words of Don were his guidance. He'd always said the big lads were just for show, and after their workouts and baby-food diets, they didn't have the energy to

157

move. From every other anecdote of the Red-Ties he'd overheard, he knew; Speed, aggression and surprise were what he needed.

Jamie was enraged by the harassment of the students in the petrol station. Sweat erupted from his pores as the anger built instead of dissipating with time. Jamie had been triggered. He hit him again with a knee to the groin snarling, 'Fucking moron!' As Wayne buckled, his throat was chopped and to no one in particular Jamie snarled, 'Explain please to this tosser why he is an arrogant, useless, brain-dead, dickhead and mentally retarded cock-womble.'

His fists battered the man to the floor, and stepping on his fingers, he used Wayne's belt and collar as a grip to smash his head into the wall.
'If I was you, I'd stop stealing oxygen from the world and not be a big fat bodybuilder cunt that bullies wee kids. I couldnae live with the shame of being as wankerish as you! If I was as fucking stupid as you, I'd just have to cut my fucking head off.'
Jamie began to splutter in rage, 'Those wee kids. Were. Let me see. FUCKING KIDS!' With his palm open, he repeatedly struck the lump on the back of his head.
'There you go Paul, I felt I needed to have a word,' he said regaining his composure, 'I shall ask Mr Walker, I mean, suggest to Mr Walker that I would prefer not to work with this thing in future.'

Crow lit up another two fags and handed one to Jamie, calling over his shoulder to 87, 'You forget how big the little lad is until he gets angry.'
Jamie lurched through the pub with gritted teeth and feigning a smile, his head swivelled left and right, scanning every square foot of the non-smoking venue, programmed like they all were in the training courses. He took long drags of the fag on the doorstep with his hand cupped over it, in obedience to the "Doormen don't smoke when working rule."

Apart from the Geordie, the rest of the Red-Ties came to the front door.
'He's gone into a sulk,' reported Paul, 'The thing is Jamie, we need him to make up the numbers. Go apologise or something. Will ya?'
'Talk him into staying, or we won't have a line of sight.'
He has a big, petted lip,' advised 87 while laughing.

Jamie flared his nostrils at the thought of contaminating himself by even talking to the Geordie, but he knew they were right. Crow nodded in calm, silent urging, and 87 pursed his lips while holding out his hands as if to say, 'I dunno.'

Jamie flicked his cigarette away said, 'Okay,' and stomped off to the rear of the pub where he explained to Wayne, 'The lads want me to apologise. So, I'll say I'm very sorry that you're a total waste of space. Now put your fucking tie on and don't even try to look at me funny.'

The wafer-thin camouflage of contempt finished with, 'Paul, give the cretin back his tie.' Paul did, but not before swapping his creased, stained, frayed version for the bright new one that the Geordie thought was his. Jamie, for a moment, took charge of the other more experienced doormen and returned to the front door. Crow went with him and lit another two cigarettes, giving one to Jamie, who drew deeply on it, trying to calm down. 'You're a lot different from the lad I met not so long ago. Good thing you don't have a mad-jock temper, innit?' he told him sarcastically.
'Nights not fucking over yet,' he replied, then paused to inhale more nicotine reflecting that he was indeed very different from the person who'd left his village. He wasn't sure it was a good thing.

***

As the evening progressed, there was no trouble, only a few random struggles when searching people as they opened the nightclub part of the place. At half past eleven, there was nothing to alarm them, and Paul walked around to tell each station, 'That's us. No more entry.'
'Good, a quiet night,' replied the Geordie.
'What did you say that for? Fucking Jinx!'
Unfortunately for the doormen, not every club patron that night was solely interested in drinking and dancing. A group of young men who usually engaged in robbing drug dealers with extreme violence for their amusement had devised a novel Friday night sport.

At exactly midnight, they attacked. Men who'd been trying to make conversation about football and offer drinks all night suddenly produced CS gas and sprayed the face of each Red-Tie. Jamie was lucky. He had slightly more time to react than the other doormen, who'd been standing shoulder-to-shoulder with their assailants. The training he'd received on the course had told him not to accept drinks, not to chat with anyone and in the succinct words of Don,

'No cunt should be closer than four feet. Keep your head on a swivel!'

It was a coordinated, timed attack that took them teary-eyed from the gas into a chaos of grabbing and punches. In one blink of panic, he saw his colleagues frantically swing elbows and stumble with their foes in wrestling matches that disappeared from his view when he was hit himself. The blow was from a beer glass thrown as a man raced towards him. It bounced off his forehead unbroken, but it gave him a surge of anger that blotted out his normal tendencies towards reason.

Trained reactions took over his muscles as a heavyweight attacker bobbed and weaved towards him with his fists raised in confidence. Jamie took half a step back and drove the edge of his leading foot into the man's knee. He heard a crack, the man's body buckled, and Jamie growled, 'Fucking boxers!' while following through, simultaneously striking upwards with his knee and downwards with his elbow to the man's head.

Crow yelled, 'The door! The door!' and the pair of Red-Ties raced down the stairs of the club towards the entrance. The scene there made him freeze for a second, Paul was trying to shut the half-closed entrance, fighting on his own with a group of four. The doorman was on his own, bent and pressing forward like a forward in a rugby scrum, and it was at that precise moment when a hand squeezed off more CS gas at point-blank range into his face.

Unsure who to grab first, Jamie's eye caught sight of a man fumbling to pull a leather cosh from his waistband and lunged at him from the foot of the stairs. His arms slithered around the man's neck for his favourite Judo technique. In training, he'd learned that heavily developed muscles were easier to inflict strangles on, but unfortunately, no one had told the guy he was choking. Still holding on, Jamie was smashed off walls and swung around like a ball on a string until his grip finally cut off the man's thinking. Concussed, winded and in pain, Jamie felt him switch off and released his hold. He turned his attention to the doorway and attempted to kick high at someone's face. It missed, his supporting foot slipped on a beer spillage at the entrance, and then he heard someone shouting, 'Fire, Fire, Fire.'

Fleeing from the CS fumes, it began as a dozen panicked patrons surging past him and inadvertently giving a reprieve from those trying to come in.

As Jamie staggered to his feet, he reached for one of the attackers and tried to place one foot between his legs to pull him in what should have been an effortless combat throw. However, as he lifted the man, he found the weight and balance greater than his skills could manage and he was hit by a stampede tumbling down the stairs. Knocked down again, first one, then two, and then a herd of feet stomped on his head and body.

He heard police sirens and passed out. The next thing he remembered was leaning against an ambulance smoking a cigarette. There were two crews from the emergency services tending to the venue's customers as they milled around on the street, coughing, choking, crying, and moaning.

As an adrenaline dump arrived for everyone, Paul conducted an end-of-the-game team talk, 'You pricks! I needed fucking stormtroopers. Not, Oh. Hi mates, do you want an ice cream?'

Once that tiny leak of frustration hissed out of his system, he returned to calm commands, 'That's it keep everyone out. Anybody hurt? Oh, yer everybody. Jamie, you've got a black eye. Has anyone seen Wayne?'

They hadn't. In fact, they never heard from him again.

Once the gas cleared, he joined the other Red-ties to sit in the upstairs bar drinking pints with the landlady. Crow smiled,

'That was 90% proof that was. Proper, proper CS gas that is.'

'Where were you?'

'Dance floor when it kicked off. They done us all.'

'They fucked off when they heard the police sirens,' said Jamie.

'True, true,' said Crow, 'That probably saved our arses.'

As they went over the night's events, Jamie contributed with what he saw, heard, and did but mostly he listened in awe to how the other two thought about things. As they verbally refought the evening, it was like the team was everything and individuals didn't exist. Instead of talking like thuggish security, they embraced the failure and began dissecting what they could've done better and where they'd done well.

It became clear that despite Paul's outward appearance as a shambolic alcoholic, it was far from the reality of who he was. It was like he weighed his work colleague's abilities down to the gram and millimetre, knowing how they thought and moved in every situation. Easing away the tension in their bodies with lager, Crow received a call and he replied with elation, 'It all sounds good. I'll see you tomorrow.'
Suddenly he stood up and said, 'Gotta go lads. Sorry,' and almost ran out of the pub.
'Where's he gone?' asked Jamie.
'Probably a burd,' replied 87.
'Fuck who's driving then?' said Paul walking from the bar with two pints, both for him.

***

Maria had a visitor, and answered her door with, 'Qué quieres coño?'
Angel replied in English in a sleazy tone, 'Hello my pretty.'
'What do you want? It's five in the morning and you're not coming in.'
'Just wanted to tell you the good news myself,' he replied.
'So, tell me, and fuck off. I've someone here in three minutes.'
Angel chuckled, 'Friend? Timings? Are you tracking him?'
'Fuck off Angel, what did you come to say?' she growled with palpable hatred for the Spanish agent.
'Just that your job is done. You are stood down.'
'Vale,' she replied and closed the door in his face.

He drove away just as Jamie was dropped off outside by a semi sober Paul. Maria opened the door to him just as he raised his key to the lock and hugged him with the words, 'I worried about you.'
'Okay,' he replied with a dozy smile and stumbled backwards, to fall out of her embrace. Then blinking and looking around as if disorientated, he began stripping off on the path, 'I don't feel well,' he said and dropped his jacket on the ground at his feet. That was when Maria noticed he had a black eye and scowled, 'What happened, what's wrong? Your face is white.'

As if in a dream state he muttered, 'Something is… with my… ribs,' while trying to tear off his chainmail before unbuttoning his shirt properly. Maria moved forward to help him and when she got to the Velcro of his bulletproof, she pulled the side of his armour open, and Jamie's knees buckled beneath him. He fell and lay on the crazy paving in the light from the hallway and she watched in horror as a cricket ball-sized hematoma grew out from under his skin.

She squealed, 'Joder!' while Jamie, in pain, slowly curled himself into a foetal position and passed out. Once an ambulance was called, she tried to remember her trauma care when the wound wasn't bleeding. Torn between slapping him awake and resting her hand gently on his side, she opted to do both, while hoping the bubble of blood didn't burst. On the way to the hospital, he woke for half a second to say, 'Hi,' and smiled at her holding his hand.

She said, 'Love you,' but he wasn't conscious long enough to hear it.

***

Outside in the hospital carpark, Petra got a call, 'How is it looking?'

'All good,' she replied, 'But half the murder wall walked past me today. It's spy central.'

Ken asked, 'Anything interesting?'

'Nah, just a student who keeps turning up. I'm texting a picture.'

Ken suggested, 'We don't believe in coincidences, do we?'

She yawned, 'Okay, I'll have to find out why I'm seeing him everywhere.'

Jamie woke under some bright lights and saw that he was in an intensive care room in a crisp, clean bed. His vision was still too blurred to read everything on his monitor, but it looked like one of his blood pressure readings said forty-six. His ignorance of medical matters wasn't total, he knew enough to be worried, as his mum had been a surgical nurse and home was often filled with the chatting of her medic friends. He said, 'That's not good,' tried to remember what his pressure should be, and fell asleep.

The next time Jamie woke, he could see the screen more clearly and comforted himself that eighty over sixty was better than nothing. Then he began checking his body from the toes up, wiggling each muscle in series, up past the thighs. At his abs, it became apparent that he had a large, hardened patch on his rib cage and a lot of pain. All he could remember after turning up on Maria's doorstep was being on a trolley with a doctor asking him if he was allergic to anything. He'd replied, 'Prawns.'

As he strained to hold up his head to look around, it flopped back against the pillow and Jamie fell asleep again before he could consider the merits of getting anxious. He woke and passed out several times, but in each cycle, he stayed awake longer and breathed deeper. When his drowsy eyes blinked open again, he noticed a cannula stuck in his arm with the remnants of drugs, and a little bit of his brain told him that his condition was serious.

He was no longer floating in and out of consciousness, instead he was irritated that there was no one around to answer the concerns that were throbbing beside the nausea inside his head. His thoughts weren't to do with the pain or the cliché of having a hand to hold because he had some urge not to be alone. His worries were about calling the Red-Tie office, calling Maria, getting something to drink, finding out where he was and having breakfast.

He heard footsteps click closer, then saw a man in purple scrubs walk in and become surprised when Jamie asked, 'Can you get this thing out of my arm please?' 'You shouldn't be awake,' the nurse had an alarm in his voice, 'They just operated...' 'Yer, can I get bowl to throw up in and maybe point me to the coffee?"
'Are you going to be sick?' he asked, scurrying, looking for a container.

'No, but I had a pre-med, right? Once I drink something, I'll vomit and I'll be fine.'

The nurse got him a bowl and water but refused to take the needle out of his arm. He began explaining something, but Jamie fell asleep again halfway through the sentence.

He woke up again at noon to find Maria at his bedside with a tear on her cheek.

'Glad you are here,' his voice rasped.'

'You left me a smiley face on the fridge!'

'Think the pain made me cry,' he told her, unembarrassed that he had been.

'Forget that. I'm waiting here all night, and they don't tell me anything and they say I am not allowed to see you. I had to watch them use the key code and sneak in. I only want you to be...' and whatever else she intended to say stuck in her throat.

Her expression was one of anguish, but she wrapped her smallest finger around his and said, 'I am so sorry. I have not been fair to you.'

It's okay,' he replied, grimacing in pain as he tried to push himself up in bed, but the effort was exhausting and he collapsed back down again, squeakily whimpering, 'Hurts!'

She leaned over him to whisper with a kiss, 'Don't talk, rest. Te amo.'

He wanted to explain the events that led him to be late home, and that trying to lift a 150kg man with an 86kg body whilst being stood on, wasn't the best idea he'd ever had, but lost concentration just as he caught a glimpse of Maria's shoulder holster when her jacket fell open. 'What's that?' he muttered and would have asked more but a doctor came in. Checking on the patient he explained that; Jamie's rib had been buckled and broken. It had caused bleeding under his skin and the only way they had to stop the blood loss was to crack him open. As an afterthought he mentioned to Maria, 'You shouldn't be in here.'

The next time a doctor was in his room it was to tell him that he'd be discharged, the pain was so bad that he didn't even want to move out of his bed to pee, but the hospital had decided the risk of an infection from a superbug was more dangerous than his stitches re-opening, so insisted he go. He walked an inch at a time out of the hospital with tiny painful steps that took him half an hour to reach her little car. Maria had poorly parked at an angle blocking a grey Jaguar, and as she turned her key in the ignition, the other driver began beeping his horn while ranting and swearing at her.

Maria wasn't the calm assertive woman he knew, instead, she was flustered by the man's continued abuse and took a dozen manoeuvres to clear the space. As they drove off at 10 mph, the Jaguar followed only a few feet behind, still beeping. After fifty metres of the driver too close to their rear, Jamie finally lost his temper and tried to get out of her car while it was still moving. He only had violent rage in his head.

'No!' Maria yelled, dragging him back, 'You will tear them!'

She reached over to grab and pull him onto his seat. As their bodies touched together, he felt Maria's pistol and realised that the weapon he'd seen earlier, hadn't been in his imagination.

'What's that?' he asked, yet somehow unwilling to know the answer.

'Nothing!' she replied and switched gears.

Jamie smouldered in the car and asked, 'Did ya phone Don to let him know?'

'Tonto!' she replied and began talking in Spanish. It sounded like she was having an angry conversation with herself. Now and then, she glanced over to burn a new hole in him with her eyes.

Finally, she calmed down as they parked in her driveway, 'This is our first argue, Cariño. It's okay, but can you remember please that I lo...' She caught herself and continued, 'You are my lovely Jamie, not a fighter. Is it good for you? Does your body feel good? I can't stop you if you want to break yourself. Can I? Shall I?'

'Sorry,' he told her, then grumbling he suggested, 'But I'm a fighter, not a lover innit?'

Maria giggled and shook her head. It was a struggle to help him from the car to limp inside and he almost fainted because of the pain.

'It was not my plan, but you were in my path. So, I have to look after you, no?' she told him, led him to her front room and helped him lower himself onto the soft sofa.

With a deep breath of relief, he told her, 'Oh, don't move me. Oh, okay, that's good here.'

He grinned, 'You said you loved me.'

'Don't think so. I said lovely. Are you hungry, Cariño?' she asked.

'Yes, you did, and please, I'm starving. Can you get my phone so I can call Don?'

'I can call him and say you are okay. I'll call the professors and say to send me the coursework. You convalesce. I'm looking after you now. Everything will be okay.'

Ten minutes later, she brought him a stack of bacon sandwiches drenched in ketchup and a pot of coffee, 'Eat, eat, and maybe you can just brush your teeth, okay?'

'Thank you, can I get my phone?'

***

The next time she walked in, he was lying on his side fast asleep with the plate of bacon sandwiches precariously balanced next to his head.

'Te Quiero mi Amor,' she purred and moved the food.

Apart from his ribcage, the hospital had changed the dressings of his Watford injuries, including a large white plaster over his nose. Feeling annoyed, that in her view the Red-Ties had broken Jamie, she took a photograph with his phone and sent it to the contact that said, 'Office,' with the message, 'I've Jamie, he safe 4 now. M.'

When Don got the text, his mistaken first thoughts were criminal, and so were the rest of the ideas that he had that afternoon. It never occurred to him to call the number back or go to where Jamie lived. For him the only possible explanation was that Jamie had been kidnapped. There was no reasoning with him. He called everyone who owed him any loyalty to meet at the now-closed Leni Quintain Pub. As each arrived, he quietly issued orders to them to hunt all the known gangsters of the city and bring them back to the pub.

'Boss, they ain't gonna be involved,' one pleaded, but to no avail.

'Oi, just do it!' Don replied, 'Gather them up!'

Running his fingers through his hair, then slowly growling his command to every Red-Tie in the pub, 'Just fucking do it.'

By six in the evening, he'd run out of names and began grabbing every low-level drug dealer, pimp or armed robber type that passed by the doors of the pub. Four were held captive in the beer garden flanked by Red-Tie guards. Each kneeling prisoner was coerced to wait with cable-tied wrists and duct tape blindfolds. Inside a man was being held down across the pool table. He whined that he knew nothing about Jamie and didn't even know who he was, but Don explained an alternative view.

Swinging a long football sock packed with three apples, he smashed the load onto his victim's stomach and told him, 'You are gonna talk, tell me where you put him.'

Ginger complained, 'Don, this is you showing who is in charge, not about Jamie is it?'

'Meh,' he replied, holding his hands up in mock surrender, 'It's the same thing innit.'

Behind him, one of the Red-Ties picked up the phone that the message had come in on and suggested, 'M might be his bint. Could be with her.'

Don's response was to continue beating the body of the man pinned down.

'Where is he,' he snarled. Perhaps he believed the man and merely wanted to be thorough in his due diligence, but the interrogation was interrupted by the arrival of a police sergeant. The officer was followed by four more cops and from their smiles, pre-drawn tasers and truncheons it seemed obvious to all, that they'd come prepared to catch the boss of the Red-Ties doing something mischievous.

The sergeant grinned and said, 'Well Don, you're under arrest for starters,' but if the cop was hopeful to slap handcuffs on him, he was soon disappointed. Don paused only to slap one of the Red-Ties on the back of the head and say, 'Dickhead! Whatcha let them in for?' then raced out of the fire escape leaving the cops behind, blocked by the bodies of his men. Fifteen hours later, he was in a villa in Spain with the clothes he stood up in, eighty Euros in his pocket, and a cheap burner phone to send messages to Walker. His first text was, 'Send someone with some cash.'

Angel couldn't find any clean clothes in his wardrobes, so he did what until then had been unthinkable and looked in a package that Denver had sent him. He took it as a sign that he was depressed, worn out and getting past caring as he dressed in the "live-the-brand" coffee attire of a company shirt, khaki cargo pants and tan deck shoes.

After driving to work, he parked behind the roastery and saw a long orange ladder wedged between pallets of Kenya AB coffee and a forklift. Thinking the production manager would probably be on the roof, he climbed the rungs knowing that it was useful to check in with him each day to see what was happening.

He'd often wondered if the manager was part of the operation, but there was no way of knowing who was taking orders from the computer in Denver and who wasn't. The minimum wage cleaner in the Singapore roastery might have been the boss of the CIA's whole Southeast Asia region, but the grim German engineer in Hamburg who told him that the afterburners above the roasting drums could be useful for disposing of bodies because they worked at the same temperature crematorium ovens, could just have been an engineer.

Angel called out, 'Hi,' as he got to the top of the ladder and saw the manager was up, and as usual on a deck chair watching the site's CCTV cameras fed to his iPad.

'Sorry can't help you. I'm busy slacking.'

'Hombre, your false modesty is not work on me,' he told with a slurred and exaggerated Spanish enunciation, it was the accent he used to encourage people to assume he wasn't very clever and didn't understand English too well. It was good that people underestimated him.

The manager asked, 'What are you after then? Help with some bean bag colours?'

'Careful, or you will sound like you think my job is the waste of time,' said Angel grinning.

'Me? Who me? Nah!' he replied laughing, 'But I gotta ask, did you write that article in today's paper from our dear leader? It said that we're more like a family, and we get on with things. And the best bit was, saying we only have a meeting if we really need one.'

'No,' Angel replied, 'But I like that. It sounds like our ethos.'

'Wow, you said that with a straight face. That's a real skill.'

'Hey man, that is sedition, don't get me involved,' Angel joked.

'Listen, I can attend meetings back-to-back for forty hours a week, and nobody would care until the coffee stopped getting to the shops.'

The manager beckoned him to where he was sitting next to a chimney stack.

'You have to go to some, surely?' Angel said, walking along the roof's spine.

'Nope, everything I can manage from here or on the back of a forklift.'

Angel said, 'But if you don't attend meetings, you'll miss everything?'

'Oh, I used to go. They'd ask me to take the minutes. And guess what? I used to change the names and dates from a previous year's waste of time and re-circulate it. No one ever noticed because it's always the same grand plans, word for word.'

'Hey, that can't be right. We are a growing company, lots of improvements on the way, lots of new initiatives,' Angel tried his best to look like the easily duped.

The manager shook his head and lit a cigarette, then held up his iPad to show a spreadsheet with annual production figures in tonnes. Next to the numbers was a graph which showed the trend as a flat line, with sales neither rising nor falling.

'Nah, don't believe the hype. Listen, I run this place by keeping out of senior management's way, and I don't believe something is happening until after it has happened.'

'Wow, man! You are way too cynical.'

'Seen them all come and go with their continuous improvement malarkey. I know how it works. I have half a dozen vice presidents, directors and weird job titles who all think I am their direct report. Everyone is 100% in charge of the whole plan I've already scheduled and delivered before they were hired, and half of them can't even use a fucking spreadsheet.'

Angel pulled a face feigning disbelief, 'How long have you been with the company?'

'Twelve years. Sit on the roof long enough and all the urgent meetings about bean bags or empowering initiatives will all come around again, without ever mentioning how us workers hate the management and pretty much have to ignore their nonsense, to get the work done.'

The conversation was interrupted by the production manager's phone ringing.

'Tell him I am unblocking the chimney. Say I can come down but explain that there will be a fire if I stop halfway through the job. If they ask how long, make out there's a breakdown in the silo system too. Oh, and bring me something to eat. Please.'

'Is there an urgent breakdown?' asked Angel once he'd hung up.

'No mate, but if I don't manage them, I will end up in a room talking about valuing workers while trying to constructively dismiss someone. Today I am up here because one of the lads spotted a burglar scoping the place.'

'A burglar, really? How do you know?' Angel asked, offering him a cigarette.

'Well, this one I went to school with. A few tried their luck last week too, arriving on push-bikes and leaving with a laptop and car keys from the place next door.'

Angel listened as the manager gossiped about the ins and outs of the factory until he held up his iPad, 'That lady has arrived, by the way.'

'Lady?' asked Angel.

'Yer the American charity lady with the big tits. She is getting out of a cab,' he told him.

'Ah yes, that's one of my meetings. Gotta go.'

Jessica was already in the room when he arrived. Pulling clothing out of a blue ribbon-tied box from a Bond Street shopping bag, she asked, 'Hi honey, what do you think?'

'Looks good, ma'am,' he replied as she held up a lingerie set and pressed it against her chest. It was hard for him not to imagine her in it, and he began to stiffen as her fingers caressed the material and her cleavage. She told him, 'I'm trying to decide which outfit to send to my hotel room. My new beau is waiting at the Tokyo summit, so all those silly bankers who want to screw me will have to wait.'

Angel's instinct was to flirt, but his training made him blush in embarrassment and behave like a nervous employee of the coffee company cornered by a VIP visitor. Just then, there was a knock on the open door, and a mousy-looking man was ushered in by one of the marketing interns.

Jessica's face seemed to sag in disappointment when he greeted her with a limp handshake and a charmless, 'Good to see you again.'

She replied with, 'Glad y'all could finally make it,' and turning to Angel asked,

'Fix us some drinks Honey,' and she pointed at a set of display cases stuffed with bottles of alcohol and packaging samples. 'The Speyside malt please?'

'Yes, ma'am he replied, picking up a dimpled bottle from behind a clutter of awards for coffee and commercial excellence. Angel poured the guest a whisky without the man acknowledging that the Spaniard was even in the room. He merely held out an upturned palm as if expecting his fingers to be wrapped around the glass for him by a servant. Angel knew him. The visitor was a self-important type. Another taxi-for-hire Minister lost without his advisors to guide him in what to say. He also knew that the man was being blackmailed by Jessica.

He knew everything about him, from where he bought his expensive suit, to what he did with the unimpressive physique he kept hidden under it. Jessica had been behind a company offering him a holiday at a Romanian skiing chalet with all the prostitutes and wine he wanted. And Angel knew, it wasn't even the photographs of him with a transsexual that she'd used to ensnare him, but the secrets he'd revealed while drunk. Angel had heard the tapes. Jessica made him wait silently until she'd slowly drained her glass before explaining, 'I want to chat about our predicament.'

The man spoke in quiet nervous tones, 'I want to assure you that our original plan is underway. The doctor could be replaced by the end of the year.'

'Could? Could? He can still talk, can't he? I hear he's a wrong and right type o' guy?'

The man nodded but offered disagreement, 'He is going. He won't be able to contradict the new report. Official secrets and all that. He wouldn't be allowed.'

'I think he's a whistle-blower type,' she replied, motioning to Angel to refill her glass.

'He will be retired. I promise you. Before the report is published,' the man was still looking around, obviously uncomfortable about how the conversation was going, 'We are managing him out due to stress, and the Government can assure you that very stringent measures have been implemented. It will be done quietly.'

Jessica dumped her glass on the table with a bang, 'All I know is that time's a ticking, and that fella hasn't changed his report, and that's a risk I do not want right now.'

She changed her tone to gentle pleading, 'This has to be managed in the right way, at the right times, by the right people. Share prices move on just one word, and God forbid the secessionists heard about this during campaigning instead of a year before the election. He nodded, 'Everything is in hand,' he mumbled, 'We don't need to...'

'I know honey,' she interrupted him. Her voice was soothing, seducing, 'You've said.'

172

The man tried to say something else, but Jessica held up her hand while sloshing whisky around her palate. She reminded him of the power she wielded,

'Finally, we've a president who understands business and just wants to git things done!'

The man nodded and smirked, 'Certainly a change from his predecessors.'

Jessica seemed to take that as bait, 'You know everyone has the wrong idea of the President. He's honestly very aware. He gets it. He knows that when you are in the Oval Office, you're going to be a little in awe of him. So, he does everything he can to put you at ease.'

She leant across the table to slam her knuckles down on its wood, staring at her prey she implied it wasn't only her project, 'He is not the mindless fuckwit that everyone takes him for. So, if he wants it, he gits it.'

Jessica was now a demon-possessed and reminded the man that the US had the biggest military budget in the world. She made a thinly veiled threat about Scottish independence and explained,

'Honey, you do know that I'm in the change of government business and that all the contracts I care about are in a place that got poorer with less infrastructure since its oil was discovered. Y'all want me to manage things different, get them onboard, push things a bit more their way?'

The man tried to speak, but she held up her hand over his face and shook her head. She told him, 'Honey, the Press need to run my stories about the accidents, radioactive leaks, drunken missile controllers and submarine running aground now, today, not tomorrow.' The spiritless Minister began to speak but she cut him off with, 'Git me my approvals!'

Angel enjoyed watching her go full evil villain with her monologues. She looked so horny when she was like that. Everything about her was a turn-on, from her voice to the wrap-around dress and how it clung to her curves. Then she stood up straight and changed tone again to speak as if giving a lecture at a seminar, 'Right now, I am sitting astride the folks in the Office of Transnational Issues and Deployed Support. I am about three ranks down in the chain of command, so I'm a dozen ranks up from ever getting dirty. I can't do that, or there'd be a whole mess of paperwork. So, I've people like Angel be all dirty for me.'

Jessica paused to sip her whisky, then she hit the Minister with her full family tree, 'What y'all gotta know is I serve my country. I'm a patriot. I don't give two hoots about red tape or what is meant to be the executive or what the goddam legislature is supposed to be up to. I serve my president and I'm the fourth generation of my family to serve a president, that's what we do. My daddy was a Marine at the end of Vietnam then he went to Lebanon for the Corps. His daddy was in Guadalcanal, and every generation, we got someone fighting for freedom. Grandpa Frank was in the first world war and his daddy fought at Wounded Knee, before him, his Pa was a brigade commander in the Army of North Virginia.'

It was something Jessica knew by heart, and she paused for only a short breath before telling him, 'His Pa got bloodied at the battle of Dernia in eighteen oh five, and guess what, his daddy was a Captain in the American War of Independence!'

The Minister tried to interrupt her, but she waved her hand at his face, 'Hush up honey, y'all been pussyfooting with this bureaucracy since I got here. Y'all light a fire under this and go get me that official green light, or I'll go get me a shot-caller that can git it done.'

'I can give you…,' the man's voice trailed off into a whisper, 'The fullest cooperation.'

'Praise the lord, Can I have an Amen!' she shrieked, standing up. From her bag, she pulled two sheaves of paper and told him, 'Sign both copies.'

And before he knew it, the man signed, thanked by Jessica for his time and ushered out the door. On leaving, he looked considerably less conceited than when he'd arrived despite being given a small fortune for non-specific consultancy work via the document he'd signed. Paperwork which had awarded him 'Nil paid shares' in an oil exploitation company.

'Is all okay?' Angel questioned, 'It doesn't seem like he came through for us?' to him, it looked like the meeting had been a failure, and another delay with nothing specific agreed on.

'He hasn't, he won't, but at least he'll be a quiet little mouse when we go with Plan B.'

'Are you sure?' Angel asked with a familiar sick feeling in his stomach.

'Yup, I can't waste any more time on this. It was supposed to be fixed.'

Angel nodded, 'Okay. Well, it's ready.'

174

'Then honey, press the button,' she told him, 'Get it done already. It's a green light. They know they're either with us or against us. Take our friendship or take our wrath. That's the bottom line. Always been that way, always gonna be that way.'

With a manicured finger, she stroked gently under his chin, kissed the air on either side of his face, and told him, 'Bye, honey. I will see y'all again. Soon.'

Once Angel saw his boss's taxi leave the car park, he pulled out a small mole-skin book from his jacket pocket and noted on a fresh page the details of Jessica's latest bribe. The encryption he used was only meant to foil the casual observer rather than be an uncrackable code. It was a basic cypher he'd learned about in a history class that used Latin, Mayan, and Arabic symbols. He used it to transcribe the details of the Minister's bribe. Her pattern was clear. By its very nature, her connections to talk to the right people and commandeer resources on behalf of the CIA also allowed her to seek out the corrupt, vulnerable, and greedy. His little book listed his glimpses of her impressive audacity in chasing profits on a monumental scale. She wanted control of business sectors, not a mere hundred million for a government contract. Jessica wanted to move governments, not work in an office for one. He knew her wicked mind and almost laughed when she'd first told him the fable that,

'The doctor will be collateral damage for the greater good.'

***

The second Jessica and Angel were out of the building, the production manager made his way to the mail order room and began packing a special delivery. At the bottom of a box, under some purple tissue paper, he placed a plastic CD case. On top, he carefully positioned an especially light roasted Sulawesi that was MI-5's regular delivery. The boffins there had taken a few weeks to theorise and build the device he used to record conversations. It was clever. They'd made the walls a sound receiver with a coat of clear metal paint. It was an old-school clockwork technology using modern engineering materials for etching recordings with a stylus onto a disk of thin 24-carat gold. The manager, who had a free run of the site, switched over disks and sent it to his contact.

Paddy texted from inside his sleeping bag, 'I've seen them.'

'Have you confirmed their faces?' Ken asked.

'Got better than that. They arrived five minutes ago. In and out fast, but I got their licence plates.'

'What else?'

'They poured some noxious shit over the parking area and disappeared. I could smell it from my O.P.,' he told him, 'At least one is dug in on the other side of the loch.'

'It's imminent then. Watch and wait,' Ken told him.

'Will do Sir. I'm sending pics now.'

So far, Ken was pleased with his newest recruit. Paddy had not even jokingly complained about being dug into a damp hillside. All previous communications from the big Legionnaire had been on time, precise and without asking any questions about what he was doing. He followed orders and merely smiled when told to lie in a hide on the western side of the loch. He treated the task of scanning walkie-talkie frequencies and watching for unusual activity as a simple one and hinted that he'd be willing to do whatever he was asked.

After looking at what Paddy had sent, he called Petra and told her,

'I need you to go to Paisley police station, give them a story about being on holiday and spotting a London villain up here acting suspicious. Put a name down in their status book and start looking for that hit team.'

'They'll see what I'm up to. It's a different system up here in Jockland,' she explained.

'No. No one will, I promise. I'm sending you another code to use as a back door. See if you can find a pattern in where they've been driving.'

'And then?'

'And then we wait. We only have some of the pawns and a few of their moves.'

'Wait? Aren't we going to get in the way of this boss?' She hadn't sounded happy since he'd told her it would only be the three of them in Scotland.

'Why do you say that,' asked Ken, sipping a takeaway coffee.

'The recon pics showed the location. That's a screw-up, isn't it?' she asked.

'Yes. Yes, it is. Actually, I hadn't thought about that bit of it, yet.'

She asked with a worried tone, 'We stop it. Right? That's the aim?'

'We follow orders from senior officers who have the bigger picture,' he told her in a harsh tone, 'Trust the system. The service always gets it right in the end.'

'Yer. Understood boss,' she replied sounding dejected, 'We aren't stopping this?

'Not at this moment. I want you to find their forward base. They're the target.'

'So, is this who we are, just playing with pawns? Not ethics,' she said scolding.

For now. But things change. Once you see their movements, come, and join me,' he told her.

'Join you with the bigger picture?' she asked petulantly.

'Yes. It's Schwerpunkt.'

'Okay,' she sighed, 'I am on it.'

When she called him back two hours later, her tone had been replaced by the giddy excitement of a huntress who'd found the lair of her prey, 'Boss, I've got them. That number plate has been up and down the A9. I sketched a little cluster map of where they've been. It's nowhere near Paddy. Sending now. Got to be somewhere around the town of Killin.'

'Ironic. But yes, good work,' he told her, 'Link up and it'll be nearly over.'

'There is more boss. You're gonna love this. The Russian redhead is here too. I have just seen her at the airport?'

Ken paused for a moment then seemed to snarl, 'What are you doing there?'

'That's where my hotel is, boss.'

'God no!' he sounded annoyed, 'Never use airport hotels to communicate!'

'Boss. It is okay,' she told him, 'I'm not an idiot. Just saying I saw her there when I drove here. I've tracker on her car. Do you want me to grab her? I mean, I'd love to!'

The old spy hesitated, torn about what to advise. He worried that his illness was causing him to lose the clarity he needed for the job, and he dithered. For the first time since he could remember, his mind was blank. He felt feeble and old for a moment but gathered his wits enough to tell Petra, 'Don't worry about her. Head to the loch.'

***

After a pill and a sip of whisky from his flask, Ken allowed himself a brief moment of happiness about how his real plan was going, and made a phone call with another burner, 'I am client Boston Forty-Two. Code is. They'll never shoot me in my own country.'

At the other end of the phone, a voice told him, 'Go ahead, Boston Forty-Two.'

He gave the anti-terrorism command Tanya's passport number and the story that she was brokering an arms-deal for an Irishman known as 'Farmer Paul.'

'It's happening soon,' he told them, 'I've not been wrong in the past?'

The identity he used was of an informant that he had disappeared himself. Ken gave just enough information to set alarm bells ringing in every department of the security services and dumped his phone.

Against his doctor's orders, he lit a cigar and enjoyed a moment of pleasure. As warm smoke blossomed in his lungs, he weighed his options in what he thought of as, 'My last roll of the dice.'

Chapter 24 - Scheduling.

'Glad I came,' declared Dr Kraus as he and Hector set off from a country gate in Milngavie along a path of glistening grassy sogginess on an unexpectedly hot sunny day in Scotland. There had been occasional drafts of crisp cool breeze and moments of rainfall to chill their sweat, but the cooling weather did not last. Gentle rain evaporated into steam as it hit the ground, leaving them panting in the heat.

Kraus was already savouring the freedom; he felt stress leach out of his body with every step as they headed north through the flatter, less scenic first stage of the West Highland Way. He was finding the walking hard in his stiff new boots, and Hector slowed his pace as they trudged onward and upward through the winding wild mushroom-littered glen.

Everyone around him, his wife, Hector, human resources, and his new boss in the Denver office that now subcontracted his government work, had all conspired against him to take a holiday. Now that he had, he loved it. Justin had argued and eventually toned-down Hector's ambitions for carrying their equipment and the idea of camping after an unrealistic twenty-five miles of hiking per day. So forced to take ten days' leave, they agreed on an enjoyable stroll and sleeping comfortably in beds near a beer tap in hotels, instead of listening unrelenting hum of biting insects from inside a tent.

To pass the time as they hiked, Hector discussed his failed marriage, identifying where he felt his wife had let him down or not supported him as he'd made his career in the army and M.o.D. Justin soon began sympathising with Hector's wife and stopped listening to the moans. Occasionally he nodded and muttered ambiguous grunts, but mostly he tuned into the crack of silver birch twigs underfoot and the quacking of ducks in a nearby stream.

Suddenly Hector stopped to look at his map, 'Not far, one more kilometre, and we're done.' 'Thank God! replied Justin, 'Thought we'd never get there.'

It took them twenty minutes to walk on tired legs the rest of the way. When they arrived outside, Justin only managed to puff, 'Oh,' and slumped to sit on a railway sleeper that walkers used to scrape their boots. To him, as the blood raced back into his legs, it felt like a soft mattress to sleep on. 'Let's book in,' said Hector.

'In a minute!' he said, not paying attention but so glad to have stopped. An hour later, they were ordering their second meals, third pints of lager, and agreeing to meet up for breakfast at six the following day.

When Justin woke the next morning, he was ready and eager for the day ahead and soon forking into a large helping of fried eggs, bacon, and buttered toast in the hotel's bar. Then came the surprise. 'Oh my god! Are you okay?' he asked Hector as his friend stumbled into the doorframe and began limping towards him, using tables and chairs for support. A waitress clattered out of the kitchen and asked, 'What do you want for breakfast? Oh, and the driver for your bags will be here in a wee minute.' Hector answered them both, 'I'm fine, don't worry, I'll help myself to a coffee.' Justin looked on in disbelief, 'What have you done?'

'It's an old injury. I must have twisted it or something,' he explained, stretching out the bootless foot. 'It's okay. Some tape and painkillers. It'll be as good as new.'

Justin's face was concerned, 'Can't walk with your leg like that. You need a doctor.'

'I checked. There is a clinic not far from here. I can get some anti-inflammatory stuff.'

'Yes, Hector, absolutely. Let a professional check it out.'

Over coffee, they agreed to meet again at the next waypoint.

The hotel made a few phone calls, and the waitress came in with fresh coffee and news, 'Well, the clinic opens at 9:30. I've spoken to the portage company, they say the driver will give you a lift and drop you off at the Drovers Inn at the end of the loch.'

Hector nodded, 'Oh, that's great. I'll catch you up.'

'You sure you don't want me to come with?' asked Justin.

'No, I'll be fine. This way, we'll both end up at the pub for lunch. And I'm not sure he's got another seat,' replied Hector. It seemed decided.

After another coffee, they stood outside the hotel. Two other walkers were also about to set off, and Justin waved to them. He was going to ask if he could join them, but Hector winced in pain and said, 'Need your shoulder to lean on while I hobble.' Justin obliged, 'Of course,' and took Hector's weight, but by the time they'd finished chatting and said their goodbyes, the other walkers had disappeared down the path. Justin didn't know that his departure time was being carefully managed. Once the portage driver closed the passenger door for him, Hector waved a final farewell to his friend and sent the message, 'T-X now,' into an old phone that had been manufactured before smart technology was a thing. While the portage driver took him to a plausible alibi, Hector chatted away in friendly conversation and dropped bits of the phone out of the window and onto the road. As the pieces fell, he sighed in relief while imagining what he might do as a good family friend when he went to offer his condolences to Annabelle. He didn't know why and didn't feel any guilt, only a little eagerness to get through the rehearsed process of bluff he had agreed to in exchange for the payment of his debts and a promotion.

***

At Maria's house, Jamie's sleep pattern was one of catching a few hours of sleep for every hour awake, and at early o'clock in the morning he was happily yelling at a TV. 'No! Don't do it. He's the baddy,' Jamie was drugged up and disturbed by the boss of a Mexican cartel in an implausible, subtitled mini-series that Maria had put on for him. She entered the room with poached eggs, rye bread, spears of asparagus and a glass of orange juice. He smelled the aroma he smiled, 'Thanks, you're the best cook ever.'

After he gorged himself on what she called, 'Good student food,' she went into nurse mode. 'Up, up Jamie,' you need to start moving a little. Just a little exercise each day I promise,' she told him while draping his arms over her shoulders to stand. 'I am a perfect patient ain't I? Maybe keep giving me the codeine,' he told her sleepily. 'With those you snore,' and as if on command, his head flopped onto her neck, and cuddling her he began to doze. He woke seconds later, with Maria lifting him gently.

Slowly she supported his weight and guided him, one tiny step at a time, to the shower. Then it became a combination of him holding on tightly to the door, and her admonishing him with, 'Shh! It's nothing I haven't seen before,' undressing him. He became speechless with something between embarrassment and a groggy fuzzy-headed excitement as she smoothed a soapy lather where he couldn't reach himself. After towelling him dry, and them both ignoring his codeine fuelled erection, she helped him back onto his cushion-strewn chair and began changing his dressing. Biting her lips, she snarled without words. Every few minutes she would breathe out sharply and flare her nostrils, but the only thing she said after she expertly cleaned the wound was, 'I look after you.'

'I'm fine now. Well, enough to go back to lectures,' he told her, 'I can move around a bit more. I only need to be careful lifting my arm or bending.'

She watched as he struggled to lift the TV remote and grumpily told him, 'Gilipollas!'

At nine o'clock, Maria called his tutor to ask for his coursework and explain again, what she'd called an accident with, 'He wouldn't be back until the start of next term.' Jamie muttered, 'You're no the boss of me,' and flashed a cheeky smile, but she stood between him and the TV with hands on her hips until he admitted, 'Oh, yeah you are.' After that, she went to get fresh supplies from a nearby pharmacy, and as she walked, she tried to understand how she could have gotten so involved with Jamie. Meeting him had been an accident and her predicament with him wasn't on her agenda at all. At first, she thought of him as respite but argued with herself about why she had embraced him so eagerly into her life. She wondered how he would react if she told him at least even a half-truth about herself, 'Probably, he'd just smile.'

By the time she finished shopping, she'd resolved to tell him something. What she was, or at least who she was. Perhaps it would be enough to stop his eyes from questioning, but when she entered her house to tell him , the only thing that came out of her mouth was a scream. On the fridge, a note, 'We've Jamie. He is safe 4 now. W.'

***

While Maria was out, Mr Walker had arrived and convinced Jamie that the firm needed him, 'Nobody else can go mate, and as you are not doing anything anyway?'

'Will I be gone long?' he asked.

'No, just there and back. Grab your passport, or we'll miss the flight.'

Jamie didn't think. He was drowsy, the codeine he was taking had made him docile. In Walker's car, they drove to Gatwick Airport and the underboss explained the plan, 'All ya gotta do is go to Spain with a bag and give it to the guy you meet at the airport.'

'Is it drugs, Mr Walker?'

With a heavy paternalistic groan, he said, 'Ya don't smuggle drugs into Spain from England.'

'Is it weapons?' asked Jamie with the cogs in his brain sluggishly grinding.

'Nothing illegal at all?' he told him, 'Absolutely legal. It's all good.'

'Mr. Walker, is it drugs?' he mumbled and fell asleep in his seatbelt.

It was not naivety that pulled him into the unknown. It was more like a developed sense of loyalty to the firm that pushed him. A feeling that he was a minuteman responding to the call and rising to any situation asked, albeit with dopey and worried curiosity. His primary motivation being that he shouldn't appear weak as a Red-Tie.

When he woke at Gatwick, he was disorientated and spoke as if continuing an unbroken conversation, 'Okay, I totally trust you, but how long am I looking at if caught?'

Walker grunted with exasperation, 'Jamie, it's not drugs, weapons or endangered peregrine fucking falcons. It's fucking legal! You're just doing me a favour.'

'Okay, so if I get caught, I can say I picked it up from you? Right?'

'No, you bloody well can't. Keep your mouth shut,' Walker's facial expression cut off the conversation, and Jamie went to Spain, medicating with codeine and four in-flight wines.

It was early evening, with the sun still bright in the sky when he arrived at Alicante. Don met him with a mischievous, happy grin and a hug that made his eyes water in pain.

Jamie groaned, 'Boss, I'm injured,' and popped more codeine in his mouth, while wondering what new carnage lay ahead.

'Mate, thanks for coming. Walker told me everything. You need a coffee or anything?'

'Got to call Maria, but I didn't bring a phone,' he replied while handing Don the bag.

'Okay. Mate, we will get that done soon as...'

As they drove, Don seemed more relaxed than he'd ever seen him. He was a rapid, enthusiastic machine gun firing out business models involving drug dealing and gun running. He even had an idea about importing stolen diggers for the construction industry. Jamie asked, 'Where are we going?'

Don explained, 'Off to pick up something, at the villa. It's a loaner from a bloke I know in London, it's a bit Costa del Crime out here innit.'

'Are you staying then?'

'Nah, I just need Walker to give me the all-clear. We'll be here two weeks max.'

Crow had been awake all night, listening to rats scurry through the bracken and ferns, so it was a reprieve to hear the observation post on the other side of the loch talking in everyone's earpiece again.

'Sunray to Highland-Charge. Radio check. Over.'

'This is Highland-Charge. All good. Received Four. Over.

'Sun Ray to Southern Cross, stay awake. Over.'

Southern-Cross was Crow's call sign, and he pressed the button of his throat-mic to answer, 'Morning Sun Ray. Southern Cross all clear and good over.'

The observation post on the western side of the loch said, 'Biker Cut off. We are on gentlemen. Go. Go. Go. Over.'

'Sun Ray, this is Biker Alpha. Received. Roger Wilco. Out.'

Crow started work and wiped the fog from his rifle scope to look around. It was one thing being awake, but now Crow needed to switch on as alert and switch off as stiff and groggy. He had a pain in his ribs, and he was desperate for a stretch, but it was still too early in the quiet of the morning to even fart. Slowly he took a long deep breath to fill his lungs and rolled his clinker-built frame onto one side to quietly piss in a bottle. As he breathed out, he felt a little rattle of mucous on his chest and told himself it would have to stay there until later. Everything hurt. The dampness of the dirty hole had sucked out his energy and seeped into his bones with his only warmth throbbing in the boots he hadn't taken off in days.

'It was normal to ache. That was the trade,' he thought as he began tensing, then relaxing his creaking joints, scarred tendons, and cold muscles in sequence, preparing for work. A light breeze picked up, and he decided the noise around him was enough to allow him breakfast, so he unwrapped a protein bar he'd prepared in cling film and gulped down the food with a sip of whisky that was meant to put some warmth into his body. The next signal was a whisper in his ear that he couldn't make out. Perhaps due to his hearing deteriorating from years of shooting, but he presumed it was the signal for four men who'd had hot breakfasts and swam across the loch, to now slip out of the cold water.

The morning mist was lifting, Crow could see it was going to be a beautiful day.

'Easy payday for a well-planned operation,' he thought while marvelling at the view.

'Southern Cross, stand by,' he heard next, and he began running through his drills.

When the target was sighted, step one was to block off the upper path. Step two let him pass on the lower track, and step three switched around which path was blocked. It was simple. But not for the first time, a horrible thought crossed his mind, 'If the timing wasn't right and the public spotted him, Matty would have to make him disappear. He knew that drill.'

He controlled his concerns and filed them in his brain under 'Paranoia due to sleep deprivation,' then he took a little slug of whisky from his hip flask, hoping it was enough to push the stiffness out from his body, at least until the job was over.

Crow reasoned that, on the balance of probabilities, it should go well. Matty had thought the easiest way to close the road would be with orange tape and a simple, official sign saying, 'Warning Forestry Operations - Path closed for repairs.'

They had spilt noxious smelling slurry on the other side of the loch at the parking place to drive away overnight campers and the team had checked every minuscule detail and practised repeatedly. If that wasn't enough for success, Matty had said he was ready to cancel the job at any moment if even a blade of grass looked out of place.

Then his earpiece told him, 'Stand to,' and one by one, the men replied with their call signs and, 'Ready, over.'

A minute after that, he heard, 'Southern Cross, this is Sunray over.'

Crow replied, 'Sunray, this is Southern Cross. Send over.'

'You are go, go, go. Over.'

'Received out,' he replied, and without moving from his hide, Crow began to pull on a length of para-cord that he'd buried in the soil.

One end looped through a pulley near him, and the other was attached to the top of a fence post on the upper path. As he tugged, a sign was dragged out of a hidden bag and the whole assembly rose to block the way with warning tape. He tied it taut and waited as the barking of hectic military code began again.

A few seconds later, Crow spotted Justin walking toward him.

'Southern Cross to Sunray. Packet sighted. Contact. Figures eight zero. Over.'

'Break. Break. Biker Cut-off. Sighted. Figures eight zero. Over.'

'Biker Cut-Off. This is Sunray over.'

'Send Sunray Over.'

'Biker, Package is in the basket over.'

'Roger that. Out.'

When Justin walked past him and disappeared behind a few tree-clustered mounds, Crow cut his first para-cord and began pulling slowly on a second line that would simultaneously block the other route and drag back into the foliage his original sign. As he turned back, he saw four divers stepping out of the loch and took a moment to admire their professionalism; one by one, they lifted their masks and placed them carefully on the rocks next to an orange marker pole. With their hoods pulled back, they began smiling and changing their body language to become friendly recreational divers.

Crow whispered into his mic, 'Sunray, this is Southern Cross. Over.'

'Southern Cross, send over.'

'All good. Can I move to BRAVO? Over.'

'Sun Ray to Southern Cross, Go BRAVO, over!'

'Received Out!' With his last order, Crow began crawling towards the sign on the upper path. Slowly sliding through the undergrowth, he heard what they all were waiting for, 'Biker Cut off. All clear,' then the words, 'Minus 30 seconds over.'

'Sunray. Seen. Out,' Matty replied.

Within minutes the upper path was clear of all evidence that a warning notice had ever hung there. All pieces of the deception were stuffed in a bag, and uncaring that three hundred metres north on the path a man was about to die, Crow retraced his movements back to his hide.

Matty took his position at the water's edge and fiddling with his wet bag he pretended to ignore the doctor as he approached.

Walking up to the group, Kraus mumbled a polite, 'Good morning,' and Matty replied, 'See the football last night?' to draw his attention. It happened so fast. Justin only had time for a sharp intake of breath before his hands were pinned to his sides, and his small body collapsed between the four veteran killers. In planning, Matty had called the operation 'Soft Tonsil' to emphasise the need to leave no marks on the doctor. They held him upright in the embrace of an anaconda, squeezing him slowly and softly as they gagged him. It was a swift and rehearsed movement when they pushed a laryngoscope into his mouth and fed a tube down his throat through a hole in his gag. Then they used a funnel to pour a decoction of psilocybin mushrooms into his stomach. It was a measured dose. Once done, they removed their utensils and sealed his mouth with a soft ball buckled in place; they never spoke to their victim, but calmly checked his pulse as they waited. All the while, Justin's eyes were wide open in panic, but he could not move as he was an elderly office worker and they were fit, muscled veterans of murder.

His wrists were then placed in cushioned cuffs and connected by a rigid bar behind his back. One of the team pressed down on his head as two others grabbed his arms to walk him forward. While waiting for the drug to work, Matty put on surgical gloves and removed a sealed bag containing a guidebook on mushrooms from his wetsuit. He rubbed the book on Justin's skin and dabbed his fingerprints repeatedly on its pages, then put the book and small zip-lock bag of mushrooms into Justin's backpack. Sun Ray from the other side of the loch kept a lookout. It was all going to plan and as they walked Justin up and down the path, one of the men took a collapsible broom and water bucket from his wet bag to scrub away their more obvious footprints.

Soon the psychedelic mixture in Justin caused his head to slump, and one of the men holding him said, 'His eyes are closing. He'll be trying to focus on reality.'

'Okay. Lads, strip him of our kit and give him a clean-up.'

One checked his pupils and said, 'Sorry mate, just orders. You're fucked.'

As a team, they began wiping the unconscious doctor down with cleaning wipes and skin softener. Matty opened a zip-lock that held a can of cola. It was pushed into Justin's fingers to hold as they swilled drink over his lips and down his gullet.

Then one of the men keyed his mic, 'Sun Ray. Time check. Over.'

'Biker Alpha. All clear. Time good.'

While Matty spoke into his radio, another slipped on a pair of smooth rubber over-shoes and picked up the delirious Justin in his arms like a baby, then walked him into a shallow stream. When he was waist-deep in water, he let him drop and calmly pressed the head down until the doctor's half-hearted struggle and bubbles stopped. The contractor gave him last rights by saying, 'You've kept me long enough without a cigarette, so off you fuck, there's a good corpse.'

Matty told them, 'Okay, we are ready,' and they worked their way back to where they'd first met Justin, removing all equipment and signs that four heavy men had ever left the water. At the Lochside one of the divers read off a checklist as if he was checking whether utensils had been left in a patient after an operation. Then the four frogmen swam back underwater to the other side of the water.

***

It was the first time Tanya had been almost sober and almost relaxed since she'd planted listening devices on her Spanish lover. She also felt in control and allowed herself some pride and happiness that her mission was nearing completion. She was calm, although somehow feeling guilty about lying to Angel when she'd said she couldn't drive. As for her orders to kill him, she didn't let that cross her mind. At a specific time, she was to park with her car window slightly open and a copy of Italo Calvino's, "Invisible Cities," on the dashboard. Then for thirty minutes she was to have a cup of coffee in a cafe. Tanya would then head back to the airport and go to London. She was only a few hours from that rendezvous, and a few days away from Moscow and being welcomed as a hero. But speeding over the Erskine bridge, the Russian agent was blissfully unaware that she was being followed by Scotland Yard's counter-terrorism unit.

Crow cut the cord that tied the sign blocking the lower path, reeled in the last of the proof that either the Lochside or higher path had ever been blocked and headed back to his hide. Then Sunray signalled, 'All teams, all teams, let's go to the pub.'

Crow took a long sip of water and acknowledged the message with a whisper into his mic, 'Sunray, this is Southern Cross. Received. OUT!'

For a moment he watched through his scope as his comrades on the other side of Loch Lomond exited in their vehicles. The last to leave was the main observation post, and although he could not see his hide, he spotted his colleague's forestry van join the main road. Crow smiled. It had been a fast, professional job.

He always knew that he'd be the last to leave, as he was the one with a long slow crawl away from the paths, back along a drainage ditch to where he was to be picked up. But just as he edged out of his hide, he saw a shape rising from the ground.

It transformed into a man wearing the camouflage of a Ghillie suit with what looked like a long-lensed camera in his hand.

Crow keyed his mic in Morse code, repeating the letters F.C. several times, then waiting. It didn't take Sunray long to check through his colleagues and find that it was only Southern Cross who wasn't answering, 'Southern Cross send over.'

Not wanting to risk even whispering into his mic, Crow tapped out in Morse code, 'Cameraman. Figures three zero. My north. Over.'

The cogs of his brain slowly turned as he tried to figure it out; when did the man get there, when did he dig in? Was it before they'd arrived?

He thought, 'Maybe hadn't seen him because of the mound and trees,' and then wondered if he'd arrived during a violent thunderstorm a few days before. It was the only explanation as to why they hadn't seen each other. The message that Matty sent back in reply was succinct, 'Take him out. Over.'

Crow clicked his mic three times and planned his new deadly task.

He sensed tightness and aches in every corner of his body, from every muscle and sinew so decided to suck half a litre of water from his water-sack to ease his dehydrated body. It helped, sweat surged from his pores as his senses began to overload with the noises of the breeze shifting through the wood and the scents of flora opening up to the morning sun. Crow watched as the man changed clothing into the guise of a jogger with a backpack and his heart froze as he realised that the target wasn't going to make it easy for him. Instead of walking out of the woods on one of the paths, the man was taking a course heading straight towards him.

He moved closer, treading lightly on the bracken, gingerly pushing it down, before rolling his feet onto the grass. First, the edge of his foot, the weight of his toes, then the heel. He was relaxed, putting his weight down and moving with his next foot. Crow began to panic; he couldn't get up, he couldn't make a noise, and he couldn't get away. Worst of all, as the man got closer, he saw he was a huge and dangerous-looking fuck with slightly almond eyes, like a Mongolian made from breeze blocks.

A startled grouse broke from the cover of ferns and flew in front of the approaching man's face, but he didn't flinch and kept moving at a snail's pace onwards along a faint line of flattened foliage that some deer had made. He tried to keep calm. Having someone to kill focused his mind but he was alarmed that the hulk would pass right in front of him.

He thought, 'It'll come as a bit of a surprise to the fat git when I slot him,' but as the man got closer, he understood that his victim was too big to do anything simple with a knife, 'Fuck, that won't work,' he thought, 'I'm gonna have to shoot him!'

Crow screwed the silencer onto his pistol which was loaded but "Made-Safe."
The adrenalin got him thinking, he knew he would have to cock the weapon to put a round in the spout, and that the man would hear the metal on metal. In his mind, he planned the event and told himself, 'I will be speed, aggression, and surprise. Sod that slow is smooth, smooth is fast, nonsense.'
His heart began racing. He forced himself to take long slow breaths and held his pistol flat against his chest. He thought, 'Ten more feet and the target would maybe see him. Perhaps, the guy would dive for cover or perhaps he'll draw a weapon and kill me?' As the man stepped past his dirty hole in the ground, Crow pressed his hand onto the pistol's slide then bet his life on how his target would react when he heard the click chambering a round.

Level with his hiding place, without hesitation, he fired. He didn't need his second clip, and he didn't empty his magazine. As soon as the sound of the slide moving hit the cameraman's ear, he began to roll. Crow's first round hit him in his arse and travelled forward along his spine, another entered his side just below his armpit, and the third round penetrated his jawbone to explode from the top of his skull in a fine pink mist. The muffled shots shattered the peace of the morning, birds flew away, but just as quickly, all was still again.

Crow licked his lips and spoke a quiet reverend prayer, 'Two in the body, one in the head, make sure the fuckers dead!' then into his mic informed his team,
'Sunray, this is Southern Cross, all plates down. Over.'
'Southern Cross. This is Biker Cut off. We are en route to you. Over.'
'Received. Thank fuck for that. Out.'
The next thing Crow heard on the radio was a quick burst of, 'Deep Fried Pizza,' messages. It was their code to signal a change in the plan and to head to alternate rendezvous points.

Any body and blood DNA at the site of an accident would be a significant fuckup, so there was no choice. Crow bagged up as much of the brain, hairy bone, and flesh as he could and began searching the dead man. There was nothing except anonymous gear, but it was evident from a blood group tattoo under his armpit that he was Russian. He sat staring into space momentarily before uttering, 'See ya in Valhalla.'
Then his radio crackled into life.
'Southern Cross, this is Sunray. Wait at CHARLIE. Over.'
He snapped alert, 'Sunray. This is Southern Cross, moving to CHARLIE. Out.'

It took him three trips to crawl with the Russian and all his gear to a position four hundred metres north. There he waited, soaked in sweat behind a small stack of forgotten logs rotting and overgrown moss. Then a horrifying thought crossed his mind, and he began looking through the pictures on the Russian's camera. There were hundreds of images, not just of the hit team putting the tube down Doctor Kraus's throat, but of Matty meeting others in various locations.

'Probably a little suspicious!' he thought, and Crow did what most people would do in the circumstances and copied all the photos onto a spare memory card he'd found on the deadman. He mused, 'Not a single picture of me,' then stuffed the copy in his sock.

***

At Crow's new hiding position, Matty arrived in a Forestry Commission Land Rover, and greeted him with smiling words, 'No plan survives contact with an enemy.' After having a brief look at the Russian's camera, Matty's normally taciturn nature became even more relaxed and jovial. It was a mood that was uncharacteristic for the grim bastard, and it made Crow immediately suspicious with an overwhelming sense of dread. Matty reported that so far, there was nothing on their police scanner about a dead body and that they were simply heading to rendezvous with hot food and showers. But when they loaded the body in the back, Crow noticed they already had weights and a large roll of chicken wire half hidden under an old army poncho. That's when panic set in. As they drove away, Crow shovelled down a cook-in-the-can beef stroganoff while his teammates in the back of the van, cut away the corpse's clothing, teeth, and tattoo.

They continued north, and by the time they pulled into a picnic spot by Loch Lubhair, the Russian was parcelled up in a wire coffin, ready to be dumped. Quickly the two men in the back changed into diving gear and slipped into the cold water with the body. Just before they submerged, one of the men stabbed the Russian's torso to let out any stomach gases that might help the corpse float. The chicken wire would do the same, as the body bloated and the steel cut through the expanding flesh. When they returned, one man lit a cigarette and the other gave only a matter-of-fact report, 'Sorted. Chained under a waterlogged tree. He'll sink into the gravel with it.'

As they drove on, Crow considered what he'd do if he was Matty, and had just discovered every member of his team had been photographed at a murder apart from his newest recruit. What Crow didn't know, was that his death had been decided on the first day he was hired.

***

Paddy's perspective of the same events was a little different. When the hit team swam back to his side of the loch, he made a call to Ken from his own camouflaged hide. He connected an earpiece to his phone and whispered, 'It's what you thought. Four on the way back. And at least one on the other side.'

Ken replied, 'Yes. Anything else to report? Have you heard anything?'

'Affirmative. They used walkie-talkies for comms. I've a few recordings but nothing incriminating on its own. But, with my pictures, it's good stuff.'

'Great work,' Ken told him.

The big English legionnaire then explained,

'Estimation is that the main team is out water and back with me in figures... Two ...Zero. So, I'm bugging out.'

'Understood. I want pictures of them moving from the loch to their vehicles. You are free to follow. Don't worry about losing him. I'd rather that than you were seen.'

'Yes sir, will do.'

'How are you feeling?' asked Ken from the comfort of his warm car.

'Cold sir and I've a very strong grassy knoll premonition going on.'

'Yes, makes sense. If you think it's a good place to observe. They will too.'

'Yup, but I'm good to go,' he said while cleaning his armpits with baby wipes.

Ken told him, 'Good. Dump that phone. Use the next one in an hour,' and hung up.

Paddy didn't care about the target he'd seen killed. He'd taken pictures of the murder and the only thought he really had in his head was, 'Interesting work. I could get used to this.'

All that bothered him was that his thousand pounds a day job might be coming to an end. Inside his hide, he quickly dressed in his biker leathers and crawled down a ravine to where he had hidden his motorbike under a tarp and bracken. Ken's instructions had been simple; take pictures and follow. He wanted a chain of evidence between the murder and who'd hired them, but not at the risk of being seen.

The old spy had told him, 'I need times, locations of phone calls, pictures of their vehicles, where they stop and buy petrol. Hopefully, they'll use something with a card I can trace back to something else.'

Still concerned that there was another observation post in the area, He waited until he saw the hit team get out of their diving gear and drive off.

Then he rolled his bike down a forestry track to the main road. He was lucky that after so long on its side in the damp, his bike started for the first time, and was soon following their trail north. If Paddy had peered out of his hide for a moment longer with his binoculars before setting off, he might have seen the other killing, but in a rush to tail the assassins, he'd missed it. As it would have been suspicious not to weave through the traffic on his bike, so Paddy took on the guise of a tourist stopping at bends in the road to take pictures. The Lochside road was busy with a tailback of cars stuck behind caravans and that was how he lost them near the town of Crianlarich. They were only two hundred metres ahead, but by the time he moved up the road again, they were gone. When he texted Ken with his update, the old spy simply replied, 'Meet me at the fire station.'

When Paddy got there, Ken's first words were, 'Jump in, we've to exchange gifts.' The old spy then explained how he and Petra had been waiting at different forks in the road, and that now she was following them West.

Their meeting lasted less than five minutes and Paddy swapped his camera for a hot cheeseburger and tracking device to clip onto his handlebars.

Ken told him, 'You play leapfrog. She's the red dot. You're green.'

'Thanks Boss,' Paddy told him and got back on his bike.

'I promise, won't be much longer. Then you'll have a good night's sleep in a nice soft bed.'

'You're alright, I'm fine.'

'Remember, better to lose contact than have them spot you. They aren't nice people,'

'Neither am I,' Paddy said with a smile and drove away.

On his bike, he easily caught up with Petra and slowed down just enough to talk to her on a slow-moving straight, 'Alright darling, where are they?'

'Land-rover about twelve cars ahead, seen?' she asked.

'Yer, seen,' he replied and sped off but at a place called Laggan, inexplicably they lost their prey and split up, taking different routes to try and find them.

Chapter 27 - Command & Control.

Upstairs on the first floor of a skiing chalet, Matty told his team, 'Alright, lads. Food is on the go. There's hot water. Debrief. Half an hour.'

Crow nodded and with a cheerful grin said, 'Ah, lovely-jubbly,' while pretending to rummage in a holdall for shampoo. Part of him reasoned that his tiredness was causing him to misread the situation and jump to paranoid conclusions, but there was another voice in his head reminding him that he was now in the darker, secrecy at all costs, side of contracting.

His escape plan was hampered by Matty in the kitchen at the rear exit, and the Smoker blocking the front door at the bottom of the stairs.

They'd tried not to make it obvious, but Crow could see that since the Russian's body had been loaded in the van it was as if he was under guard with one of them close by, at all times. He unlaced his boots, stripped to his boxers and considered his options. The building was too far off the main road for anyone to hear anything untoward which was bad, but Matty was the type to leave keys in the cars for a speedy getaway which was good.

That was enough information for Crow to come to a decision, and he folded up his pistol inside a towel and sauntered off to get clean with a fresh set of clothes under his arms. With the door an inch ajar, he washed away a week of dirt while singing and keeping the pistol near to his hand. Once dressed he peered out into the hallway to check if anyone was near and yelled, 'Have I time for a shit?'

Matty replied from the stairwell, 'Yer Mate, ten minutes,' and Crow smiled knowing no one was close enough to stop him. He flushed, ran a tap, and stepped onto the sink to slither out the small toilet window. A slice of skin peeled off his hips as he twisted through the gap, with worse to come as his landing. Even though it was only fifteen feet to the ground, he fell like a buckled bike onto a set of stairs and spilt, winded and bleeding into the wheel arch of the Land Rover. He didn't lie sprawled in a heap for long. He checked keys were there and sent, 'Phht, Phht,' from his silenced pistol into the tyres of the cars he wasn't going to steal. Within seconds, he put the vehicle into neutral and used all his strength to push it down the dirt track towards the main road. As the car gained speed at fifty metres from the building, he jumped in and turned the key to drive away. There was one familiar ping of hot metal on metal and when he looked in his rear-view mirror to see muzzle flashes, he laughed and said, 'Yer, Mate. At this range, you've no fucking chance.'

Crow slammed the car through the gears and hoped he was seen heading north, then he came off the main road to feel his way south via a maze of farm roads. When rejoining the dual carriageway, he slowed to the speed limit and turned west at the next big junction. It was only when he was an hour and fifty twists and turns of the road away that he thought about calling his MI-5 handler to tell him what had happened. Crow only said, 'Hi, this is...' before reminding himself to trust no one and hanging up.

***

'I dunno,' Paddy moaned into his phone, 'Maybe they switched cars.'

'Yes, I think you are right,' replied Petra, 'They've gone.'

'Been all over the place, seen nothing. In other news, my tracker has jacked.'

'We may as well quit then. My tracker's quit on me too,' she said.

'I'm at a place called Da-la-win-neh, I'll wait here for you.'

'Not what it's called, but I know where you mean. See you soon,' she told him and hung up. Paddy had a piss in a service station and filled himself with junk food before lying down on some grass to wait for Petra. He was just about to chug down his second Coke when a licence plate he'd previously photographed drove in and parked up next to him. Still lying on his back, Paddy texted Petra, 'I have spotted one of them. I am following.'

Chapter 28 - Networking.

Angel had gone to sleep at three in the afternoon after a coded message from a withheld number. It said, 'Delivered-Pizza.'

From that, he knew that Matty's job had been a success but that there had been some complications. An hour later, he got an email from the Denver HQ with an instruction to attend a charity event that night in Parliament.

All he had to do was go to Portcullis House, drink free wine and listen to the corporate PR people talk about the godly works they did around the globe.

He dressed in the company brand, caught a train to London and began thinking about Tanya again, hopeful that she was in town and they could meet.

She'd gone quiet even though he'd been texting her relentlessly, telling her he missed her. Tanya had turned into an oasis of relief he felt in the sickening world he lived in. He did not like what he had become, and it was she who could reach into his soul to smooth away the pain and anxieties that hid there. She had something on him, and he hoped maybe she felt a connection too. In his mind, he thought of her as the one person in his life who wasn't some corrupt spy or mercenary doing something despicable and relaxed into a warm, happy stupor flicking through some pictures she'd sent.

When he arrived in Westminster, he found it to be a busy event with several MPs and their staff attending, so he skulked in a corner by a drinks trolley. It wasn't long before he was discovered by two elderly baronesses determined to be sociable and friendly. One asked him, 'Don't I know you from Africa?' and as she looked at his name tag, she paused and told him, 'So glad you could make all this happen.'

'Such a great company to work for,' he replied attempting a smile.

The other eighty-year-old lady moved in with a gentle stroke of his arm to ask him, 'Did you have anything to do with the press pack? Apparently, something sweet might trickle over my palate tonight. Say there might even be a nice sugar cane on my lips.'

Angel wasn't relieved when the first Baroness giggled and asked him, 'You're a soldier, aren't you?'

'No, sorry. Not at all,' he replied and only escaped their interrogation when the lights dimmed and the video presentation of the evening was projected on the north wall.

The film was about the work of the MPs and the sponsoring corporations standing in the room. It soon became a tear-jerker movie showing artillery strikes and the debris of war with a merciless manipulation of emotions using mutilated corpses, burned-out desolation and the walking wounded of a previous year's African rebellion. It was reinforced by a ticker tape of statistics at the bottom of the screen listing the deaths, disease, and destruction. Then the tone of the video changed, and hope began. A half-dressed child staggered along a muddy path crying in anguish towards an aide worker's welcoming arms.

The horror scenes morphed into a section with dawn breaking over a beautiful landscape and the music of Wagner's Gotterdammerung changing into Beethoven's, 'Ode to Joy,' with the video cutting to farming in sun-drenched fields and happy beaming smiles. Western and African faces posed at every stage of a coffee harvest and drying process while earnest-looking charity volunteers did pieces to camera wearing comical baseball hats and company t-shirts that said, "I love my team," or emblazoned with quotes from Marcus Aurelius.

Then the film went to the credits, showing a montage of corporate and NGO logos mixed with the faces of doctors, nurses and schoolteachers who were working to help. A girl's face appeared, smiling, and holding in her hands a flower. She spoke earnestly about her future and Angel recognised her as a teenager he'd seen earlier by the drinks trolley, serving coffee grown on the plantation to attendees and handing out leaflets.

It was part of the event company's vision to fly her from where she worked in Africa to London, have her mingle with the guests and tell her traumatic story and rebirth as a manager of a coffee cooperative. As the movie ended, a spotlight switched on to show that it was no longer a recording of the English narrator but the famous lady in person. She was a big deal for the organisers and stood at the podium beckoning the teenager to be hugged. The speaker, an accomplished human rights lawyer and wife of a famous Lord was there to enthral and excite listeners. The gig was to pitch the coffee company's charity in Central Africa and stir consciences on health, education, women's rights, and the business initiatives that supported local communities.

Angel yawned. He'd been bored since entering the sea of grey glassy stares and was just about to reach for another drink when one of the baronesses said, 'She's so very good!'

He tuned in when the other old lady replied, sounding shocked, 'Oh my god, I have never known you to make a complimentary remark about another lawyer. Ever! The media make out she is a scatter-brained weirdo?'

'No, far from it. She's actually brilliant. We consider her as the best legal mind of our generation!'

'Oh wow, that is praise coming from you,' her friend smiled both returned to the speech, listening intently.

From the podium, the presentation was enticing eloquence. She thanked the benefactors for their funding while creating an image of a fragile post-genocide tribal homeland that was now blossoming into a beacon of optimism. As an impassioned orator, she drew connections between infrastructure and social mobility while explaining that the charity needed a little help and only £180 million from the UK government. She spoke brilliantly for precisely eight minutes before packing up her notes and brushing past her many fans and be halfway to the exit by the time the lights came on.

The old ladies left and as Angel's eyes adjusted to the new brightness, Jessica arrived with a man who was a perfect chinless piece of dandruff in a black suit. Standing between them, she didn't bother with her usual pretence of southern charm. She seemed more anxious than usual. Without looking up from the game she was playing on her phone she whispered,

'Angel, you okay honey, this is Smith. He's with me.'

Angel knew the name. It was her liaison officer in MI5. A name tag stated that he was a communications manager which was more or less true, but Angel recognised the type. He'd be an apex predator if the world was, survival of the most devious.

'So why are we here?' Jessica asked, still playing the game on her phone.

'There were complications with your thing,' Smith explained.

She sighed, 'Honey, you better spell it out, as you'd not believe the documents, I had to fill out just to stand here. I've expense claims, purposes, replies to guidance and all that hooey.'

Smith leant in to whisper several sentences in her ear, and Jessica's expression changed to one that Angel hadn't seen before. It was fear. When her eyes darted towards him, Angel's instincts told him that he was in trouble, and perhaps his days were numbered. He chatted amiably, 'It's bad news. Only a matter of time before things are asked. Unless we can do something about damage control.'

'What might that be?' she asked pocketing her phone and picking up a glass of wine.

'An illegal turned up. It seems, they took photographs. Our boffins checked a camera and found that copies had been made. We presume those to be with a team member. Who is now, also missing.'

'Understood. Who else knows,' she replied with her nostrils flaring.

'No one yet.'

'Any idea about where our missing things are now,' she asked.

Smith looked at Angel, 'No, not yet. I thought your colleague here might be able to help some of our specialist trackers with that question?'

She sipped her wine and told him, 'I guess,' then breathed in as if smelling her favourite perfume before smiling at Angel to say,

'It'll be fine Honey. Y'all work together on this now and keep me posted.'

Angel nodded, but with a sense of alarm in his stomach and the urge to throw up while Jessica asked Smith, 'Anything I should know about?'

The MI5 officer gloomily replied, 'Two similar issues. In the last few days.'

'Which issues?'

'Do you remember the Minister we met in Paris?'

Jessica purred, 'Oh yes, I remember his economic advisor. I doubt she had a primary school education, but she had great tits.'

Smith coughed and cleared his throat with a glass of wine before replying, 'I was asked about it. Nothing too specific, and it all seemed too casual.'

'So, someone is looking?' She asked.

'Because of where it came from. I think it's your people. But I can't ask anyone about it. If it is something, I'll have to wait for a team to wade through whatever it is, before being told about it in a briefing.'

'My people can investigate me all they like. They won't find anything. It all went through,' she paused and nodded at Angel.

The MI-5 man muttered, 'Okay then. As far as I know, the records on my side are impartial and accurate. There is nothing amiss.'

Jessica breathed deeply and asked, 'And the other thing?'

'A webpage was asking about Scotland this morning. It's gone now, but it was there for an hour.'

Now Jessica seemed calm and serious, 'Who was behind that?'

Smith shrugged.

Jessica snorted and scowled before turning to Angel, saying, 'Okay Honey, we need to put all of this behind us, why don't y'all go with Smith? He is our partner in this and so might have a few little questions. So, y'know, work together then y'all can disappear on that sabbatical I've always promised you.'

Angel's mind swirled when she said that, but he presented his best attempt at appearing unbothered and replied, 'Sure Boss, no problemo.'

As far as he could tell, a button was being pressed on Jessica's world.

He walked with Smith to Westminster station. As they were about to cross the road a car pulled up next to them and made it obvious, he had to get in.

Angel sat in the back, flanked by two large thugs. They didn't say a word until they arrived at a safe house at the end of an overgrown track in rural Essex. The place looked like a stone mason's workshop, with slabs of marble stacked neatly around a cutting table. The whole place sucked the heat out of his body, and Angel feared the worst, as it was the perfect place for disposing of bodies. Smith started his interrogation by asking,

'Sorry about all this, it's orders. Your boss and I want to know about the Russian illegal you've been fucking.'

The questioning went on with different and grim old men until the following day. It didn't seem routine, and he thought he overheard an American accent during one of the breaks in his ordeal. A sign that confirmed to him, someone was looking into Jessica's activities.

Chapter 29 - Profit & Loss.

Jamie was not happy; he couldn't remember Maria's mobile number and when he tried calling the house phone she didn't answer. Worse still, he'd run out of codeine and Don was taking him on a maniac's tour of dodgy meetings in pubs. 'This is the last one. Right?' he asked as they stopped at a white-walled beach bar.

It was the kind of place where no one arrived without a cheery wave from the bar staff and everyone wore a smile because they were happy, rather than it being ordered for their shift. The decor reminded Jamie of an old movie where the hero visited heaven, and all was draped in flowing white, gently kissed by a soft celestial wind. The furniture was white, the floors were white, and the uniforms of the tanned staff were a white blend of casual chic and trendy.

Wide canvas sheets hung lazily above all the couches and wicker beds served as shaded comfort to lounge on. It was perfection with little rose petals from a wedding party being bleached white as they tumbled around on gusts of cool sea breeze.

Jamie though, was unable to relax as he constantly thought about how he'd left in a hurry and that, 'Maria will be worried.'

They ordered drinks and found a table in the sun facing the hazy glare of the Mediterranean but when the waitress brought their lagers, she handed them a tube of sun cream and said, 'Please, put this on or sit under in shade. Okay?'

It felt more like a command than a request, and besides, she was right . Even though it was getting close to dusk, the sun was still strong, so they happily smeared on factor forty and ordered a second pint. Then Don spotted someone he knew and said, 'I'll be right back.'

The next time Jamie looked up from his glass, he saw Don beckoning him urgently from the doorway, blood pouring from his eye. It looked like he'd have to go to casualty for treatment.

Jamie muttered, 'Fucking typical,' remembering that Don could find mayhem in even the most serene locations. He looked back and forth between the waitress and the door, reluctantly paid the bill, and left.

Outside in the carpark, Don handed him a set of keys and pointed to a blue Toyota hatchback. He didn't ask how or where the additional vehicle had come from, and Don didn't explain. His instructions were, 'Jamie, Mush. Stick close to his bumper, headlights off.'

It wasn't a fun trip. Don drove at 90mph along winding unlit roads using his boxer's reaction speeds to throw his car around corners, a skill Jamie struggled to match. It was hard for him to keep up because of his injury, every gear change and jerky manoeuvre brought pain and tears to his eyes, while the car handled as if it was overloaded.

Once at the villa, Don gave him serious instructions on the first aid for his wound, 'Fuck this up, and I'll kill you.'

'Yes boss,' Jamie replied, giggling inanely.

'Your hands clean?'

Jamie shook his head while Don continued with a manic lesson plan.

'Right, first you get the needle and roll it up in a tea towel.'

'Yer, I dunno if threatening to kill me is going to make my hand that steady.'

'Shut up and listen! You bend the tea towel like this,' he told him then unrolled the towel to reveal a semi-circular needle.

'You need Brandy,' he said pouring three glasses, then more into a saucer.

'Drink your glass,' he said, and Jamie gasped as the spirit hit his throat.

'Look, Don, my hands are still shaking,' he said holding out his palms, but Don poured brandy on them and said, 'Now ya thread the needle.'

Don's instructions were clear, loud, as an order, and punctuated with grunts, 'Put the needle and thread in the saucer then pour a shot over my wound.'

He winced as the alcohol stung and told him, 'If you do a shit job, it will open every time I get in a fight.'

Jamie shook his head, 'Simples. Don't get into any more fights. You considered yoga?'

'Shut up,' he replied and jokingly, again threatened Jamie with painful death if he screwed up. Chuckling with nerves, his fingers slipped on the blood. The first stitch was the worst, but slowly, with quiet words of encouragement from Don, he managed proper spacing and depth.

When it was done, Don conceded, 'Not a totally shit job.'

'Thanks…But I have to ask. When am I going back?'

'Don't worry. Walker will sort things.'

'So can I go back tomorrow?'

'Soon. As it goes, we just need to do a few things first.'

'What do you mean, am I going back or not?' asked Jamie petulantly.

'Course mate. You're back home, as soon as I pick up some more money. Has to be cash. They can trace plastic, innit?'

Jamie was flustered, 'Can I phone now?'

'Sure. I just need to drive you somewhere. We gotta use a call box.'

They found one at a service station near Gandia, and Don went to buy a couple of bacon sandwiches and cans of beer.

Jamie called Maria's house again, but when she didn't answer, he dialled another number, 'Hi Mum, you okay?'

'Yes. Darling, we've been waiting for you to call,' she sounded anxious.

'What's up?'

'Och Jamie, you need to get one of those mobile phones. There's a laddie here for you.'

'What? Who?'

'A friend of yours, Sean. He seems to be in a bit of trouble, so I let him stay in the back room. It's nice to have someone to go to the shops for me, but he seems in a bit of bother.'

'Sean? What does he look like?'

'Paratrooper tattoos. Very polite. He says things like stay low, move fast a lot.'

'Yes mum, I know him. He is one of mine.'

'I'll give him the phone,' there was the noise of her wheelchair clattering against a doorframe and he heard his mum fumble with her frail fingers as she passed the receiver over. After the sound of fumbling he heard Crow, 'Alright, Jamie?'

'What are you doing at my mum's? I mean, what the fuck?!'

'Had no choice, sorry. It's all gone pear-shaped.'

'How did you know where to find her?'

'Just cos you are boring doesn't mean I don't listen to you. You banged on about how in your village there are only three digits to call in your number. I was in Scotland and looked at a map. I knew sooner or later you'd phone home.'

'Pear-shaped?' Jamie asked.

'Suffice to say I had to change my trousers. Can ya get a hold of Don?'

'Don is on the run, and hello, my mum's house?'

'Can ya get a hold of Walker then? Please mate, I am a bit desperate,' he sounded frightened.

'It's okay. I can get Don.'

'Haven't much time, mate.'

'I mean, gimme a sec, I'll get Don,' he said wildly waving across the forecourt.

'What do you mean, where are ya?' asked Crow.

'Spain, the wee pointy bit next to the Bally-are-ricks.'

'With Don?'

'Yer he is walking towards me with food.'

Jamie shared the handset with Don as Crow highlighted his plight, 'I am being hunted by some serious blokes. They want to take my birthday away from me. I can't say much, but reckon I am already on a database or ten.'

'Do you know what firm is after you mate?'

'Yes, government but they aren't plod. They're contractors I was working with. Think they wanted me slotted all along.'

'Do they know where you are?'

'Doubt it Don, I'm in Jamie's village. No traffic cameras in this part of the world. I got nuffink here apart from a bit of incriminating, and they can't track me on that.'

'What do you mean?'

'Well, I took a memory card from a camera. Luckily, it has 'em on it but not me.'

'You're an idiot,' Don told him, 'Okay, stay still, stay off the phone. I'm on my way.'

'Thanks, Don,' he replied sheepishly and hung up.

Standing outside the phone box on the dirty tarmac, Jamie was irate and stressed. It took Don all his verbal manipulation skills to calm him down.

He said, 'Listen, if it's as bad as he says, we'll need money. And I've money waiting on the border.'

Jamie whined, 'I can go myself. There must be a flight from Madrid to Glasgow.'

Don told him, 'No mate if you go on your own, and you lead the bastards to him. Then what do you do on your own?'

The first thing they do when looking for someone on the run is check their known associates. Think about it. I was only gone two minutes, and Walker says they raided my cousin's boatyard. They could nick you at an airport or something, so let's plan this for half a second.

He changed to a more compassionate tone, and explained what he thought might work, 'Okay? I have to go 'cause I'm the boss. You have to go 'cause it's your mum, but it'll be better if we go mob-handed. I'll get us some new passports and we'll get the lads. Okay?'

***

Don had a radar that picked up on all criminals, it was like he could feel their presence in the same way that a shark could sense blood in the water. And he'd used that dubious gift since he'd arrived in Spain. Don's idea was that they delayed travelling long enough to meet a Serbian gangster in another pub. It was a meeting about something Jamie didn't want to hear, but Don made him sit in on it anyway. 'If you give me another few days, I can get you a better one, bre,' said a man while sliding two Russian passports across their table.

'Nah, mate. We can't wait. There was no time,' Don replied picking up his passports, 'In fact, the boy here is in a hurry.'

With that, they shook hands with the gangsters and headed north in two cars. Don took the overloaded one with its rear scraping across speed bumps and Jamie drove behind, uncomfortable with the schedule and his latest non-specific, general orders that stated, 'Stay behind me. If anything happens, be ready to ram them but don't drive off without me.'

Jamie was very far from being ready to do any of that.

After the French border, they both sped through until Bordeaux where progress stalled at a long line of slow-moving traffic. Don leant out of his window to yell something, but at three cars behind, Jamie couldn't hear.

Then he saw it. A Gendarmerie checkpoint, searching. There were eight officers. They'd blocked the motorway with a chicane of cars and police motorcycles and there was no way to avoid it without causing suspicion even if they had the room to turn around. Don was only two cars away from the police, and Jamie knew that whatever crime they were up to, he wasn't prepared to ram cops in his car. Suddenly a miracle happened, and the police packed up to leave with blue lights flashing. There were no further worries until ten hours later they arrived at a village outside Lille and Don was greeted by two grim-looking hoods in leather coats and woolly jumpers. As mafia types, they looked like they could easily carry a horse on their backs and two more just like them loitered next to the car they'd arrived in.

Jamie's suspicions about what Don was doing were confirmed when he opened the boot of his car to reveal it had been smuggling weapons. 'You crazy man!' said one of the big men, 'We not think you bring them yourself.'
Don was euphoric, grinning like a junkie with a fix, 'I only trusted me for this job.'
One of the lumps, smiled toothlessly at Jamie and asked, 'Who you?'
But before he could answer, Don answered for him as if wanting to change the subject, 'He's a jock. I had to take on at least one to the firm as I'm an equal opportunities criminal.'
'Ajock? He is Ajock?' they replied not understanding.
'Yer, I vouch for him. Vouch yer? Ya understand?' replied Don in a tone that suggested he was done with small talk. Money changed hands, and everyone had a shot of vodka from a Goon's hip flask. Excuses were then made about why they couldn't stay for any more drinks, and as a courtesy, the buyers dropped Jamie and Don off at the train station.

It was only when clear of the unlawful situation that Jamie sulkily voiced his ire, 'You can't help yourself, can you?'

But he felt guilty when Don told him why he'd taken the risk of crossing a border with a boot full of Tavor assault rifles, 'Listen Mush, I don't wanna get nicked either, but we needed the wedge for the Crow situation. Not enough to get to him, we need to set him up somewhere.'

They bought tickets to Amsterdam, and Jamie was morose after that, staying quiet for the rest of the journey north. There wasn't an opportunity to talk anyway, as Don spent most of the next hours using his phone as a one-way communication device to make arrangements.

Chapter 30 - Boardroom Strategies.

Phil, with his arm still in plaster, greeted them at the train station with, 'Oi, Oi fuckers. What've ya done now!'

Shaking his head, Don said, 'Not here. When are we going back?'

'Couldn't get the Newcastle ferry, we need to be in Hook about six in the morning.'

'What we doing now then?' Jamie asked.

Phil grabbed him in a headlock and began rubbing his head, 'Happy hour innit!'

Jamie squealed, 'Fuck off Phil, you'll pull my stitches!'

'Put him down!' Don growled in a serious tone, 'Has Ben turned up yet?'

'Nah he's meeting us in a pub,' he replied letting go of Jamie.

Phil led them to a minibus where Ginger and six other Red-Ties were parked at a supermarket and having a picnic of French sticks, cheese and fruit juice. When they'd left Spain, Don had said they'd catch a ferry and be in Scotland in a day. Jamie had agreed, but twenty-four hours later, they'd only got as far as Amsterdam. He thought the plan was to catch some sleep on the Newcastle ferry, not head off to the Red-Light district, drink lager and window shop, but Jamie was stressing less as Don seemed to know what he was doing, even if he explained only a little of what was in his head while demanding specifics from everyone else that he spoke to. When Don spoke on the phone it sounded like a code, and he used obscure references and mumbled slang to communicate as he became a walking, talking, constantly evolving plan.

Using the phones of different Red-Ties, one minute he'd be calling someone and speaking with Gypsy words, the next he'd be chatting in fluent Dutch. The impressive thing wasn't that he was a linguist, but that he kept the hundreds of telephone numbers he used in his head. After being refused entry at a sex club, they had a minor scuffle with other English tourists on a bridge, which was where Jamie found out what noise city police cars made. As the Red-Ties fought around him, Don relieved himself into the canal and, for no apparent reason, hurled insults at the two coppers that arrived. One of the officers drew his pistol, and spluttering with rage, pointed it at Don's head to say, 'Fucking English! Fucking English!'

It might have been Ginger's presence that influenced matters, but no arrests were made, and they walked on to another pub with the Red-Ties chorusing, 'Fucking English,' at Don.

At their fourth pub, they were joined by a small piece of hard wire that Jamie recognised from England as a former Royal Marine called Ben, and as someone who worked in a kind of security that he never talked about. After buying a pint, Jamie, Ben and Don went to a quiet corner to discuss what they were all there for.

The first thing the marine wanted to do, was call Crow and get a fuller understanding of the problem. Jamie obliged by calling home. The conversation was brief, littered with military jargon and one that made Ben's face contort with worry. His first words when he hung up were, 'I never met you today, and I don't even want to be in the same country when this goes off.'

'That bad?' Jamie groaned.

Ben replied, 'You're fucked. Doubt you'll get in the country.'

Don asked, 'But if we find him and get him to you. You set him up somewhere?'

He replied, 'I can hide him in Europe, I can even pick him up from a beach and take him across the North Sea in my rib, but the ex-fil isn't the problem. Getting to him is.'

While draining their pints, he outlined what he thought the difficulties were, 'Your enemy will be at the top of their game, maybe the kind you get once in a generation. You've no proper resources. And no offence Don, but y'know, the lads have no chance against them. If it's like Crow says, ya can assume they've the names and addresses of everyone he's phoned in the last year and their pictures. They are gonna be watching everything.'

'Let them,' he said, 'Not the first time I planned a job with cops listening in.'

Ben scowled, 'Mate these ain't cops, they've got kit the cops ain't even allowed to hear about. Computers that analyse face and voice recognition all day long.'

Don was worried but focused on the positives, 'It'll be a simple grab and go.'

They sat looking at each other for a while in silence, occasionally drawing deep breaths to sigh, until Ben made a suggestion that sounded reasonable and almost encouraging, 'What Crow has got involved in. Sure, it goes on, but it is not all that legit. Even the spooks can't go around killing people on the UK mainland that much. It's a big deal when they do, and all the old-school ties in government start looking over their shoulder. They get to worrying if they've covered things up properly. So, if you get trapped by them, make it messy! Let Phil off the leash.'

Don grinned, 'That I know how to do.'

***

The next morning on the early ferry back to England the doormen were suffering. Don told the lads who were all slouched in various hung-over positions of discomfort around a table, 'Healthy grub, this is. It's what I used to eat when I was boxing,' He'd arrived from the ship's restaurant with a tray of liver, bacon, steaming hot dauphinoise potatoes and vegetables. It was an assault of freshness and flavour on their ambient scent of stale beer, body odour and cigarettes. Without raising his head, Jamie opened one eye in response to the smell that wafted into his nostrils and groaned, 'Uhhhhh.' He wasn't even sure he could move. It was as if his body had shut down; his wound hurt, he hadn't slept properly for days and without his codeine, every movement was making him gasp in pain.

Now half awake, exhausted, and sprawled across the furniture like a lumpy, untidy duvet, he just wanted the world to stop moving until he felt human again. Phil, who was spread across a sofa with his eyes shut, asked, 'You money left?' Don told him, 'Nah. None left. And we can't use cards remember.'

'What about the envelope?' Phil asked, with a bit of hope in his voice.

'Not touching that. It's for the job,' then holding up a bottle of summer fruits smoothie, he declared, 'I was down to my last tenner. Had to shoplift this.'

Jamie groaned as Don sat beside him and banged the food tray next to his head. Like everyone else, he'd drunk the last of his wallet, and as the taste of hot food wafted over him, his stomach rumbled. As Jamie's slack jaw hung open, he looked up at Don from the tabletop and saw him holding a knife and fork above his head. It took him a few seconds to understand that Don was urging him to move, but before he could find the energy, Don declared, 'Cunts,' and stood up.

'Eat,' he ordered.

'No, Don, it's alright,' Phil replied, 'We're alright.'

'Eat, or I'll throw you over the side,' he growled and left to walk around the ship. Jamie looked at the food, but although hungry, it all seemed too much effort and he closed his eyes. Other more active hands leant in to pick up bits of liver and fingerfuls of potato from Don's plate.

Ten minutes later, still with his brain throbbing, they heard the ship's Tannoy system announce, 'Security to Deck C. Security to Deck C. Sports Bar. Sports Bar!' Ginger was first to move, 'Shall we lads?'

'Why not?' replied Phil, 'It's probably Don innit. So, we better go.'

Ginger pulled Jamie up by his shoulder, and they all ambled towards the ship's bow. Rubbing their eyes, yawning and stretching their joints as they moved. The Red-Ties reached the top of the stairwell and Ginger pointed to a sign, 'Pub ahoy, full steam ahead and damn the...'

He never finished his sentence as a fat old man dressed as security and a skinny youth who didn't quite fit his uniform rushed past them, bumping into Phil as they went by. He bellowed, 'Oi-Oi, party time!' and the Red-Ties followed.

As they approached the doors of the bar, they naturally spread out to about one arms-length apart behind Ginger to create a loose V-formation.

Jamie's injury forced him to hobble along at the rear and it seemed the logical place to be. He knew he couldn't do much in a fight as it was clear that if he tried to change direction too suddenly, he'd fall over. As soon as he stepped into the bar, he saw the problem and sensed the tension. The air felt as if it was charged with static electricity and the sounds of a braying mob of football fans, all hurling abuse and beer mats at the bar staff with a complaint about flat, warm lager. Confronted, the ship's security looked scared and stood motionless unsure of what to do.

With a grin, Don asked them, 'Want some help? Looks to me like you has got thirty wannabes up for a fight, and same again as wanker spectators.'

The security staff didn't answer but Don put his hand on top of his head as a sign for the Red-Ties to move towards him. Jamie felt a slight sense of pride. His comrades didn't seem worried by the odds, so he resolved not to be either. Apart from bringing a power-lifting giant with them, the Red-Ties knew each other so well that they could anticipate each other's strikes and timing. Then the fight in earnest began, Don yelled, 'You like the odds, lads?'

Ginger moaned, 'Cheers Boss,' while the team formed a semicircle around Don and the security staff, to begin unloading their classically trained Berserker behaviours. Jamie was also kept to the back.

'Thirty to one. Yer, fekkin brilliant boss,' said Phil sarcastically as he punched someone and Don chuckled, 'Where would ya rather be?'

'Nowhere boss. Honest,' replied Ginger as he threw a man into his hooligan mates. Despite Don threatening to beat his men, if they didn't let him into the front rank, he was soon laughing, watching the violence unfold. 'Fuck off out the way, Jamie! Can't you see we're working?' yelled Phil while smashing someone in the face with his cast. With the ship's staff, Don stood against the bar to watch as opponents came in waves. As predators, the football fans were baying for the Red-Ties, but they became prey and hesitant to be smacked, after witnessing how brutally systematic a giant could be. It was a relaxing workout in the gym for Ginger as he crushed men's bodies and their spirits. Football replica tops surged forward in vain attempts to assault the ever-taunting Don, and each charge failed on the ends of Red-Tie fists. It became a game for them, calling out points as they scored knockouts. When finally, half a dozen troublemakers were lying at their feet, and no one was trying to help them away, it was all over and Phil yelled, 'Aw come on. I wanna play some more.'

Ginger grinned and began walking amongst their battered opponents, making eye contact with them. All turned their heads away, beaten.

The ship's Captain and his first officer arrived, they stood out amongst the torn and broken scene as pressed, polished professionals in pristine white shirts with braids. 'Who is responsible,' he asked his bar manager, a man still cowering behind the till. In a frightened stutter, the employee replied in French with a full report. If any Red-Ties had understood a word of it, they'd have heard him explaining how the football supporters had abused his staff, and Don had valiantly stepped in to defend him and his barmaids. To Jamie's amazement, the captain turned to ask Don with a kindly smile, 'I'd be honoured if you would be my guest in the officer's mess?'

Don replied, 'Sure,' but pointed at the football supporters strewn around the bar amongst wrecked tables and smashed glasses, 'What about them?'

The Captain looked at his security, then at Don and back at his security before asking, 'There'll be damages to pay. I've called the police. They'll be detained at port.'

'You got a brig on board?' said Don with a smile spreading on his face as if he'd won the Euromillions jackpot. The officer nodded and the Red-Ties volunteered themselves to herd the football fans below decks. It was a task made easier by the threat of extreme violence and Ginger's towering stature, making every man in a football top a spiritual prisoner, long before being pushed into a storage hold.

Once done, Don and the Red-Ties filled their bellies with all they could eat from the captain's table and drank the cool lager that their hangovers had been missing. At Harwich, the Captain wanted to turn the ship around as soon as possible, so they were again asked to help with the football fans. This time, to take them to the police who'd soon be arriving at the dock. Don enjoyed the task, and during the escort off the ship, he broke the jaw of one of their prisoners for the crime of, 'Looking at him funny and mumbling.'

It was their ring leader's face he hit. One that'd already been shattered by Ginger. 'There you go matey, given ya something to mumble about,' he told him, but even Phil winced at the sound of the jaw's destruction.

When the police met them on the quayside, it seemed pretty evident that their instincts were to arrest the Red-Ties and not bother about the men in torn football shirts, which was a cue for all except Jamie and Don to fade away and get to the minibus on the car deck. One of the cops glared at Don suspiciously and asked, 'Can I see your passport, please?'

Don's jacket had been ripped by Phil during the fight, and his fake passport had fallen out, so he decided to bluff, 'Lost it in the punch-up. One of these pricks will have nicked it.'

He rolled up the sleeve of his t-shirt and said, 'English mate, Look English.'

The captain, already charmed by Don over breakfast, spoke on his behalf, 'Not him,' he said, then pointing at the football supporters, 'Those men. Those are the ones who assaulted my staff.' Don smirked and stayed quiet.
'This man,' indicating Don, 'Kindly assisted my staff and was assaulted by them.' Obviously reluctant, a cop asked, 'Do you want to press charges, sir?'
Don laughed, 'No mate, wanna get home. It's all been very upsetting.'

As the police began handcuffing the football fans, Don nodded to Jamie, and they tried to saunter away quietly, but a cop called them back to make statements. What followed was an endless series of private conversations between various members of the ship's crew and border agency staff. All of which made Don increasingly impatient. Finally, they took note of Jamie's passport and let the pair walk off to enter England across the tarmac and past the vehicle exits. Escorted by four police officers and a border agent, they reached the final gate just as the minibus came off the ship's ramp. After a few dry-mouthed seconds, Jamie passed through without issue and disappeared, citing an urgent need to find a toilet.
Only the lads in the minibus noticed the ship's purser running along their queue of traffic towards Don. He thought he was helping return a lost passport to the man who had assisted their security, but as he handed it over one of the cops who said, 'English is it?'

Don was taken away for questioning. Glancing backwards Jamie panicked. Barely able to control the urge to run he kept walking until he cleared of the port. Unsure whether the other Red-Ties had been stopped, and in a haste to see his mum, he stuck out a hitchhiker's thumb and was almost immediately picked by a fish-lorry heading north to Aberdeen.

Chapter 31 - Trade Competitors.

At London Bridge, two men waited on a jetty for a boat. Although they worked in the same industry, at the same level, on the same project, they couldn't be any more different.

'You know you look like a 1970s porn star, right?' said Smith in a grumpy tone. Angel chuckled, 'What is wrong with my clothes?'

Since meeting in Westminster, he'd been able to change from his company-appropriate attire back into his familiar jeans, cowboy boots, bright parrot shirt.

They saw Matty sitting at the stern of a River Taxi and boarded. The soldier looked out of place amongst the commuters; he was wearing a Chelsea top and looked the embodiment of a grumpy old tourist lost in London. They kept quiet until the boat pulled away from the pier, but once chopping through the waves Smith leaned over and whispered out of the side of his mouth, 'Event is confirmed. I've got the marketing plan.'

'What the fuck are ya on about, ya dozy Rupert?' barked Matty. Watch too much TV!'

The hood for hire turned to Angel to apologise, 'Sorry, but looks like it's gotta be.'

The Spaniard replied, 'She got close enough to plant electronics, so I fucked up.'

'Yes, you did,' Smith added as thin sprays of horizontal rain lashed his face.

Matty growled, 'Spare us. Like it don't happen to you masters of dysfunction every day.'

Smith smirked, 'You'll need to keep me regularly and closely informed of outcomes.'

'Yer good luck with that. Need-to-know innit,' Matty told him and winked at Angel saying, 'I report to the monkey grinder, not the organs. And we are off after this shit.'

Smith retorted in a petulant tone, 'I have the authority to oversee anything related to Crow.'

'Alright,' snapped Matty, 'Come with us? Stand next to me if ya want?'

Smith shook his head and edged a memory stick he concealed in his hand towards Matty. 'Oh, for fucks sake. Just give me the fucking thing?' Matty snatched it and stuck it in his shoe. Smiling at Angel he said, 'Bit of a cock with real humans, ain't he?'

The river taxi pulled into its next dock, and the three of them waited for passengers to get on and off before starting up their conversation again.

Smith explained, 'The handbook for the system is on the stick. But it's quite simple. You just plug it into a laptop, and it will do everything automatically. You will see everything, your phone, their phone, anyone that Crow has called or texted. It will look for other phones in his vicinity; it even lets you see deleted messages or any GCHQ recordings linked to it.'

Matty replied, 'I just need to find where he is hiding.'

Smith became agitated, 'And how long will this take you?'

Matty told him, 'I'll call who I usually call. Next one's your stop, Rupert.'

Smith's face twitched with anger when he heard the term of abuse and stood up to say, 'You don't have to speak to me like that. Keep me informed. I am still in charge.'

Matty snarled, 'Yer whatever, Rupert! I've known you since before you lost your bits in Afghan. To you, we will always be servants. You meddle in plans and fuck them up. Yer, your type are just as likely to send us off to collect your laundry as do a hit.'

There was silence after that until Smith walked down the gangplank and off the boat. Angel lit a cigarette and Matty snarled, 'At least in the mafia, bosses sometimes treat you well. But this lot, they'd talk bollocks about patriotism, then slip me basic pay with stoppages if I let them. They need to be kept in line from time to time about pay and conditions.'

'We pay you?' Angel said, 'The arrangement is okay, no?'

'Actually Mate, the payments side of things is a grey area that no one needs to talk about. Technically we still work for Smith's lot, and now and then we're let off our chain and told who to savage. I try not to intellectualise it. Points to note. Fuck him and the horse he rode in on.'

Then Matty took the cigarette from Angel's grasp and flicked it over the side, 'It's no smoking on the boat. For fuck's sake, you're sitting next to the sign.'

Angel groaned, 'You're not making this day fun at all are you.'

Matty gave Angel a friendly pat on his shoulder, and told him,

'For what it's worth, I argued against doing this. It all seems a bit unnecessary. But no choice. They'll have people watching us.'

'So where am I going now?'

'Well, the plan is that you're nicked, and you're meant to be taken to an American black site. Smith says you are to be marked down as a rogue and disappear, as far as MI-5 is concerned.'

Angel lit another cigarette and said, 'I wish it'd turned out different.'

Matty shrugged, 'Me too, but it is what it is.'

At the next port for the River Taxi, just as the vessel pulled away from the pier, Angel elbowed Matty in the face and leapt ashore to run for all he was worth.

***

Angel was in flight. He'd booked into a hotel, left through the room's window, and caught a taxi. Then he repeated the process several times with a credit card, at several locations before calling Tanya to say, 'Sorry, I just wanted to say goodbye. I have to go. I don't know when I will be back.'

'What? What is going on?' she asked him, 'Are you in trouble?'

'I'm leaving' he told her, 'I have to pick up something from my flat first.'

Tanya's sounded alarmed, 'Not home. That's the first place people will look for you. I'm sailing in Hamble. Come and see me. We can meet for a drink and talk options?'

Angel refused, 'I am sorry. I just can't. I will miss you. Goodbye.'

'Wait. Wait. Listen, I want to see you!' she demanded.

Her words sounded shrill at first, then soothing, 'Maybe we can go together. I have a friend sailing to Vigo in a few days. I'm owed holiday, and my project has just finished. So hey, we can go together? And if you need something from your flat, I'll go?'

'I don't know. I'm sorry. Erm, you meant a lot to me,' he told her.

'Meant? What do you mean meant past tense? Tell you what, you decide. I'll text you an address. I'm house-sitting for a friend, and when she gets back, we can go to Spain.' She now sounded upbeat as if discussing a party, 'It'll be fun! C'mon?'

'I don't know Tanya. I have to go now?'

219

'Okay, I care about you and think about it; if you're in trouble with the police, you won't need to show your passport. We could drop you off on a beach?'

'I have to go, bye,' and Angel hung up, but four hours later, he texted Tanya from a Yachtie pub on the Solent, 'Does your offer still stand?'

She called back, he told her where he was, and she raced to meet him, arriving breathless. Tenderly caressing his shoulder she said, 'Together, we are in this together.' As the sun began setting, Tanya and Angel ambled down a cobble-stone lane to a small cottage on the outside of the village. It was a traditional fisherman's home of low wooden beams and thick stonework. Inside, it had plain walls and a sparse array of sofas, as if whoever owned it hadn't finished moving in furniture.

Suddenly she was perky and suggested, 'I'll make supper.'

Half an hour later, he was drinking gin and feeding on some pizzas she'd thrown in the oven. He told her, 'I do like you, y'know!'

'You sure? You look bored, You want to sleep, instead of fucking me,' she said giggling.

'No, I want you,' he mumbled.

'The last time you did me, but now, I think I'll do you,' she told him, 'You'll like that?'

'Yes,' he replied, sluggishly leaning over to kiss her.

She moved away before his lips reached her and said, 'Okay, get in the shower, hurry,' and Angel groggily walked to the bathroom.

Under the sound of hot water streaming from the faucet, he thought he heard two words in Russian, 'On gatov.' It was something like, 'Are you ready?' but he couldn't remember the little he knew of that language and dismissed worrying about it as if it was a daydream. He nearly dozed off standing in the shower and had to remind himself, 'Don't quit now, nearly there.'

He was too tired, not just from the last few days but from living undercover and manipulating everyone around him. At least that's what he thought.

Outside the bathroom door, Tanya asked, 'Don't you want me?' and finally, the part of his slothful brain that wasn't an idiot, told him that he'd been drugged. With an effort to concentrate, he reached for the Ruger LCR pistol concealed in his jacket. That was the last thing he remembered.

***

Angel woke up groggy and stiff, ropes secured his wrists and ankles to her bed. He raised his head from a pillow and tried to gather his thoughts, but only saw Tanya crying. She was shaking, biting her lips, and groaning softly like a mad animal while staring into space as she paced around the room in high heels wrapped in a black silken dressing gown.

He croaked wearily, 'It's not you, it's me. Maybe take a break. Think we need space?' She turned towards him, wiped her eyes and said, 'Oh good, you're awake.'

He inhaled a deep breath, 'I've no time to give the relationship a special woman like you deserves. I know you'll find someone who'll make you happy one day.' Tanya looked puzzled, 'What are you saying?'

Angel grinned, 'I don't think our relationship is healthy and I'm maybe too young to be tied down. And besides, you're a crazy fucking bitch.'

Tanya giggled and wiggled seductively, then untied the belt of her robe to reveal the sexy outfit beneath. She wore a tiny black basque that barely held in her large breasts, stockings, and suspenders. It wasn't her neatly trimmed pussy that caught his eye though, but the Makarov fitted with a silencer in her hand. He kept his eye on it as she walked around the bed checking his restraints, but lost sight of the pistol when she leaned over him and brushed her breasts in his face while asking, 'You do like me don't you?'

Angel grunted, 'Of course, what's not to like?' Despite the situation, he was horny.

Then Tanya sat down next to begin stroking the cold metal of the barrel against his temple, and with a sad smile, she murmured, 'A clean-up team is coming.' 'Joder, not this way,' Angel joked, 'At least, let me have my last cigarette.' Then he sighed and relaxed as if accepting his fate, 'I have always known I would die like this, even as a kid. Oh well, at least I'll keep my reputation.' Tanya didn't laugh, although her words were calm, her expression screamed in panic, 'I'm ordered to kill you all, but I have missed the opportunity. If I don't, I'll be replaced.'

'You can untie me if you like. I could go talk to them for you?'

'It's too late. I am to go home for a medal.'

Mocking her, he looked down at his crotch and erect cock, to say with a wink, 'Hey, it's hard all over.'

Tanya told him, 'You better be quiet,' and buckled a ball-gag to his mouth.

As a clock tick-tocked in the background, she read texts on her phone and told him, 'They will be here soon. Five minutes.'

Angel grunted. He felt fear and anger, but also a sense of relief as he stared at the doorway through which her associates would enter. He was tired of his life, so very tired of everything. Tanya began rocking in the chair next to the bed and reciting her killer plan as if it was a memorised mantra, 'I want them to see me prepared to do my duty, I want them looking at my tits. I have a Glock pistol for this job. I have screwed in the silencer, I have checked the magazine, and I will sit next to my lover, tussling his hair until I have to pull the trigger. I am fine. I am fine.' Then more frighteningly for Angel, she asked, 'Do you care about me?'

'He nodded,' but in his head he thought, 'Why the fuck did I talk to her on the train.'

Angel heard a car pull up outside, and his face went white. Tanya's expressions cycled through a range of emotions. Tears began to well up in her eyes, her nostrils flared, her jaw clenched, and she told him smiling, 'I need you to be still. Once I shoot, I will untie you…A little!'

Then as if in a trance she told him, 'It's all your fault what I've to do.'

Bizarrely, with the pistol still on his temple, she leant towards him to stroke his cock and balls as if a tender lover.

A few minutes of waiting seemed like hours, until eventually, two severe-looking thugs in black Adidas tracksuits came through the door. One said, 'Suka, kak…?' but never finished his sentence.

Tanya's wrist swung around, but just as she squeezed the trigger, a flash-bang grenade exploded in front of them all.

Chapter 32 - New Sales Territories.

At the same time as Angel had travelled to meet Tanya, the Red-Ties met with Walker in a Harwich pub. Most of them were to return home, but he took Phil, Ginger, and Paul Gantt aside for a private conversation.

'I've spoken to Don. They got him in a sweatbox, but he smuggled himself a phone.'

'How is he?' asked Phil.

'Good news and bad news. Whatcha want first?' asked the second in command.

'Bad news,' said Phil.

'Looks like Don is off to an internment centre for illegals. Which is mad, of course.'

'What's the good news?' asked Ginger.

'Looks like Don is off to an internment centre for illegals,' he replied, laughing, 'Fuck sake, lads. We all love him to bits, but he's a hand grenade with the pin pulled. And you never know when he's gonna go off, do ya?'

There was nodding agreement as Walker continued with his briefing, 'I've brought another minibus for ya. It's nicked but don't worry, the owner isn't back from holiday for two weeks. I've also put a few presents in for you and taken out a few seats for Ginger.'

'We still doing this then?' asked Paul.

Walker ignored the question and told them, 'Crow is at Jamie's mum's, but we don't know where that is because you lost Jamie. You lot can't risk phoning anyone, so go to his town. Have a butcher's and find Crow. If you see the bad guys, have a very strong word with them.'

Phil grunted, 'I'm alright with going, but Crow needs a strong word.'

'Yer mate, I get what you're saying, but we don't got a choice. Don says he is family.'

'Anything else we should know?' asked Ginger.

'Basics are still the same; we'll all probably get gathered, the lads we are up against are a proper-proper team that are tooled-up-to-fuck and when I say we, I mean you, cause I'm not going.'

'I'm fine. With that, one less person telling me what to do,' said Phil sticking his tongue out. Walker explained, 'There will be more of them. They will be faster, stronger, fitter, better armed, better trained, and probably smarter.'

Phil, at the scent of danger, became more playful and excited. He began singing, 'We're all gonna die, we're all gonna die. We're all gonna get sliced up, we're all gonna die!'

'Not bigger cocks though?' said Ginger unzipping his jeans.

Walker growled, 'Take this seriously, for fuck's sake. Please!'

They talked for the duration of another pint, and suddenly, the ordinarily serious Paul got up from the settee where he'd been slouching and shouted, 'Less talk, more doing lads in. Leave the pints, cry England, Harry and St. George and let's fucking go! Let's go!'

He stood erect, downed his drink, then began swinging and flailing his arms. 'Let's fucking have it, let's have it.'

With a heavy sigh, Walker put his head in his hands and shook his shaven skull from side to side.

He told them, 'Listen lads, take the back roads so don't flash on any cameras and you better hand in your phones too.'

'What, how do we call anyone?' Phil complained.

'I put a few burners in the minibus, and they're just for emergencies. It's a mission. Cops have clever metadata stuff to track you. Use once and throw away. Keep changing the number plates I made up for you.'

'Bit over complicated!' suggested Phil.

'It will be fine. The plates match car sales on eBay but keep off the main roads and traffic cameras just in case.'

As they parted, Walker told them, 'Don't let Phil drink all the money. The clock is ticking. Try to be back by Friday night. Remember, whoever wants the responsibility of this going to shit can be in charge, but if you find Jamie, it's him! Cause it's his mum in the frame.'

His last advice was, 'Don't worry, you'll know what to do when you get there,' and they drove away with Phil and his fractured arm at the wheel.

Ginger declared, 'I'm gonna slap that Para when I see him.'

Communicating in grunts with his hand on the dashboard, Paul contorted his palm into shapes and held out fingers to indicate the speed and angles of junctions. That left Ginger looking backwards to confirm they weren't being followed and the duty of occasionally flicking their ears to keep them awake.

Little was said until at the border, an exasperated Phil asked, 'What fuck is Ecclesfechan?'

'Why can't they write fucking English on the road signs,' moaned Paul who then asked, 'Why can't Crow just get the train?'

Ginger told him, 'Behave. We know our jobs. If we find Jamie, he's our local tribal guide. He'll make sure the oatmeal savages don't eat us and you can fire up your superpower.'

'What's that?'

'Inability to see reason.'

Slumping against a window, Paul looked in the wing mirror and with a yawn asked, 'Do you think any of us are coming back from this?'

'We are,' snarled Phil, 'I dunno about Crow, though.'

'No prisoners?' asked Ginger.

'No prisoners!' yelled Phil and Paul in chorus.

Suddenly motivated, they began screaming at drivers who were not excessively fast in the slow country lanes, and the mood in the vehicle changed into impatient aggression as if on a trip to Watford. Each manoeuvre became a concern as Phil drove on pure instinct without attention to his mirrors or any page of the highway code.

'We need more fags,' said Ginger from the back, 'Before Phil kills us.'

As they approached the town of Irvine, they stopped at a supermarket to fill the minibus with petrol and shopping bags with, hot pies, cooked chicken, potato wedges, and smoothies. Then they stopped again for fish and chips in the town of Gourock because Ginger complained, 'I'm still hungry.'

On the boat over to Argyll, they switched drivers. Paul took the wheel, and Phil finally fell asleep snoring at Ginger's feet in the rear.

Once off the Clyde ferry, they parked at an old people's home next to a police station, and the giant joined Phil snoring while Paul wandered off to do some reconnaissance.

***

An hour later; Paul left Ginger snoring and led Phil to a grubby dive bar in town. The pub's low roof and heavily stained floor presented itself as a ship's hold with flaking paint and random nautical bric-a-brac on the walls. It seemed whoever installed the décor, did so with a Pirate fetish in mind, but it was their kind of pub. It had sturdy barrels for tables that couldn't be broken in fights and thick ropes anchored to the walls to guide the drunkenly unsteady to the toilet. Paul had already sniffed out the criminals in the town and was now negotiating with a rat-like teenager in a Manchester United top for the contents of a cheap nylon sports bag. Phil ignored the local thief as if the vermin was beneath contempt, and he couldn't bring himself to recognise the rat's existence.

'Open it up, Mush,' ordered Paul.

'It's all there! Eight hundred,' the rat hissed.

His reply was quiet and matter-of-fact, 'Open the bag or I'll open your fucking head.'

The rat tugged at the zip to reveal a camera, a long zoom lens and a bag of cables and plastic boxes as Paul opined, 'So you think this is eight hundred quid?'

Without waiting for an answer, he shifted in his seat to pull out a roll of bank notes. He grabbed the thief's arm, slapped two hundred in cash on his palm and told him, 'That's your lot. Now fuck off, before I tell your ma you're wearing her earrings.'

Paul snarled, and the rat left in a hurry.

'What do we need that for?' asked Phil.

'Jamie told me last night that all this was because Crow nicked a memory card from a camera, so I got one so we can see stuff.'

Phil grunted, 'That's wasting beer money. You can put them in any PC.'

Then the pair shifted seats to sit against a wall with their backs angled to keep an eye on the door as well as street activity through a dirty window. Phil liked the place, it smelled of stale beer and it had a slight tang of weed blowing through vents from the beer garden. It took him only a minute to analyse the pub's clientele who were mostly slumped on bar stools, facing an abyss of boredom that was their typical afternoon. It was obvious that the other clientele in the pub were forestry workers with chainsaws at their feet, a postman, and a man who was probably the local heroin addict.

The locals sat in a row but weren't drinking together, it was more like they happened to be there at the same time, trying not to notice each other or be drawn into any conversations except when they stumbled outside for a smoke. The big berserker was happy about the scene and commented, 'My natural habitat, this place,' as he farted out the smell of a dead horse.

'You are an animal Phil,' complained Paul who moved under a fake porthole for some fresher air.

He was about to begin a lecture about why he thought everyone was over thinking what they had to do when a new stranger walked into the bar and began grinning at them. The man then walked up to the Jukebox, selected 1-3-4 for THE CURE's 'Love-Cats,' and bounced off to the bar, still looking over his shoulder at them with an inane smile on his face.

Phil and Paul didn't know what to make of it as he spun around three times and squeezed into a space in the line of men at the bar.

'Hello Agnes,' he shouted slightly loudly, disturbing the communal depressed silence.

'What you want doll?' she replied.

'Lager,' he answered, 'What about you, Lachlann?'

'Lager.'

'Lachlann?' he asked, working his way down the line.

'Lager.'

'Lachlann?'

'Lager,' another replied.

'Lachlann?'

'Lager,' they all rocked backwards on their barstools. Looking around each other's faces, realising for the first time that they were all a Lachlann.

'Lachlann?'

'I am not a name. I am a number,' the last one bellowed.

'Lager for number 6 then, please Agnes.'

With the pints pulled, they turned back to staring at the gantry and occasional glances at each other's newspapers, as that was about as sociable as the Uigskibar Pub got.

The strange man took his pint, and sat next to the Red-Tie tourists, asking, 'How?'

'Who the fuck are you?' barked Phil in reply.

'Oh, fuck me! an English, we better be aff tae find a translator.'

The Red-Ties stood up in anger, but just in time, the man told them, 'Jamie sent me.'

Twenty minutes later, three Red-Ties were bouncing along a winding loch-side road with the Lachlann leading the way in an old Humber Sceptre. They'd started the journey with their guide explaining, 'It's only twenty minutes away,' then speeding off out of the town, into the country. Braking hard right at a lonely petrol station, Lachlann raced along a tight winding road that hugged a hillside's contours.

Following behind Paul struggled to keep the vehicle between the ditches as he jerked the steering around unfamiliar corners.

He mumbled, 'I tell you what is good, haven't seen a single cop. Do we phone anybody?'

'Nah no need,' replied Ginger as the minibus swerved for a dog walker.

Phil's head clattered off the window he was leaning on, 'You still learning to drive?'

'Where is this mum's house then? Where are we going?' asked Ginger, 'Cause y'know we are just following a random fekkin' stranger into a trap. Right?'

'Yer. So what?' said Phil, 'It's what I live for!'

Ginger growled, 'I don't trust this Jock.'

Paul added, 'Yer, might be a trap.'

As they drove past a church, their guide slowed down to the speed limit then suddenly turned off the road and up a sloping driveway to what looked like a disused pub, the Red-Ties followed.

When they clambered out of the minibus, Lachlann explained in his peculiar dialect, 'Aye well, there's a car ootside his hoose. I don't recognise it. So youz betta stay here 'till I check it oot. A'right? Place is closed anyways, so chust hide roon the back fir noo.'

Ginger grunted, 'Stay,' and grabbed Lachlann's shoulder.

Phil went to a large, padlocked door and began kicking it while saying to the team, 'The sweaty is right. Hide here till we suss it out.

'F'sake Phil, could you be any more noisy!' said Paul walking to the rear of the building and a minute later, he opened the door from inside to declare, 'Security's shit! Alarms are off.'

They followed him inside and made for the front of the building where there were windows overlooking the nearby houses. Paul was the first to peer out from behind heavy tartan curtains. He laughed and told them, 'Oi lads, there's a car alright. I knows who it is.'

Ginger sang out, 'Jamie's in trouble, Jamie's in trouble!'

Phil had a look around the corner and sniggered,

'Ah! Mary drives an Audi-TT, don't she?'

At Lachlann's suggestion, they took the back way to Jamie's house along a drainage ditch on the hillside. Phil moaned every step of the way as they stumbled through the bracken. It was so rural, with only about thirty houses per mile, that they didn't think anyone would notice them even if they'd walked along the main road, but Lachlann insisted and told them, 'You brought a giant with you. That kinda gets noticed.'

Chapter 33 - Setting Limits.

Paddy called Ken to report, 'The lads you wanted me to watch have arrived.'

'Have they spotted you?'

'Nah, they've parked up down the road at a pub and not come down to the cottage yet.'

'Any other changes? How does the situation look to you?' he asked.

'No movement until now, it's been so quiet that Petra went to the garage for le casse-croûte.'

'What about phone calls?'

'Nope, not once. I used the laptop you gave me. Nobody has any digital stuff in there, at all.'

'Have you managed to put up any more cameras?'

Paddy replied, stifling a yawn, 'No. It was too risky, but they've not been out of our sight. Mostly they've been sat in the porch drinking tea.'

'Okay,' Ken told him, 'New orders. I need you earning your pay today.'

'What am I doing?'

'First, I want to know how you are feeling. If you are okay?'

The ex-soldier replied in typical good humour, 'I'll sleep when I'm dead.'

'Thank you,' the old spy told him. Both pleased and impressed by his new hire. Ken then explained his plan, 'Now that they are in the area, I need them to stay put.'

'I can try, but have you read the file on their giant? I'd have to hit him on the head with a tank battalion to even slow him down,' he replied while reaching for a meat pie.

'I don't mean physically. Just convince them it'd be stupid to leave.'

'Yer, fair enough. Have you got any ideas?'

Ken did. It was a horrible idea, but Paddy agreed and once parked at the cottage he declared, 'In position,' unlocked another phone and texted what the old spy had told him to say, 'Still looking for cat. GPS not working.'

Ken replied 'Okay. Good luck. Don't oversell it.'

'Oh fuck. They're all at the cottage. I'm spotted. Wait Out,' he said and threw the phone he was talking on over the sea wall into the loch. Clambering out of his car, Paddy saw the woman he'd been watching step out of the porch and stare straight at him. He didn't have time to assess whether she seemed surprised or not, because suddenly from behind the cottage, two large men and the giant appeared.

Walking towards him, the first one came with a friendly welcome in his eyes. He was limping slightly and scratching under a plaster cast on his arm.

Paddy calmly played his part acting dumb as he held up Crow's picture to ask, 'I'm looking for...' but never finished the sentence.

The first man-made a half-hearted effort to distract him by chatting about the weather and moving to his left. The giant stepped to his right to grab him by the collar of his jacket, while the third gracefully slip-stepped between his partners and hit Paddy with an eight-punch combination to his torso.

Winded and gasping for air, his pride made him struggle out of the giant's grip, but he felt as much use as a salmon launching an attack on a grizzly bear feeding in a stream. It was no surprise when the giant slapped him with a paw to his shoulder and lifted him in the air.

Paddy hung there for a second on the end of two massive arms, then he was slammed down onto his car's roof. He felt his brain flicker in and out of consciousness, then heard the giant bellow, 'IPPON! That's judo, that is!'

The one he knew as Paul yelled,' Don't break him. We need him. Get him inside!' and the doorman with plaster cast added, 'Take him back to the pub.'

***

Ginger didn't fancy trudging up the hill and through the undergrowth again. Instead, he bounded up the driveway in his size thirteen trainers to greet Maria.

'Alright, my lovely. Fancy meeting you here.'

'Hello Meester Giant, so happy to see you. Can you help search his car?'

'Yer, course,' he replied, 'Good idea.'

Lachlann, who'd arrived with them but kept away from the fight, jumped into Paddy's car and crawled it in first gear into the cottage's garage. Being a petrol-head by nature, he couldn't resist exploring the controls, pressing buttons on the dashboard and declaring,

'Radio doesn't work.'

'What are we looking for,' asked Ginger.

'There are usually secret compartments,' she replied, and the three began looking with Ginger tearing all the plastic fittings off the interior.

Lachlann was excited, 'What? What are you lot into?'

Ginger replied for her, 'We is looking after Jamie innit,' then he began pulling the car apart while Lachlann was bounced around inside.

Within minutes, and without use of a spanner, they found a storage unit that contained, amongst other things, a laptop and a pistol.

Sometime later Jamie came outside looking for Maria and was surprised to find Ginger in his mum's garage, deadlifting the front end of a car. Confused he greeted his colleague with,

'Ginger, when d'you get here? Where's Maria?'

'Oi. Mate. She's fine. Went with your mate Lachlann. How come she's here?'

'She was worried about me. Didn't know I'd gone to see Don. So, she phoned my mum.'

'Oh, you didn't tell her you was in Spain?' Ginger asked shaking his head.

Jamie looked embarrassed, 'I couldn't get a hold of her. I only knew the house phone.'

'She's pissed off at you, ain't she?'

'No! No. She was concerned. Anyway, where did she go?'

'Something about the laptop we found. There was a wrong'un outside your gaff. This is his car. We got it here for safekeeping.'

'Wrong'un. Who you got, a neighbour?' asked Jamie, worried.

'Course he is,' grunted Ginger as he slammed the car up and down, 'Phil's just having a gentle word...You training?'

'Having a word? Fuck no. Where?' he whined, 'They can't hurt people?'

The giant dropped the vehicle's front end and grinned, 'Nah, don't worry. They are good at chats. They won't kill him. Anyway Mush, ain't you glad to see us then?'

'Well, yer...But.,' Jamie stuttered. He was completely alarmed by Ginger's nonchalant attitude, 'You sure it wasn't one of my neighbours.'

'Nah, he's an Essex boy from the sounds of him. Anyways, you joining me? I need one more set, and I can pretend I've done something today.'

The Giant only stopped lifting when Jamie asked him, 'Was he looking for Crow?' which prompted a change in attitude and a growl to say, 'Yer...him. I better say hello innit.'

Entering the cottage was a tight fit for Ginger, which he managed only by bending at the waist and twisting sideways through doors. Even hunched over, he still managed to bang his head on a light fitting and plunge the hallway into a shadowy gloom. Jamie's mum then wheeled through from the kitchen on her electric chair. She didn't seem to be too bothered by a giant in her house, and simply asked, 'Would anyone like a cuppa tea?'

'Yes please,' replied Ginger, 'I'd love one. You Jamie's mum then?'

That was when Crow emerged from the other side of the hallway. Unfortunately, he walked into Ginger, who elbowed him away with an attitude adjustment, 'Tart! I'd to drive here with Phil 'cause of you!'

There wasn't a lot of power put into the blow, but it was enough to send Crow stumbling backwards through the door and onto the floor.

'Sorry Ginger, I deserved that. Thanks for coming to get me,' Crow said sheepishly.

'Yer, well, about that,' Ginger told him, 'We ain't going nowhere yet.'

Chapter 34 - Ethical Considerations.

Paddy woke up with a slap across his face and the words, 'Alright Mush, wakey-wakey. We got some questions. And guess what, I found a blow torch in the tool shed to help ya answer.'

Tied to a chair in a cluttered pub's cellar he'd no idea how long he'd been unconscious, but he recognised the situation as well as the type of thug that was standing in front of him. It was someone just like himself, a grinning hood with not an ounce of mercy in his eyes.

As he scanned around for a way out of his predicament, a blinding arc light was switched on. Painfully, someone behind him began wrapping his mouth in duct tape, and he slowly suffocated while a voice in front suggested, 'Sack him, please.' A clear plastic bag was pulled over his head with the words 'So ya don't see our faces.'

Paddy began to panic, out of breath he groaned and whined.

The shadow in front swung a fist into his face, and told him, 'Shut up. Stop moaning,' and from behind a voice laughed, 'Use your words. Use your words, deep breaths, calming breaths Phil. Remember, if he don't wanna know, we'll cut our losses.' The thug in front replied, irritated, 'For fuck's sake. Why d'you tell him my name?' 'He knows our names. Had our police files in his car!' said his partner, who grabbed Paddy by the throat from behind to ask, 'Who are you?'

Paddy regretted that he'd only briefly glanced at their files. Petra had passed them to him in a lay-by and said, 'These are his known associates.' At the time, he'd dismissed the dossier as too big to read and mused that it was just in the movies that agents remembered everything in a file that they'd only seen for a short time. Knuckle-draggers like them should never have found the documents, and because they had, it meant that they'd found everything else. And that was a problem. Strangely, the idea that things had gone badly wrong was comforting.

In his experience, things always went badly wrong. The whole job was making decisions without proper information and making mistakes on a conveyor belt of improvisation. Real work was about having fuckups and correcting them slightly faster than a target made and corrected theirs. He couldn't say anything coherent and muttered through the tape for them to un-gag him, but the voice behind him said, 'I think he swore, and that is so rude!'

Paddy fought to breathe, and while he bucked and struggled against his bonds, the thug in front of him turned his back and declared, 'I'm not loving this. I'm not feeling woke yet?'

'That's not what woke means,' replied his partner.

Paddy was about to black out again, but just in time, his captors pushed a hole through the tape with a biro and one purred in a soft, conciliatory voice, 'There all better.'

'It's interesting stuff in your car, mate,' said the other.

He shook his head and then nodded, still sucking desperately for air.

A voice whispered in his ear, 'Can't hear you. Please answer the question. Do that?'

The bigger man asked, 'Would you like a smoke mate?' and he lit fag and stuffed it through the hole, forcing Paddy to inhale for a few seconds. Seconds later, a shadow screamed, 'Prisoners don't smoke,' then slapped his jaw making the cigarette fly away.

'That wasn't nice, Phil,' said his partner, 'Think of his human rights.'

'Don't give a fuck, he's only the right to find a solution we can all live with. If he don't, he's gonna end up in a scrap yard car crusher the size of a loaf of bread!'

Another punch arrived, followed by a knee to his chest. Each would have sent him flying backwards, if not for the man behind him, holding him in place. Ironically, he was ready to confess, yet the men holding him were not letting him speak. It was completely mad. He was supposed to be beaten, act afraid and then start talking. His last thought before passing out again, was that it didn't feel like the start of a typical good cop-bad cop routine. To Paddy, as he was knocked unconscious, it was two very bad cops.

The next time he woke, he was ungagged and pleaded in character, 'Let me go. Why have you done this? Untie me! Please!'

The man called Phil, slapped him on the head and said, 'I don't like cops.'

Paddy whined and pretended to be more afraid than he was. He wanted to explain to him that he and his mates, were just a bunch of idiot doormen with a million ways to lose if they went against the intelligence services, but Ken had advised him to keep it simple.

To be plausible, he knew he'd have to resist, at least for a while. His orders were to drip-feed the idea that, 'Cops were watching every road in the area.'

It never occurred to him that the thug in front of him was also acting a role, one for which his previous resistance to interrogation training, had not prepared him.

Paddy pleaded, 'No point asking me anything. I don't know anything.'

The shadow chuckled, 'If ya don't knows nuffink. We can't make a deal, so we can just cut your throat and leave. Right?'

Paddy reminded himself that the doorman in front of him was as thick as paint, and his defiant pride caught up with him.

He yelled, 'You're in a lot of trouble. Just turn yourself in.'

'Why? We read the texts,' replied the voice behind him, 'Looks like you're on your own.'

Paddy feigned fear and surprise, 'They know where I am. I've called in.'

'Ah, that would be a lie. Hit him please.'

'With this?' his partner replied, holding up a sledgehammer,

'I could learn to golf, innit.'

'Nah, not yet. If he doesn't talk, then you can play?'

Once again Paddy's mouth was wrapped in duct tape and another hole was punched through to let him breathe. Still blinded by the bright white bulbs, a voice whispered in Paddy's ear, 'It's all very stressful. I am having a bit of a mental breakdown at the moment. It would help if you told me your name, please. Pretty please with sugar on top!'

Paddy was still baffled as to why they asked the question while his mouth was taped, more so as they'd already had his wallet and ID.

'Why are you following Crow? I mean, when we got up this morning, we thought we were looking for our mate. But nope, you put us straight. Looks like you who wants him.'

'You cleared that up. We feel very foolish, don't we,' said the man at his back.

'Where are the rest of you?' asked the big shadow, who dropped the hammer on his thigh. As he made a muffled scream, the voice asked in a dulcet sing-song tone, 'Hiya sweetie do I have your attention now?'

Paddy nodded in pain and breathed rapidly in and out through his blowhole. The other man leaned over him and barked, 'You is with the Federales. You has got badges. Badges, badges we don't need no stinking badges here!'

'Can we torture him,' asked the bigger man. Then shaking his head madly, he replied to his own question in soft murmurs as if a patient hearing voices, 'No, you can't! Haven't time!' The same man feigned a sulky tone and asked, 'And later? Can we torture him?'

Paddy, gulped in real fear as the voice again yelled like he was out of meds, 'No, you fucking can't, you lunatic. Not until he tells us something.'

Then he began licking his face and asked, 'We thinks you are a ninja and trained to show no emotion. Mary says you're a grey man or something.'

Tapping Paddy's shins, using the sledgehammer like a croquet mallet, he asked, 'Does he have any rights!' and with each stroke, he sang, 'Human rights, human rights.'

The voice behind him reached over his shoulder, put his finger to the hole in the duct tape and said, 'Shhhh. Señor Badges. Imagine a logo on goods that said that a country of origin complied with the Universal Charter on Human Rights. You know free elections, votes for women, not being tortured for politics or unions?'

Paddy closed his eyes against the glare, anything he had assumed was unravelling. They weren't acting like interrogators, it was insane.

'Explain human rights to Señor Badges, please,' asked the man behind.

Then Paddy felt a fist crack his jaw while the hitter explained, 'Imagine that sanctions do not work. And evil dictators still send their wives to Geneva to shop, while the peasants die of hunger and lack of proper medicine. Can you imagine?'

This time Paddy grunted, and he nodded his head vigorously.

The man behind him began humming a John Lennon song while his colleague suggested with a laugh, 'Imagine that instead of changing packaging every month for Christmas, Easter, World cups and Mother's Day, manufacturers added something else to their packaging. We could have a free trade logo on the packaging to show what products came from nice places.'

Weirdly, as if forgetting about their prisoner they began discussing world trade, 'Without the logo, naughty dictators would have a slow erosion of their profits because people buy the nice chocolates instead of the mean ones?'

'I'd buy that chocolate bar, mate?' said the voice behind, now tapping lightly on his air hole.

'Thank you, but suppose it was more expensive.'

'I'd still buy it because I'm a nice person. I care about other people's human rights.'

'Pinkie Swear?' asked the voice behind.

'Yes, I pinkie swear,' he replied, leaning across Paddy to curl a finger.

'That's right, and we wouldn't need sanctions, as the profit motive pushed behaviours.'

'I totally agree. What about you, fuckwit? Would you buy that chocolate?'

Paddy nodded, but the shadow to his front dropped the hammer on his knee, yelling, 'Liar!'

He still couldn't speak. He just closed his eyes with his face twisting into fear. The voice behind him snarled, 'Phil! He won't engage in a meaningful way. Do something!' His partner replied, 'We don't need to talk to him. He won't anyway.'

'If he won't tell us it. Just kill him and dump him at sea. Loads of boats around here to nick. Mary said that if we couldn't get him to talk within an hour. To give up.' The shadow chose that moment to sit on his lap, 'Hiya, can I be your friend? And, I promise if you tell us stuff, we'll only torture you a little.'

For twenty minutes, the pair carried on with insane, stupid questions and repeated, 'Why are you following Crow? Why are you following Crow? But still, they did not remove the gag, no matter how Paddy tried to mumble sentences in answer. It dawned on him that his captors were either mad or high on something, maybe both. 'Do you want to play?' the bigger man asked, 'Are you some special forces lad? Go on, tell us! Because like, you know, you're in a cellar, and nobody can hear ya scream.'

Paddy shook his head in disbelief as the man licked his face again.

The doorman standing next to the light, hissed into his other ear to whisper, 'You want to arrest us and steal our nice things?'

Paddy's eyes were now full of fear as an adrenalin dump drained his body of strength. 'We are going to play a game,' said the voice behind him, 'Nod once for yes and shake your head and whimper for no, no, no. Please, God, no! for no. But we want a real story. Where are the other bad guys?'

'We want to know everything,' stated his partner.

Paddy just wanted to speak but one of them kept telling him, 'Tell us, we'll let you go.' The other one repeated, 'We won't let ya go. We won't let you go.'

Paddy was relieved when they finally tore off his gag but then panicked as they fired up a small blowtorch, 'Tell ya what, we'll give you one last chance to answer questions. If you still can't be bothered to be nice, I'm going to burn off your cock.' The tape was ripped off his mouth and he responded by shaking his head vigorously from side to side while trying to tell them, 'Just stop! I'll tell you anything you want to know!'

'It's a shame you wouldn't talk,' said the man with the torch.

'Shame,' the voice behind him replied, 'I guess he is useless.'

'I'll talk. I'll tell you everything,' he squealed, hoping to keep to Ken's plan.

That was when Maria stepped in to say, 'Everything? You'll tell us everything.'

Her interrogation was at a different pace, she spoke with a calm, sweet voice and her pistol pressed against his forehead. She promised to,

'I pull the trigger if you hesitate to answer.'

Then she asked, 'Go on, tell us how many in your team watching the roads. You've twenty seconds,' and in a space of two seconds, she counted down to fourteen.'

'Three!' he replied, and Paddy began to spill his knowledge in a hurry.

The Red-Ties flanked him with well-rehearsed menace and each new question was asked with a similar urgency before Maria rapidly moved on to a new threat and a new query. Paddy was given fewer seconds to think. Unsettled and under pressure from the new tactic, he finally broke.

His time from capture to leaking his secrets had been only forty minutes, but it had felt like hours. He was exhausted, and although he didn't mean to let anything slip from his lips. The softening up and his lack of sleep for the previous week made him blurt out mistake after mistake. Under pressure, he mixed up the details of who, what and where was being watched.

To cover up his error, he explained, 'As soon as I found you, I was to stand down and just listen into your phones.' That slip of the tongue caused him to divulge what he meant, and he told his interrogators about the spy software on his laptop and the password to open it. Too late, he realised he was a half-broken man at the nadir of a fuck-up, and he resolved that when they started the interrogation again, he'd die like a soldier and tell them nothing more. But he'd already revealed that although he knew where Crow was, Matty didn't.

Paul stayed behind to guard Paddy and everyone else gathered back at the cottage where Crow anxiously asked, 'Did he tell us anything?'
Maria nodded, 'We can't go anywhere yet, someone is watching the exits. Not your friends but it's not good for us. We need to draw them off first, and I think I know how.'
Phil grinned, 'See, I told you we wouldn't need to hurt him.'
'Oh, fuck off, don't gloat,' Crow replied.
In the porch, Maria began exploring Paddy's laptop. She said, 'Looks easy to use.'
Crow wasn't so sure, 'It's just fucking icons. Why can't they write what the buttons do?'
'It's okay.' She told him, 'I used something similar before, but mine didn't steal Wi-Fi signals from whatever had the best signal nearest to it. It's years ahead of what I used.'

Maria began typing a number, and suddenly a map appeared with the laptop tracing a phone. She continued to click buttons, but within a minute there were tens, then hundreds of icons flooding the screen. It was as if a virus had taken over the map of the UK. Then the laptop crashed, and Maria declared, 'We need to go back and talk to him.'
Crow grumbled, 'Fucking hell, it just gets worse.'

As they got up to go back to the former pub, Jamie's mum battered through the storm doors of the porch to scold her guests. 'How about someone tells me what's going on?'

Crow tried to say, 'Mrs C, it's...'

She shook her head and cut him off by saying, 'It's all very nice having my son and Ginger making bread as a wee distraction, but I wasn't born yesterday.'

Then she flicked a button on her wheelchair, zoomed forward to look Maria in the eyes and say, 'You do know I can see out my window, so, if no one minds, I'd like to meet everybody that's been tramping through my garden. Including the man that Ginger threw into the air.

Chapter 35 - Resource Planning.

Fifteen minutes later, Paul was making tea in the kitchen while Ginger was squeezing Paddy into the half-space next to him on the living room sofa. Mrs. C struggled with her wheelchair's brake and Phil stood up to help her. He was waved away by Maria, who said, 'We don't do that. Jamie's mum likes to do things herself.' For a moment the room was silent until Mrs. C. declared, 'You know, I wasn't always like this. I was brought up by my uncles, who didn't know what to do with a wee girl. They'd all been to war and couldn't settle down after that, so my earliest memories are of cleaning firearms at our kitchen table and chats like the one we are about to have.' In a gentle tone she explained, 'And just so as you know, my uncles would make you wanna-be gangsters look like Teddy-bears. So, who wants to bring me up to date?'

It was Ginger who explained, no one else seemed willing.

'Well, Mrs C, it's like this. Matey-boy here belongs to some kinda government agency. Unless we can take Crow somewhere safe and hide him, he's dead.'

Phil chimed in with his take, 'All Crow's fault. He took a job to hit someone. And being a thicky squaddie, didn't know that hitmen pretty much get hit by their employers after a job.'

Ginger nodded and continued, 'Yer and we don't know exactly how many are after him, but it looks like it'll be the lads he used to work with. And we can't go anywhere yet because somebody is watching the roads. So, we're a bit stuffed. Only good thing today is that Mary thinks we can track a phone call or two and find out who is watching for us.'

Mrs C replied calmly, 'Oh well,' as if it was nothing out of the ordinary for her. That's when she surprised them once again by wheeling towards Paddy and accidentally smashing into his already damaged legs, 'You know something, don't you?'

Paddy whined in pain, 'I'm just a spotter.'

Mrs C replied, 'You're a bit more than that, aren't you dear? Tell me something new?'

He said, 'I don't know. I don't even know where my people are. And I don't kill people!'

Flicking a switch on her chair, she rolled back a few inches and told him, 'Well that I don't believe. You smell of death. You and Sean could be two peas in a pod.

To me, you look like a nasty little order follower. So, tell me what you know, or I'll ask young Ginger to pull your head off. And trust me, neck breaks aren't much fun.'

Maria reinforced the threat by pulling open the lapel of her jacket to reveal a pistol.

Jamie smiled at her, 'A gun...I knew it.'

'You should marry her!' said Phil, 'I mean, how the fuck did ya pull her?'

Jamie's mum tutted and said, 'Stop that Phillip, or you can go outside.'

Maria told him, 'Is not a gun Cariño, it is a revolver,' then looking at Paddy, she counted, 'Five...four....'

'I don't know where they are!' Paddy blurted out, 'There are just three of us watching you. I don't know who is coming. I got sent here to watch. That's it.'

Crow asked, 'So how do you stay in contact?'

Paddy hesitated as if lying, 'We're using burners. I use it once and dispose of it. I don't even know my boss's number, only he has the full list. So, I can't track anybody for you.'

'Prove it, track your phone,' Mrs C said, as an order, 'Show Maria who you've called.'

He typed in a number the same way Maria had, then added, 'TRACEX before clicking a blue icon and declaring, 'See! Anyway they won't be where they last called from. That's basics.'

She told him, 'Thank you,' and took back the laptop and said, 'I've an idea.'

Crow whined, 'Hey, guys. Let's just run! We could...'

Ginger didn't let him finish and roared over the top of him, 'Mush, everyone is in the frame because of you. So, everyone gets an opinion, apart from you. Is that alright? Yer?' then in a tone that told the other Red-Ties in the room that he was grumpy and that they should listen to Maria, he said,

'Alright, Mary-doll, what do you think?'

To punctuate his point, the giant slid his massive arm around Paddy's neck and slowly applied pressure like an anaconda until the agent passed out.

Then he shrugged his shoulders and told everyone, 'Well, can't have him listening in?'

Once Paddy had been tied up and dumped in the cottage's scullery, Maria presented her proposal. She made it sound like their only choice and led with the words, 'Crow is bait! Without time for a good plan, we need agree an Okay-now plan.'

'What we doing then?' asked Phil.

Maria's idea was to draw in those hunting Crow to one place, while everyone else sneaked away. But the way she talked, it seemed to be only Maria who was taking any risks. When she suggested to the Red-Ties, 'You need to stay out of this. It's dangerous,' they started laughing. Ginger almost choked on his tea, and he told her, 'Mary, ya don't understand. We live for this sorta craic! Okay, it would've been nice if Crow wasn't an idiot. And yer, we didn't want to come. But now that we is here, there's no way we'll let some squaddies stand over us and give it the big un.'

Paul grimly declared, 'I won't have anybody looking for me. Better to take them now than sleep with one eye open.'

Phil then proposed a revised, riskier plan, 'We got our own tools and there's a plant-hire place up the road. Funnily enough, Ginger here steals diggers for a living. We can use one to ram them if they turn up. Like Don told us, be flexible. Use landscape and whatnot.'

Paul smiled, 'Yer, that's right. Flexible and whatnot! I'm fine with lots of whatnots.'

Jamie's input was, 'We make it messy. Very messy!'

Everyone had a say, even Jamie's mum who said, 'Now the place up the road where Lachlann is working. It has a Gaelic name. Guess what it means in English?'

When she explained the word Ardentinny, it gave them a wonderfully terrible idea. One that needed a few more people involved. Maria drove into town for some supplies that she'd insisted they needed. Her shopping list included the kind of glass globes that a gardener used to slowly water their plants, and as many fish suppers as she could buy from the chip shops in town. Jamie and Lachlann took Crow three miles north to contact his old comrades. There he made a panicked phone call to a former comrade in the Parachute regiment.

It was part of their planned ruse, but when they arrived back, Crow was still anxious and holding his head in despair, 'He's gone full-on mental straight Jacket!

'Listen, it'll work, I know this place more than you!' replied Jamie.

Phil who was lounging in the porch asked, 'What's up? You flapping again?'

'I'm not flapping, Cunt,' replied Crow, 'I just don't believe Paddy's story about anybody watching us, if they were, Matty would be here already. We should all go now. Right now.'

Phil shook his head and slouched on the sofa, 'Not sure running works for Mrs C.'

Once Maria got back, Paul got the golf bag they'd brought from Harwich. Inside, was an odd collection of firearms that he spread out on the kitchen table. When Lachlann saw the weapons, he gasped, 'Jeez, that's five years for possession,' and stated, 'I can help a bit, but honest, this with the guns it's a bit out of my league.'

Paul nodded and told him, 'It's alright mate. We didn't bring nuff for you anyway.'

Crow muttered, 'This lot like they've been buried or stolen from an antique shop.'

'Joder,' said Maria, 'Do they even fire?'

Ginger promised, 'I checked them, but figured Crow would enjoy cleaning them.'

Paul added sarcastically, 'And maybe show us what end to point, him being a squaddie like.'

Almost simultaneously, Crow and Maria sighed as they looked at the assembled resources and Ginger pointed at the weapons to ask, 'What one do you want Mary?'

Maria grinned, 'I've my own,' she said, opening her jacket to show her .357 Ruger.

'I meant to ask about that,' mumbled Jamie, 'How come you've one already?'

'I was in the army once,' then she smiled and said, 'I still have to carry.'

'But, like a medic or something?'

Her nostrils flared, 'What do you say? Because I am a girl. Gilipollas! I was an infantry officer. We have them now in Spain. En realidad, yo era comandante a los veinte siete.'

'What? You're twenty-seven!' asked Jamie, remembering his Spanish numbers.

'Ayee...So you only hear that! That I am twenty-seven?' kissing him on the cheek.

'Well...I,' he was stuck on what to say, mumbling, 'Didn't know. You look younger.'

The atmosphere was more like they were preparing for a church picnic than conflict, but Crow did his best to remind them all about what was coming.

'You dunno what they're like. This is still crazy. We could still get out of here. Now!'

His whinging had become so routine that the rest of the lads had begun to ignore it, and they started chatting about the sweets that Jamie's mum had laid out.

'So, Mrs C, it's really made from potatoes?' asked Paul incredulously as he chomped down on a sugary-tasting white bar wrapped in chocolate and coconut sprinkles.'

Have you tried tablet?' she replied, full of friendly calm.

Crow sighed and handed over an old Lugar and a rusted Sten gun to Phil, telling him, 'Keep it on single shot. Don't hold the magazine.'

'How come Phil gets two?' asked Ginger.

Crow smirked, 'They have the same ammo. And we've only one box of sweaty rounds, so one will probably blow up in his face. What I'm hoping for anyway!'

'Phil can have them. What do I get?'

'You, Ginger, have this,' Maria told him, handing over a very robust-looking sawn-off and two full boxes of brand new 10 gauge.

Paul was given a Kalashnikov, but he wanted the S.L.R assault rifle and asked Maria, 'You're not going to give it to Jamie, are ya?'

Crow replied, moaning, explaining, 'It's mine! I've eleven rounds. I need three to zero.'

'What do I get then?' asked Jamie walking back to the living room with a coffee.

'Sorry, you're injured.' Maria told him, her voice soothing.

'So is Phil!' he complained, 'Uch, that's no fair. Everyone will have a shooter but me.'

'Shooter?' Paul laughed at his use of slang, 'Ginger, kindly get Jamie a shooter?'

'Why I don't mind if I do get a shooter for him. Jamie, which shooter do you prefer?'

Crow sneered, reminding everyone, 'Bad enough I got us here without arming Jamie. No offence mate, but it ain't gonna be like Braveheart. It'll be better if you stay with the laptop.'

Crow appealed to Jamie's mum, 'We'll be outgunned. Outmanoeuvred. Tell him.'

'Yes dear, you've said already,' replied Mrs C, 'But I'd rather not have him flinch.'

Chapter 36 - Exception Reports.

'Wake up,' Matty told him while holding a small bottle of ammonia salts under Angel's nose. His eyes opened briefly, but he was too groggy to recognise where he was or even who was talking to him. The Smoker asked, 'You okay mate?'

'What happened?' he asked, 'It's like an elephant is standing on my chest.'

'Well, the main thing is, you're dressed now,' Matty told him with a chuckle.

Pieces of information fluttered back into his mind and he said, 'She was going to...'

'She was gonna slot you,' Matty told him.

'Not sure. I think she wanted to defect. But thanks for getting here in time anyway.'

'Yer mate, about that. Police were here before us. Smith tried to argue the toss about who this arrest belonged to, but there was a guy here he couldn't pull rank on. So, the cops took everyone into custody. Well apart from you. You were in an ambulance when we got here.'

'That wasn't the plan,' Angel replied, now even more confused.

Matty explained, 'We were detained by a Police firearms unit a mile from here. Surrounded our car and held us until Smith came to our rescue and we were let go.'

'I see. Why is my arm like this...and this?' Angel asked, rubbing a large chest bruise.

Matty replied, 'Sorry they lost you for a bit.'

'They?' Angel was puzzled.

The Smoker took a long drag and frowned, 'A bit of a coincidence?'

Matty clarified, 'Counterterrorism. They told Smith that you were flapping about like a mad fish. You'd died for a minute.'

The Smoker lit two cigarettes and handed one to Angel, 'They used a ballistic shield fitted with a bank of tasers, just like a claymore. It does the whole room. It sounds brilliant. I want one!'

'And I died? Joder.'

'Yer,' Matty told him, 'It was experimental kit. They had to jumpstart you and stick an adrenalin needle in your heart.'

Angel took a minute and sat kitchen table with the cigarette hanging off his lips. Between puffs, he asked, 'And next? We found Crow yet?'

'Yup,' Matty told him, putting a blanket around his shoulders, 'The idiot is waiting for the cavalry, but no one is going except us.'

'Piece of piss,' said the Smoker, 'He won't know what hit him.'

'Okay, we better go,' Angel replied, standing up.

Matty pushed him down and offered sympathy, 'You're still in shock, and as much as we might be in a hurry to grab the fucker, you need to take a minute.'

'I can curl up later. Where is he?'

'Some village in Scotland. Smith is getting us a background.'

Angel looked puzzled, 'How did we find him?'

Matty explained, 'Smith has been watching most of Crow's old Para mates. He called one of them sounding terrified. The Muppet left a message on his answering machine. Soon as the call came through, they had his position. Looks like he's living rough out in the sticks.'

'And this guy he contacted? What's he know?' asked Angel, still dizzy.

'Nah, he's out the country. The message wiped. Crow has nobody to his rescue.'

**

When Angel called Jessica, she sounded calm but told him something that alarmed him, 'It will get worse in the next few days. People are asking questions!'

'How much worse?' he asked.

'The British Prime Minister phoned the coroner's office within minutes of the body being discovered. The cops hadn't even arrived at the scene.'

'Joder. What an idiot.'

'I want to contain this. We'll take my plane. I don't want the Brits managing any more of this mess. Nobody talks. Nobody at all. Do you understand?'

Angel tried to suggest, 'We got this. We're already moving. Wheels up in 20 minutes.'

'Wait for me!' she told him then flew into a temper demanding they, 'Hold position.'

Angel could only reply, 'Yes boss,' and agree to what Jessica wanted.

She was brutally succinct, 'Fuck them. I will regain control of this Op,' and hung up.

The instruction to delay departure was worrying, not least because it was the first time that he'd ever heard her sound totally panicked. She also wanted to meet them at a small civilian airport. Matty had planned to fly between military bases with their equipment, then hire cars with false identities before watching Crow for at least two days before closing in on him. Jessica however, wanted Crow in her hands within a few hours. Worse still she wanted to come with them and use armoured Range Rovers provided by the US consulate in Scotland.

Although annoyed, the team had no choice, except to wait in a VIP lounge and hope that no sniffer dogs were making the rounds that day. Their weapons were vacuum-packed in briefcases which in turn had been sprayed with a masking agent, but the added risk of being arrested was making the team furious. Even if Smith could get them un-arrested later. As they waited with complimentary food and drinks, the only thing Matty said was, 'Still not moved,' and every ten or so minutes he checked Crow's position on his laptop. Occasionally, someone would moan sarcastically, 'Great,' or, 'Well, I'm having fun,' until a Phenom jet landed and taxied to the refuelling point. The plane's doors didn't open, paperwork was passed in and out of the cockpit while a ground crew came and went. Matty declared with his nostrils flaring, 'That'll be her,' yet still they waited and Jessica wasn't answering her phone. As each minute of inactivity ticked by, Matty's team became increasingly infuriated. The Smoker muttered, 'Fuck, we could be there by now, but here we are. Stopped so that a no use Yank can tag along and get in the way.'

'Sorry amigo,' replied Angel, 'At least we have vehicles at the other end.'

'Yer, I know. Her arrangements, not mine,' Matty growled. He did not look happy.

Half an hour later, Jessica appeared at the plane's door and Matty snarled, 'Bitch!' When they were finally let on board, she greeted them in her familiar cooing voice, 'Hey boys, how y'all doing,' and to Angel said, 'It'll be okay. I've made calls.' They nodded grimly, but none of Matty's team answered, and sullenly they took their seats. Once in the air Jessica carried on with her relentless southern belle charm and dangled a lure, 'It ain't your fault is it now, so I guess y'all deserve some kinda bonus for all this Hoo-ha? Can I fetch y'all a drink from my refreshment centre?'

The team took cans of coke rather than the whisky offered by her, and as she sipped on an 18-year-old Islay, a call came in.

She spoke without her usual haughtiness and listened more than talked. For a long time, she just nodded, with her face looking progressively paler. She ended the call with a calm, 'Oh Honey, that's too bad,' but the moment she hung up, her phone was thrown past Angel's head to smash against the toilet door.

'She declared, 'We are on our own. No imaging and no local support.'

'Fine,' replied Matty with a dig at his employer, 'I prefer no outsiders.'

'What happened, Boss?' asked Angel.

Her answer was for everyone, 'The British are giving Tanya back to the Russians in exchange for someone they wanted. They aren't interrogating her. They don't even think she is important. She's just an added extra in a deal to hand back a Moldovian defector.'

'What?!' bellowed Matt, seemingly disappointed that she'd got away.

Angel however was torn, part smirked at the news and part of him was annoyed.

'Makes as much sense as anything else,' growled Matty.

Then in a chirpy tone, she asked, 'Do you have a plan for when we arrive?'

The Smoker answered for the team, but it wasn't delivered in a tone she was used to hearing, 'You want us to rush in, kick down doors and hopefully not be seen. That is our whole, non-existent stupid fucking plan. We tracked his phone, but don't even know if he is still with it.'

The surprise was that Jessica only replied with, 'Hmmm.'

It was obvious that Matty's team were seething about being rushed, and maybe it was a good decision of hers not to get into an argument with a team of killers on a small plane. But it was totally out of character for his boss to accept someone talking to her like that.

Instead of reacting she quietly retrieved her phone with its cracked screen. Sitting next to Angel, she acted more like a lover on a honeymoon trip, encouraging him to act the same. In hushed tones, they whispered in each other's ears and touched playfully.

'Why can't we have a sexy boss,' joked the Smoker loud enough to be heard.

Jessica ignored the comment and reached over to tussle Angel's hair feigning lust for her operative. She purred in his ear, 'We can't trust these for damage control?'

He replied in a whisper, 'We can be close when they take Crow.'

Jessica moaned and squirmed in her seat, 'We have two vehicles. You and I will take him and the Intel.'

'Yes, darling,' he replied, knowing what she was thinking. Matty would want the pictures destroyed as soon as he got them, whereas she'd want to use them as blackmail.

Then they chatted about his apartment and how much he was still drinking, sliding her hand along his thigh murmured, 'We just need to eliminate anyone Crow has talked to. Then I'll have you on that sabbatical for a while until this mess quiets down.'

'After that?' he asked, trying to sound as if he believed her lies.

'Oh Honey, after that a couple more years working for me, you'll be able to retire. Remember that. The few, the brave, the well-rewarded.'

Angel smiled when she said but assumed that a sabbatical meant a shallow grave and not a pause before a pay-off.

Then just as Angel looked at his future as being short and painful, a miracle happened, Jessica pulled out her laptop and flipped open the screen. He snuggled closer and looked down towards the keyboard. His heart raced in excitement, hoping that he might catch a glimpse of at least a part of her password. She mistook what he was looking at and leant back to ask, 'Like what you see?'

Angel flashed a sleazy smile and attempted to conceal his hatred for her. It was a reliable deception that he'd used from when he'd first been handed over to her by Rivera. As he stared down Jessica's cleavage, he licked his lips but in his mind was memory of the hits he'd arranged for her and thoughts about how he might steal some of her fortune.

Angel's expression lit up for real, as out of the corner of his eye, he saw Jessica log on to her laptop and move funds from her bank account using only her thumbprint. Sweat streamed out of his pores as he stayed in his role as 'Tranquilo

Hombre,' and tried to hide his excitement by leering at her breasts. Finally, he calmed himself and changed from a man frightened about his own future, into a bastard who was planning to end hers.

***

Apart from Lachlann and the tied-up Paddy, everyone gathered in the front room again. Maria typed in the decoy phone's number and the code suffix she'd got from Paddy, 'It worked. Look at the screen.'

The display now showed a blue icon at the position Crow had made his call from, and another in the south of England.

When Maria zoomed in, she said, 'Someone's cloned the phone.'

'Who?' asked Jamie. On the map other icons lit up, representing other phones nearby.

Excitedly she clicked on a list of commands from a drop-down box and said, 'Can you get me a pen and paper? I need to write this down.'

It was a learning experience, whoever had designed the program had used acronyms like AXML, CDEM, and RFRT instead of anything useful like, 'turn on the microphone,' or, 'track the last number called,' so she kept clicking icons in an attempt to understand how it all worked. Finally, she got the sound on but immediately turned pale. It was a familiar accent that she heard say, 'We are to kill them all, right?'

Another man replied, 'I'm afraid so. No witnesses. A gas explosion, a car catching fire, an overdose. Take your pick, long as it gets done. Anyone he's talked to gets dead.'

'Fuck, that's Matty's voice,' declared Crow.

The voice Maria recognised as Angel asked, 'Has he moved yet?'

'No, not yet. And I've just had a message from Smith. We've a cottage to visit en route.'

The following silence could have been a solemn moment if not for Ginger loudly crunching through a packet of biscuits, and growling, 'Teddy-bears.'

'I can see them moving north,' Maria explained, 'I hope we're ready.'

Mrs C said, 'Time to go then,' and burled around in her wheelchair.

Automatically, everyone in the room shrunk backwards in the knowledge that to be in her path was a bruised ankle.

'See you when it's over Mrs. C,' said Crow but this time when he spoke, there was no fear in his voice. It was like, with the decision made, he was now filled with steel resolve. Taking his rifle in hand, it was he who looked most determined to see through what they'd agreed. The former paratrooper was psyched and in a robotic voice, he told them all, 'Okay, remember who ya are!'

Paul offered, 'No Prisoners,' but despite the bluster, his face was a picture of concern. It looked like Crow had stolen all of the Red-Ties' heroism for himself and Jamie squeezed past Ginger to close on Maria and say, 'Love you.'

'Si, don't worry. I will take your mum. She is safe with me,' then she bit her lip and told him, 'Cariño, there is something else.'

It was like all of the time since they'd met at the cottage had been an angry rush, without time for any tenderness. Now time slowed and Jamie brushed the long hair from Maria's face and kissed her cheek,

'It's okay, I already know.'

'You know? What do you know?' she asked.

'Oh, I've always known you were a soldier or kinda dodgy acronym.'

'No, you didn't, and no, not that Tonto,' she said, burying her head into him.

'Well, what? And it's okay, whatever it is.'

'I love you,' she replied calmly, 'I love you with all my heart.'

They kissed, and it could have lasted for an eternity, but the moment was spoiled by Phil tugging on his jacket and yelling, 'C'mon Cunt, we're in a hurry; Fuck her later.'

Chapter 37 - Project Variables.

When everyone left Mrs C's cottage, they didn't know how long they'd have to wait, only that Matty's team had already passed Carlisle in the air.

As a precaution against intermittent phone reception in Argyll, Lachlann was in an Edwardian hotel called the Culag Bar.

It was a place habitually missed by tourists as it was sunk beneath the level of the road and lay hidden behind a petrol station and tearoom. It was the kind of pub that had rooms but no hotel guests and quietly shuffled between bank payments propped up by farmers, fishermen and woodcutter drinkers who were struggling themselves. Whatever the weather, the patrons would shelter from it and rest their drinks on solidly wonky tables by a log fire.

It was the weather that was worrying Lachlann. Early morning there had been a little rain of the type that was halfway between soaking fog and light drizzle, but it didn't last, and he felt reassured that the land was still dry as tinder and begging for clouds.

He was waiting with a man called Jeff, an elderly woodcutter who despite being German, had adopted the exaggerated speech of a caricature Highlander.

Few knew that the old rogue had once been a soldier, and fewer still knew which country's armies he'd fought for.

Jeff was aware of the plan and quietly commented,

'It's a nice enough place to wait for assassins.'

'Shh! For fuck sake!' Lachlann huffed.

'Och don't worry. Any word from the boat?' the old man asked, referring to other friends who worked on the ferry and were watching for what they'd been told were, 'Police from Glasgow.'

Lachlann and Jeff were both admiring the most recent landlord's attempts to upgrade. For them, hiding the dark décor of woodworm and peeling wallpaper by lining the walls with stuffed animals and farming implements wasn't an improvement. For the fifth time since they'd got there, they discussed the unseasonably hot weather, 'Is it, not a beautiful day?'

'It is,' replied Lachlann, 'Are you still okay with this?'

'I am. Do I not look okay?' replied Jeff.

Jeff looked like a medical cadaver that had once died of old age but was still staggering around on baggy corduroy legs wrapped in a frayed and torn wax jacket. His face was a map of burst thread veins, and all his stubble was of different lengths in testimony to the craters and creases of his features. The long-abused body looked very, very far from okay. He told them grinning, 'It'll not be my first time, y' know.'

'I know,' Lachlann replied and concluded that he must have been a terror in his youth. It was easy to imagine the old man looking the same in war as he did now. He was feral, jovial and sly yet whatever his actual age, capable of darting up and down a tree line to use a chainsaw as deftly as an office worker with a pen.

Jeff put on a serious face and leant in to say, 'There's a lot of nonsense said on war, but any situation where you can get a blowjob for a loaf of bread is not at all that bad!' Lachlann coughed into his pint with a little bit of laughter leaking out and asked, 'What did you actually do?'

'Uch Jeez, that was such a long time ago, it's hard to remember. And I don't think I was sober once from the day I landed until it was all over.'

Just at that moment, Lachlann's phone beeped. It told him bad news, 'Two blacked-out Range Rovers on the ferry.'

He relayed the message to Jeff, who exclaimed, 'A toast then!' and lifted his dram to say, 'You eat every day, you sleep every day. No one is shooting at you. What more ya want?'

'How about we do our bit and stay out of the way?' Lachlann replied.

'Och suppose you're richt?' replied Jeff.

Lachlann's face squirmed, 'We better go.'

'Alright, alright, you heathen slave driver you!' replied Jeff as he stumbled from his chair, 'Let's go and don't forget the fish.'

Lachlann picked up a 20lb salmon he'd found lost in a stream and said, 'I'll drive.'

Although it was Jeff's car, he was not known for driving with the haste they needed, as he drove at 20mph everywhere. Drunk or sober.

Lachlann took the car eastwards along a winding loch-side road averaging sixty to where they'd parked the tractor, winch and caravan that the pair used for timber harvesting jobs. Looking in the mirror, Jeff mentioned a black storm cloud stuck on a mountain behind them, 'Looks like proper Argyll rain is coming, and coming fast. That's not good, Lachy. That's no good at all.'

'Och, not to worry Jeff, it will be fine. I can't see it raining till we finish.'

They ended up at a long stretch of sandy gravel seven miles away, a place that was flanked by a steep wooded hill and a sea loch.

At either end were ravines, and furthest away from the entrance was a large barren cliff of granite with an old water tower perched on it. Normally visitors could drive in and park almost anywhere on the three hundred yards of grass, gravel and road that wound in through a long loop of picnic tables under the trees.

Due to the fire risk, the beach was deserted. Access had temporarily been blocked off with a warning sign hanging between two fence posts. The only sign of life was a few deer scurrying away from them as they replaced the chain that closed the narrow winding road.

Crossing a small concrete bridge that was the only access to the picnic area, Lachlann beeped his car horn and yelled out the window, 'We're here!' and parked next to where Jeff's timber harvesting had been closed down by the forestry commission. Despite the probation notice for safety violations, the old man started up his tractor and began to drag a steel cable from its winch towards the caravan. Lachlann worked in jeans and a t-shirt with his chainsaw to drop a tree in front of the caravan and sned its branches into long stumps.

He cut deep trenches into the length of the fallen tree, some as deep as a foot and Jeff then wove his cable through the handles of some nearby jerry cans before shackling a coiled end around the wide end of the log. He said, 'You know anyone looking at this will think something is wrong. It's too tidy. We've even stacked the timber on the hill.'

'Don't worry. It'll be fine,' Lachlann replied and lit a fire on the log.

'But will this work?' Jeff asked while looking at his watch.

'Yer, it'll be like we are having a beach party,' Lachlann told him while skewering the salmon on a thick branch positioned above the flames.

Their efforts weren't for a barbecue however, Jeff had suggested they build a fire in front of the caravan to stop anyone from using thermal imaging properly. As for the cable, they were hidden with the debris of branches and sawdust for an entirely different reason. When Lachlann switched off his chainsaw's vibrations, insects began buzzing around and he lit a cigarette to keep them away. That was when Jeff saw a figure in camouflage walking towards him from the cliffs.

He was used to strange wee soldiers out training on the hillsides, but this one was familiar, and he called out, 'Jamie, you're meant to be hiding.'

Ginger and Paul appeared behind him, clumsily moving through rhododendrons and bracken accompanied by the noise of cracking twigs and his muffled grunts with every step.

'I am ignoring 'em in case they'll be wanting to ask for a cigarette.' said Jeff smiling.

'Giant is still here then,' said Lachlann as the big man plodded up to him.

'He's gonna be more like a troll today,' said Jeff.

'I'm a poacher by trade; I can hide behind a blade of grass if I needs to,' he told them holding his shotgun in front of his nose, 'You can't see me now, can ya?'

Jeff found a flask of whisky in his jacket, took a sip, and told them, 'Their vehicles might be armour-plated, don't let them use them as cover. Let them come in the open.'

'It's gonna work, isn't it?' replied Jamie taking a cigarette from Lachlann and nervously pacing back and forth.

Ginger whispered to Jamie, 'Don't worry me, old Cacker.'

'We've only ever agreed it might work,' replied Jeff, 'We still have to trust in a hundred years of British Army training and them being awfy professional!'

'It'll be fine,' replied Ginger,' They are only expecting one frightened Crow, innit?'

'Where is he by the way?' Jamie tugged on the cigarette with a deep lungful.

Ginger bellowed, 'Crow! Come out. You need to make the next call!'

'I'm just worried this is all too easy and simple looking,' said Jeff taking another sip.

Jamie replied, 'It doesn't feel simple. I am worried about them coming back on us; we don't want that do we, but it's legal, innit? It's self-defence?'

'Well, if it's not, the lawyers will have a lot of fun with my photos,' said Paul brandishing the camera he'd bought.

'It will not be coming to that,' said Jeff, 'Anyway, It's you or them. Remember what I said, lads, they'll come in for a look first before getting too close.'

'What if they don't?' asked Jamie. Every part of the plan worried him; he wasn't even sure if Maria staying with his mother was a good or a bad thing. She'd have to greet anyone who came looking for trouble, all alone.

Jeff reminded them all, 'And don't get cocky. They'll still outshoot the lot of you. Those sorts practice ten hours a day on targets. When they see the danger, they'll take cover and move fast. They'll be great at that. Don't get dead, or your mother will never forgive me.'

Jeff looked at his watch, 'Aye, right we got to go; once they pass us, I'll drop a tree across the main road; the way home for you is up through the forest. And, and one more thing. Keep the TV on, it's not just the body heat you need to obscure. They'll ping a laser off a window to try and hear who is inside. It's what I'd do.'

As per the plan, the two woodcutters got into their old car and drove off, just as Crow appeared in an old 1968 pattern army smock that Jeff had loaned him, festooned with clumps of grass and leaves. In keeping with their plan, he made his last panicked and begging call to a former comrade and left the phone in the caravan.

It was all going to schedule. Five minutes later, they heard Jeff beep his horn then they saw two black Range Rovers turn a bend in the coast road. The vehicles disappeared behind a wood for a few minutes before reappearing to rumble across the bridge next to Jeff's tractor.

Once in the picnic area, the first vehicle drove forward into a parking space, while the other stopped mid-span on the crossing to block access. Jamie's throat dried and his stomach knotted as he watched from a disused pump house on the hill overlooking the beach.

Even with Crow a few metres to his left in a shallow trench, and Phil to his right behind a steel water tower, he still felt very alone.

When they exited their cars, Jamie saw that there were six people who'd come looking for Crow. In the distance one looked like a woman in a black business suit, there were four men in hiking clothes, and someone dressed in a Hawaiian shirt.

They split into three groups of two and got closer. The woman sat down on a picnic bench with a man who produced a set of binoculars from inside a green waxed jacket and scanned the tree-line. The bright shirt and a man in a green fleece stayed by the vehicles near the bridge, and the other two spread out on either side of the road and walked slowly towards the caravan. As Jamie peered out from a fist-sized hole in his hiding place, he guessed what they were doing.

So far, everything they'd thought might happen, was happening, even down to how far their visitors would be spaced apart as they walked. But when Jamie saw the military contractors draw short assault rifles from under their coats, the full reality of what was unfolding hit home and he began mumbling, 'Fuck, fuck, fuck!' One of them moved forward and crouched near the half-open caravan door. He probably had just enough time to see Paddy's warm body tied to a chair before his own body was hurled backwards by the force of Crow's first press on his trigger.

Ginger walked out from under the cover of the bridge to shoot both barrels of his shotgun into a man wearing a fleece and Paul moved from his hiding place to shoot the man in the Parrot shirt. Then his Avtomat Kalashnikova did the unimaginable and jammed. With their weapons temporarily spent, the man in the gaudy shirt was able to slide down the banks of the gully and stand beside them by the bridge. There he levelled a small pistol at Ginger's head and smiled. He said, 'Hola, Coño!' and the pair of Red-Ties knew they were done.

***

'Where are they?' asked Jamie, peering from his hiding place.
'Fuck knows,' replied Phil, who stepped out from behind the steel water tower to fire aimlessly with his submachine gun, then jump back again behind his protection.

Crow shouted, 'Wankers!' to confirm where he was and fired two tracer rounds in the rough direction of where they'd all last seen his would-be hunters, and as if on cue the log burst into flames along its length.

Jamie then heard three short bursts and saw dirt fly up accompanied by the sounds of metal hitting metal next to Phil.

Looking around, Jamie spotted Crow slither into a ditch behind him.

'They're flanking. We need to regain the momentum,' he told him.

'Yer mate,' said Phil from his water tower, 'Once again in English huh?'

Crow shook his head and arched around a tree to fire off a round.

Phil shouted, 'Look. They're there. One's just run across.'

Crow sneered, 'Brilliant target indication mate,' then it became obvious where their enemy was, from a steady beat of muzzle flashes amongst the foliage.

Phil barked, 'They're getting closer and keeping us pinned while they move. Where the fuck's Ginger?'

Jamie pressed play on a large boom-box stereo, and bagpipe music belched out from its speakers. He then opened a picnic cooler box and took out a small Crème Brulee torch. With the press of a button, he lit another cross-cut log that started burning like a flare. 'Fall back! Fall back!' yelled Jamie, now giving away his position too. Nobody moved, but at two hundred metres away, the men firing at them crossed a line of orange tape fluttering in the breeze. Crow had taken it from where it had marked trees for harvesting and moved it so he could measure wind speed for shooting. When Jamie saw they'd reached that far, he panicked, 'Ginger should be firing by now!'

'Have they stopped coming?' shouted Phil, who poked his weapon around the side of the water tower and fired it again without looking.

'I see them,' yelled Jamie, who then drew the only weapon he'd brought with him to the gunfight, an old Ka-Bar knife that he'd previously used as a multi-tool when working as a lumberjack.

'What da fuck are you gonna do with that!' growled Phil.

'Fuck off. They're getting closer,' shouted Jamie,' who could now see them making short dashes between trees, only slowing down as they crossed another small chasm running down the hill.

'Where's Ginger?' shouted Phil, but as the words left his mouth, they saw him. Halfway along the beach, behind the caravan, the giant fired the first shot from the Red-Tie's secret weapon. It arced in the air to land behind the assault team and set fire to the grass. And the last part of the plan started falling into place.

The idea for it came about as Phil had started talking about using Molotov cocktails and Maria revealed what she'd seen in Jamie's bedroom. On his wall was a Mongolian horse bow with arrows he'd fletched himself, including ones with steel baskets that could hold gel-soaked cloth. Fire arrows.

Due to Jamie's injury, the bow and twelve shafts were handed to Ginger with a little bit of hurried instruction, 'No need to be accurate. Just lob them in amongst the trees. In front. Behind. All around them.'

As soon as Ginger released his first shaft, Paul pulled on the levers of Jeff's tractor. It started the idling drums turning, which in turn made it haul in slack. Slowly steel cables were dragged through pulleys on the hillside. First, the tethered jerry cans tumbled and spilt petrol, then the flaming log followed their route twenty metres behind to bounce through the undergrowth and ignite everything in its path. 'Now?' asked Phil as bullets smacked into steel and concrete that he was hiding behind. 'Think so,' replied Crow, while crawling in the ditch to lie next to him at his feet. 'God, yes!' howled Jamie and he carefully unpacked then lined up two dozen glass globes. Each had been filled with a mix of petrol, sugar, and washing-up liquid, each had a small piece of cut denim protruding that had been soaked in a gel for lighting barbecues. One by one, Phil loaded the globes into an ancient-style slinger, lit the wick over his flaming log and launched them nearly 80 metres like David swinging at Goliath, without a clue where they'd land. It was a team effort, coordinated with Mother Nature who'd provided a long dry summer. More globes flew in the air, landing amongst Matty's team and the flames began to spread faster than a man could walk. The hunters had nowhere to go that wasn't a fire.

Phil yelled, 'Second line. Second line,' then he and Crow lit the last two garden globes and threw them as grenades. This time the three Red-Ties retreated for real. Meanwhile, Paul saw the hillside in flame and assumed the danger was over, so went to get Paddy. But as he opened the caravan door, he heard the Range Rover's door slam shut. In alarm, he spun around and sent a burst of rounds towards movement and managed to slice a thin red line across Jamie, who fell with a squeal.

Chapter 38 - Negotiations.

'This is not happening,' whimpered the once proud CIA boss. She watched in shock what was meant to be a simple extraction, unravel into chaos. She'd never been this close to an operation before and her inexperience with the actual dirty work she authorised was showing. She recovered quickly, but her fear of being shot kept her silent, motionless, and hidden behind a tree. But when the firing stopped, she'd kicked off her high heels and ran for her life.

Reaching the nearest Range-Rover, she locked the doors, and yelled, 'Yes!' relieved to be sitting behind its B4 bullet-resistant armour. But then, as her silk-stockinged feet hit the pedals, she felt sick, knowing something was savagely wrong. There was a noise that she thought was the engine running, but there were no keys in the ignition, only a cooling fan that had stayed on after the car stopped. In a panic, she called Smith.

He picked up immediately and seemed to mock her, 'Honey, how are y'all doing? Are you having fun yet?'

'They are all dead,' she was whining near tears now.

'Phhhtclunk...chTing!' a round ricocheted off the car's bonnet into its front window.

'Jessica dear, just chill and tell me what is going on, Honey.'

She whimpered, 'We have men down, and a sniper is shooting at us.'

'Dang, is Matty there with you?'

'No, he is dead, I am safe inside the car, but I have no keys.'

'Well honey, you stay safe now y'hear,' and he hung up.

She tried calling him again, and again, but he didn't answer. Then rounds began to cook-off and fly in all directions from the charred remains of the hillside. Five minutes seemed like five hours, during which time she counselled herself that the fire brigade or police would be en route for such a mass of smoke that could be seen for miles. She weighed her options, 'It would be okay; she could wait.'

A trickle of fear ran down her back, and she turned around in her seat to see that all around were men with automatic weapons in their hands. The youth in the vest top she'd seen fall was now limping with blood leaking from a wound in his leg.

Another one walked towards her and called out, 'Oi Oi!' while grabbing his crotch and shaking his hips at her.

'Fuck. Fuck, I am still safe,' she thought and tried calling Smith again, 'He could send the cavalry.'

But there was no answer. She was trapped. Around the car were grinning animals, not soldiers, not intelligence operative she could bargain with but laughing hyenas.

She saw hope walking towards her Range Rover from the beach. It was Angel, and the gathered thugs all had their backs to him. He had a short assault rifle in his hands and all he had to do was open up with a burst of fire and her problems would be over. Then a giant appeared next to him in baggy knee-length shorts, flip-flops and a torn t-shirt carrying a sawn-off shotgun in his arms like a baby. They walked past the other men and stood next to the rear passenger side door, both smiling. Shouting through the glass, Angel asked, 'Hola Jessica, would you like to come out?'

'What are you doing? Bastard!' she replied.

Angel lit a cigarette and laughed, 'I made an offer to my friend here. I don't shoot him, and he gives me you.'

'That's right girl, we is mates now,' said the Giant, 'Nice of him not to kill me really.'

'Bastard! You could have been rich!' You still can,' suggested Jessica in panic.

'Don't think this is true. Dead maybe, but not rich. Anyway, are you coming out?'

'Fuck off!' she replied, and a third man with a Kalashnikov stepped up and tapped Angel on the shoulder and said, 'I'll do this bit.'

'Bang!' another brute his hands down on the bonnet of the car and grinned as he drew his thumb across his neck.

The rough men began arguing outside. The one armed with the Kalashnikov pointed at the line of trees in the carpark and yelled, 'Lads, stand back while I do this. We only need a police chopper to come look at us, and we is fucked; go stand under the shade.'

Jessica guessed from the first shot till now, had been ten minutes. It could only be another ten minutes at most until sirens and flashing lights arrived. She thought,

'Someone must have called the emergency services,' but didn't know that, even if they were coming, trees that Lachlann cut down across the road would delay them.

Still in shock, she tried to process what had happened. It was incredible that a forest fire could've moved that fast. It had been the speed of a car in first gear and in denial, she thought, 'Maybe the men on the hill had escaped?'
Jessica considered all the possibilities, 'They could've run up the hill. Regrouped?' Then she bypassed any guilt about her part in the operation and began to think about bargaining with the men outside, 'Tell me what you want! We'll make a deal!' The man with the Kalashnikov shook his head and squeezed the trigger, 'Chu-unk' echoed all around. 'Chu-unk, chu-unk, chu-unk,' and after eight rounds on the same spot, the window turned opaque as frosted glass and a small hole with a tiny indentation appeared. There was a pause with a camouflaged man assessing the damage, 'Nearly through,' and the Kalashnikov man began again, 'Chu-unk, chu-unk, chu-unk.'
Jessica felt terror as he calmly called out, 'I'm through. Gather round.'

That was when she progressed to anger and took out her pistol. With gritted teeth, she fired it through the hole, and men around her vehicle ducked for cover. In her mind, she knew she could hold them off and she thought back to a short course she'd attended in Florida to prepare her for any kidnapping attempts. Summoning all of her mental strength, she told herself, 'I am trained for this,' and began composing lies in her head for a report that would explain away this catastrophe on a beach. One of the men climbed on the roof, and with growing horror, realised why he was being handed a piece of garden hose and petrol can. 'As you're a bit slow, remember to get off the roof!' one of them hollered.
'Stop being a cunt. You're not even funny,' replied the man above.

All around, Jessica could see the men pointing weapons at her, their faces urging her to open the car a crack to fire out so they could fire in. She knew it. They yelled, kicked the car, and banged on it with their fists like a pack of baying hounds. Frantically looking for something to block the hole. She found an adhesive bandage from the car's first aid kit to tape over it. Unfocused and hysterical, she didn't see the giant sneak up behind the car and point his shotgun at the hole. The first she knew he was there, was when he bellowed, 'Hello my lovely?' and pulled his trigger.

Jessica saw a limp lump of flesh hanging from her elbow where her hand used to be, but she couldn't hear her own screams because of the ringing in her ears.

As the petrol can sloshed its contents down the tube and into the hole, she began to accept that death was imminent. In a final act of defiance and pride, she squealed in pain, 'You won't get away with this. Don't you know who I am?'

From around the car, they chorused, 'SHE DOESN'T KNOW WHO SHE IS!' and laughed like maniacs.

Another round cooked off and whirred by the car prompting one of the men to shout, 'We better hurry!' and a few seconds later Jessica heard a loud, 'Shluump' as flames ignited. Paint began to crackle and blister around the window. It was the thick steamy smoke, not heat that drove her to reach for her exit and fumble with the slippery, blood-soaked handle. She took one last look of self-pity at her torn arm, opened the door, and fell out onto the ground gasping for breath.

Jessica felt a hand grip her leg and pull her away from the fire across dirt and grass, and when she looked up, it was Angel in his Hawaiian shirt with a cigarette hanging out of his mouth. He asked, 'What do we do with you then?' and pressed his pistol against her eye socket.

She whined, 'Angel, you prick!' and it was the last thing she ever said.

Chapter 39 - Closing a Project.

The Red-Ties and a tied-up Paddy travelled in the mini-bus while Angel followed with the spare Range Rover and Jessica's thumb in a plastic bag.

Phil insisted on driving, but as he followed Jamie's directions along the twisting single-track road he snarled, 'Fuck this, you're driving,' and they stopped to switch. As Jamie threw the vehicle around sharp undulating corners, he began to flap and told them, 'We left stuff behind, with our fingerprints on it.'

Crow smiled, 'Mate, I picked up my brass. Everything else is burnt.'

'Yer, about that,' said Paul, 'That Angel cunt was a bit weird.'

'Do you know who he is?' asked Phil.

'Nah! He just turned up, and pointed a pistol at my head,' said Ginger.

Paul added, 'Yer, then he told us he was a friend of Mary's and started picking up our shell cases.'

Phil slapped him on the chest and smiled, 'See mate, we're all good. Just gotta burn our clothes now. We already cleaned up the pub.'

'Yup place smells of bleach now, so we're all good mate,' said Crow, 'Well apart from you being a getaway driver that's fucking incapable of driving more than thirty miles an hour.'

Jamie barked back angrily, 'Do you know this road then?' then he moaned, 'And by the way, I was shot in the leg?' and drove along the twisting single-track road over the hillside in silence until they arrived at a small tearoom at another Loch.

Under a few parasol-shaded chairs were Mrs C and Maria. His mum was leaning back in her wheelchair in a pair of sunglasses. She looked happy and rested as if simply enjoying the early evening sun.

Maria, however, looked angry and agitated. She was pacing up and down in a light blue summer dress, and when she saw Jamie, her mood seemed to grow worse. He limped towards her in bloodied jeans to hug her, but she scolded him,

'Why did I bring your vest if you weren't going to wear it?'

'It was too hot and hurts my ribs. Besides, plan had me hiding, so I gave it to Paul.'

Her hands rose to push him away. She said, 'No cuddles, you'll get blood on me.'

As the rest of the Red-Ties spilt out of the mini-bus Phil grinned at her and explained, 'Not grassing anyone up, but it wasn't me, okay.'

'Who is he,' asked Ginger, pointing at Angel as he parked up next to them.

Maria shook her head and didn't answer but it was obvious they knew each other.

'So, is he alright?' asked Phil.

She nodded, then as an afterthought she said, 'Meester Ginger, por favor if you see my Spanish associate talk to my Jamie, I'd like you to hit him very, very hard. Okay!'

Angel groaned, 'I bondage him!' and declared, 'Es solo un pequeño corte.'

'Bandage! Bandage!' she snarled, 'Why're you here? You don't need to be.'

'I know,' he replied, 'But y'know. Maybe I can help.'

'So, you know him?' asked Ginger as if he'd forgotten Maria's previous answer, 'Cause he just turned up and said he was your mate pointing a gun at my head.'

'Si, I know him, we work sometimes together, but I don't trust the cabron.'

Ginger went to speak to the solitary staff member of the remote tearoom and order drinks. He couldn't fit through the doorway, but when she shrieked at the sight of him, he put on a gentle and polite voice to ask her for a menu, 'Ma'am, it's fine if you are busy, but would it be okay if you made us like a dozen pizzas?'

'It'll take a long time, the ovens not on?' she replied.

'Take your time, any chance you've got those sweeties that are made from potatoes, and scones, and those meringues, and?'

He glanced down at the menu and ordered, 'Nine teas and banana muffins please.'

When the tea arrived, Angel sat by himself on the grass and chatted with a stray cat. Everyone else leant in towards each other to speak in hushed tones, about, 'What to do next?'

'We go home!' said Phil, 'Hand Crow off to Walker.'

Jamie argued, 'But, that Paddy bloke said he was watching. We ain't got his mates yet.'

He never finished his sentence, as the discussion was interrupted by a female visitor. She walked towards them smiling, holding up her phone as if it could stop bullets, then handed it to Maria to say, 'Hi, I'm Petra and this phone call is for you.'

Unsure of the diplomatic etiquette, the Red-Ties grabbed the woman, albeit with a little more care than they'd shown Paddy. Maria waved frantically for them to calm down as she told the caller, 'Speak.'

'You can call me Ken…Miss Hernan.'

Maria was a little shocked that he knew her name and said, 'Ah, what do you want?'

'Nothing at all, just letting you know about a tragic car accident setting fire to woodland.'

'So, we just walk away. No marines, no helicopters or police from across the loch?'

'Absolutely. **You** can walk away, but I'll keep the rest,' Ken told her, 'Don't worry, he'll be extradited for trial when we finish with him. We are allies, after all.'

Maria chuckled, turned on the phone's speaker and said, 'Okay, but if I give you the civilians, they'll be back on the beach, no? So, it's no deal. Everyone walks free.'

Ken sighed, 'No one would agree to that variable. Besides, I was just being polite; this isn't a negotiation. You're surrounded. Every exit, I'll take you all in. Officially.'

She hoped at least some of what Ken was saying was a lie, but before she could say another word, Angel held up his hand reaching for the mobile phone and chuckled, 'Okay, Cariña. So I can help. Who is it?'

Maria shrugged and handed it to him, 'He thinks I am in charge. He thinks I will trade in Jamie and his friends for safe passage. He wants you in a cell for interrogation. He maybe wants everyone else back to the beach for an accident. Mostly he says that I can go free. Just me!'

When Angel spoke to Ken, his voice was slurred and languid as if he didn't have a care in the world, 'Oyez Tio. I am Angel. I have the alternative.'

Ken asked, 'Okay. I'm listening. What do you propose?'

Angel was tired and struggled with the correct English words, but was still clear in intent, 'Is a problem, but you can't have them. I have good reasons for saying this.'

'Go on,' replied Ken.

'So maybe, you are already talking to Spain or maybe you think I am, or Maria is a rogue agent? Maybe she was never going to walk safely out of here, and maybe you plan to take her in. But I know her very well, and if she doesn't take everyone, she will never agree to a deal.'

Ken chuckled, 'And I care because?'

Everyone's eyes were on him, as he explained, 'First of all. I am a loyal soldier of Spain, and my real boss has already booked my flight home. First-class.'

'Go on,' Ken replied sombrely.

Angel chuckled and said, 'My job was Jessica, nada mas.'

'Ah.' Ken replied, 'You wanted this?'

'Si, claro. Didn't you? Nobody wants this Jessica Puta here, but nobody can tell her no. I did not plan this, but I don't mind the O-K corral or if Everybody gets well.'

Ken sounded surprised, 'Yes but, still. There are still loose ends.'

Angel told him, 'Mira Señor. You will care because the giant has my pistol now, so even if I have Jessica's operation in my head he might shoot me. I have her contacts, who she pays, who she blackmails and what businesses she controls. I even have what share prices she made move up and then moved down. I know where her bank accounts are and how to access them. But the giant has my pistol.'

The old spy replied, 'Well that just makes me more eager to have a chat with you.'

'I work for Spain,' was Angel's blunt reply, 'They know I am here and will want me back. Luck for me, you want to be my friend and not detain me. You'll be my friend.'

'No deal,' said Ken and Angel shook his head and handed the phone back to Maria.

'Hola, what do you say?'

Ken told her, 'I think, upon reflection, everyone is coming into custody for interrogation.'

Maria was calm and cold as ice when she spoke again,

'Mira, if you've researched me at all, you'll know I'll happily shoot Angel in the head, and destroy what Jessica had on her. I'll take the consequences. Instead of my friends on the beach and burnt, I'll leave your Paddy and the unlovely Petra here dead. You see I know you. I know all people like you. Es la mierda.'

It was a bluff, she hoped that Ken only knew her name and no more.

'You'd shoot him?' It sounded like a revelation he didn't expect.

Maria snarled, 'Trust me; I'm not fond of him. I might pull the trigger regardless of what we agree. But if you want anything from this. Everyone walks.'

Angel groaned and looked up to the sky and complained, 'It was one time!' But it didn't look like he was worried, even when Ginger draped an arm around his shoulders, commenting, 'Oi Mary doll, how come you speak good English all of a sudden.'

There was a long pause on the other end of the phone.

Maria guessed it wasn't the conversation Ken had expected, but when he finally answered, it was an abrupt, 'Like I said before. I don't believe you!'

That was when Maria almost laughed, 'I am not Spanish intelligence today. Angel, you know he is loyal always to Espain, but I am here against my will. I don't mind to shoot it out and make a diplomatic mess.'

Then she grinned and told him, 'After all, you did steal Gibraltar!'

Chapter 40 - Holiday Entitlement.

They made the deal. Ken didn't know she was lying, and Maria didn't realise Ken was already getting more than he'd hoped for in exchange for their safe passage. Paddy was cut free of duct tape, and everyone went to Mrs C's cottage where Ginger asked, 'Can we trust him?'

'Because there's no police at the door, and he knew we were coming.'

Maria didn't explain everything to the Red-Ties, just enough to ensure that they didn't take hostages and try to shoot their way out of Argyll. Some parts of the story the Red-Ties couldn't get their heads around and it wasn't until she revealed Gabriella switched Crow's watch for a tracking device at the slave auction, that they understood and started calling her, 'Bond.'

She told them, 'I was in England to study. I wasn't involved, but Angel asked me to do a favour.' Pointing at Jamie she said, 'And this, he happened!'

'So, your pistol? Jamie asked looking perplexed, 'You'd shoot him?'

'I was never going to shoot him. I'm not allowed. The bastard knows this.'

Angel smirked as if whatever the issue was between them, it was no big deal, and he declared, 'Mi honour es mi lealtad,' which seemed to cause a brief argument with Maria. She snarled, 'No me importa nada,' and crossed the room to hold Jamie's hand. Crow broke the room's tension by asking,

'And the pictures? You know, like a guarantee?'

Maria snorted, 'They are not so important,' then sarcastically told him,

'But yes, why not? Email them to a newspaper; no one will print a word. I promise you'll end up in a cell with a different name, drugged up to the eyeballs. It was never about the pictures; you were dead from the moment you took the job. You know this.'

'Bueno. Is over!' She declared, 'We all to go home, I think. It never happened.'

Ginger escorted Paddy to his car but he couldn't resist a last dig at the man he'd kidnapped, 'You need to get yourself to the gym Mush, you're a bit too weak for your line of work.'

Jamie took a shower and dressed again in a t-shirt and pair of shorts so that his cleaned wound could be inspected by Maria and dressed properly with less haste. After the other Red-Ties waved goodbye, Angel took an airport taxi and was gone. Maria said, 'I talked with your mum, and we'll stay a few days.'

'Oh, okay,' he replied, 'That's good. That way we can hear if there's any gossip.'

She then slipped her arms around him and supplied the last surprise of the day by saying, 'After that, I was thinking we could go meet my daddy. Maybe. Before term starts?'

'Your real father or a cover one like your best friend Gabriella,' he said laughing.

She winked, 'Well, does it matter?'

'Suppose not. As long as you love me. I'm happy.'

Maria flushed red and cuddled him, 'Oh, and I already have the tickets.'

***

At Alicante airport, he switched on his phone to receive a voice message from Don. It was a bit rambling as if he was celebrating.

The gist of it was that after two weeks of telling the internment staff that he was English while showing them his Union Jack and British bulldog tattoos.

They finally released him. At his local police station, when he'd tried to turn himself in for the Lenny Quintain incident, the desk sergeant told him,

'Nothing happened Don, nobody's looking for you.'

Everything felt like it was going to be okay, and Jamie committed himself to embracing each moment of happiness with Maria. He had no questions about anything. He didn't ask why she showed two passports at customs, why their random taxi driver knew which hotel they were booked into without being told, or why their suite had a bottle of Cava already chilling in a bucket of fresh ice when they got there. Maria had a shower while Jamie lazed on the room's balcony, sipping wine and gazing at the hazy vista of the Balearics.

'Lovely room innit?' he said, 'I could sit here all day watching the sea.'

'We are out of here in an hour,' she said, peeping around the doorway.

'Okay,' he replied.

'Well get ready.'

'You said an hour? What's up, you've been stressed all morning!'

Maria didn't answer. Instead, she stomped around getting dressed growling in Valencian. Buttoning up a white blouse she grumpily told him, 'You're not moving.'

Jamie looked puzzled and asked, 'What's up? You said he'd be alright with us?'

She replied, 'I said he was probably alright with us!'

'Put the wine down and get ready. Joder. Por favor.'

Standing up he said, 'People were trying to kill us and you were calmer than this.'

Reaching out to tenderly entwine her fingers in his, she pulled him off the balcony and back into the room. Then without warning, she pushed him over onto the bed, 'Please hurry!'

Sprawled on his back and looking up at her soft curves, a lump dried in his throat. It wasn't lust he felt, it was more like a warm serenity that he held him transfixed as he said, 'You're beautiful.'

Maria ignored his slack-jawed, glazed expression and sighed, 'Okay, but get ready?'

'I'm totally ready. Look!'

'You can't wear that,' she told him.

'Why not?'

'It's not pressed. You're crumpled. Please!'

Jamie didn't move, but said, 'It's all a bit overwhelming. This emotion stuff, huh?'

'You are such a girl,' she giggled, 'Am I going to have to wipe away a tear?'

Jamie scowled, 'Nope, and that's last time I do the openness about feelings malarkey.'

'Cariño, I'm teasing,' then she laughed, 'If you wanted to, we could hold hands later.'

Jamie stuck his tongue out and in a sulky tone told her, 'Don't wanna.'

She sat down next to him, took a deep breath then spent an age looking at him before saying, 'I love you! Love you with all my heart. I love you more than pizza, more than wine!'

Jamie grinned and replied with a new phrase he'd learned and been waiting to use, 'Vale, guapa. Esto es exactamente lo que necesitaba.'

A flash of annoyance rippled over Maria's face as she picked up a pillow and smacked him across the head with it, 'Que? So now. Now! you can't say you love me?'

'Listen. This is serious,' Jamie replied laughing, 'You can't throw yourself at a woman and say you love her when you've just met. Ya gotta play hard to get! Treat 'em mean, keep 'em keen! And hey, Maria, can you not get all girly and needy on me? It's a bit of a turn-off.'

The pillow rained down on him while he chuckled and spluttered, 'I kinda like you.'

Maria twisted his nipple in her fingers until he said, 'Love you. Love you!' then she let him up and he changed into an identical white linen shirt and a slightly lighter shade of tan chinos. Neither had come out of his suitcase any less creased than what he'd worn before, but Maria was calmer. He suspected that she'd stay that way as long as he didn't sit down anywhere and have the audacity to appear relaxed or say anything for a while. When the concierge phoned to say a taxi had arrived for them, she used her soft purring voice to say, 'I love you,' one more time, and they left the room holding hands.

***

Twenty minutes later, they were waiting in a small bar-restaurant.

The place looked familiar, with tired blanc walls marked with faded light blue lettering. Everywhere he looked were white awnings, white-attired waitresses, and an atmosphere of friendly mirth. Then Jamie remembered that he'd been there before and suddenly looked worried.

'You okay? Remember I'm with you,' Maria said as they looked at the menus

'I am a little nervous. I've been here. With Don!'

'Oh, joder. That is so cheeky of him.'

'What do you mean?'

'It means you're watched all the time, and my dad tries to be funny. Don't worry.'

'Don't worry? But I was doing something illegal with Don.'

'Is fine, he doesn't care.' Maria said shaking her head slightly.

'You said he owns a chain of supermarkets or is that your real dad who owns those?'

Maria smiled, 'Is what he calls it, more like a butcher shop. Oh, look, here he is.'

Jamie turned his head, and his jaw dropped. The man was an escaped gorilla.

'Daddy-Daddy!' she squealed and dragged Jamie behind her.

'Daddy-Daddy?' he replied slowly, sounding irritated, 'Maria, Joder!'

She ignored his gruff tone and pulled them all in for a hug. Her "father" was the scariest looking man Jamie had ever seen and clearly unused to any public displays of affection, but any defences he may have had, buckled under the infectious happiness of her sweet assault.

His reserved expression then changed to one of sighs, 'Si, Si. Okay, we hug. Okay,' and Maria bounded like an excited schoolgirl pulling him to their table. It was so out of character, but Jamie assumed she must have a reason for the act.

It took several beers and tapas portions before the large man finally stopped groaning and grunting in a sweary mix of English, Spanish, Arabic and French to smile. He became friendly, gripped Jamie's hand and asked in faltering English as if a real dad, 'So, what is it you want to do as work? Is boring to be in the office no?

Maria screeched, 'No! I said no!' and raised her finger to the gorilla's face in anger. She had already prepped Jamie on how to make a good impression. Her instructions were, 'Say nothing too definite, don't agree to anything, no matter what, I'll do the talking.'

Under the shade of a parasol, she talked and talked and talked almost non-stop. It was relentless, a steamroller of Spanish for minutes at a time, while he replied with either single words or short grunted sentences. The real surprise was when Maria asked her pretend dad, 'Is still okay to stay in England? You say for Jamie to understand. Please.'

'Si, claro que si... Hija...Joder. You can stay in England, but you're still a Legal. Vale?'

She hugged him and replied, 'Of course. But I get to study. Okay?'

Maria's pretend father then glowered at Jamie to say a gruff, 'Yes.'

After that, Jamie tuned out of the conversation and slumped in silence with his drink while Maria snuggled against him cuddling his arm.

The grim gorilla spoke with occasional English words about shopping and deliveries, but it was as if he was telling Maria something in code.

Jamie was happy. It was a moment of bliss. Maria had made the deal she'd told him about. In a week he'd be back at university, living with the woman he adored, and everything would be okay. At least that is what he thought. He didn't see the drab old spy in the corner of the bar, a man who had taken an interest in the couple. But of course, nobody ever really saw Ken.

THE END

Glossary.

Alba gu bràth -Scotland (until Judgement Day) Forever.

Ardentinny -A village name. Gaelic for a hill fire (Beacon).

Bampot - A word for someone of foolish & erratic behaviour.

Yir a pure fud - A slur for person assumed to have low worth.

Gonnae no dae that - Please desist from fud-like behaviour.

Casse-Croûte - A French expression for something to eat.

Kalhoznik -In Russian a slur word for a peasant.

Praporshchik - Russian rank of Regimental Sergeant Major

Segda gatov -Always Ready. Motto of 'Soviet Pioneers.'

Gilipollas - Spanish for Dickhead.

En realidad, yo era comandante a los veintesiete - I got promoted Major at 27.

Gamberros - Folk who aren't sticklers for authority or legality.

Chulo Puto – A worthless man +/or exploiter of womens' sexuality for profit.

Guardaespaldas asertivo -A security guard who is full of it.
La que tu me haces - What you do to me.

Me gustas aqui todos los días - I like you here every day.

Y no trates de ser amable. Eres stupido Tambien - Don't try to be nice, dumbass.

M'importa. No em vaig adonar que eres important per a mi, fins que et facis mal -
Means 'I care, I didn't realize you were important to me, until you got hurt.'

'Qui etstuie bé que és el teu anglès?' – How do you study/How good is your English?

Character List.

Don - A charming & criminally inclined boss of a security firm.

Walker - Don's second in command. The man who manages all.

Ginger - A giant, power-lifting gypsy doorman who forgets things.

Phil - An intellectual who hides behind the guise of a psychotic.

Paul - An alcoholic boxer & standard bearer of the security firm.

Jamie - A student struggling to balance the two worlds he lives in.

Mrs. Dora C - Jamie's mum. Not her first time with a pistol on the table.

Lachlann - A lumberjack Jamie once worked with.

Jeff - An old feral wood cutter who was once a soldier.

Crow - A well trained paratrooper and military contractor.

Jessica - A bad CIA lady who manipulates everything for profit.

Smith - An ambitious MI-5 officer and Jessica's liaison.

Matty - A mercenary who is seconded to Jessica's plots by MI-5

Angel - An intelligence officer who is a wee bit deceitful.

Maria - An intelligence officer of Spain who is so tired of her work.

Ken - An officer in MI-11, tasked with policing MI-5 activity.

Petra - Ken's assistant& protégé. A former Special Branch officer.

Tanya - A sad honey-trap spy from the Russian security services.

Mishka - Tanya's boss in Russia. An old school government hood.

Dr Kraus - A scientist unwilling to falsify a report.

Annabelle – The lovely wife of Dr Kraus.

About the author.

J.K. Scot was born in Dalmuir, Clydebank, Scotland.
His teenage years were spent in Argyll and after moving to England he
worked in primary, secondary & tertiary industries in a variety of roles.

The author has a dilettante interest in combat sports and rioja, but their main
hobby is what was best described by James Stewart in the 1962 movie,
'How the West Was Won.'

The author will, *"Always go look at that varmint."*

www.ingramcontent.com/pod-product-compliance
Lightning Source LLC
Chambersburg PA
CBHW051419170626
46809CB00006B/2228